A HUNDRED VICIOUS TURNS

A HUNDRED VICIOUS TURNS

LEE PAIGE O'BRIEN

AMULET BOOKS • NEW YORK

Content warning: Internalized transphobia, moments of gender dysphoria, anxiety, mentions of death, missing persons (in a fantasy context), physical harm, brief animal death

Cataloging-in-Publication Data has been applied for and may be obtained from the Library of Congress.

ISBN 978-1-4197-6515-5

Text © 2023 Lee Paige O'Brien
Jacket illustrations by Corey Brickley

Book design by Deena Micah Fleming

Published in 2023 by Amulet Books, an imprint of ABRAMS. All rights reserved. No portion of this book may be reproduced, stored in a retrieval system, or transmitted in any form or by any means, mechanical, electronic, photocopying, recording, or otherwise, without written permission from the publisher.

Printed and bound in USA
10 9 8 7 6 5 4 3 2 1

Amulet Books are available at special discounts when purchased in quantity for premiums and promotions as well as fundraising or educational use. Special editions can also be created to specification. For details, contact specialsales@abramsbooks.com or the address below.

Amulet Books® is a registered trademark of Harry N. Abrams, Inc.

ABRAMS The Art of Books
195 Broadway, New York, NY 10007
abramsbooks.com

TO ALL OF THE TRANS KIDS WHO WANT
WITH TEETH AND CLAWS

CHAPTER ONE

RAT FOUND THEIR WAY THROUGH THE HOUSE, THE BEAM of their phone's flashlight trailing over the carpet ahead of them, but they didn't let themself think about where they were going until they'd made it back to the staircase that didn't exist.

The staircase rose up out of their family's archive amid the aisles of spellbooks and reference texts, the steps curving impossibly upward even though Rat knew that there wasn't anything above them in this part of the house. A thin veil of dust drifted over the mouth of the steps, glowing dimly in the darkness of the stacks, and the faint scent of magic hung in the air.

Rat always thought of them as dead passages—the staircases that no one else could see and hallways that snaked off the edges of the map.

Some of the passages were strange, shifting things, but this one was there whenever they looked for it and it always led to the same place, even though they hadn't been up in months.

Rat cast the beam of their flashlight over the bottom steps. Usually, as a rule, they kept clear of the passages now, but they hadn't been able to sleep. Tomorrow, they would be on their way to Bellamy Arts, and they wouldn't be back home for a while.

"It's fine," they said under their breath. "Go up, get your things, come back."

With a pang, they wished that Harker was there. He could have cast an actual light, and if nothing else, at least Rat wouldn't have been going alone. But it was past three in the morning the night before move-in day, and they refused to think about texting him.

Rat looked over their shoulder one more time and then stepped through, the veil of dust breaking around them.

On the other side, the air turned cool and dry, but otherwise, crossing into the dead passage didn't feel like anything. There had always been something unsettlingly easy about it.

They'd asked Harker what he saw, back when he was still talking to them, if he ever noticed the passages. He'd told them that it was like catching a glimpse of something in the mirror, but if he moved to try and get a better look, the angle changed and it was gone again.

Rat didn't know why that bothered them so much, but they hadn't brought it up again after that.

When they'd asked Elise, maybe because she was their mother, she'd just said, *"Whatever this thing is, I promise you we'll deal with it."*

It wasn't, they understood, the way that magic was supposed to work. But in spite of the fact that Rat was heir to the fourth oldest arcane bloodline on the East Coast—the second oldest in New York, Elise had reminded them more than once—it worked that way for them.

Their hand went to their compass as they took the stairs, the familiar weight of it tucked into the pocket of their pajama pants. They thumbed the cool metal of the case, letting it ground them, even though they knew that if they took it out here, the needle would sweep one way and then the other, never finding north.

Once, before Rat had understood how out of alignment their magic was, they would let themself wander, just to see how far the passages led. Sometimes, they stumbled onto small, tucked-away rooms or winding book-lined passages leading away from the shelves of their family's archives.

Sometimes, to places farther than that, like sprawling fields and far-off towers.

Back then, they'd still believed that the passages were empty.

Rat shoved the thought away as they came to the top of the stairs. They barely cast anymore. Usually, they preferred to pretend that they didn't have any magic at all.

Above them, the staircase opened into a wide, circular room with a domed glass ceiling looking out onto a sky full of strange stars. An intricate ring of sigils marked the floor, but whatever it was, Rat had never had anyone to ask.

As far as they knew, no one else had been here in years, if ever. They didn't know where the observatory had come from or who had built it. Just that it was always there at the top of the steps, like another piece of the house.

A heavy, preternatural silence hung in the air. The place might have seemed wholly abandoned, if not for the pile of books and papers heaped in the corner from last spring, and their sweatshirt still crumpled on the floor where they'd left it.

"Thank god," Rat said under their breath.

They paced across the room, their footsteps echoing around them. A few spellbooks had been left out, scattered across the floor, since they hadn't been back to clean up after Harker had stopped coming with them.

Rat knelt down to grab their sweatshirt. Some of the tension in their chest unknotted as they pulled it on, pushing up the too-long sleeves. If they were being technical, it was actually *his* sweatshirt, and the twined smells of magic and burnt paper still clung to it. Harker's magic—in its most basic form, before he could will it into something else—had always been fire, and it came to him like breathing. He conjured sparks the same way that Rat found hallways.

They thumbed the protection spell that he'd stitched into the pocket for them. Since Harker wasn't going to Bellamy Arts with them anymore, they doubted that he'd be asking for it back any time soon.

Rat moved to get up, and then stopped again as they caught sight of one of the still-open spellbooks.

Tucked into the fold of the pages was a sketch of a tower, its crooked battlements jutting against the sky. Seven black marks spotted the space around it, a little like faraway birds and a little like stars.

Rat reached out, their fingers hovering just above the page, but they didn't touch it. Everything about the image set their teeth on edge, maybe because they were the one who'd drawn it.

The first time that Rat had seen the tower, it had been in a drawing buried among their father's old notes. Elise never spoke about what kind of magic he'd done, but with all of the maps and sketches he'd left behind, they'd always had an inkling that in some way, maybe, it was a bit like theirs.

There had been drawings of the campus and a few loose illustrations of the ruins of the Ashwood House overlooking the school's grounds from the foothills above. And then, amid everything else, the tower rising out of a field of grass and fallen stones. Ruined and glorious.

That was the real reason Rat was going to Bellamy Arts, even though they barely cast anymore. Not because they were a legacy, and not because it was a good school. As soon as they were inside the campus wards, nothing would be able to follow them.

Last year, after the Council of Hours had finished casting protection spells over their house and Rat had finished their senior year remotely, it had all been decided. They'd expected to be withdrawn, but Elise had put in a call to the dean to discuss the details, and that had settled it. Bellamy Arts, she'd promised, would be the safest place for them.

If Rat had learned anything, it was that some doors were best left shut. Once they were at Bellamy Arts, they could see to it that they remained on their side of the passages, and everything else remained safely on its.

Pushing down their unease, Rat took the sketch and folded it in half so it wouldn't smudge into the book, then flipped the cover shut. They didn't know if it was the drawing or just the thought of heading out tomorrow, but suddenly, they felt like they'd stayed too long and they wanted to get back to the house proper.

When they finally made it back to bed, their sleep was fitful and shallow, and they dreamt of seven stars that were also seven black birds, tilting in orbit around a tower all autumn light and jagged stone.

It wasn't until Rat woke, breathing hard with the sheets plastered to their skin, that they remembered they were safely back in their room, and nothing was chasing them.

CHAPTER TWO

ELISE'S HEADLIGHTS SWEPT OVER GRAVEL AS THE CAR pulled through the school's gates. Bellamy Arts lay an hour's drive north of the Evans place, half hidden in the Appalachian foothills.

They'd passed the concealment spells a few miles back, where the valley opened like a split seam. To anyone from the outside, it would have looked like an unbroken ridge rising toward the mountains, where the road tapered into nothing and GPSes had a tendency to fail. But, for them, the way down was green and winding and touched by the first hour of dusk.

In terms of places that Rat dreaded, Bellamy Arts easily ranked second or third on the list, starting with the fact that it was a university and ending with the part about how it taught magic.

Over the summer, Rat had spent enough hours studying campus maps that the schools' pitched rooftops and roving footpaths were pretty much burned behind their eyes. Being there, though, that all felt immensely inadequate.

As a rule, Rat did their best to stick to places they knew well. No matter how many maps they studied, whenever they set foot somewhere new, they could never shake the feeling that there might be something lurking around the corner or hidden in the angles of a building that no one else could see.

"So much gothic architecture," Elise said. "I forgot how hard it is to tell the buildings apart. I think they add more turrets every time I come back."

"Right. Yeah." Rat peered up through the window, fighting back a fresh wave of anxiety. They pictured the bird's-eye view from the maps—the clock tower at the center of campus with the library, freshman dorms to the south, senior apartments north by the woods that circled the edge of the grounds. Classroom buildings and casting spaces between.

In the distance, the clock tower rose above the jumble of steeply pitched rooftops, sharp-edged and gray against the deepening sky. Rat had been hoping that if they arrived late enough, they could miss the move-in crowd and just appear in class tomorrow without anyone noticing them. Probably, that had been a mistake. It wasn't night yet, but in another hour or two, it would be too dark for them to make a sweep of the campus.

Their phone buzzed. Rat jumped.

"Is that Will?" Elise asked. "Is he settled in?"

Rat glanced down and swiped the message away without reading it. Will had been a family friend for about as long as Rat could remember. He'd come up with his parents in the morning to move in, and he'd been texting them selfies and pictures from campus since he'd arrived. So far, Rat had barely been able to make themself look.

Elise slowed the car and turned into a driveway in front of a sprawling Queen Anne house surrounded by neatly kept shrubs.

"Hey." Something in her face softened. "Still feeling alright?"

"Yeah, of course," they managed, fighting back a fresh pang of anxiety.

"Miranda." Elise reached over the center console and touched their hand.

Rat sank back. It wasn't a deadname, even if Elise was one of the only people who still used it. It was just that something in the way she said it always made them feel like a child who'd gotten lost in the supermarket.

"You're going to be safe here," she said. "The minute that stops being true, I'll be right here to pull you out. Do you understand?"

"I'm really okay."

"I know you are." She gave them a reassuring smile, which made Rat wonder exactly how not okay they looked.

Before they could say something that would probably definitely convince her to turn the car around, Rat pushed their door open.

A woman had appeared in front of the house, dressed in a neat, violet suit. She had light, age-lined skin and her long gray hair was swept back in the same tidy way that Rat recognized from her photographs, even though they'd never met her face-to-face. In the light, it was hard to guess how old she was, but there was an unmistakable whisper of power about her that most arcanists only came by with years of study.

"That's Vivian Fairchild, the dean of Magics and High Arts," Elise said, letting herself out of the car.

"Vivian. Please," the woman said, which Rat would absolutely not be calling her. "And this is . . ."

"I go by Rat," they said quickly.

Rat glanced up, half expecting her to ask them if that was short for something, in case they had a more satisfactory name on hand, but she just smiled a little wider.

"Excellent. Come. We have lots to talk about." Motioning to them, Fairchild started back toward the building with the sure air of someone who was used to being followed. "There's tea and coffee in my office—just something light while we finish your registration. I thought I'd handle this one myself since it's something of a special circumstance."

She led the way into a small, well-lit lobby, empty except for the boy at the front desk.

The original campus of Bellamy Arts had been leveled and rebuilt at the turn of the twentieth century, and the Historic Founder's House was meant to be a replica of Margaret Ingrid's living quarters. The inside of the building looked like a home that had been retrofitted as an office space, with dark wooden paneling and the kind of heavy carpet that drank sound.

Fairchild leaned across the reception desk. "The Evans family is here. Could you send someone to transport their luggage? Their room assignment should be in Mallory Hall. And the registration forms—" she turned back to Elise as the boy behind the desk slid her a manila file folder. "There are a couple of extra things to sign off on, given the circumstances. I understand that Rat will be coming in as non-casting. Is that correct?"

Rat shot a sideways glance at Elise.

Non-casting was usually a nice way of saying someone's powers had never fully come in but they still had a trust fund. Given the options, it was technically the most accurate term for what Rat was, but it always took them off guard whenever they heard it aloud.

It sounded ordinary, like Rat might not be the ideal choice, but they could still be an alright heir to the Evans family archives. Or, at the least, like they could walk down a hallway without having to count all the doors and check twice over their shoulder.

"Yes," Elise said. "We decided that would be best."

"Of course," Fairchild said.

As she spoke, a small group of faculty came down the stairs behind her like they'd just gotten out of a meeting.

Fairchild looked up, following Rat's gaze. "Ah, perfect timing. I was hoping we'd cross paths. Arthur—"

She waved to the group, and one of the professors turned toward them, with a leather briefcase slung over his shoulder and his graying locs tied back in a low ponytail. He had warm Black skin, and a pair of silver reading glasses were clipped to the pocket of his tweed jacket, like he expected to need them.

"Vivian," he said, with a small nod. "Elise." His gaze fell on Rat. "This is—"

"Rat Evans," he finished, holding out his hand. "Vivian was just telling me about you. It's been a long time since we've had an Evans on campus. Or a Holbrook, for that matter."

"Sir." Rat drew themself up and shook his hand. They had never been sure if it was their blond hair, cut like a boy's, or just the fact that they

9

looked nothing like Elise, but something about them always made people think of their father first, even though the Evans name was older.

"This is Professor Frey," Fairchild said. "He's with the Department of Higher Magics, but he's taking on some introductory classes this term."

He nodded to them. "I'll look forward to seeing you in class. I'm sure you'll do great things here."

"Oh. I'm on bookwork." Rat's face heated. "I don't actually do any magic."

"I've been told," Frey said. He gave them a small smile. "Still. Your father always had a particular talent for finding trouble. I wouldn't expect any less of you, magic or not."

Behind him, the other faculty had begun to make their way toward the door. He gave them a last nod before he excused himself, weaving back into the crowd.

After he'd gone, Fairchild turned back to Elise, paperwork in hand. "I imagine you'll want some time to read everything over while Rat and I discuss their situation," she said, passing her the forms. "Would you meet us when you finish?"

Fairchild led Rat up the stairs to an office that looked more like a small, bookish living room that happened to have a desk in it.

"Now then," she said, settling into the high-backed chair. "Tea? It's raspberry. I find that it helps soothe my nerves."

"Oh. Uh, thanks."

Her eyes flickered over them, and Rat realized how tensely they were holding themself. They took a seat as she poured a cup of tea from the pot on her desk and slid it across to them.

"Tell me. Have you thought at all about pursuing magic?"

"I . . . no," they said quickly. "I already have an agreement with Elise, and we both thought it would be better if I didn't."

"Of course. Naturally, that's between you and her, but I'm curious what you think."

Rat hesitated.

"You know, I taught when she was a student here," Fairchild said. "Your father too, actually, before he became a professor. He was an accomplished formal caster. They both were." She waved her hand, stirring the air. "I imagine you might have a bit of catching up to do, but there are other things that you could learn here outside of your own . . . particular abilities. If that's of interest to you?"

"It's not," they said, then immediately felt rude. Magic took many forms. If Rat wanted to, technically, nothing stopped them from casting spells. At one point, they'd even been okay at basic casting exercises, the kind of simple spells that consisted mostly of waving their hands and willing their power to do things. If they had a head for more advanced casting and the right spellbooks, nothing would have stopped them from doing formal magic, either.

They hadn't wanted to. Magic—any magic—still drew on their own powers. Most of what they'd once learned, they'd forgotten on purpose.

Fairchild looked them over, considering. "Perhaps we could start you on small magics and some minor spellwork. Something that wouldn't require much power. Or, theory, even? I've known formalists without a spark of their own ability who derived the most brilliant spells without ever casting."

"I meant what I said before. I really have no interest in learning magic."

"Of course," she said. Disappointment flickered across her face. "It does make our work simpler, I suppose."

Rat took a sip of their tea so they wouldn't have to reply.

Across from them, Fairchild settled back in her seat. As she did, a seam on the wall behind her caught Rat's eye.

She glanced back to follow their gaze, and Rat stiffened.

"Ah," she said, and they realized that she saw it, too. "That was the next thing I wanted to talk to you about. Bellamy Arts is a very old school, and the campus can be somewhat . . . particular. Some of the buildings still have old maintenance passages. We've sealed them off where we could, but if you happen to find any, they're strictly off-limits."

"Of course. I'll remember that."

She nodded once, but her gaze stayed fixed on them. "I've been told that you have a knack for getting places. I have no doubt that if you tried, you might find any number of strange, tucked-away corners of the campus," she went on. "I think you might have an incredible gift, if you chose to use it, but I'm well aware of why you've come here. You won't find many places safer than Bellamy Arts, but no matter how vigilant we are or how many wards we cast, none of that will do you any good if you wander out of the school's reach. For the time that you're here, I need to ask that you don't go looking."

"I can't control the dead passages," Rat said quickly. "They just happen."

Fairchild studied them for a moment, then clasped her hands together. "All the more reason to err on the side of caution, then."

"You really won't have any problems from me."

Finally, Fairchild's posture relaxed. "I understand that you've already been sent maps, and Elise told me that William Chen agreed to show you around. We've put you in the same core classes, so you should be able to walk with him between buildings, and your professors have already been notified that you're exempt from any casting requirements."

"Right," Rat said. "Elise mentioned that."

Fairchild gave them a small nod like she might go on, but before she could say anything else, Elise knocked at the door.

"Paperwork's taken care of," she said, poking her head in. "And they gave me your room number in Mallory Hall. We just have to collect the key from the front desk. How is everything?"

"We were just finishing up," Fairchild told her. "Could I speak to you for a couple of minutes?"

"Of course. Rat could you . . ."

They pushed their cup back across the desk and got up. "I'll be in the hall."

"It's so good meeting you," Fairchild said to them, folding her hands. "I think you're really going to do well here."

CHAPTER THREE

AFTER ELISE HAD LEFT TO HEAD HOME, RAT JUNKED THEIR backpack on the floor of their dorm room and collapsed onto the bed.

Mallory Hall was built like an old estate house. Inside, it was a sprawl of common rooms and dorms that housed most of the incoming girls, plus Rat, since they hadn't been sure that living in the boys' dorm would be any less daunting. Tucked away behind a staircase, their room was easily big enough to be a double, with a set of matching hardwood furniture and a window overlooking the campus. It was fully dark outside now, and the foothills rose up in the distance like the swell of a wave.

Automatically, Rat slid their compass from their pocket, grounding themself. They'd found it among their father's things a long time ago. There wasn't any magic to it aside from a spell to keep it from tarnishing, but it was cool and satisfyingly heavy, and they liked having it on them.

They watched as the needle found north.

Safe.

They thought of weeds, and grass, and crumbling stone, but they were behind the school's wards, now. Nothing would find them here.

"You're fine," they said under their breath. "You're here."

The compass bit into the heel of their hand, and Rat realized how tightly they were holding it.

Before they could think better of it, they put their compass back and took out their phone, swiping back to their message thread with Harker.

Hey, they typed. *So, you can probably guess where I am right now, but*

They stopped and stared at the screen, guilt twisting in the pit of their stomach.

They'd sent him a volley of messages last spring after they'd left Highgate Prep, in case there was any chance he'd ever speak to them again after how badly they'd left off. They'd been met with a wall of silence, which Rat was pretty sure was Harker Blakely for *fuck you.*

They took a deep breath and started the message over. *I get that you probably don't want to hear from me right now but*

They deleted it again. *I never got the rest of my books back and you still owe me breakfast you flaming marshmallow, I'm calling you*

Rat raked a hand through their hair, still messy from traveling. "It's fine," they said under their breath. "You're fine. You're here."

Behind them, someone knocked on the door.

"Fuck." Rat's phone slipped out of their hand as they whipped around. "It's open!"

Will let himself in. He was wearing a blazer even though it was still hot out, the sleeves pushed up to show his muscled forearms, and his dark hair was rumpled from the humidity. He flashed them the easy, lopsided smile that usually got him free refills. "Am I interrupting something?"

"Hey. Hi. I thought you were still moving in," Rat said, sitting up.

Both of their families were old allies for political reasons that Rat had never completely grasped, and Will was probably one of the nicest people they knew. He could also definitely pick them up and throw them, since he was built like a lacrosse player. He'd been pretty much the only person they'd spoken to while they were shut up in the Evans place all summer.

They flipped their phone over. "Are you dressed for something?"

"There's a new student reception in Galison Hall," he said, leaning against the desk. "A few people asked if you'd be there, so I thought I'd drag you out of hiding to say hi to everyone. Or, you know, grab some cake and finish texting Blakely a dossier on old blood social politics, or whatever it is you're doing." He nodded to their phone on the bed. "So? Dessert and intrigue?"

"I was checking the weather," Rat said, shoving their phone into their pocket. "I told you, we stopped talking. There's no intrigue, Will."

"Is that also a no on dessert?"

Rat opened their mouth to say that speaking to people was the last thing they wanted to do, but they didn't want to be in their room anymore, either. "When do you need to be there?"

"It runs until curfew," he said. "Some people are waiting for us, but I could tell them we're running late. Why?"

"I wanted to get a view of the campus," Rat said, deciding as they spoke. "I thought I saw a way onto the roof when I was coming in. Did you . . ."

"See anything?" Will was one of the only people outside of their family who knew the details of Rat's powers, since he'd grown up close to them. They'd never told him the full story about the tower, but he knew most of the broad strokes about the dead passages, and he'd covered for Rat with the other old blood kids more than once.

Rat nodded.

"Maybe? Is it on the map?"

They gave him a hopeful look. "I was thinking I could check it out? So I'd know?"

Will hesitated, which wasn't a no.

"I'll be fast," Rat said, grabbing their sketchbook from their backpack, amid their half-unpacked things.

Will followed as they slipped out into the hallway. Rat glanced at the line of closed doors to one side, the stairwell to the other. Then, satisfied that they were alone, they motioned to him. "I'm pretty sure I figured out how to get up, if there's a way up."

"This feels dangerous," Will said. "Is it dangerous?"

"It's definitely fine," they said, starting into the building.

Will trailed after them. "Everyone's asking about you, by the way. I already ran into a few of the guys from Highgate, and they're all excited that you're back."

"Oh. Right." Rat fought the urge to duck their head. Based on how they'd left school last year, they were pretty sure that *excited* wasn't the word.

"I ran into the St. Augustines, too, during move-in. Both of them are here, and one of the Mendoza kids is with the New England crowd. And the Van Sandts, obviously."

Rat pushed down a fresh wave of anxiety as he spoke, letting the names wash over them. The oldest bloodlines typically kept to themselves, and blooded society wasn't a particularly large pond. There was only a small handful of arcane universities on par with Bellamy Arts, and Rat had nearly allowed themself to forget how many of their classmates from Highgate had set their sights on it and, unlike them, actually had the abilities to back their applications.

"Oh," Will said. "And there's this girl."

Something about the way he said it pulled Rat's attention back.

"She's new," he went on. "Everyone's saying she's ridiculously good. One of the guys on my floor has an uncle on the admissions board, and apparently Fairchild hand selected her application. But far as anyone knows, she didn't come from any of the major prep schools. It's like she appeared out of thin air."

Rat released some of the tension in their shoulders. A talented new girl was good. If they were lucky, everyone in their year would be too busy with her to even notice them.

They slowed as they reached another staircase, this one rickety and narrow, hidden away at the back of the building. A line of old electrical sconces lit the way up.

When Rat turned back, the concern in Will's face was a punch to the gut. They tried not to let it show. "I know you see this staircase," they said, jabbing their sketchbook. "It's on the map."

"Yeah," he said. "No, the creepy deserted staircase is definitely there. And we're here, in an empty dorm, about to climb a hundred-and-fifty-year-old pile of building code violations."

"Hundred and twenty max." Rat tucked the sketchbook back under their arm and grabbed ahold of the handrail. "The whole school was pretty much rebuilt around the start of the 1900s."

"Right," he said behind them. "This is cool. Like an adventure."

Swallowing their fear, Rat started up the stairs.

They'd done some sketches over the summer, but they needed someone with them while they were mapping the campus, at least until they got their footing. If they caved now and went to the reception, Will would take it as a cue to skip over other parts of the campus that were out of the way. The good vantage points and the hiding places. The dark corners that something might crawl out of.

Rat pushed the thought away. They couldn't worry about that here.

They checked over their shoulder one more time to make sure the stairway was empty before they dug the compass from their pocket and kept going.

According to the floor plans, the staircase should have ended at the third floor, but instead Rat came to a flat landing. Above, the row of sconces ended and the stairs narrowed, leading up to a wooden doorway, half hidden in the shadows.

Rat held up their compass. The needle swung neatly into place.

"I see it, too," Will said. "Um. Is this the part where we run out there and go exploring?"

"I'm expressly forbidden from exploring. You're just helping me with my maps." Rat put the compass back into their pocket, afraid that if they held it out any longer, Will would see their hands shaking.

With a deep breath, they opened the door. A damp gust of night air blew in, carrying in the cut-grass smell of late summer, and all of their fear evaporated.

Past the rail of the widow's walk, the steep rooftops and angled turrets of the campus raked the sky, their silhouettes speckled with squares of light. Streetlamps glowed all along the pathways, growing fainter and fainter as each path wound away from the heart of the campus, until they gave way to the dark sweep of the woods. Farther than that, the soft glow of the main wards rose out of the trees, hemming the school in.

Farther still, the mountains sprawled in the distance like long-sleeping giants.

"Will, holy shit. You have to see this. It's—" Rat looked back, only to find he was already behind them, his jacket in his hands.

"Definitely out-of-bounds," he said, but he was grinning now, too. He set his blazer down to prop open the door. "What happens next?"

"I don't know. I've never had to map somewhere this big."

Will crossed to the edge of the platform and leaned against the rails, the campus skyline sprawling behind him. "What do you have so far?"

"I've got an okay idea of the general layout, but I'm still getting my bearings." Rat hesitated, then took their sketchbook from under their arm. Will had seen their maps before, but only the finished ones. Once Rat had realized what the dead passages were, they'd stopped showing their rough drafts to anyone, with the exception of Harker.

Will tilted his head slightly, like he was waiting for them to go on.

"Right now it's just the basics," Rat told him. Using their phone's flashlight, they flipped through the pages. When they found their sketch of the main campus, they angled it toward him. "So, the clock tower is in the middle of campus. Like, dead center."

They tapped the page, then looked back up. In the dark, all of the rooftops ran together, but the clock tower was easy to spot. It rose out of the skyline, taller than the rest, the face of the clock stark white, like a second moon.

"On the west side, the Drake Library kind of wraps around it, and then that building on the east is the student center."

"Galison Hall, where the reception is."

"Right. Dessert and intrigue." Rat glanced down at their map. "It's hard to see right now, but the infirmary and the old chapel are also near the middle. Um, but I think they use the chapel for something else now. Those buildings kind of make up the core, and then there's a ring of classrooms and practice fields around that."

Will nodded. "And then those are the dorms around the outer edge?"

"Right. And Armitage and Mallory Hall are in this corner." Rat tapped their finger against the page. "I think that's all more or less correct. The only hard part is that a few of the buildings don't have floor plans. Like, I can't find anything for the Drake, and I think the dorms have been renovated since the original maps."

"Huh. Do you think—" Will's phone buzzed. "Hold on."

"Who's that?" Rat asked as he glanced down at the screen.

He flipped it toward them. A photo of pastel petit fours filled the chat window, with the words, *get down here loser i'm not saving you any <3*

"Should I say we're on our way?"

"You should go," Rat said. Some of the excitement of being on the roof drained out of them. "I need to finish checking some things. Most of the people down there are your friends, anyways."

"They're your friends, too."

Rat gave him a meaningful look.

He pointed at Rat. "I don't know why you're looking at me like that, but I'm not going to read into it." His phone buzzed again. "Let me know if you want to join us. It's not a long walk and I'm happy to come back for you."

Rat's chest tightened as he turned toward the door.

Will was leaving them. Alone. On their first night at Bellamy Arts. The widow's walk was a blank spot that had been left off the campus maps, and no one else knew that they were up here.

Rat spun around. "Will!"

He stopped on the landing and looked back at them. "Yeah?"

"I—" Rat stopped themself. They nodded to his blazer on the ground. "You should take that," they said, pacing back to the door. They twisted the handle. "It's unlocked."

"Good call." He grinned at them and scooped up the blazer. "Text me if you change your mind, okay?"

As soon as Will had gone, Rat paced back to the rails.

A steady stream of lanterns trickled up the path toward Galison Hall below. Again, Rat swept their gaze across the campus, taking it all in.

It should have been a relief, being there.

Elise had all but warded them into the Evans house last summer, though even she didn't know the full story. In the version Rat had told her, something had followed them out of one of the dead passages. They'd shown her the piles of crow-gifts that they'd found on their windowsill over the months—the oil-black feathers, and lengths of tarnished silver chain, and tiny, sun-bleached bones. Yellow chrysanthemums and shoots of mugwort and yarrow, kept so long that they'd turned brittle with age.

In that version, Rat hadn't even made it as far as the outlying fields, and they'd never laid eyes on the tower itself.

In that version, nothing had tried to bring them back to stay.

They shoved the thought away.

They were at Bellamy Arts. Safe. It didn't matter if the school kept them under watch, or if they hated almost everything about this place. They would spend the next four years behind the wards, and they'd learn exactly as much magic as they needed to make certain that they never opened another dead passage again.

From the corner of their vision, a flicker of motion caught their eye in the courtyard. Instinctively, they glanced down.

At some point, a small group of students had appeared on the grass below, though Rat couldn't tell which direction they'd come from.

Rat leaned out over the railing, curious, and then everything in them ground to a stop.

There were only three kids in the courtyard. There were two girls whispering to each other, one of them wearing a leather bomber jacket, and the second one, pulling at her arm to draw her attention, who Rat guessed had to be even shorter than they were.

The third person, Rat would know anywhere.

Harker Blakely had, at one point at least, been their best friend, and he easily held the record for Most Times Saving Rat Evans's Life in One Calendar Year. He didn't come from a bloodline the way Rat did, but he'd been the only other trans kid in their year at Highgate, and unlike them, he was obnoxiously good at magic. Even though they hadn't spoken to him in months, he was probably Rat's favorite person on the face of the planet.

He also hated them.

Rat hadn't even realized he would still be coming to Bellamy Arts. Elise had told them over the summer that she'd heard he was going to be changing schools, but Rat hadn't been able to help wondering if something had happened with his admission. The last they'd heard, he'd barely been allowed to finish the year at Highgate after how badly everything had ended, and he would have needed a scholarship just to make it past the front gates here.

But now he was standing three stories below them in the courtyard with a pair of strangers, dark hair tied back in a bristly almost-ponytail like whenever he was casting. Absently, he drew a flicker of spellfire out of the air as he listened, the light catching on his pale skin as it wove between his fingers. It was a casting drill he'd practiced until it became a habit, and something about it made Rat's chest pull.

As if he'd sensed them watching, he glanced up toward the roof.

The girl in the jacket tapped his arm, and the spellfire in his hand flickered out again. Harker drew back like he'd burnt himself.

Even that felt off somehow, maybe because Rat knew how much he hated being touched by people he didn't know.

Rat didn't know what the three were doing, but Harker said something back to the girl and then started walking out of the courtyard. This time, if he had noticed anything, he didn't look back.

For a long moment, all that Rat could do was stare at the space below, waiting for Harker to come back and give some kind of sign that it had really been him down there.

But they knew.

Even if they were told he'd transferred. Even if Rat had assumed his silence meant they'd never see him again. Even if they hated themself for being surprised.

Harker Blakely was at Bellamy Arts.

Rat was still staring into the dark when the girl in the jacket walked back into the courtyard.

They tightened their grip on the phone, and then they realized the flashlight was still on. "Shit," they muttered, fumbling to shut it off.

They looked back down as she made her way across the lawn, the moonlight soft on the rim of her glasses.

Her gaze swept upward, to the roof. To the place where the light had been.

Rat's stomach plummeted.

They stood there, rooted to the spot, but the girl only looked in their direction for a moment. Then she turned and headed back toward the building, leaving Rat alone once again, this time for good.

CHAPTER FOUR

AT ONE POINT, THE IDEA THAT HARKER WOULD BE COMING to Bellamy Arts had been the only thing that made it sound manageable. Rat had spent most of the summer wanting to be back in his dorm room at Highgate, even though they knew he didn't live there anymore. They'd spent the rest of the time imagining that maybe Elise had been wrong, and he'd still show up in the fall, probably with a cup of dining hall coffee in hand.

That had obviously been a mistake.

Harker couldn't be here. He knew everything about Rat, and everything about the tower, and they hadn't left him with a single good reason to keep their secrets.

"What do you think you're doing here?" they asked the ceiling as they lay in bed that night.

The heavy quiet of the building prickled around them in answer.

"Fuck," they mumbled. They pulled their pillow over their head, hating themself a little more than they already did.

As the sky faded to gray outside, Rat finally gave up on getting any real sleep and slipped out into the hallway with their sketchbook. They needed to be somewhere else.

They didn't realize where they were heading until they'd made it outside to the courtyard. This early, it was still empty, the campus quiet around them. The damp from the grass bled into their sneakers as they paced across the lawn, surveying the area.

They had no idea what they were expecting to find.

Finally, letting out a breath, Rat dropped down against the side of the building and flipped their sketchbook open to a bird's-eye view of Mallory Hall, so they could at least have a reason to be there.

Sometimes, they forgot they hadn't actually become friends with Harker until last year.

At the start, when Rat had first asked him for help, they were pretty sure that he hadn't even liked them that much. Rat had basically cornered him in a stairwell because they hadn't known where else to turn, and he'd been the only person they could think of who wouldn't try to go over their head to Elise or the Council of Hours.

"I can help you with your applications. My family knows the admissions board at Bellamy Arts, so I know what they read for," Rat had said in a rush, and then, because those might have been the most disgustingly privileged words to ever leave their mouth and they'd been sure they couldn't humiliate themself any further, they'd shrunk back and said, *"Please."*

They still didn't know if it was because of how desperate they sounded or if he'd just needed it, but he'd hesitated and then said, *"Okay, Evans. Talk."*

They'd ended up in a booth at the twenty-four-hour diner a few blocks from campus still in their uniforms, since they were less likely to run into any of the other Highgate kids there. Harker had given Rat what might have been the most suspicious look they'd ever gotten from anyone, and then, somehow, they'd found themself stumbling through an explanation about the tower while he'd picked warily at a stack of pancakes.

By the end of it, Harker had become as much a part of the whole thing as they were.

He was one of the few boarding students at Highgate, and Rat spent most of their afternoons camped out in his room, discussing protection spells and distracting him from studying. Whenever Elise went out of town, he was the first person they'd call so they wouldn't be alone in the Evans house. He'd cast wards and gone through dead passages with them. Once, to the foot of the tower itself.

Rat stopped themself from following that line of thought any further.

Elise had been furious when she'd found out about Harker. That Rat had been sneaking him into the house. That they'd told him about their magic. That he'd been through their father's old notes.

That Rat had taken him into the Evans Archives had been the worst part. Higher magics were kept behind closed doors, and the older, more powerful spellbooks were rarely shared, even among other arcanists. Even their family's closest political allies hadn't set foot inside their archives. To say that old blooded society wasn't particularly welcoming to outsiders was like saying that the ocean was a bit cold and a little deep.

"You need to understand," Elise had said as she dragged Rat back up to their room afterward. *"That boy isn't like you. He's just looking for a way in."*

On the lawn, a dark shape cut across the edge of Rat's vision. They looked up as a black bird lit on the grass a few feet away.

Their pulse jumped, and then they caught themself. *Safe.*

The bird blinked.

Rat eyed it blearily. "What do you want?"

With a caw, it leapt up, catching the cold morning air.

Rat thumbed the binding of their sketchbook. This, they decided, was a terrible place to work on their map.

"It's fine," they said under their breath. Harker was actually talented, so probably, he would never even cross paths with them again. They needed to get upstairs before Will came to find them.

Rat tucked the sketchbook back under their arm and started back toward the building. They were at Bellamy Arts, they reminded themself, and literally everything was going to be fine.

It was fully light out by the time Rat made their way back to the stairs.

They were halfway up when the girl in the leather jacket appeared on the landing above them, backpack slung over her shoulder. Instinctively, Rat ducked back as she passed them.

"Thanks," she said with a nod.

"Wait!" They spun after her. "You . . ."

She turned around and looked up at them through her too-big glasses, and Rat immediately wished they hadn't called attention to themself.

She was really, disastrously pretty.

She looked like morning itself, with round, freckle-dusted cheeks and eyes the color of fog. She was built in a way that seemed plush and powerful at the same time, from the soft, strong lines of her shoulders to the full curve of her stomach to her thick thighs and scraped up knees, and her hair spilled down her back in a briar of loose, rust-colored curls.

She wore a flannel shirt under her jacket, tucked into a pair of high-waisted cutoffs, plus what might have been the most battered pair of Docs Rat had ever seen, caked with mud like wherever she'd been last night, it hadn't been the new student reception.

Rat wanted to hide. Speaking, they realized, had been a horrible mistake.

"Yeah?" she said, and Rat realized they'd been staring.

"It's, um, kind of chilly outside," they told her, fumbling over themself. "Uh, you might want to bring a sweatshirt or something."

Her lips twitched into something halfway between a smirk and a frown, and Rat immediately felt ridiculous.

"Thanks for the heads-up, but I think I'm good," she said, tugging at the corner of her leather jacket.

"Right." Rat hesitated.

When they realized that she didn't have anything else to say, relief rolled through them.

She didn't recognize them.

"Thanks, though," she said, then she paused like she was waiting for a name.

"I'm Rat," they said, heading her off. Then, quickly, "They pronouns."

"Jinx. She/her," she said.

Rat didn't know that name.

They weren't friends with everyone like Will was, but they'd brushed elbows with most of the major families on the East Coast at some point, and a few that Elise had ties with on the West Coast. But the longer that they thought about it, the more certain Rat was that they'd never seen her before last night. They would have remembered.

Like she appeared out of thin air.

Finally, it clicked. She was the girl Will had told them about.

Her eyes went to their sketchbook. A moment too late, Rat realized it was still open, with the floor plan of Mallory Hall that they'd been working on in full view. "Is that the dorm?" she asked.

"It's a hobby," they said quickly, flipping it shut. "I like architecture, I mean. Mallory Hall is a weird building."

Her eyes flickered over Rat's face again, like she was really seeing them for the first time, and then the corner of her mouth tugged in a way that made Rat's stomach drop out. "We should trade notes some time. I might be able to point out a few places, if you haven't already found them."

Rat tried to answer, but before they could find their voice, a group of girls came down the stairs. Rat edged back to let them pass, but as the girls reached the bottom, more voices echoed down from above.

"I live on the third floor," Jinx said. "Maybe we'll run into each other."

Rat bit back a nervous laugh. "Um, yeah. Maybe," they said, but before they could decide if her offer was a good thing or not, she'd already turned and started down the stairs again.

CHAPTER FIVE

ONCE RAT GOT BACK TO THEIR ROOM, THEY HAD ALL OF fourteen minutes to throw on real clothes before Will showed up to walk them to practicum.

Up until last night, first-year practicum would have easily ranked in the top five things that Rat dreaded most about Bellamy Arts, somewhere after magic and talking to people. It met every day of their first semester, with its focus split between theory of magic and practical casting, and it was required for all incoming students. For Rat, that translated to an entire semester of sitting uselessly at the back of the class.

The basement classroom reminded them a lot of the chemistry lab at their old high school, except emphatically disaster-proofed. Floor-to-ceiling supply cabinets lined the walls, and rows of high, rubber-topped lab desks filled the room, arranged in front of a set of blackboards that looked like they'd been firmly bolted to the wall. None of which was reassuring.

"So, I was thinking," Will said as they stopped in the doorway. "Since you won't need a casting partner, I was speaking with James Singh and he said I could join his group if you want to sit with us, and . . ."

He trailed off as something caught his attention across the room.

"Will?"

"Nothing," he said, before they could follow his gaze. He took them by the elbow and pulled them into the room. "Sorry. We should find an empty table. And maybe stop blocking the door."

Rat glanced over their shoulder as they followed him in, half expecting to see Harker conjuring sparks or sitting at one of the lab tables and being generally unapproachable.

Instead, they found Jinx, lounging back against one of the lab desks, her legs stretched across the aisle like it belonged to her. Rat's pulse jumped. They hadn't expected to see her again this soon.

It took them a moment to register that the seat beside her had been claimed by the same girl from the night before. Unlike Jinx, though, Rat could swear they'd seen her before. Today, she wore a lace dress fitted to her small frame, her hair falling loose down her back in long, black waves. She perched primly on the lab stool with a paper-wrapped Danish in her hand, even though Rat was pretty sure there had to be a rule against food in the practice rooms.

"Hey," Will said, steering them back a bit too deliberately. "Are you—"

"The two girls by the back of the room. Do you know them?" Rat asked.

"Not really," he said, like he did.

"Who are they?"

He let out a breath and shot another furtive glance across the room. "Alright. So that one"—he nodded to Jinx—"is Jinx Wilder. She's the girl I told you about yesterday."

Rat eyed him, catching the leading edge in his voice. "And the girl next to her?"

He leaned in, dropping his voice. "That's Agatha Cromwell Rivera."

"Wait. Like—"

"Yes," he said. "That one."

Rat shot a breath through their teeth.

They knew the Cromwell family. Agatha's uncle was friends with Elise, and he'd handled their case for the Council of Hours. Agatha had taken after her mother's side, with the Rivera family's delicate features and rich olive-brown skin, but she had the Cromwells' same self-assured bearing once they knew to look for it.

They'd known that he had a niece their age, but they'd never actually met her.

Over the years, Rat had heard whispers that Agatha had taken an apprenticeship or left school for private lessons, but there were other rumors, too, that her magic had a sharper bent to it. Some arcanists were inclined toward the kind of spells that worked on muscle and bone. But others, still, took to magic that worked on something even deeper and more human than that.

Rat had never learned the full extent of what that kind of power could do, but there were stories about arcanists who could kill with a look and shred a person apart at the core in ways that could never be fixed.

Rat usually tried not to speculate about what kind of magic Agatha got up to on her own, since they weren't exactly a stranger to ungrounded speculation themself. In spite of that, though, they thought of her in the courtyard, and the way she'd looked at Harker, like they were both in on the same secret.

Unease pricked across the back of their neck.

"I have no idea what her deal is," Will said, reading the look on their face. "Last I heard, she was going to school in London."

"Then why isn't she there?" Rat asked.

He shifted his weight. "So, I'm noticing that the theme for today seems to be Questions that William Chen Does Not Want Answered."

"I'm serious."

"That's all I know. Maybe her parents had a change of plans?"

Rat glanced back. Next to Agatha, Jinx's eyes flickered to them.

She tilted her head to the empty spot at the table behind her, a question on her face.

"Wow," Will said. "Look at us, solving mysteries. Now that that's tied up, we should probably grab seats while there are still some free tables."

"Hold on. I just—I know the girl speaking to Agatha. Jinx. I met her during move-in," Rat said before they could stop themself. "I, actually, there was something I had to ask her about. With the dorms."

"Rat, are you—" he started.

"I'll catch up with you, okay?" they said, pulling out of Will's grip.

Their chest tightened as they started across the room.

They considered bolting instead, except the only thing worse than approaching Jinx and Agatha would be for both of them to see Rat bolt.

"I thought it was you," Jinx said, turning toward them. "We're not taking you away from anything, are we?"

"Will? No. He's joining some people." Rat slid onto the open stool at the next table, trying their best to look collected.

She tipped her head. "Have you two met yet?"

"Agatha," they said. Then quickly, "We've just seen each other around. Our families know each other."

"I told you," Agatha said to Jinx, propping her chin primly on her fist. "Admit it. I'm infamous."

"Alright, Cromwell. You win," Jinx said, nudging her back. She turned to Rat. "I was telling her about how you make maps."

"Oh," they managed.

"No, it's cool. We've been doing a bit of exploring, too. It's an interesting campus." She studied them for a moment. "There was something I was wondering about, though. Maybe you can help me with it."

Rat fought down a fresh wave of panic. "Shoot."

"I saw a light on the roof last night. I've been trying to figure out how to get out there. When I saw your maps earlier, I thought it might have been you." She said it casually enough, but she watched them with a keen, unmistakable interest.

Rat was used to being looked at by strangers, but not like this. Most people looked at them like they were a puzzle to be solved, or something fragile that had to be handled delicately. Jinx didn't.

She looked at Rat like she thought that they might have something in common, and she wanted to be right.

They swallowed hard. "Actually, I—" they started, and then their voice died all over again as Harker appeared in the doorway.

All of the air went out of Rat's lungs. They hadn't expected him to be in their class, maybe because he was exceptional and they weren't, or, maybe because until twelve hours ago, they hadn't seriously considered the possibility that they'd ever be in the same room as him again.

Seeing him last night from the rooftop had been like glimpsing a ghost. Now, in broad daylight, it was a punch in the solar plexus.

Harker had always been skinny in a sleepless, black-coffee-and-all-nighters kind of way, but something about him seemed sharper now in a way Rat couldn't place. His hair had gotten longer since the last time Rat had spoken to him, hanging past his jaw where it had slipped loose from his hair tie, and fresh burns marked his hands from whatever spell he'd been practicing.

He met their eyes, and they didn't know if they wanted to launch themself at him or duck under the desk and stay there.

He stared at them, and even across the room, they could swear they heard his breath hitch. Then, just as fast, his jaw tightened, and his whole expression iced over again.

Something in Rat's chest sank.

Like he hadn't noticed them at all, he fixed his gaze on Jinx and Agatha and made his way to their lab table.

Jinx raised her eyebrows at him behind her glasses. "You're late."

"Yeah. I—" His gaze flickered back to Rat before he looked away again. "I was at the library. I ended up taking the morning shift."

Rat guessed that meant he'd gotten the work-study he'd applied for.

"Remind me to build a memorial to your lost sleep," Agatha said, tearing off another piece of her Danish. She held it out to him, and he looked back at her unamused.

She raised her eyebrows at him as if to say *suit yourself* and then popped the piece into her mouth. "Have you met Rat yet? They make maps."

Rat waved, fighting the urge to flinch. "Hey."

"We went to the same school," Harker said, like they weren't there. An unmistakable chill crept into his voice, and that told Rat everything they needed to know.

They ducked their head.

Out of the corner of their eye, they could swear they saw Jinx and Agatha trade glances.

"We were just talking about the campus," Jinx said, less sure. "Apparently Rat knows a way up to the widow's walk on Mallory Hall."

"Really," Harker said flatly.

"I don't," Rat said. "I was just going to say that I didn't know you could go out there."

Disappointment flickered across Jinx's face.

"Sorry," they said before they could stop themself. "I walked around a bit last night, but it's basically just broom closets and service staircases. I'm probably not even going to finish the whole mapping thing. It's really nothing."

"Oh," Jinx said.

Before they could say anything else, the same man Rat had met at the Founder's House appeared in the doorway dressed in a tweed blazer, carrying a cardboard box under one arm and a leather briefcase in the other.

"Professor Frey," they heard Jinx say to Agatha under her breath.

"I didn't think he taught first-years," Agatha said back.

"He doesn't."

Harker followed their gaze. Then, as if he'd finally realized he couldn't put it off any longer, he collected himself and slipped into the back row, next to Rat.

He set his backpack on the floor and took out the course books and a fresh composition notebook, the cover already filled out in his spindly handwriting. Without looking at them, he flipped it open and became very interested in writing out the date.

At the front, Frey finished arranging his desk. His eyes swept the room, lingering on Rat before moving on.

The class quieted.

"A few people still need to find their way in, but we're already past time," Frey said. He picked up a piece of chalk, tapped it against the board, then turned back to the class. "And before I forget. Cromwell, we've spoken. Evans." He pointed the chalk at Rat. Every eye in the room followed. "I have an extra reading list for you. Make sure you pick it up at the end of class."

Jinx glanced back at them, her brow furrowed like she was trying to decide something. Then Agatha leaned in and whispered to her. Rat had expected her to laugh or turn away again, but whatever Agatha had said, her frown only deepened.

Worse, though, was Harker, not looking at them at all.

Frey turned back to the board and wrote the words *Introduction to Formal Casting Techniques*.

"By this point," he said, underlining the words, "I expect you've all encountered classical spellwork. That is, workings that rely only on the caster's own power, with no other components. An advanced enough caster can accomplish a great deal with little else, although classical methods are usually best for spells that are very physical and only need to last as long as the caster can maintain their focus—moving an object, conjuring light, and what have you.

"Formal casting, on the other hand, covers a range of techniques to support more complex workings. I would advise you all to think of it as supplementary rather than a separate system of magic, though it can operate quite differently at higher levels." Frey tapped the chalkboard. "To start us off, can anyone remind us all of the five basic principles of classical casting?"

A few hands went up, and Rat realized how eminently prepared they were to fail this class. They didn't remotely know or care what the five basic principles were.

As far as Rat could tell, classical spellwork meant anything that could be cast with their hands. As soon as spellbooks and casting chalk were involved, it became formal magic. Beyond that point, all that Rat knew for certain was that it turned into something thorny and unyielding, full of sigils and rituals and spell diagrams that had to be carried out precisely. Most of the more complex spells were locked away in private archives, which, as far as Rat was concerned, was probably safer for everyone.

Harker had taken to it naturally, though, maybe because he was also thorny and unyielding, and he knew how to puzzle out the rules in a way that Rat didn't.

Rat tapped their pen against the paper and then set it down again. They stole another glance at him.

Harker sat forward, eyes on the board. Absently, his hand went to a stray burn on his wrist. The leather bracelets he used to wear, tooth marked and burnt black in most places, were gone, probably because they'd been from Rat, after they'd watched him chew, burn, or otherwise wear through about a dozen string ones.

Their stomach fluttered. "Hey," they said under their breath.

Ignoring them, Harker scribbled something down in his notebook.

They swallowed hard. "I thought . . . I heard that you weren't going to go here anymore. I mean, I'm glad you are. I really . . ."

A frisson of power rolled through the air as Harker's magic slipped away from him, before he could tamp it back down again.

Deliberately, he shifted away, still not meeting Rat's gaze.

They tore a scrap of paper from their sketchbook.

I didn't hear from you all summer and I really

They stopped, staring down at it as the lecture washed over them, and then scribbled over it.

What happened? After I left school? Are you okay? they wrote and slid it over to him.

They stole another glance at Harker. He watched the front of the room intently.

They tore another strip of paper. *Elise told me you'd decided to go somewhere else. I didn't know you'd be here.* And then another. *I tried to reach you.*

They passed those across the desk to him, too.

He made no move to open either one.

Before Rat could make things worse, Frey crossed the room, pulling their attention back.

They looked up as he opened the cardboard box he'd carried in at the beginning of class. From it, he produced a glass ball so delicate that it looked like a trick of the light. "We're going to begin with a classical casting drill that some of you may have done before. You'll be using a simple retrieval spell, from a distance of ten feet."

As he spoke, he traced his fingers through the air, and the orb floated neatly from one hand to the other. All the hairs on Rat's arms pricked up as they caught the dust-and-sunlight scent of magic on the air.

"Preferably, without breaking anything," Frey added, turning the orb in his hand. "If someone could demonstrate . . ."

A few hands went up around the room.

Rat looked back at Harker. "Look," they said under their breath. "I just—"

Heat pricked the air around him. His hand shot up, and Frey's gaze settled on him.

"Ah," Frey said. "Excellent. And you would be . . ."

"Harker," he said, stepping into the aisle. "Blakely, sir."

At the front of the room, Frey held up the glass orb, perched neatly on his fingertips. "This is a simple spell I expect many of you are already familiar with," he said. "Blakely, if you would."

Harker traced a spell on the air, the motion crisp and practiced. The orb lifted out of Frey's hand and floated across the room before settling lightly in Harker's palm.

"Very good," Frey said. He studied Harker like he was considering something, and then took a second orb from the box on the desk. "Do you think you could do another one?"

With a small nod, Harker traced his thumb over the orb in his hand, marking the shape of a spell, and then released it like he was setting it on a shelf. It hung in the air beside him as he returned his gaze to the front of the room.

"At its core, classical casting relies on concentration and intent," Frey said. As he spoke, the second orb floated across the room to Harker, following the path of the first. "While a formal spell can last on its own, ordinary workings are limited by the caster's ability to focus, often more so than their innate power."

Light glinted off of the orb as Harker caught it out of the air.

Frey lifted another and held it up, a question on his face.

Harker sharpened like he'd understood the rules of the game. Effortlessly, he released the second orb, leaving it suspended, and nodded.

He cast again, and the third orb came to rest in his palm.

"There are limits to spreading your power too thin, of course," Frey went on. "But as I'm sure many of you have already found, power counts for very little without the skill to channel it."

Frey took two more orbs from the box as he spoke.

Methodically, Harker drew the next one to himself, and then the next. The orbs around him drifted slightly as he worked, like planets in orbit.

Frey held up a sixth, and Harker traced another spell.

The air warmed around him as the faintest trace of his magic bled out between the cracks in his focus, subtle enough that Rat wasn't sure they would have noticed if they hadn't known what to look for.

They'd forgotten what it was like to see him really cast. They thought of him drawing spell diagrams and flipping frantically through spellbooks in the observatory, the scent of smoke and magic hanging in the air around him as he worked.

"I swore she wouldn't find you, and she won't," he'd promised, his voice desperate and low.

As if Harker had felt their eyes on him, he drew himself up, his shoulders tense as he set another orb on the air. At some point, Rat had stopped counting, but the air had heated around him, the glass orbs roving from their paths.

With a start, they realized that they'd leaned in to watch. They pushed themself back as Harker extended his arm to cast again.

Rat could swear that his eyes flickered back to them, and then the spell broke. The glass orbs crashed down around him and splintered against the floor. Wisps of spellfire curled over the glass, where his magic had spilled back over in the wake of the spell.

"Excellent," Frey said, making his way back up the aisle. He waved his hand over the wreckage, and the spellfire died away. "And an affinity for fire workings. We'll need to work on your control, but really, excellent work. I can't remember the last time I saw a first-year get to nine."

Harker's composure slipped back into place, like he'd remembered the whole class was still watching him, and some of the tension went out of him. "Thank you, sir."

Frey drew a spell on the air as Harker returned to his seat, and the broken glass clicked back together. One by one, the orbs drifted across the room, bobbing on the air like they were being carried on an invisible current before they settled on the desk in a neat row.

Frey made his way back to the front of the room to finish giving instructions, but Rat had already stopped listening again. The casting exercise wasn't for them.

Around the room, the rest of the class began to get up and shuffle toward the front for materials.

Jinx swiveled around in her stool. "Blakely, should I get you one?"

"I'll come with you." Harker got up and slipped into the aisle, moving past Rat as if they weren't there.

"Wait," they said, before he could follow. "Harker."

They caught him by the wrist, stopping him short. His skin was still feverish from casting. He looked down at them, impassive, and something in their chest tightened.

"I just—all summer I was . . . are you okay?"

"Why wouldn't I be?" he asked crisply.

"I—"

"We had an arrangement," he said. "You got what you wanted out of it. I'm pretty sure we're done here."

They sank back.

"I don't need you, either, Evans," Harker said. Then neatly, he pulled out of their grasp and started toward the front of the room without looking back at them.

The moment class let out, Rat bolted.

They made it past all five sets of fire doors and out into the too-bright wash of midday sun before they let themself slow down.

They could barely sit through the casting drill. They couldn't *think*.

"I barely know him. We just had an arrangement."

Those had been their words to Elise.

Obviously, Harker hadn't forgotten the last time they'd spoken.

Rat wanted the earth to swallow them, but even that still wouldn't be enough distance.

They got as far as the clock tower before Will caught up to them. "Hey. What happened in there?" he asked. "Are you okay?"

"Fine," Rat said. "I just, I needed air."

"Was it Blakely? Did he say something? I mean, what's he even doing here, Rat?"

"I don't know."

"I thought—"

"I don't know," they snapped. "He isn't speaking to me. We're not even friends, okay?"

The air had lost some of its chill from the morning, and clumps of students spotted the lawn. Rat felt people staring.

Will took them by the shoulder, and they realized that their knees were shaking.

Rat smudged at their eyes. If they kept talking, they were going to break down, and they couldn't start crying here, in front of everyone.

They exhaled. "I just . . . let's please get inside."

Before Will could argue, they turned back toward the clock tower. They started toward the door, but he pulled them back.

"Rat," Will said, so gently that it hurt.

Then they realized their mistake.

They'd seen pictures of the clock tower in the brochures. It was a relic from before the school had been rebuilt, and whatever strange, tireless magic kept it running, the entrance had been walled off decades ago.

When they looked back, the door was gone, replaced by a wall of sun-faded bricks.

"Fuck. I hate this place." Rat collapsed against the side of the building and slid to the ground, in case by some small mercy the earth actually did swallow them.

With a grunt, Will knelt down next to them. "Why do you always have to sit on the ground? You know we're like ten feet away from a bench, right?"

Rat made a noise that was halfway between a snort and a sniffle. "Leave me alone. I'm gay."

They wiped their nose on their sweatshirt. At least most of the students on the lawn had stopped staring.

"Alright. What's wrong?" Will asked.

Rat drew their knees to their chest. "I thought I saw Harker with Jinx and Agatha last night. That's why I went over there in class. I just . . . fuck, I don't know." They tipped their head back and let out a breath. They had no idea what they'd expected to happen. "Does it seem off to you? That he's with them?"

Will glanced away. "I'm sure it's nothing."

They sat up. "What?"

He shifted his weight. "Look. I'm not going to say something isn't up, but . . ."

"Do you know something?"

"No. Just." He exhaled. "Look, I know you don't want to hear this, but Blakely is ambitious and this actually sounds like exactly the kind of thing he would do. I mean, last year he attached himself to you. And, this year it's Jinx Wilder and Agatha Cromwell, and whenever they get tired of him, it'll be someone else."

Rat let out a strangled laugh. "What?"

Will looked away.

"Will. You know that isn't how it happened, right? I approached him. He was helping me."

One of the worst things about last spring was that everyone had more or less assumed that Harker had used them as a stepping stone to get closer to the old families. It would have only been worse, Rat reminded themself, if they'd tried to convince Elise that he was actually friends with them.

They knew that Harker was ambitious. They *liked* that about him. It meant that there was no spell too complicated to attempt, even if he hurt himself trying. If he hadn't been ambitious, Rat doubted they would've survived the last year.

Something in Will's face softened. "Okay," he said. "Forget I said anything. What I'm trying to say is, of course Harker is up to something.

He's literally always up to something. But maybe we should just leave him to it, and the less we know, the better?"

Rat rested their chin on their knees. "Maybe," they mumbled.

Overhead, the clock chimed the hour.

Will rested his hand on their shoulder. "Come on. We should get back." He flashed them a small, hopeful smile. "Some of the kids from practicum were going to grab lunch. You should come."

"You go ahead. I'll be right there. I just, I need a minute."

"I'll hold you a spot."

They watched until Will had made it back to the path before they slumped back against the building.

They wanted to grab Harker by the shoulders and ask him what he could possibly be up to.

They wanted to never have to look him in the eyes again.

Rat scrubbed their hand over their face. They'd come here to forget that the last year had ever happened.

A cloud drifted over the sun.

With a sigh, Rat picked themself up to go. As they started across the grass, they took a last glance back at the clock tower. For a moment, they caught the faintest flicker of a doorway carved into the brickwork. Then it was gone again, like it had never been there at all.

CHAPTER SIX

HARKER WENT BACK TO IGNORING RAT AFTER THAT.

As it turned out, Agatha was also bookwork only, so he partnered with Jinx, and Rat got to sit quietly at their desk and not touch anything. Which, they guessed, worked out for everyone.

When they weren't in class, Rat tried to keep their head down and steer clear of anywhere they might run into Harker, which, because they didn't know his routes here the way they had at Highgate, turned out to mean most places.

They only managed to add a few buildings to their maps that week: the sprawl of the library, but only from the outside; the clock tower, stark and now doorless; the route down to the casting rooms for practicum; and the lower floors of Galison Hall, where the dining room and student union were.

"Some of us are going to check out the east woods after this. You can come with us," Will offered on Saturday over breakfast. "We're going to prep for Lake Night, but I bet you could put it on your map, too."

Rat's stomach knotted. "Oh. Right."

Bellamy Arts had two major events every fall. The school's Whisper Ball in October, being an alumni event, was decidedly the more official of the two. Even if Rat wasn't looking forward to it, they at least had some idea of what to expect. Lake Night was something else entirely.

Every year, after classes had started but before the autumn chill could settle in completely, teams of students took their cloaks and headed out to the woods at dusk, to the muddy banks of Lake Amory at the edge of campus. Rat didn't know the rules of the game that went on, besides that it ran until sunrise or until there were no teams left, and that the school was usually content to overlook whatever went on, as long as everyone was safely back for breakfast.

Up until last spring, Rat had assumed that if they played at all, they'd probably pair off with Harker and let him do all of the casting, since he was about as bad at teamwork as they were at magic. Or maybe just hide in the dorms because the whole thing sounded suspiciously like sports.

They weren't sure what they were supposed to do now. They'd barely thought about it in months.

"We just started putting together a team," Will added. "You could join us. You don't need to cast or anything. You could always, you know, strategize and run around."

"I might just cheer," Rat managed. They picked up their sketchbook. "I actually wanted to look around campus a bit while it's still quiet. Maybe I could text you when I'm done?"

After he'd left for the woods, Rat set off, following a hallway toward the back of the building. They didn't have anywhere in particular they needed to go, and there were still parts of Galison Hall they hadn't had a chance to see.

A bird lit on the windowsill as they passed.

They stopped.

It eyed them from the other side of the glass, its feathers oil-black in the early light.

Without meaning to, they thought of the low retaining wall that snaked across the tower's outlying fields, black birds perched along the crumbling stones.

The tower had lots of messengers, but birds had always been foremost. Crows and rooks and ravens, and sometimes common blackbirds not much bigger than Rat's hand.

Like nothing, the bird on the windowsill dropped a rock from its beak and took off again, its dark wings catching the morning air.

Rat stared after it, their heart in their mouth. It was a *bird*. They were fine.

Their hand went to their compass.

It's over, they reminded themself, shoving away from the window. Now that Harker wasn't speaking to them, they could almost pretend that the last year hadn't happened at all.

In spite of themself, Rat looked back at the open window one more time, but there was nothing there.

Rat took off toward the stairs without thinking of where they were going and kept moving until they were deep in the upper floors of Galison Hall.

Above the dining hall, the building turned into a maze of reading rooms and common areas, and then farther up, to private casting rooms, which were only available to more advanced students. Everything was still quiet and empty, and Rat took their time, winding between the rooms until their pulse came down and they found themself in a hallway full of old class photos, somewhere on one of the higher floors of the building.

Each of the pictures showed a group of students gathered on the main lawn, the familiar lines of the campus rising behind them. The oldest were grainy and faded in a way that even preservation charms couldn't fix. Rat trailed their fingers along the wall, their eyes flickering over the pictures as they went.

"Rat?"

They turned to see Evening of the Council of Hours standing behind them, his pale skin still slightly windburned from the morning chill. He was tall and angular, his white-blond hair parted crisply to the side.

Edgar Cromwell had always fallen somewhere between a family friend and a political ally, although Rat knew him best in his capacity as one of the four Greater Hours. Maybe because of his closeness with their parents—or maybe because the tower fell under whatever nebulous domain of formal magic the council had given him charge of—Evening had been the one to head up Rat's case last year, after some version of the truth had finally come out. Over the spring, he'd spent almost a week in and out of the Evans house, setting new protections on the property, and had been back a few times since, to make certain that all of the new workings had held.

Rat might have resented him for it, but he'd grudgingly agreed to leave most of Harker's spells intact, and he hadn't breathed a word to Elise.

"Oh," they said. "Hi. What are you doing here?"

"Council business. We have a travel spell anchored in one of the casting rooms upstairs." He looked at the wall of photos, and then, like he already knew, reached out and tapped one on the frame. "Were you looking for this one?"

Rat started to say that they hadn't been looking for anything, and then stopped.

It wasn't the full graduating class, even though the years at Bellamy Arts were relatively small. Instead, a handful of students stood clustered outside one of the classroom buildings dressed in their arcanists' cloaks, a few with matching school pins clasped at their throats. At the edge of the frame was Rat's father when he'd still been a student, slight and summer blond in a deep, dusk-blue cloak that marked him as a Holbrook.

"They're by department," Evening said. "Alexander and I were both in Higher Magics."

He tipped his head at the picture, and Rat realized that he was there, too, standing beside their father, imposing even then.

"You know, he was almost on the Council of Hours," he said, thumbing the picture frame. "We were offered apprenticeships at the same

49

time. He always had a knack for finding things—he was a bit like you, actually. I think they were eyeing him for Dawn."

Rat looked up. "What happened?"

"He chose to stay on here instead." Evening tapped the picture a few frames away. "Elise was a year above us. She was a scourge. Once she raised a full-size castle out of the ground in the middle of the campus as a joke and refused to put it back."

They found her in the picture, almost as tall as most of the boys, her dark hair tied back with a length of satin ribbon the same red as her cloak.

"Anyways," he said. "I should take off. Fairchild's expecting me."

Rat glanced back at the picture of their father as Evening started down the hall. Their hand went back to their compass as they thought of the notes they'd found in their father's office, from when he'd worked at the school. The roughly drawn maps and sketches of the campus, and more of the ruins of the Ashwood estate, in the foothills beyond. The tower itself, amid a sprawl of grass and crumbling stones.

A knack for finding things.

Unease tugged in their chest.

They started after Evening. "Wait," they said, before they could stop themself. "I—Could I ask you something? About the school?"

Evening looked over them, considering. "It's a decent walk from here to the Founder's House, if you have a few minutes."

Rat nodded, and they started back through the building.

Outside, the last of the morning's fog had broken away and a handful of students had appeared on the grass. Evening took to the gravel pathway that led across the center of campus.

"I just . . . it is safe here," Rat said, keeping pace. "Right?"

It felt almost ridiculous to ask. It was daylight, and they were behind the wards. But, something pulled at them, and if they took the question back now, they wouldn't get an answer.

Evening frowned slightly. Rat drew themself up, forcing themself to hold his gaze.

"I trust Elise's judgment," he said smoothly. "She wouldn't have sent you here if she thought that you'd be in danger."

"But?" Rat said, catching the leading edge in his voice.

He paused, like he was trying to decide how to explain. "You found your father's notes on the tower."

A chill pricked across their shoulders, and for a moment, they were back in the tall grass, out among the blackbirds and scavengers and fallen stones, a gloved hand raised to their cheek.

"You look just like him."

"Not many people can reach places like that without higher magics," Evening went on. "But some of those places are . . . closer to certain parts of our world than others, you might say." Reading the flicker of panic on Rat's face, he shook his head. "The campus is very safe, of course. I don't think you'd find anywhere that's better warded. But, things have been known to happen."

"Things?"

"You're a particular case, Rat, but suffice it to say that if you were to wander off somewhere, it wouldn't be the first time a student had vanished from their room. Uncommonly talented young arcanists. Most of them never found. It's been a few years now, but one of the Breton-Fox girls—" he stopped, catching himself.

Rat looked up at him, a question on their face, but he shook his head.

"Ah. Sorry. I'm not allowed to disclose the details of a sealed case, even for an Evans." He pushed his hand through his hair. "Elise knows the faculty here. I fully trust that they'll do everything in their power to keep you safe, but you are your father's child. Given his work and your abilities, it was only a matter of time before something found you. And, sending you here . . . I can only hope that Elise is correct that this is the best place for you. I don't doubt her judgment, but I sometimes wonder if she puts too much faith in Vivian Fairchild's oversight."

"Your niece goes here," Rat blurted before they could stop themself.

"Agatha," Evening said, with no small amount of rue. He rubbed his eyes. "She does. To be honest, I don't like her enrollment here much more than I like yours."

"Is that why you're here?"

He looked surprised, then shook his head. "No. I'm afraid it really is council business. We're a bit outside of my usual hours, but there's an investigation I've been keeping a close watch over. It's . . ." He paused and then frowned. "Well, I suppose you have a right to know. Something went missing from the school's private archives in the Drake last week. Ordinarily, I wouldn't be at liberty to say, but seeing as you have right of succession over your father's property, I believe that makes you an interested party. Unofficially, of course."

Rat furrowed their brow. "What?"

"It was a Holbrook map," Evening said. "That was the only thing stolen, actually."

"A map of what?" Rat said, hesitant.

"It was a personal project of your father's, the final years that he worked here. My understanding is that he was mapping the campus, but he turned it over to Fairchild for safekeeping before he passed."

"But what would Fairchild want with a map of the school? I mean, why would it need safekeeping?" they asked.

"It's a peculiar piece of magic, and Bellamy Arts is an old school with a long history. I imagine that in the wrong hands, someone could find all manner of things," Evening said.

As he spoke, they thought of Fairchild in her office, the service door at her back. *I have no doubt that if you tried, you might find any number of strange, tucked-away corners of the campus.*

Something about it set Rat on edge.

Evening paused, studying them, and his frown deepened. "I'm sorry. I assumed your mother would have mentioned it."

"I . . . no," Rat said. "It never came up."

Elise never spoke about their father's work, but he'd spent half of his life at Bellamy Arts. Rat didn't know if it bothered them more that the Holbrook Map had been stolen or that they'd never known it existed to begin with.

Before they could even begin to form another question, though, Evening waved his hand. "Of course. I didn't mean to trouble you. Forget that I said a word."

At the end of the path, the Founder's House came into view, rising out of the trees. Sun glinted off the cars parked in the gravel lot out front.

"This is me," he said, nodding toward the doors. Then he stopped and turned back to Rat. "I suspect that I'll be on and off campus until this whole thing is sorted out. If you do happen to hear anything, about the case or otherwise . . ."

"Right," Rat said. "Of course. I'll let you know."

He rested his hand on their shoulder. "The Breton-Foxes have a reading room in the library. If you ever find yourself there, I've been told it gets good light in the mornings."

Rat blinked at him. "What?"

"Look out for yourself, Rat," he said. Then, he turned and started into Founder's House, leaving them alone on the lawn.

CHAPTER SEVEN

RAT DREAMT THAT NIGHT ABOUT STOLEN MAPS, AND TALL grass, and the cool press of leather gloves against their cheek.

When they woke up, they lay still for a long time, breathing hard. The taste of mugwort and dust coated their throat. Their skin was slicked with sweat, but the air had gone cold around them at some point in the night.

Rat grabbed their phone off the bed.

Automatically, they opened their message thread with Harker.

Hey, are you

Rat closed it before they could do something awful and desperate like sending Harker a text at five in the morning to ask if he was awake. Without thinking, they swiped over to their browser instead. *Bellamy Arts Missing Student*, they typed into the search bar.

They rolled onto their side and scrolled through the results. There were corners of the internet that were hard for anyone outside of the magic community to find, but the glamours always seemed to recognize Rat as an arcanist, or at least enough of one to let them past. Rat wasn't sure what would have come back for anyone else, but for them, it was all student life articles and school policies.

They tapped their fingers against the side of their phone, trying to remember the name that Evening had given them.

Breton fox bellamy arts, they typed. Nothing.

Breton fox girl missing. Still nothing about the school.

Bellamy arts missing person.

Rat thumbed through the results so fast they could barely read the entries. They already knew that what they were looking for wasn't there. It wasn't like blooded arcanists to air their personal affairs where everyone could see, and Rat didn't even have the missing girl's full name.

Holbrook Map, they typed.

Rat stared at the words in the search bar. They didn't know what they were expecting to turn up. They'd never even heard of the map before yesterday.

For about the twelfth time in as many hours, they thought of the sketch of the tower they'd found in their father's notes back before they knew what it was, and the whisper of wind over the dry grass. If he wasn't like them, he'd been something close.

They didn't want to think about the possibilities for where a map like that might lead.

They didn't want to think about what it meant that someone had stolen it.

It has nothing to do with you, they reminded themself. *The school is handling it.*

They tossed their phone back down.

Outside, the sky had just begun to get light at the edges, but they already knew that they wouldn't be falling back to sleep. Rat pushed themself up and grabbed their compass from the bedside table, slipping it into the pocket of their pajama pants.

They needed air.

Before they could think better of it, they gathered up their sketchbook and slipped out into the hall, toward the stairs to the widow's walk.

Rat had been up a few times since they'd gotten settled, usually in the mornings. No one bothered them there, and it was the one place on campus where they could draw without being seen.

Usually, they worked over the campus, checking the scale of their maps and sketching thumbnails of the academic buildings. The sprawl of the library, and the pitched roof of the Founder's House just beyond it.

The not-a-chapel-anymore, with its high windows, and the clock tower rising above it all.

Today, though, Rat found themself sketching the field of old stone.

They still dreamt about it all the time. Sometimes they were out in the tall grass among the crumbling boulders, the sky around them deepening to the color of a bruise. Sometimes, they dreamt about the tower itself.

Sometimes, though, they just dreamt about *her*, standing in the overgrowth like a knight from a fairytale, the dark snarls of her hair crowned in autumn flowers, with her worn leather gloves and a traveling cloak draped across the broad line of her shoulders, her eyes cold and bright like a carrion bird.

That was how they always thought of her—the knight, with the tower rising at her back and her pale skin etched in evening light. She only looked a few years older than Rat, but there was something about her that seemed untouched by time, like the years passed differently for her, or maybe not at all.

The nights Rat dreamt of her, they had to remind themself that they hadn't gone back with her when she'd tried to take them.

They still lost sleep, wondering what might have happened if they had.

"It wouldn't be the first time a student had vanished from their room."

Rat's pencil snapped against the page, and they realized they'd worn a hole in the paper. Slowly, they released the tension in their shoulders.

They shouldn't have been thinking about the tower at all.

They were safe here.

They stared down at their sketchbook. The whole situation made their skin crawl. The missing students. The stolen map. The way that the theft had been timed with their own arrival on campus.

They felt like they'd stepped into the middle of something that was already in motion.

Like, maybe, some part of this had been set in motion because of them.

They pushed their hand through their hair. "Holy fuck, get a grip, Evans."

Their phone chimed. Blearily, they glanced down at the screen to see three new messages from Will.

Probably, he wanted to know if they were heading to breakfast, or whatever it was that well-adjusted people did before noon on the weekend.

Go away im sleeping thx they mashed out, then stopped, their thumb hovering over the send button.

With a twinge of unease, they looked back out at the campus.

They deleted the message. *Hey*, they typed, pulling their knees to their chest. *Is there any chance you're going by the library?*

Three dots appeared at the bottom of the screen, and then a new message. *Meeting some people there during the week maybe. Why?*

CHAPTER EIGHT

THE DRAKE LIBRARY SPRAWLED AT THE FOOT OF THE clock tower like a slain beast, except with a pitched roof and substantially more turrets. Rat had spent hours poring over brochures, but for all the pictures of sunlit reading rooms and leather-bound books, they couldn't find a cohesive map anywhere.

They followed Will, allowing him to lead them through the building.

Something about libraries had always gotten under their skin—the faint, musty smell that could be magic or could just be old paper, the maze of self-same aisles. They could never shake the feeling that they were just about to turn down the wrong row of books, and the shelves would close behind them.

The Drake, they could already tell, was one of the worst of its kind.

"You're looking for books," Will repeated, leading them up one of the library's too-many staircases.

"I read things. Sometimes." They hadn't told him about their father's map, or the investigation, or anything else. Will worried about them enough as it was, without them making up new problems.

He gave them a dubious look.

"I wanted to see the building," they said, a bit more convincingly. "I haven't been inside yet."

Will hesitated, and his eyes flickered over them like he could tell that something was wrong. "Are you okay?"

"Yeah. Great," they said.

"Hey." He knocked their shoulder as they came to the top of the staircase. "You're welcome to crash our Lake Night meeting if you get tired of making maps."

Rat looked up at him. "Wait, is that what you're doing here?"

He grinned. "It's still our first strategy session, but we're thinking of playing a strong defense," he said, turning onto a wide, well-lit corridor. High arches lined the way, opening into the stacks. "Some of us were talking about fortifications."

In spite of themself, Rat let out a small laugh. "What?"

"One of the St. Augustine sisters is in the engineering department. She's drawing up schematics for a fortress. The sophomores aren't going to be able to lay a hand on us." As he spoke, he took a glass bauble from his bag and held it up to them, like the one Frey had them use in practicum. Deftly, he tossed it and caught it again.

Rat guessed that it had to be a part of the game, but they also didn't know how to ask without admitting that they knew exactly nothing about what kind of game this was.

Will stopped near a set of open doors and waved Rat into a large reading room lined with shelves. A pack of kids they recognized from the New York crowd had already claimed the high-backed leather chairs by the window, laughing loudly about something.

All of them stopped and turned toward the door as Rat entered.

"Hey guys," Will said with an easy smile.

Fighting the urge to duck their head, Rat waved, their eyes flickering around the circle. There were five kids in all.

One of the St. Augustine girls sprawled on the window seat where she was idly levitating a glass orb, her long, dark hair bound back in a length of satin ribbon. The other one shared an armchair with Viola Nguyen, who Rat was passingly familiar with since she was one of the few other trans kids in their year at Bellamy Arts, though she'd gone to a different prep school in Manhattan. The other two were a pair of boys who Rat had seen in their practicum class.

One of the boys lit up. "Do we have Evans?"

"Oh," Rat said. "Um, no, I can't actually—"

"I already offered. They're just stopping in right now," Will said, then shot Rat a hopeful look. "You're welcome to stick around though, if you want."

The St. Augustine girl on the window seat released her spell, letting the bauble drop into her hand. "We're only allowed to start the game with three, but we managed to get extra from the practice rooms," she said, swinging her legs down. "Will, how are you with earthworking? Vi wants a moat, but I'm worried the battlements will cave in if the ground gets too muddy."

Viola gave him a hopeful look and mouthed, *Moat.*

Unsure of what else to do with themself, Rat perched against the side of one of the study tables. They stayed like that for a bit, letting the discussion wash over them but not really following any of it, before they finally excused themself and ducked back into the hallway.

As soon as they left, a tension they hadn't realized they were holding went out of them. Rat never knew if it was the old blood kids in particular or just meeting new people, but they could never seem to relax.

They didn't even know why. Will's friends were nice. If Rat wanted a place, they knew they'd have it. Somehow, though, they could never figure out what to do with themself, which always made it worse since Rat was all too aware that if they kept hiding from people, eventually, they wouldn't be invited back.

Still, there was a part of them that was just glad to know that Will was somewhere in the building, like at least, if they made a wrong turn and vanished into the stacks, someone would know where they'd last been seen.

They made it all the way around the bend and up another flight of stairs before they allowed themself to stop and think about where they were going.

They'd ended up in a long, window-lined hallway overlooking a courtyard. Squares of cool morning sunlight striped the ground ahead of them, and the faint smell of paper and leather hung in the air.

Rat settled against the windowsill and drew out their sketchbook, but their maps of the library were sparse at best.

Even if they tracked down the right reading room, they had no idea what Evening was hoping they'd find there.

If Harker was with them, he would have three new leads and a reading list by now. He was always the one who knew what to look for. Rat's job usually involved creating new problems and occasionally providing snacks.

They forced out a breath and drew their compass from their pocket, letting the steady weight of it ground them. They refused to need him.

"Lost?"

Rat looked up with a start to see Jinx in her too-big jacket and battered Docs.

Since the first day of class, she hadn't tried to speak to them again. Apparently, that had ended.

Quickly, their hand tightened around their compass.

Her mouth quirked. "You know, for someone with so many maps, I kind of expected you to know your way around better."

Their face heated. "If I knew my way, I wouldn't bother with making maps," they said, which really wasn't the comeback they'd been hoping for.

She came over, leaning her shoulder against the wall. "Where to?"

"Nowhere," they said. They pocketed their compass and flipped their sketchbook shut. "I'm just looking around."

Jinx watched them, considering.

"Actually, do you know where the Breton-Fox room is?" Rat asked before they could stop themself.

She furrowed her brow. "Why that one?"

"I . . . heard it gets good light," they managed. "Why? Is something wrong with it?"

She eyed them carefully, like she couldn't tell if they were joking or not. "What?"

"Nothing. No one ever goes up there."

"But you know where it is."

"I've been around the building."

Jinx regarded them impassively. With a pang of frustration, Rat realized she was waiting for them to ask her a second time.

After a long moment, she turned, her boots squeaking on the hardwood floors. "Well, anyways—"

"Wait," they said.

She glanced back at them, and they could swear that her eyes glinted behind her glasses.

Rat huffed a breath. "Can you tell me where it is? Please?"

Her gaze went to their sketchbook. "I'll trade you."

They opened their mouth to protest, but they could feel the sheer size of the library, sprawling out around them. They could spend the whole day wandering and probably never find it. The stacks would open up and swallow them, or, worse, they'd run into Harker and have to ask him for directions instead.

"One map," Rat said.

"Two," Jinx said.

They ground their teeth, which Jinx took as a yes.

She put her hand out.

"One, and I get to pick."

She lifted her eyebrows at them, because apparently negotiating was only fun when she did it.

They riffled through the pages, holding the sketchbook close enough that she wouldn't see anything. The last thing they needed was Jinx catching a glimpse of the tower nested between their sketches of the campus.

They stopped at a floor plan of Mallory Hall, completed, without any stray marks or extra doorways that might give them away. Their thumb brushed the sketch of the third floor, stopping at the staircase to the roof.

Drawing themself up, Rat tore it neatly from the binding and handed it to her. Maybe because they knew it was what she wanted.

Maybe because a small part of them wanted her to know she'd been right about them.

Recognition flickered over Jinx's face, and when she looked back at them, something in her gaze sharpened.

Rat fought the urge to look away.

Jinx tucked the map neatly into her bag. "This way," she said, nodding for Rat to follow her.

She led them to the end of the corridor, where three wide, stone archways were cut into the wall, each branching off in a different direction.

"You'll want to go left," Jinx said. "It'll take you to a set of stairs. When you get there, straight up." She nodded to the second archway. "The other way takes you deeper into the stacks."

Rat nodded, and then they heard what she was saying. *The other way.* Singular.

Rat looked back at the passage in the middle. Then the one on the far right. Both looked real, and the heavy scent of aged paper and furniture polish was enough to mask the attic smell of a dead passage entirely.

In the light, they hadn't noticed at all. Despite the sun-warmth of the hallway, they suddenly felt cold all over.

"Thanks," they said.

They took off before they could give themself away completely.

They made it most of the way to an old, stone staircase at the end of the hall before they slowed again, their heart beating too hard against their ribs.

Rat scrubbed their hand over their face.

They weren't going to think about it.

They settled against the rail of the stairs and forced themself to breathe, pulling their sketchbook to their chest.

Maybe because they were in the library, maybe because they hadn't really stopped thinking about it, their mind turned back to the Holbrook Map.

Rat glanced back over their shoulder, but they had already lost sight of the mouth of the hallway, and Jinx with it. They remembered the intense way her eyes had flickered over the map they'd given her.

Do you know something? They wanted to ask. *About the school?*

They pushed the thought away.

Whatever cloak-and-dagger secret-society bullshit Harker had gotten himself into with Jinx and Agatha, it was emphatically not their business.

Rat hadn't known that the Holbrook Map in the library existed until it was stolen. They didn't even know for certain what was in it. If there were places on campus that were stranger or harder to find, there was no reason why Jinx would know about them, let alone care.

Harker might, a voice whispered in the back of Rat's mind.

They shoved that thought away, too.

They weren't going to think about Harker at all.

They tightened their arm around their sketchbook and started up the stairs, and this time, they didn't allow themself to look back.

The common room was tucked away at the top of the stairs, with a sloping ceiling and an out-of-use fireplace with a painting over the mantel.

As soon as Rat found it, they understood why Evening had sent them there.

The girl in the painting sat stiffly, her hands folded in her lap like she'd been posed, a single mum held between them almost as if she'd forgotten she was still holding it. She had the Fox family's fair skin and square jawline, and her hair had been swept back, falling over one pale shoulder in chestnut-colored waves. She looked like she wanted to be somewhere else.

Below the picture, there was a small, gold plaque with a set of dates, but a part of Rat already knew who she was.

"Piper Breton-Fox," they read under their breath. The last missing student.

Goosebumps pricked up their arms.

Absently, they traced their hand over the mantle. A handful of small trinkets had been left out on the sill—not the strange crow gifts that Rat used to find on their windowsill, but the kind of superstitious offering that students left. Butterscotch candies in yellow cellophane. A silver ring. A deck of playing cards and a fresh book of matches.

From their pocket, they took a nub of chalk that they sometimes used to mark their route and set it down amid everything else.

Then their eyes pulled back up to the painting of Piper, the mum clasped in her hands. From the dates on the plaque, she'd been missing for the better part of a decade now.

They tried to picture her wading out into the field of grass, but it didn't make sense. They couldn't imagine how the knight had found her or what she possibly could have wanted.

What happened to you? they wanted to ask.

But no matter how hard Rat tried, they couldn't think of an answer.

CHAPTER NINE

RAT SPENT THE REST OF THE WEEK PORING OVER THEIR notes on the campus whenever they weren't in class, but if there was any hint of what, exactly, the stolen Holbrook Map might have been of, they couldn't find it. They added a few more buildings to their map and checked through all of the sketches they'd done, but there wasn't anything else.

When they slept, they dreamt that they were wandering the twisting corridors of the campus, until everything around them opened into grass and unfamiliar stars. They always woke up in the dark, the sky still fading outside of their window.

Even before the knight had tried to take Rat back with her, they'd never known what exactly she wanted from them. Sometimes, they still lay awake at night wondering what would have happened if they'd followed her.

All that Rat knew for certain was that if they had, they wouldn't have made it home again.

By the time Lake Night came around, the first hint of a chill had stolen into the air.

"Obviously, you'll be cheering for us," Will said when he found them in the dining hall Friday morning. "Since my team has already decided we're going to win."

"Obviously," Rat told him, fighting a smile in spite of themself.

At least the lake would be noisy and crowded, which meant Rat could disappear into the sidelines as soon as the game started.

That night, after they'd gathered up their things and shut their sketchbook in their desk, they dug their cloak out of the bottom of their trunk.

Most arcanists had one, although Rat hadn't had occasion to wear theirs, maybe because they weren't much of an arcanist. The oldest families usually passed theirs down the line, the cloth stitched with enchantments that had been added across the years. Protection workings and spells to keep off the weather, but more intricate magic, too.

Elise had given them hers to try on before they'd come to school. It was a brilliant shade of crimson stitched with gold thread, and easily one of the most striking things Rat had ever laid eyes on.

It wasn't the one they'd packed.

This one was blue, so deep it was a shade off from black, closed with a simple silver clasp.

Rat had found it in an old cedar trunk amid their father's belongings a few years back. They didn't know why they'd taken it, but they'd never shown it to Elise. They'd only worn it a few times, and never out of their house. They just knew that it had felt like *theirs*, in a way that almost nothing else did.

Cautiously, like the cloak might break apart in their hands, Rat unfolded it, letting it drape over their arm. They only needed to wear it tonight if they were planning to join the game, though they knew that most of the other students would come dressed for it, playing or not.

They glanced up at the floor-length mirror, and then, uncertain, they drew it around their shoulders. They braced themself for it to be wrong somehow, like they'd only imagined that it had fit them. But it wasn't.

It was perfect.

Alexander Holbrook hadn't been tall, but the cloak fell so exactly that Rat knew someone must have added a tailoring spell at some point. They traced their hands along the inside of the silk lining, to a pocket just deep enough for their compass and maybe a few sheets of paper or a stick of casting chalk. Then another, beside it, big enough for a small book. If it wasn't for the faint smell of cedar oil still clinging to the fabric, the cloak could have been made for them.

Studying their reflection, Rat pushed their hair back, sweeping their bangs away from their face.

They looked like a Holbrook.

They looked like a boy.

Not a boy, they thought, tilting their head. They looked like something magnificently *other*, valiant and terrible and shrouded in the last hour of dusk.

Their chest pulled. Rat was used to wanting things, but this was the kind of want with teeth and claws. The kind that it would be dangerous to put words to, because if they said it out loud, they'd have to admit to how badly they'd wanted to be seen this way. They wouldn't be able to pretend that it didn't sting when they were inevitably told no.

They touched their fingers to the cloak's clasp. Suddenly, the idea of being perceived made them want to crawl under the bed and stay there.

Their phone buzzed. Rat glanced down to see a new text from Will, asking when they were coming down to meet him.

Just getting my stuff, down in five, they typed.

They looked at the mirror one last time, and their reflection looked back, strange and familiar at the same time.

Letting out a breath, Rat folded the cloak and shoved it back into the trunk. They grabbed a sweatshirt from the foot of their bed, and the compass from their nightstand, and went down to meet him.

A wind swept across the path as they followed Will out toward the edge of the east woods. Rat was realizing they hadn't thought the whole outing all the way through.

They didn't particularly like being in the woods after dark, any more than they liked the idea of getting near the lake. There was something about water that made them feel especially directionless and unmoored. They badly regretted not taking Will up on the chance to map the area in the daylight.

Up ahead, a wave of shouts rose up from the trees. Rat ducked their head, pulling their arms tighter around themself.

"I promise you're not going to get thrown in the lake," Will said.

"I might," they protested.

"If anyone tries to pick you up, I will personally sink them into the mud." Will slung his arm over their shoulder, pulling them forward. "You're going to be fine."

They were not going to be remotely fine.

Before Rat could come up with an excuse to turn back, they came to a break in the trees.

"I swear on the Chen family name and all of the stars I was born under," Will said, "you will not get thrown in the lake."

Ahead, the woods opened up into the wide sweep of the lake's banks. Candles hovered over the water, bobbing lazily on the air. Rat didn't know what kind of enchantment it was, other than that it was far beyond their skill level. A group of students in cloaks had gathered at the end of the wooden dock, laughing about something as they cast ripples across the lake, and more kids had gathered along the shoreline, some dressed for the game and a few in jackets and sturdy shoes like they'd come to watch.

Farther out, the glow from the party gave way to the far shore and the dark rise of the foothills beyond.

The faint scent of magic and lake water hung in the air, but there was something underneath it—mugwort and turned earth and night air.

Rat's chest tightened. *Because you're in the woods, Evans. Get a grip.*

"Hey." Will tagged their arm, and Rat realized that a few of the kids they'd met in the library had already found him. "The rest of the team is here. They're meeting a bit down the shore. Want to come?"

"You go," Rat said. "I think I'm still kind of . . ." they gestured to the clearing.

"If you need me—"

"Don't worry. Really, I'm good," they said, waving him off.

They just needed to breathe.

As soon as he was gone, Rat dipped back toward the edge of the clearing. Automatically, their hand went to their compass.

They turned it between their fingers, grounding themself.

This was what they had come to Bellamy Arts for. To put everything with the tower to rest and to forget that they'd ever had any magic of their own to begin with. To make the right friends and finally get on with their life.

Not to start digging it all up again.

"You're fine," they said under their breath. "You're here, and you're fine."

In spite of themself, their eyes flickered across the crowd before they realized who they were searching for. Who they were always searching for.

Even if he was here, he wouldn't want to talk to them, they reminded themself.

Someone's arm settled on Rat's shoulder, jarring them back. They jumped.

"Hey, Evans," Jinx said.

Rat turned.

She'd traded her leather jacket for a long cloak the color of a storm that brushed the top of her Docs, and she carried a camping lantern, though the lake wasn't yet dark enough to use it.

"Find what you were looking for?" she asked.

Before they could answer, she was already off, her cloak billowing after her on the breeze.

They watched as she picked her way across the lake bank to where Agatha Cromwell Rivera was standing by the water, with a crown of reeds woven into her hair. She'd chosen an ostentatiously white cloak—somehow clean in spite of the trek through the woods—open over a satin slip dress, like the Lady of Shalott in hiking boots.

Rat forced the tension from their shoulders. It was officially time to find Will again before the night got any worse.

Rat turned to go, and then froze.

At some point, Harker had appeared at the edge of the clearing, in the same faded black cloak he'd had at Highgate. His hair was still tied back, a sprig of grass tucked behind his ear.

A breeze caught the edges of his cloak as he drew a flicker of spellfire absently between his fingers. The grass rippled around him, and in the fading light, for a moment, he looked like he'd stepped out of one of Rat's tower dreams.

Unbidden, Rat thought of him kneeling in the field of grass and fallen stones the one time they'd brought him there, gathering a handful of dirt for a warding spell while they watched from behind the low line of the old retaining wall.

Their pulse kicked against their ribs, and Rat pushed the memory away before they could follow it any further. It wasn't something they liked to remember.

Harker glanced up at Rat and raised his eyebrows at them pointedly. Heat crept up the back of their neck as they realized that they'd been staring.

Then, like he didn't remotely care what they did, Harker looked out, surveying the crowd like he was waiting for literally anyone else.

A nervous flutter rose in their throat.

The smart thing to do was go. Will was waiting for them.

They thought of the tower again, and the Holbrook Map, and the missing students.

Before they could think about what they were doing, they started toward Harker.

"Hey, can we talk?" Rat asked, closing the last of the distance between them.

Heat pricked the air around him. "Sorry, I'm meeting someone," he said as he moved to leave.

"Wait." Quickly, they grabbed his cloak. "Please."

He looked down at them, unimpressed.

"Look. I know you don't want to see me, but—"

"No. Rat, what do you think you're doing?" he said, dropping his voice. Some of his composure fell away. "I thought you didn't want to be seen with me."

"No, I—"

He pulled his cloak back from them. "Elise tried to pay me to pick a school I was *better suited for* so I wouldn't be in your way. You know that, right?"

"*What?*" they breathed. "Harker. I didn't—"

"No, you just let everyone else do things for you." He drew in. "Maybe you don't want to be here, but this is literally the only thing I have. I'm not losing it over you. You clearly weren't going to lose it over me, either."

"I talked to her as soon as you were gone. Elise promised she'd leave you out of it," they said in a rush. "I was trying to protect you."

He looked down at them, and his voice was all ashes. "Oh. Is that what that was?"

Their face heated. *Yes*, they wanted to tell him. Rat was sheltered and powerless, and no one would have believed that someone as ruthlessly capable as Harker would ever actually want to be friends with them.

He must have known that.

"I—you ignored me all summer and then traded me for Jinx and Agatha," Rat blurted. Their voice came out high and plaintive, and they hated themself for it.

Immediately, they wanted to hide, but they drew themself up, holding his gaze.

"I—Look," they said. "I don't care what you're all up to, I just need you to tell me something and I'll leave you alone. I found out that my father made a map of the campus. It was stolen from the school's private archives and I just . . . and maybe it's nothing, but you've seen his work before. I don't know if you've noticed anything about the school, but . . . have you? Noticed anything?"

Their heart beat hard in their chest.

They didn't want an answer from him. They wanted him to ask them what they knew about the map, or how someone could have gotten into the school archives. They wanted to be sitting on the floor of their room in Mallory Hall explaining everything to him over late-night coffee.

They wanted to be wrong.

"That sounds like a personal problem, Evans." His voice ran cold.

"Harker—"

"Then again. If there was something here," he said, drawing it out, "I guess it would be safest for you not to go looking."

Rat stilled.

"That's what you wanted, right? To be safe?"

A chill tracked down their spine. "You do know something."

He regarded them impassively. "Rat. What could I possibly know about your family's secrets?"

"You—"

Before they could get another word out, Jinx appeared from the crowd, Agatha in tow.

"Hey," she said, and Rat realized how close to him they were standing. They stepped back as her gaze shifted from them back to Harker. "Are they with us?"

"No," he said decisively. "They're not. We're going." He pulled away from them and started toward the tree line.

Rat stared after as he vanished into the woods.

Behind him, Jinx and Agatha traded glances. Agatha leaned in and whispered something, then started after him.

Jinx cast a last, curious glance back at them, like she was waiting to see what Rat would do.

Then, after a too long moment, she turned and followed, her cloak billowing after her.

Rat's face burned.

It didn't matter if Harker had left them a trail, because they were a coward, and he knew it. He was being obvious because he could be.

Their eyes stung.

"Fuck," they breathed.

They scanned the trees. At some point without them noticing, night had nearly fallen around them, and the woods were darker than before. Jinx's lantern glinted in the distance, the light receding up the path as she walked.

Will had promised that the game kept close to the lake, but Harker had cut straight back into the trees.

Rat grit their teeth. They weren't letting him have this.

They stole a glance up the shore, where Will was standing with the rest of his team.

Then, regretting it already, Rat took off into the woods after Harker.

Rat picked their way between the trees, their heart in their mouth, but they couldn't let themself slow down. The faint glow of Jinx's camping lantern flickered between the trees ahead of them. If they stopped, they would lose sight of it entirely, and then they would be completely alone.

There was still some light left, but they were losing it quickly. The trees grew tall and close, the canopy arching overhead, and it was darker than it had been along the banks of the lake.

Overgrowth crept in along the edges of the trail. Ivy and sumac, mugwort and flowers gone to seed.

"You're fine. You're here," Rat said under their breath, pushing down a swell of panic.

You're in New York. In the woods. Things grow here.

They glanced back the way they'd come, but they couldn't see the lights over the lake anymore.

Their hand slipped to their compass, their thumb brushing over the cool metal of its case.

"You're fine," they said again.

They forced themself forward, and then, with a start, they realized that the glow from Jinx's camping lantern had stopped moving.

Rat hurried to close the distance.

When they couldn't get any closer without being heard, they ducked behind a tree. Their heart threatened to crawl out through their throat.

Carefully, they peered out.

The group had come to a stop.

Ahead lay a low brick wall, split in the middle like there had been a gate there once, before it had been brought down by time and weather. Beyond that, in a small dirt clearing, there was a pair of cellar doors set into the dirt. Grass sprouted up around them, sparse and brittle.

A door in the woods.

Harker leaned in to say something too low for Rat to hear, and Jinx and Agatha started up the path without him.

He waited a long moment for them to leave before he turned back toward the path, then traced his hand through the air to cast.

Before Rat could move, a pale will-o'-wisp of spellfire flared over his hand, throwing shadows across the path.

Except it was wrong, the spellfire cold and flickering where it had always been steady and bright. If one of his spells had been abandoned in a field, this was the ragged, left-behind thing that it might have grown into.

The wind caught the edges of his cloak, leaves skittering around him.

And then, the pieces finally sliding into place, Rat couldn't unsee it.

They didn't know if it was the spellfire, or the woods, or the way Harker caught the last dregs of the fading daylight, but traces of the tower clung to him like a pall of smoke. It was written into the too-sharp line of his jaw, and the tension in his shoulders, and the wisp of spellfire still wavering on the air.

"No," Rat said softly.

They were the one the knight had been after. Rat had barely even spoken to Harker in months. She wouldn't have come back for him.

Harker cast a last, searching glance up the path.

Finally, he lowered his hand. He looked up at a crow perched on a low branch like they were in on the same secret, and then, unreadable as ever, he turned and started back up the path after the others, leaving Rat alone in the weeds.

CHAPTER TEN

RAT DIDN'T ALLOW THEMSELF TO STOP MOVING UNTIL they were back in their room in Mallory Hall. They fumbled to lock the door, and then they realized that it didn't matter, because the knight was *here*.

No matter where they went, no matter how many wards Rat put between themself and the tower, always, she found a way back in.

She'd found Harker.

He was the only person who'd ever felt really safe to Rat. If they vanished off the face of the earth, he was the one they always knew would find them and drag them back.

Or at least, he had been, once.

Rat dropped onto the bed and reached for their compass, except it wasn't there. With a pang, they realized they must have dropped it somewhere by the lake, but they couldn't make themself go back out.

Again, they thought of Harker in the east woods, with the day fading around him and a sprig of grass tucked behind his ear.

He'd been going somewhere. Looking for something.

Again, they remembered him at the tower, one knee to the dirt where he'd knelt in the field of old stones, the knight's hand clasped around his wrist. Caught.

"You're theirs, aren't you?"

Rat shoved the thought back down.

They didn't know if it scared them more that she'd found him again or that she'd left him unharmed.

Without thinking, they opened their phone.

They had a handful of missed texts from Will, but they swiped past to their message thread with Harker.

What did she do with you? they typed.

They stared at it for a long time without sending, and then they deleted it and opened Will's messages instead.

Sorry, they typed. *I didn't want to take you away from the game. I wasn't feeling well, just made it back to the dorm.*

That one, they sent.

Rat shoved their phone under their pillow and curled on their side with the lights still on, and they stayed that way for a long time.

CHAPTER ELEVEN

RAT HAD TAKEN HARKER TO THE TOWER EXACTLY ONCE.

It had been close to the end, right before Elise had found out and everything unraveled, when they'd come back to find a rabbit curled at the foot of their bed wreathed in mums and Queen Anne's lace, too still to be sleeping.

It had been late, but Elise had been out of town until the weekend, and they'd known that Harker would be awake if they called him.

They'd let him wrap the rabbit in an old towel and carry it out to the woods behind the house, the birds watching from the low branches of the trees, and then they'd sat on the floor of their room while he'd redone the wards on the bedroom window.

"It's really bad," they'd said after he'd finished sealing the spells. "Isn't it?"

It had been after midnight, and they'd both ended up in the kitchen. Rat sat perched on the counter next to the stove, their feet drawn up since it wasn't like Elise would see them. They hadn't stopped trembling, and Harker had put on water for tea, even though they were probably supposed to do that, because it was their house.

"I added another layer to the wards, but I don't think the spells are working anymore," he'd admitted. "I don't know if she's figured them out, or if she's had it from the beginning and she's just showing her hand now."

"We could summon something worse," they'd offered unhelpfully. "You know. Find a bigger fish. Like, with more teeth."

They'd bared their teeth at him to demonstrate, and Harker had given them a look that said absolutely not.

"I have an archive. I bet there's a book."

"You have enough monsters, Evans. You're not summoning another one."

They'd flashed him a shaky attempt at a grin. "Technically, you'd be summoning it. I'd just supervise."

In spite of himself, Harker let out a small, bitten-off laugh. "Rat. No." Then, just as fast, he caught himself and the reality of the situation set back in.

He hesitated.

"What?" Rat had asked.

"There's another spell," he'd said. "One that we haven't tried yet."

They'd looked at him. "Why are you saying that like I won't like it?"

He'd met their eyes, and they'd known from the look on his face that it was because they wouldn't.

"Say it," they'd said.

"We would need dirt," he'd told them. "From the tower. And we'd need to be as close as we could get. Not just to the world, but . . ."

"The tower itself," Rat had said, understanding, and he'd given them a small, grim nod. "But, it would work?"

"I can keep searching for a different working. There has to be—"

"No," they'd said, feeling small. They hadn't known how to explain it to him. The knight was toying with them. She would keep toying with them until she grew bored, and when she did, she'd bring the game to a close. Rat didn't want other options. They wanted it to stop. "I can get us through. If I can open the way to get what we need, can you cast the spell?"

For a moment, they'd thought he might lie and say that he couldn't, but then, maybe because he'd heard the desperation in their voice, he'd said, "I can try."

They'd let him talk them through the spell while the water finished boiling, but Rat barely heard anything he'd said. It was going to be okay, they'd told themself, and even though they didn't believe it, it didn't matter. If there was a chance it would work, they'd go.

They'd taken Harker the same way they'd gone the first time, through a dead passage from their father's study.

It had been months since they'd been back, since the last time the knight had finally asked them to return with her, but the way had opened ahead of them into the familiar sprawl of the outlying fields, the first evening stars pricking against the coming dark. The tower rose ahead of them, its crooked battlements stark against the sky.

A wind had rippled across the tall grass, warmer than where they'd left and smelling faintly of mugwort.

Behind them, Harker had drawn in a sharp breath, and his grip on their sleeve had tightened. They'd taken him through dead passages before but never this far.

Never here.

They'd come out just behind the low stone wall that cut across the grass. There had been maybe a hundred yards between them and the tower. It hadn't been as close as they'd wanted to be, but it had been the best they'd been able to manage.

Harker had eyed the distance. "If I can make it there, can you hold the way open?"

Rat had swallowed hard and nodded.

Beside them, Harker had let out a shuddering breath. "Stay here, okay?" he'd said, raising his hand to a casting position, and then he'd started forward, into the grass.

"Wait." They'd caught his sleeve, pulling him back. "Harker. I—"

This whole thing had been a mistake. They shouldn't have brought him.

They'd wanted to go with him into the field so they wouldn't have to let go of his sleeve.

They'd wanted to grab him by the arm and drag him back to the safety of the study.

Something in his face had softened. He'd take them back if they asked, and if they did, they wouldn't have had the resolve to come back.

"Be fast," they'd said. "Okay?"

81

He'd given Rat a small nod and then slipped ahead of them, through a break in the wall of stones, one hand already working a concealment spell on the air.

As soon as he'd gone, Rat had sunk down at the foot of the stone wall that cut across the field, not daring to move from the passageway.

They shouldn't have come back. Any moment, the knight would come wading through the grass, her dogs at her heels. She would appear on the wall, perched on the crumbling stones. She would smell them on the wind, and somehow, she would stop them and they wouldn't make it back this time.

They'd wanted to go home.

Letting out a breath, they'd peered around the edge of the wall.

A bird had swept overhead, black against the sky. They'd drawn their knees in, following it with their eyes as it circled low over the field.

It had banked toward the ground, but before it could land, something shifted, like a trick of the light, and then she'd been there, standing over Harker in the grass. She'd looked the way that Rat remembered, a crown of flowers gone to seed woven into her dark hair, the lines of her traveling cloak etched in the fading light.

Her hand had closed around Harker's wrist. On instinct, he'd drawn back, but she'd wrenched him forward.

Appraisingly, she'd pressed her gloved knuckles under his jaw, tilting his face up to hers. "You're theirs," she'd said, just loud enough that the wind carried her voice over the grass. "Aren't you?"

Heat had rolled off of him in waves. He'd looked up at her, helpless and furious, like he'd already known he wouldn't be able to fight.

Rat had shifted forward, their heart in their mouth, and something in her face had sharpened, almost as if she'd known that they were there, watching.

She'd leaned in close and said something into his ear, too low for Rat to hear.

And then, she'd folded her hand over his, the dirt still clasped in his fist, and released him.

He'd shoved away from her, but she was already gone. The wind had stirred the grass where she'd been standing.

Heat had rippled the air around him, but he was alone.

Still clutching the handful of dirt, he'd started back across the field. Rat had caught him by the arm as soon as he'd cleared the retaining wall to pull him through the passage, and they hadn't stopped until they were back in their father's office, the way to the tower closed behind them.

It had been the only time Rat had ever seen Harker more shaken than they were.

"You should stay here," they'd told him in a rush before he could try to take off. "Please. Elise doesn't get back until tomorrow night, and I don't really want to be alone here."

They'd expected him to argue, but Harker had hesitated a moment too long. "Are you sure?" he'd asked, uncertain, like he was afraid they might change their mind.

"Really," they'd said, pulling him back toward the stairs. "You can take the bed if you want. I just, I'd feel a lot better if you were here."

In the end, he'd insisted on taking the floor. Rat had given him an unnecessary number of pillows, and then, because they hadn't really wanted to be on the bed, either, as the sky got light they'd curled up on the ground next to him.

"Harker?" they'd whispered.

They heard a slight catch in his breath, and they'd known he was still awake.

"It's going to be okay. Right?"

"I won't let anything happen to you," he'd said softly. "I swore."

Something in Rat had fallen. It hadn't been what they'd meant. He'd already protected them enough.

"I swear, too," they'd said, but his breathing had already leveled out again.

They'd lain there for a long time after he'd drifted off, thinking of the tower, and the rabbit, and how, like an opening gambit, the knight had closed Harker's hand over the fistful of dirt that he'd gathered and let him go.

Rat jolted awake.

They pushed themself up, then remembered that they were alone in their dorm. It was still dark outside, and the room was cold around them, the last dregs of a tower dream already ebbing away.

They didn't remember what had happened. Just that it had been bad, and that Harker had been there.

They felt hollow.

They just needed to find him.

Without bothering to check the time, they grabbed their phone and then reached for their sweatshirt, before they realized they'd fallen asleep still wearing it.

They swung the door open and stopped in their tracks. A single crumpled mum lay on the threshold, left like a declaration.

Down the hall, the window creaked on its hinges as a draft rolled in. Rat turned to see that at some point in the night, the window had been unlatched. Outside, a black bird blinked at them from the branches of a tree. Then, in a flurry of movement, it took off.

Rat shoved the mum into their pocket and took off down the stairs. They barely stopped to think about where they were going until they crossed the pathway into center campus, the sprawl of the Drake breaking through the morning fog ahead of them. Harker might not even be working today, but if he was still in his room, they already knew he'd never open the door for them.

They stormed through the lobby, the same way they'd come in with Will a few days ago, except now, everything was quiet.

The front hall opened into a long, shelf-lined reading room, paneled in dark wood. Gray morning light streamed in through the skylights, washing over the neat rows of tables. The last time Rat had come through, most of the spaces had been taken, but it was deserted now, except for a pair of people at the back of the room, reshelving books.

Rat almost turned back, but then they realized that they'd come to the right place, after all.

Jinx leaned against the row of shelves, thumbing idly through the titles while Harker worked, a cup of dining hall coffee perched on his side of the book cart. Her mouth tugged into a small not-smile at something he'd said, and frustration pricked under Rat's skin.

Jinx's eyes ticked up, and they realized they'd been spotted. The dimple at the corner of her mouth deepened, her not-smile now directed at Rat, full force. She raised her eyebrows, and it occurred to them how obvious it must have been that they'd barely slept last night.

Rat opened their mouth to say something, but they couldn't find their voice.

Whatever mix of fear and urgency had carried them into the library threatened to tip into panic. They should have waited outside of Armitage Hall until Harker returned, so at least he'd be alone.

They should have gone back to the woods and just jumped in the lake.

They swallowed hard and forced themself to close the rest of the distance. "Harker," they said, putting as much force behind it as they had.

He turned back from the shelf and stopped cold.

Rat drew themself up. "I—"

"You can leave your reading list at circulation like everyone else, Evans," he said crisply. "I'll pull the titles for you when I'm done."

He went to take another book from the cart, but they reached out and grabbed his sleeve. "We need to talk," they said under their breath.

"I'm pretty sure we did that already."

They tightened their grip. "Harker."

A note of panic slipped into their voice.

For a moment, Harker stilled. Then he removed his hand from the book cart and gave Jinx a glance that said he'd be back in a moment.

She nodded slightly, and he motioned for Rat to follow.

Rat started after him, hurrying to keep pace. Harker was only a few inches taller than them, but he always managed to make it feel like more. Especially when he was angry with them.

At the first fork, he veered off into an empty passage, the walls lined with shelves.

"Let me guess." Harker drew something out of his pocket.

Their compass.

Rat's pulse skipped. "That's—"

They reached for it, but before they could take it, he closed his hand. "You dropped it in the woods," he said, turning the compass between his fingers. "You should be more careful. I'm pretty sure it's a Holbrook family heirloom."

He looked down at them, a challenge on his face like he was waiting for them to reach for it again or worse, ask him to give it back.

They shoved him, and surprise flickered across his face. "Harker, you walking trash fire."

He stumbled back half a step, and they closed in. "Hey—"

"Are you in danger?" they said in a rush, and for a moment they didn't know if they were scared or just furious with him. "Those were her birds last night, in the woods. Why the fuck didn't you tell me?"

He stared at them for a long moment, stricken. Heat pricked the air around him. "Excuse me?"

They drew themself up. "This is serious. If she found you—"

"Please," he said. His voice ran cold. "What makes you think she found me? Maybe I went back to her."

Rat thought of him kneeling in the grass, the knight's hand locked around his wrist.

"What did she say to you? When she let you go?" they said. "Harker, if there's something—"

"Maybe I wanted to," he said. "You were too afraid to go with her, but maybe I wasn't."

"But she's—"

He looked down at them, and they remembered that of all people, Harker knew exactly what she was.

Their thoughts turned back to the ragged flicker of spellfire in the woods.

She was teaching him.

No matter how Rat tried to forget, she'd offered to teach them once, too.

They might have hated magic, but they'd been born into it. Harker had chosen it with everything he was. He'd had to earn his place, first at Highgate, then at Bellamy Arts, and Rat had nearly cost him both. They weren't sure if he even had anything else to go back to.

If the knight had offered him a chance to scrape by in this world a little bit longer, he'd take it.

"Whatever arrangement I have with the tower, it was my idea," he said. "I'm capable of handling myself."

"You can't do that."

"I'm pretty sure I already did. You were right before. What she's looking for is here on campus. For your sake, you should hope she doesn't find it."

"Harker—"

He held up their compass. "As much fun as it's been having the one and only Rat Evans chase after me, I think we're done here."

Before he could pull it away again, Rat snapped their compass back from him, the metal case still warm where he'd touched it.

They held his gaze, hot and cold all over.

Finally, Harker nodded down the hall, and Rat realized that he'd taken them to a set of doors. "You can see yourself out," he said.

Then he turned, leaving them where they stood.

CHAPTER TWELVE

RAT MADE IT HALFWAY ACROSS CAMPUS BEFORE THEY stopped. They didn't want to go back to their room yet, but they couldn't return to the library.

They couldn't be here.

They couldn't breathe.

They lowered themself to the ground under one of the trees that lined the path and pulled their knees to their chest.

Rat opened their phone, and then realized they were about to call Harker.

Immediately, they hated that he was still their first reflex. They wanted to shove him again, and they wanted him to tell them that he knew how to fix this.

They punched in their home phone number and then remembered what Harker had told them last night about Elise asking him to transfer. They couldn't speak to her, either.

"Fuck," Rat muttered. Their eyes stung.

They swiped back to their contacts. Before they could think about what they were doing, they pulled up Evening's number and hit call.

"Rat?"

"Are you on campus?" Rat asked in a rush.

He paused, and they could almost hear him furrow his brow. "Did something happen?"

"I don't know. I just—"

"Rat. Breathe," he said on the other end of the line. "Can you tell me what's going on?"

"I—the school, I just—" Rat curled in on themself. "I don't want to be here. I can't—"

"It's okay. You did the right thing calling me. Have you spoken to Elise yet?"

They pressed their heels into the grass, grounding themself. "No. I don't want her to know. She'll pull me out of school for good and—I just, I don't want to talk to her."

There was a long pause on the other end. "Alright. I'm going to send a car to bring you back to the Council Chambers so you can get your bearings. We can figure out what to tell Elise once you're here."

"Okay," they said, feeling small.

"In the meantime, I want you to pack a bag with anything you think you might need for the next few days. I'll inform the school once you're on your way."

"Okay," they said again. "Right."

"Rat."

They sniffed.

"I need you to trust me," he said. "I promise, you're going to be okay."

Then, the line went quiet again.

Movement rustled in the low branches of the tree above them. Rat looked up to see another black bird, peering down at them.

They flinched back.

And then, like it had seen all that it needed, the bird ruffled its wings and took off.

Rat went back to their room and took down their overnight bag from the closet. They grabbed an extra sweatshirt off their bed and shoved it to the bottom of the bag, and then they took it out again and tossed it back on the covers.

"Fuck," they breathed. It shouldn't have even been a question. They couldn't stay at Bellamy Arts anymore.

It had been a mistake to allow themself to believe that they might be safe anywhere. The knight had never actually stopped chasing them. She'd been playing a long game, waiting them out while they were under the Council of Hours' protection all summer, and now she was here, circling in on them again.

The school had never been safe.

She'd wanted them here.

They sank back onto the bed and thought of the Council Chambers in Manhattan, with its polished stonework and echoing marble floors. It was the safest place for them to be.

It wasn't like they were leaving Bellamy Arts for good, they told themself. It would just be a couple of days, until they figured things out. Harker would have hated them no matter what, and they hadn't even wanted to study magic in the first place.

"It's literally fine," Rat said under their breath.

Somehow, though, the thought of leaving made their chest sink.

They shut their eyes. "You're fine."

Automatically, their hand went to their compass, and their fingers brushed something else. They picked it out of their pocket, only to find the mum from earlier, just beginning to wilt.

Rat turned it between their fingers. Again, they remembered the way the knight had tilted Harker's face to hers, her fingers to the line of his jaw, and the rabbit with its eyes like frosted glass.

"Maybe I went back to her."

They didn't believe that. Whatever the knight had told him, whatever she'd done to convince him to take her side, Rat knew her too well to think she hadn't nudged him into place.

The knight had closed her hand around the one person Rat couldn't allow her to take. She had never planned to let them walk away.

They looked back at their suitcase, still open on the bed. They'd left Harker behind once already. They didn't care if he never forgave them for it. They refused to let the tower have him.

Clutching the mum to their chest, Rat shoved themself to their feet and drew the curtains. They turned the lights out.

Magic flickered in the hollow of their chest, quiet, but still there.

There was another version of the story about the tower that Rat had never told to anyone but Harker.

It was a version that they didn't even like to tell themself.

In this version—the real one—the knight had never found them at all, because Rat had found her first.

They had wandered down dead passages before, but that had been the first time they'd ever gone looking for somewhere specific, farther than their own home. They hadn't known where they were going then, except that they'd seen it in their father's sketches, crumbling and magnificent, and they'd wanted to be there.

They'd never stumbled onto a passage to the tower.

They had opened one.

Each time after that had been easier. What little they knew of their powers, the knight had taught them. Sometimes, they met her in the field of grass, where they'd find her perched on the old stone wall or picking her way through the weeds, and she would tell them the names of stars they'd never seen before or teach them the low, chittering language of the birds that came to roost in the tower's crooked battlements. Other times, she'd let them lead the way through the dead passages to the ruins of the Ashwood House, to walk the bones of the crumbling estate while she told them of worlds farther still.

"You already know the way," her voice said in the back of Rat's head, crisp and cool, like turned leaves. *"Don't think so hard about where you're going."*

Rat let out a breath. Steeling themself, they pressed their hand to the wall of their dorm room. It had been months now since they'd last tried to open a dead passage on purpose. They didn't know if they could anymore.

"Imagine that you're coming home."

"Please," they said, their voice barely a breath. "Just this once."

They imagined old stone and fading light. They imagined the tower, its broken battlements jutting up against a sky pricked with unfamiliar stars.

Faintly, their power rose up in answer. For a moment they could sense the seams and edges of the world, like a puzzle box the moment before the pieces slid into place.

Panic rolled over them in a wave.

Before Rat could pull their magic back, the wall in front of them gave way, and they stumbled forward.

The veil of dust broke around them as they fell through, out into the morning. Rat caught themself against a rail, slick with condensation.

Their breath came out harsh and ragged.

As fast as it had come, their grip on their power slipped away again, and their sense of the world around them collapsed back into the cold rail and the damp boards beneath their feet.

They stared out. The campus spread out below them. The high spire of the clock tower. The rolling sprawl of the foothills in the distance.

They had ended up out on the widow's walk.

Rat's legs shook. They sank to the ground, hating themself for it. They didn't even know what they'd thought they would do if they found her. They weren't sure that they cared.

They took their phone out and typed a message to Evening to apologize for earlier and tell him not to send anyone.

They sent it, and their phone buzzed as a new message appeared at the bottom of the screen. *Did something happen? Are you sure you're alright?*

Rat drew their knees to their chest. *I'm really sorry. I think I just panicked earlier, but I'm ok,* they typed. *Really, though. Thanks.*

As soon as the message went through, their phone buzzed again, but Rat turned it over, setting it facedown on the widow's walk without looking.

Somehow, they promised themself, they would stop her. They would find a way to pull Harker back, and they would make sure that whatever the knight was after, she never found it.

A cold, damp wind rolled over the walk.

With the last dredges of courage they had left, Rat grabbed the mum, crumpled it in their hand, and cast it out over the rails.

CHAPTER THIRTEEN

IN THE WEEK THAT FOLLOWED, RAT CAME UP WITH A new plan.

"So," Will said, when he finally caught up to them, camping out in a common room of Mallory Hall with their sketchbook. "Who's the girl?"

"There isn't . . ."

"Boy? Person? You're in Mallory Hall, so I'm guessing—"

"I'm not looking for anyone," they said. Which might have been more convincing if it wasn't entirely false.

The problem with Jinx Wilder was that now that Rat actually wanted to get her alone, she wasn't anywhere to be found. They had no idea how she spent her time, and they'd started to regret that they hadn't been able to get up the courage to just ask for her phone number in class.

Will exhaled. "Look, is everything okay with you? You've been weird since Lake Night."

"Yeah. Fine," they said. "Why wouldn't it be?"

He paused for a moment, then shook his head. "Nothing. Listen, some of the New York kids were thinking of doing a mountain weekend over fall break. You know. Cabin full of teenagers in the woods. Campfires. Scary movies." He rubbed the back of his neck. "I mean, okay, the last thing you probably want is scary movies, but we could take a break and, you know, make friends with people who are actually nice?"

"That sounds great," they managed. "Can I think about it?"

He flashed them a dangerously hopeful smile, which Rat was pretty sure meant he already knew they were out. "We're heading out the morning after midterms end. I can hold a space in my car in case you want it."

As soon as Will left, they picked up their sketchbook and headed back into the hallway. They hadn't thought about the break or midterms at all since Lake Night.

They were probably going to fail out after their first semester and get eaten by blackbirds or something. If Harker had been born with a sense of humor, he'd probably think it was hilarious.

Rat ended up on the back staircase.

They opened their sketchpad to a drawing of a service passage on the landing they'd started the other day, but they couldn't focus.

The knight was baiting them. They knew that, and they were going to do what she wanted them to anyways. She'd bet that they wouldn't be able to leave Harker behind, and she'd been right.

Whatever her game was, the only thing they could do was play.

Rat tapped their pencil against the page.

The stolen map.

The door in the east woods.

The missing students.

"What are you after?" they said under their breath.

"Passing interest, huh?" a voice said behind them.

Rat whipped around to find Jinx a few steps above them, hands in her pockets, the cuff of her jeans rolled just above the top of her boots.

"I was—"

"It's good," she said. She tipped her head to the sketchpad. "You should put it in an art show. You could call it 'Broom Closet.'"

Before Rat could collect themself enough to answer, she slipped past them, toward the landing.

They shut their sketchbook and rushed to their feet. "Jinx, wait!"

She turned back to them, a question on her face.

"I—" Rat started. They swallowed. "I was actually hoping I'd catch you. What you said, about maybe trading notes. Does that still stand?"

Her eyes flickered over them appraisingly. "I thought you weren't planning to take the whole mapping project any further."

"What if I changed my mind?"

"Hmm," she said. She took a step up, back toward Rat. "Why?"

"Because." They drew themself up, fighting the urge to shrink back. "Whatever you're doing, I want in."

"Wait." She furrowed her brow. "You don't know?"

Rat hesitated. They had no idea how to answer that, and they knew that they weren't going to be able to bluff their way through.

"Oh. Wow," Jinx said, half to herself. "You really have no clue." Her frown deepened. "You were mapping the school."

They ducked their head. "And?"

"You followed us on Lake Night."

"You were goading me."

Unless it was a trick of the light, a flush crept across her face. "You're a Hol—" she stopped herself, but they already knew what she was going to say.

A Holbrook.

"I am," Rat said. The words felt strange on their tongue, maybe because they were used to qualifying it. "I know that you could use me. Tell me what we're looking for, and I'll do whatever you need me to."

She studied them. "You and Blakely don't get along," she said, but not quite like a *no*.

"Well, I'm not helping him. I'm helping you."

"What if it's horrible?" she asked.

Rat faltered. "What?"

"What I'm after," she said. "You said it yourself. You don't even know what this is about. What if we're looking for some terrible piece of magic, and you're the one who helps us find it?"

"Maybe I'm okay with that." Rat lifted their chin. "Maybe I'm horrible, too."

They held her gaze, not daring to breathe. It didn't matter where this led. They just needed Jinx to take them there.

Jinx let out a small laugh, and Rat realized how they must have looked to her, and also that their knees were definitely shaking again.

"Alright then, Evans." She nodded to the sketchbook tucked under their arm. "Can I?"

"Please," Rat said a bit too quickly, handing it to her. There was nothing for her to find, they reminded themself. They'd gone through it twice to make sure.

They watched as she flipped to the middle of the book and riffled the pages.

"The final versions are dog-eared," Rat told her. "It isn't complete, but I've got a few other maps of Mallory Hall in pretty good detail, plus Galison Hall and most of the major classroom buildings."

"How detailed is detailed?"

"There's a service passage in Fairchild's office detailed." Some of the tension in their chest unwound. If nothing else, their maps were good.

Jinx flipped back a page. Her brows drew together. "Have you been back there yet?" she asked, angling the sketchbook toward Rat.

She'd stopped on a sketch of the service corridor they'd just been working on, the door cracked open to reveal a sliver of passageway on the other side.

"No. I mean, not far. It looked like it went pretty deep," Rat lied, because it was easier than admitting that after they'd opened it, they'd been afraid to go in. "Why?"

"Nothing," she said. "It's an old building. That door just usually locks."

"Wait, have you been?"

She studied Rat for a moment, then closed the sketchpad with a decisive snap. "Here's the deal. If I bring you in on this, whatever I show you, you have to map. No questions asked. I choose where I take you, and no matter how strange any of it seems, it's up to me how much to explain and when."

"Okay." They reached for their sketchbook, but Jinx tucked it neatly under her arm.

"I'm keeping this as collateral," she said.

"Wait. You can't—"

"This whole business is secrets all the way down, and not all of them are mine to tell. If I'm going to bring you in on this, I need to know you won't speak." She held the sketchbook out in front of her, challenging them to take it. "But if you don't want to go, say the word."

If they left now, no one would have to know they'd ever asked.

No one but Jinx.

She eyed them, waiting.

"Fine." Rat dropped their hands. "But we start soon. Just us."

Satisfied, Jinx tucked their sketchbook back under her arm. "Please, Evans. We start immediately."

Start immediately, it turned out, meant grabbing dining hall coffee at Galison Hall while Jinx thumbed through their sketchbook.

"How long have you been doing this?" she asked from the other side of the table. She'd found a place by the row of tall windows at the back of the room. It was late enough in the day that most of the other students had cleared out, and at some point on the way over, it had started to rain.

"A while?" Rat said.

She looked up at them through her glasses like that wasn't what she'd meant.

"I honestly don't know." They pushed their hand through their hair. "Maybe it's a Holbrook thing?"

"He was your father," Jinx said. It had the air of a question, but one that she already knew the answer to. "Alexander Holbrook, I mean." She stopped herself. "Sorry. If you don't want to talk about—"

"It's really fine. I just didn't realize you knew about him."

"Just bits and pieces. He's a bit famous in the department of higher magics."

"Oh. I never really knew a lot about his work," they admitted. "I was pretty young. But I found some of his maps around the house. Scraps, mostly." Rat stopped as they realized what they'd just said. "Not that I'm like him. A formalist, I mean. Or really anything. I'm just not that useful with magic."

Jinx frowned, and Rat realized that really wasn't a ringing endorsement for why she should let them in on her plans. Suddenly, they weren't sure if it would be worse to let her assume that they didn't have any aptitude for magic or to explain that they'd stopped casting on purpose.

"Why would that matter?" she asked, glancing up from the sketchbook again.

"That I'm useless?"

"If you ask me," Jinx said studying them, "useful is being able to walk into a place, and knowing no matter how many times you get turned around, you'd still be able to find your way back."

She watched them, intent, and a fresh wave of anxiety rose in their chest.

"I . . . maybe," they said, dropping their gaze. They looked back to the sketchbook. "But, the maps. Are you using the service corridors to sneak around campus?"

"Nope."

"Then—"

Jinx shook her head. "No questions."

They huffed a breath. "You need to tell me something."

"That's not the deal," she said, obviously amused.

"You have my sketchbook."

"This coffee is terrible, and my favorite color is gray." Casually, she turned the page. "Satisfied?"

Rat made a small, indignant noise from the back of their throat.

"You're thinking in the wrong direction," Jinx said, setting the sketchbook aside. "Blakely said you saw us in the woods?"

"There was a door," Rat said, remembering the cellar doors set in the ground, away from any building. "There are tunnels."

Jinx raised her eyebrows at them, like she hadn't been the one to say it. Then, she paused again. "What exactly is it with you and him?"

Rat winced. "To be fair, I'm pretty unlikable," they said. "I think I've got one of those faces."

"You went to the same private school, and your sweatshirt has burns on the cuffs."

"Fuck," Rat said under their breath. Automatically, their hand went to the burn marks on their sleeve, where Harker must have singed himself at some point before they'd stolen it. They considered crawling under the table and staying there. "What did he say?"

"Not a lot," she said.

Rat sank into themself. If Harker hadn't told her, it wasn't to defend them. He probably just didn't want anyone knowing that he'd been abandoned, and by Rat Evans of all people. He would die before he let Jinx and Agatha pity him.

Jinx let out a breath. "If we're really doing this, I need to get Cromwell and Blakely on board. You don't have to like each other, but I'm not going to have you tearing each other's throats out. So how bad is it?"

"It's . . ." Rat shifted uncomfortably. "It's a really long story. Can we just, like, garden-variety not get along?"

Jinx gave them a look.

"There was no malfeasance involved, and we weren't dating," they told her. "Happy?"

Her mouth twitched. "What?"

"No. I answered you. Your turn," Rat said. Their whole face burned. "I knew him last year and he hadn't met you. How do you know each other?"

Jinx held their gaze across the table, and they had to fight the urge to sink any lower in their seat. Finally, she said, "We both moved in early. He was after the same thing I was."

"And what's that?"

Jinx looked them over. Then she took another sip of her coffee and flipped the sketchbook shut.

"Not bad, Evans," she said, rising to go. "You'll hear from me."

CHAPTER FOURTEEN

THAT NIGHT, RAT DREAMT THEY WERE BACK IN THE FIELD of fallen stones, and when the knight offered her hand, they took it. They dreamt about black birds perched on the tower's far-off battlements where the stonework crumbled into sky, and yellow flowers, and her gloved fingers clasped around their own as she led them through the tall grass. And as they followed her, they knew with a bone-deep certainty that they wouldn't return again.

It was still dark when Rat jolted awake. A cold sweat stuck their shirt to their back as they lay there, breathing hard.

They pressed their hands to their ribs.

It wouldn't end like that, they promised themself. They'd bring Harker back and fix this, somehow, and then they would be done with the tower for good.

Rat drew another breath, and then took their compass from the bedside table, letting the familiar weight of it steady them as the last of the dream ebbed away.

Out in the hall, there was dull thud outside of their door.

They went still, their face half buried in the pillow, eyes wide open.

They'd lived at the Evans place long enough to know the sounds of an old building settling. This wasn't that.

A minute passed, and then another as they waited. Silence rung in their ears.

Slowly, Rat rolled onto their side, facing the door. The mattress creaked beneath them, painfully loud.

They listened.

Still nothing.

The carpet muffled the sound of Rat's bare feet hitting the floor. They picked their way across the room, still half asleep. Their hand closed on the doorknob, the metal cool against their palm.

Steeling themself, they pushed it open.

The hall outside stretched away into darkness. The curtains on the window were pulled back, and squares of moonlight spilled over the carpet, etching the corridor in silver.

There was no one there. Not the knight. Not one of her black birds, or her hunting dogs come to find them.

Shaking, Rat braced their hand against the doorframe.

"When you go back to the tower," they said into dark, to whatever might have been listening, "tell her that I'm going to find out what she's planning, and I'm going to unravel it."

But nothing answered.

Finally, they closed the door and went back to bed, the quiet of the building pressing in around them, but they didn't sleep for a long time after.

CHAPTER FIFTEEN

THE NEXT MORNING, RAT STEPPED OUTSIDE TO MEET WILL, only to find him kneeling in their doorway in a pile of rumpled flowers and torn paper that definitely hadn't been there the night before.

He jumped back, his fist closed around whatever he'd been holding. "Hey. I was just about to—"

"What's that?" Rat asked.

"Would you believe me if I said it's nothing?"

"Give it," Rat said, putting their hand out.

He held out a small carving of a tower. It was a *rook*, they realized, from a game of chess. The yellowing ivory had cracked down the middle, and the tower was missing a chunk off the top, leaving a handful of crenellations that stuck up like crooked teeth.

A chill pricked up Rat's arm as Will placed the figure in their open palm. They ran their thumb over the still-sharp edge of the break. "Oh. Wow. Good morning to me, I guess."

"Do you know what it is?"

"Maybe someone lost a chess match?" They forced a laugh, but everything inside of them had turned to ice.

What it meant was they were getting closer.

"Do you think it could be a secret society thing?" Will asked, but not like he believed it. "I mean, you're an Evans. That kind of thing is supposed to happen to you, right?"

"Honestly, if any secret society is willing to have me, that isn't a ringing endorsement." Doing their best to look natural, Rat dropped the rook into the pocket of their jeans. The attic scent of magic clung to the hall, but there was a sharp note of mugwort and cold air lingering beneath it.

Will hesitated. "Rat. If something—"

"Come on," they said, kicking the pile of scraps into their room. They dragged their sneaker across the carpet, raking up the thin coat of dust, and then they pulled the door shut behind them, like nothing had happened at all. "We're already running late."

When Rat arrived at practicum, Jinx, Harker, and Agatha were already at their spot near the back of the room, whispering furiously.

Even before Rat made it out of the doorway, they could tell that something had shifted from yesterday, and not in the way they'd hoped.

". . . didn't agree to this," Harker said, just loud enough for them to hear. "Jinx, you've spoken to them twice."

Perched on the desk beside Jinx, Agatha leaned in, her voice almost too soft for Rat to make out. "We still don't know where . . ."

"Which is exactly why we need them. You've seen their maps. I can—" Jinx broke off as she caught sight of Rat.

"Don't stop on my account," they said, dropping into their seat.

The three traded glances.

When nobody spoke, Rat took their notebook out and set it pointedly on the desk. They flipped it open to a fresh page and began sketching in the margin, waiting, but the conversation was over.

Jinx flashed them an apologetic look, then Agatha caught her by the sleeve and turned her back to face the front.

Their chest sank as they realized that as fast as they'd gotten Jinx on their side, they were about to lose her.

They glanced over at Harker. He gave them a smug look, and then, before Rat could protest, he turned back to his book like he hadn't just deliberately sunk their only lead.

Rat took a deep breath and ripped a scrap of paper from their notebook. *I don't care what you're up to, I'm not leaving you to the tower,* they wrote, then crumpled it up and shoved it under the cover.

I know about the tunnels, Rat wrote instead.

They tore the strip of paper out of their notebook and slid it to Harker. He didn't touch it.

At the front of the room, Frey finished sorting the things at his desk and walked up to the blackboard.

I can find out where they lead on my own, Rat wrote as he started the lecture. They tore that note out, too, and passed it across the desk.

Harker propped his chin on his knuckles, gaze fixed ahead.

Your taste in books is awful and you smell like a house fire that someone put out with body spray, they wrote. *If you're trying to scare me, you don't.* Rat crumpled the note and stuck it next to the others.

Frey tapped the chalk against the board. "Now," he said. "If you'll all take out your workbooks and turn to page seventy-two, I'd like to go over a few of the examples."

The sound of turning pages filled the room.

Rat shot Harker a last *stop me, I dare you* look, then reached into their backpack and dug out a map of the woods for Jinx they'd started in their spare sketchbook. It probably wouldn't help much, but they didn't care.

Help wasn't the point.

Rat folded it and passed it over the table to her. Harker didn't look down, but his shoulders tensed as Jinx took the paper.

Good, Rat thought.

They spent the rest of class drawing hallways in their notebook and trying not to think too hard of the door in the woods or where it led.

When the bell rang, Rat took their time shoving their things into their backpack, the room slowly emptying out around them. They had twine and marking chalk that they used to use in the dead passages. They could use their phone as a flashlight.

Rat wasn't going to give Harker the satisfaction of knowing he'd scared them off so easily.

"Hey."

With a start, they looked up to see Jinx standing on the other side of the lab desk, her bag slung over her shoulder.

"Oh. Hey. I—"

"What are you doing tonight?"

Rat blinked at her. "I . . . coming by your room to get my sketch-book?"

"Why would you do that?"

"Because I'm not invited?" they hedged.

"Cromwell has an independent study before class tomorrow, and Blakely is working in the morning, so they'll both be back in their rooms by midnight," Jinx said. She set their map on the lab table. "If I show you a route, how well do you think you can draw it?"

Rat eyed her warily. "A route where?"

Jinx gave them a look.

"It depends on how involved it is," they said. "But I could at least get you something rough."

"Can you draw it well enough to convince Cromwell?"

Rat opened their mouth to answer, and then understood what she was saying.

"Look. You already know that we're searching for something," she said, dropping her voice. "Cromwell is sensitive to magic. It's . . . you can say it has something to do with her powers. She usually just picks up residues of old spells and minor enchantments, but she has a way of knowing when she's close to something . . . else."

Rat stilled.

"I went through your sketchbook. Cromwell and Blakely don't think we need you, but I think they're wrong," Jinx said. "If you don't want to do this, say the word and your sketchbook will be back in front of your door tomorrow morning. I'll leave you alone and we can pretend that we don't know each other. But I need to see what we're dealing with." She glanced back at the door, like she'd already stayed behind for too long, then looked back at them. "Twelve-thirty, broom closet. It's up to you, but I'll be there either way."

Then, without waiting for an answer, she grabbed the map off the desk and turned back toward the door, leaving Rat alone in the classroom.

CHAPTER SIXTEEN

RAT SPENT THE REST OF THE DAY UNABLE TO SIT STILL.

The hall lights had already gone out by the time they arrived at the stairwell, and moonlight from the window spilled over the steps. Jinx hadn't arrived yet, and the whole building had gone quiet around them.

They hiked up their backpack and climbed down to the landing. The door to the service corridor stood out against the wall, narrow like a closet, just out of reach of the moonlight. Letting out a breath, Rat rested their hand on the doorknob.

It was unlocked.

Cautiously, they pushed the door open.

A gust of damp air rolled out as they peered into the corridor. Goosebumps pricked up their arms.

Rat slid their phone from their pocket and turned on the flashlight, but it didn't seem as bright as they'd thought anymore. It had always been enough for walking around their house at night, but now the light seemed weak and shadowy. They angled the beam down the passage, casting a circle of pale glow across the weathered floorboards, before it was swallowed up again.

Whatever was back there, it would be an easy place to get lost. The kind of place no one would even know to look for them, if they didn't come back.

Their mind flickered back to the knight, her hand outstretched to lead them away.

Footsteps pounded down the stairs. "Going somewhere?" Jinx asked.

Rat let go of the doorknob and jumped back.

She stood at the top of the stairs, her backpack slung over her shoulder, holding the kind of heavy flashlight in her hand that doubled as a defense weapon.

"Hey," they said. "Hi. I was waiting for you."

She raised her eyebrows.

"So," Rat said, gesturing to the door, "I really don't think that lock is what you think it is."

"Well. That saves us some time at least." She stepped past them into the musty darkness of the service corridor. "Come on. It's a long way down."

"Wait," they said.

She looked back at them, a question on her face.

"I just . . . you're sure this is safe?"

"I'm pretty sure I never said that." She paused. "If you changed your mind, this is the best time for it."

Rat peered down the corridor. They were playing into the knight's hands now, and they knew that. Whatever they found, however far in they went, if they weren't careful, they wouldn't make it back out.

Absently, they thumbed the burnt cuff of their sweatshirt. *Make it count,* they told themself.

They drew themself up. "I'm in."

She nodded to the passage, and they stepped in.

Then, she switched the flashlight on and pulled the door closed. Rat's breath caught as it clicked shut.

"You, uh, never told me where we were heading," they said.

"Yes, I did." Jinx shouldered past them. The beam of the flashlight lit the passage, washing the narrow corridor in cold, white light. "Down."

"Down where?"

"It's easier if you see. Trust me." She motioned for them to keep up. "If you wander off and disappear, I never met you. So, stay close."

Rat stole a last glance behind them, but already, the door had been swallowed up by the dark.

They ducked their head and stepped a bit closer to Jinx. Whenever they'd needed to sneak somewhere with Harker, it was usually the narrow aisles of their family archives or the dimly lit corridors of their own house. Places they knew well.

With a pang, Rat wondered how many of the students who'd gone missing over the years had made it to the tower, and how many had never actually left the campus at all.

Rat followed Jinx until she came to a rickety spiral staircase, anchored to the ground with a set of heavy, industrial-strength bolts that seemed out of place, even in the half-built service corridors.

"Um, who put this in?" Rat asked, peering over the rail. Below, the stairs curved away, vanishing into the dark.

"Remember what I said? About how, no matter how strange things seem . . ."

"No questions," they finished. "But look, if I'm going down there—"

"I promise you, it's going to make a lot more sense once you've seen everything," she said. "I told Cromwell to mount a rescue mission if we're not back by four, so the clock is ticking. Come on." She started down, the steps clattering in her wake.

Rat took a breath through their teeth. "Right."

Below, Jinx vanished around the curve of the stairs, her footsteps growing fainter and fainter, until they stopped.

For a moment, they could almost feel the passages opening up around them, branching like roots.

Wherever they were, this was the mouth of something.

"You're welcome to stay where you are," Jinx called, a metallic echo resonating through the stairwell. "But there's only one real flashlight, and I'm holding it."

The darkness yawned around them. The only thing worse than going in would be for Jinx to leave them at the top of the stairs alone.

Rat hurried down to her, their hand skipping over the railing. "There are words for people like you," they said, half panting as they rounded the staircase.

"And a special place in hell, I'm sure." Jinx leaned casually against the rail. She'd stopped partway down the steps, the rest of the staircase curving away below her. They weren't even close to the bottom, Rat realized. As if she'd sensed their panic, something in her face softened. "If I offered to turn around, right now, and walk you to the door, would you want to go back?"

"Please don't offer," Rat said. They gripped the rail so hard that the rust bit into their palm. "You don't have to be nice to me. I'm not scared."

"Rat," she said, and then her not-smile was back. "You're a pile of laundry with a trust fund. If I'm ever nice to you, you have my express permission to wash my mouth out with soap."

"I—did you call me—"

"You're welcome to fight me, but maybe wait until we're off the stairs."

Rat stared after her. She'd called them *Rat*. Jinx hadn't used their first name since she'd learned they were an Evans.

"Come on," she said, motioning to them. "It's not as far down as it looks."

Rat followed close behind her as the stairs wound lower into the earth, the air growing damper and heavier with each twist of the staircase until it bottomed out in a wide stone corridor. A series of archways bolstered the walls, the vaulted ceiling rising into darkness overhead.

Jinx leapt from the bottom step, the low thud of her boots echoing back through the corridor. All over, Rat was struck by the feeling that wherever they were, they'd barely scratched the surface of it.

The beam of Jinx's flashlight played over the walls as she led the way, throwing shadows over the crumbling masonry. Loose stones jutted from the path ahead as the ground sloped downward.

"Straight ahead?" Rat asked as they passed a fork in the tunnel.

"Unless you see another way to go."

They stole a glance over their shoulder, but the extra branch had already vanished behind them. The telltale shimmer of dust curled in the corner of their vision. Uneasy, they quickened their pace, keeping close behind her.

She came to a stop as she reached a set of doors at the end of the hall, resting her hand against the doorknob. "Wait here."

Before they could answer, the doors swung open with a low groan, and she slipped inside, the glow of the flashlight disappearing after her.

And then the lights came on.

A net of string lights and lanterns hung from the ceiling, zigzagging over a large octagonal room that looked as if it might have been a study in another lifetime. Rings of water damage crept out from behind the high bookshelves that lined the walls. A circle of mismatched armchairs had been dragged into the middle of the room, arranged around a table cluttered with stacks of books and takeout cartons from the dining hall.

"The War Room," Jinx said, motioning broadly. "This is our center of operations."

Rat stared, trying to take everything in. "And you all . . ."

"Me and Cromwell go back pretty far. Long story, don't ask. And, like I said, Blakely ran into us when he got here, since we all moved in early. Lucky for us, he'll do pretty much anything for a cup of coffee. Not even good coffee." She frowned. "It's actually kind of upsetting."

"Oh," Rat managed, trying to put together what Jinx had just told them.

"The room was already set up when we got here," she added, like that was the biggest question. "Whoever managed the electricity spells is a saint. But if I tell you anything else, Cromwell's going to demand that we give you a full initiation ceremony."

"And that would be bad?"

"Cromwell. Running a ceremony. If you feel the need to be officially inducted into the Bellamy Arts Society for All Things Lost and Found, I'll throw you her way when we're done here." She paused, seeing the look on Rat's face. "It's what Agatha calls us, but I still think it's a mouthful." She motioned for them to get out of the doorway. "We're just crossing through here. Come on."

Rat stepped into the room, and the smell hit them head on, like vanilla and wood rot. It was almost too much, but Rat still couldn't miss the familiar smoke-and-ashes smell of singed paper beneath it.

Without stopping to think, they turned toward the chairs. Their eyes went to the floor, as if they already knew where to look.

A stack of leather-bound books leaned up against the side of an armchair, beside a plastic jar of instant coffee and a couple of half-spent votive candles. Rat could almost see Harker sitting on the ground, open books spread out around him as he worked late into the night on whatever it was he was doing down here.

Jinx followed their gaze. "Most of the books are Blakely's. Working in the library has some advantages."

"What's it for?" Rat asked, skimming the titles. They glanced from the books on the floor to the ones on the table, half expecting to see the Holbrook Map lying out somewhere, and then realized that they didn't even know what it looked like. It could have been a leather-bound atlas, or an astronomical globe, or a murder of directionally inclined crows.

"Some of them are formal references," Jinx said. "But it's mostly school histories and history of magic books. I honestly have no idea how he reads them. They're pretty dry."

They glanced up at Jinx.

For the first time, it occurred to Rat that whatever Harker was up to, Jinx might not be as in on it as they'd assumed.

She grabbed a cloth pouch of casting chalk off the far side of the table. "It'll make more sense once we're going. Can you catch?"

Rat reached their hand out, and then a book off to the side of the pile caught their eye, a sheet of folded notes sticking out from between the pages, the way that Harker usually did when he was working on something.

"Seriously, we should get a move on," Jinx said when she saw Rat staring. "If you still want to talk after we figure out what's in the tunnels, we'll talk."

"In that case," Rat said and slid the book out from the bottom of the pile.

"That's—"

"Collateral. Since we're going all the way into the tunnels and I'm still not allowed to ask questions. That's how this game works, right?"

Jinx looked them dead in the eyes, unamused.

They hugged the book to their chest. Even if Jinx turned them around—even if she refused to take them any further and they had to brave the tunnels alone—they finally had something of Harker's. The thought of putting it back ached.

Rat planted their feet and stared back at Jinx, as if their knees weren't shaking.

"Fine," she said. "But only because I have your sketchbook. What do you know about Margaret Ingrid?"

They furrowed their brow. "The school founder?"

"It's a long story," she said, motioning for them to follow. "I'll tell you while we walk."

CHAPTER SEVENTEEN

"INGRID WAS A COLLECTOR OF THINGS," JINX STARTED, with the steady cadence of a story that she'd told before. Her voice echoed faintly through the dark.

The aging stonework of the passage had given way to roughly carved earth as they walked, the tunnel sloping deeper into the ground ahead of them.

"Things, like . . . ?" Rat drew another trail blaze on the wall as they passed. They'd loaded the book into their backpack so they could hold their chalk in one hand and a lantern they'd taken from the War Room in the other.

"Magic," Jinx said without looking back. "Every kind of it. Spell-books. Enchantments. Maps of distant stars, the scales and feathers of impossible creatures. The last bottled breaths of a dying god. She amassed an archive—a powerful one. Depending on who you asked, she was either a brilliant formalist or an absolute vulture, though I'm not sure those things are mutually exclusive." Jinx paused to tag the wall as she passed through a bolstered archway. "Then, one day, she disappeared."

Rat straightened.

"It wasn't that unusual for her to vanish for a few days here and there, but this time was different. Her rooms were untouched. She took nothing with her and didn't tell anyone where she'd gone."

"Where did she go?"

"Where does the smoke go when you blow out a candle?"

Rat frowned.

Jinx paused for the briefest fraction of a second and then shook her head. "No one knows. She was just, gone. Like she'd dropped off the face of the earth."

Something in the way she said it made Rat go cold, maybe because they'd imagined vanishing the same way so many times.

They *knew* where.

They wanted to stop Jinx and tell her to say it, to at least give the tower a name, but they couldn't find their voice. She still didn't know about their powers, and they couldn't ask without showing their hand.

If they were honest, they weren't even sure anymore how much she really knew. Harker hadn't actually told them that Jinx and Agatha were involved in whatever deal he'd made with the knight. Rat had just assumed.

Jinx turned a corner into a new hall, moving slowly. Following after, Rat marked another blaze on the wall.

"Months went by," she went on. "When there was still no word, the school appointed an interim head of affairs to watch over things in her absence, and then a permanent one. And then, seven years later, at the first light of dawn, Ingrid returned the same way that she'd left. Except she'd changed. She refused to tell anyone where she'd gone, and she never stopped looking over her shoulder, almost like she was afraid that something had followed her back."

Jinx paused, the steady cadence of her footsteps echoing up the narrow passage.

"She set up protections all around campus. Supposedly, she cast a seal over the school." Jinx said something in a language that might have been Latin, and Rat made a small noise of confusion. She glanced back. "*That which can't be taken back.* A deathworking. It's an old kind of magic that comes at the cost of the caster's life."

Rat's stomach knotted. "Oh," they managed.

"It isn't done anymore," she said, reading their expression. "Most of them are kept under lock and key now, but once a spell like that is in motion, they're almost impossible to break. Magic is driven by intention, and to cast something like that, that closes every other possible door—it's irrevocable. There aren't many things that can overpower that, besides another death."

They fought back a prickle of unease. "Right."

"It could just be a legend at this point," Jinx said. "According to the story, Ingrid didn't survive long after she finished the seal. Once she had everything ready, she called everyone to the clock tower. She had the staff pull all of the students out of bed and drag them to the middle of campus, with instructions to search and clear all of the buildings. The faculty who still knew her rushed to talk her down from whatever she was about to do, but by the time they arrived, she had already locked herself inside."

"I thought there wasn't a way in," Rat said.

Jinx glanced back at them and raised an eyebrow.

"The clock tower," they said, then remembered how they knew that. "I, um, tried to map it. There's no entrance."

"Not anymore," Jinx said. "She spelled it so no one would be able to find the way in, right before what she did to the old campus."

"Wait. Old campus, meaning . . ."

"That everything above us is the new campus?" Jinx stopped again, this time at an archway where once there might have been a doorway. "Hold that thought. We're here. This is where we were right before Cromwell made us turn back."

She looked one way, then the other, but everything around them was still. All at once, Rat remembered exactly how far underground they were.

Jinx touched them on the wrist and motioned for them to follow her in. On the other side, the tunnel turned back to the smooth masonry from before, opening into a cavernous room with a high, arched ceiling and a row of floor-length windows. Behind the tattered velvet curtains, dirt pressed in against the glass.

"What is this place?" Rat asked, raising their lantern to see. A layer of rubble dusted the wooden floor, and roots had grown in through the walls, twisting over the stonework like vines. "There are—" they stopped, unsure of what she saw.

"Windows?"

They nodded.

"Because," she said. "It used to be a ballroom."

"Wait, are we—"

"Shh. No spoilers." Jinx paced to the middle of the room, her footsteps echoing through the expanse.

"What are we looking for, exactly?" Rat asked.

"I don't know. I just know there's something here."

They studied her. "Agatha couldn't tell you?"

Jinx looked up again, avoiding their gaze. "Her magic might be more complicated than I let on."

Rat was pretty sure that meant she'd lied to their face.

"It's not what the rumors say," they asked, "is it?"

"You'd have to ask her," Jinx said. "She started most of them."

"What?" Rat bit back an incredulous laugh, and Jinx's mouth quirked.

Then, just as fast, some of the humor went out of her. "She catches glimpses of things. Sometimes the past. Sometimes bits of the future. I asked her, but she said it's difficult to tell them apart. Sometimes, though, when she's close to a juncture—somewhere too many things have happened, or too many things could change—it gets . . . murky," she said. "Powerful magic makes it worse. She said it's like shining a beacon through fog. It doesn't make the way ahead any clearer, just . . ."

"Glaring," Rat finished.

"She wouldn't tell me what she saw down here. For all I know,

whatever it was happened a long time ago. I just know that it was a lot."
Jinx surveyed the clearing, and then exhaled deeply. "Maybe it's another
dead end."

"I'm sorry." Rat walked to where she was standing and knelt down,
marking an *X* on the floor. Their chalk scraped across the boards.

Dead end to what? they wanted to ask.

They looked up to ask Jinx if she wanted to head back and tell them
the rest, and then stopped as a shape at the edge of the room caught
their eye.

Jinx followed their gaze, turning the beam of her flashlight to the far
wall. "Rat. Hold on."

Shadowed by the fallen wreck of a grand piano, a pair of hinges
gleamed on the floor, where a hatch had been installed. A set of stars had
been marked on the wall behind it, low enough to the ground that Rat
might have missed it if they hadn't known where to look.

"Just like she said," Jinx murmured. Without waiting, she made her
way across the room. The taste of dust stuck in the back of Rat's throat.

"Wait." Rat started after her, their hand tight on their lantern. "Agatha
said something?"

"No. It's— The stars. Supposedly they were made by another group of
students, years ago, but we've never found any before."

"For what?" Rat said, hesitant.

"That's the question. Isn't it?"

Jinx knelt down beside the hatch and pulled on the handle.

"Are you sure we should go down there?" Rat said in a rush. "I just,
we're already in pretty deep and we have no idea where that goes."

She stopped and looked up at them, and they realized how tensely
they were holding themself. "I can come back if this is too far for you. Do
you want to go back to the War Room?"

They did. Badly.

But they also knew that she was right. There was *something* down there, and if there was any chance it would get them closer to finding out what the knight was after, they needed to know what. Their hand went to the strap of their backpack, the weight of the book they'd taken resting against the small of their back.

They could make it a bit farther.

"No," they said, hating how small they sounded. They tapped the hatch with their foot. "Is it open?"

Jinx studied the hatch like she was considering something. "I think it's just stuck," she said after a moment. "Maybe you could try?"

Rat knelt down beside her and took hold of the handle. They pulled back, and for a moment, they thought it wouldn't give, but then the hatch creaked open.

Below, the beam of the flashlight glinted off the rungs of a ladder.

Rat peered down, but everything else was dark. Not dark the way that cellars or crawl spaces were dark, but the vast, sunless dark of caves.

"So, you know that part of the horror movie where the group of teenagers goes into the basement alone?" Rat said. "I'm just putting it out there that I'm way too gay to live past the first half hour. Like, if we go down there, I'm definitely going to die."

Jinx craned her neck, following their gaze. "Same." She moved past them and climbed onto the ladder. "If I scream, start running."

As she descended, Rat perched at the edge of the opening, listening to the dull clang of her boots.

Same, *like she was also going to die,* they wanted to ask. *Or same, like, she was gay, and going to die?*

Not that it mattered if Jinx was gay, because she was only on their side for the moment, here, dozens of stories underground, deep in a hulking mass of structural hazards, where they were surrounded by every kind of darkness and both very, very likely to die.

Far below, Jinx's boots hit the ground with a hard thud.

She turned her flashlight on the ladder. "Rat! You need to see this! God, I wish we had Blakely. I could really use more light."

The words hit Rat like a sack of rocks.

"At least I'm less likely to set the place on fire!" they called back. Their voice echoed through the expanse.

"Just get down here!"

Rat climbed onto the first rung. The steel was rough with rust and cold to the touch.

I'm making a mistake, they thought as they lowered themself down, one step at a time. *This is a mistake.*

They locked their hand around the rungs a little tighter. And climbed.

"You're going to have to fall the last couple feet," Jinx called up. Her voice was closer than they'd expected. "It's not as far as you think."

Above, the trap door had vanished into the dark.

Rat dropped.

For one terrible moment, Rat was weightless, and then the ground came up to meet them.

A few feet away, Jinx leaned against what looked like a wardrobe covered in a dust cloth. She pointed the light at them. "Okay?"

Rat flexed their hands. "Okay," they said, wishing they didn't sound so surprised.

As they got the lantern back out of their backpack, Jinx swept the beam of the flashlight around the room.

"Take a look at all of this stuff," she said. "What do you think this place used to be?"

Heaps of old furniture rose up all around them—chests of drawers, traveling trunks, desks, scuffed cabinets and shelves crammed with odds and ends—all of it coated in a layer of dust. The real, gray kind. Makeshift aisles led off between the gaps in the furniture into a maze of castoffs.

"I think I saw a chandelier back that way," Jinx said, pointing with the flashlight. "You're sure you couldn't, you know, conveniently turn out to be really good at light workings?"

"I am. I'm just really committed to hiding it." Rat turned toward one of the bookshelves. "What is all of this?"

They traced their thumb along a shelf of empty liquor bottles, most of the labels too dusty to read. The cabinet beside it was filled with half-burnt candles, and textbooks, and tins and tinctures with the labels worn off. Rat reached out and flipped one of the books open. It was only a few years old.

Frowning, they brushed the grit from the cover and set it back down. As they did, they caught a hint of something else on the air, cutting across the smoke and dust and earth. A sharpness, faint but unmistakable.

Rat sniffed. "Jinx?"

"Hey, check this out," she called. She stood at the edge of the light, by an old vanity with a cloth draped over the mirrors. A strip of duct tape ran across the line of drawers, holding them shut, but the top of the makeup table was covered in clutter.

Jinx held up a rusted blade, pinching it carefully between her fingers.

Rat held up the lantern, but if anything, the blade only seemed to darken. "Uh, wow. Not that I haven't always wanted tetanus, but maybe you should put that down?"

"There's a bunch of chalk, too. Looks like ritual components," she said and turned the blade. "God, no wonder this place was marked. I bet there's like a hundred years of contraband down here."

"Yeah, that's definitely one way to avoid a room check." Rat started toward her, but as they passed the mouth of the aisle, they were hit by the smell again. Fresh air and late summer. Mugwort and mums and things that didn't grown in the dark. "Hey. Jinx."

She set the blade down.

"I really—it's going to be hard to get out of here if we run into something. Maybe we shouldn't be here."

"Definitely shouldn't be here," she said and glanced up at the ladder. "I wonder if the original doors are still passable. How big do you think this place is?"

She stepped toward Rat, then stopped. She sniffed the air. "Do you smell that?"

Rat tensed. If the scent had been coming through a dead passage, Jinx wouldn't have noticed it.

"Jinx, I don't—"

"Come over here. There's a draft, and it's definitely fresh air. We've got to be half a dozen stories underground right now." She pointed down the aisle of shelves just ahead of her. "This whole place must open up out there. This might be what we're looking for."

Rat started to argue, but they couldn't get the words out. They couldn't explain the tower, and they couldn't let her see how scared they were.

If they panicked now, Jinx would take them back up like she'd offered. She wouldn't finish the story about Ingrid, and she probably wouldn't take them into the tunnels again.

"Right," Rat said, fighting back their nerves. Holding the lantern steady, they closed the distance to the mouth of the aisle, where Jinx was standing. "You're going first, though."

"If we run into anything, you have my express permission to run."

Rat swallowed hard and raised the lantern. The circle of light extended a few feet out, catching on the stacks of furniture piled up around them.

"Stay close." Jinx stepped past them.

Rat looked back at the ladder one more time, then started after her.

The twined smells of dust and mugwort grew thicker the farther they went, and even with the lantern humming in their hand, the shadows grew deeper all the time. Whole aisles branched into darkness, and Rat couldn't stop to figure out which were real. They held out the chalk, letting it skip over the furniture as they walked.

A slash on a display cabinet with broken windows.

A hurried line on the side of an upturned end table.

Rat's chest tightened. They wanted to stop Jinx and pull her back. They imagined the knight, waiting at the end of this to carry them back to the tower.

If something happened, Agatha was the only person who knew where they'd gone. No one else would even realize they were missing until morning.

Jinx planted her foot on the scuffed wood of an old storage trunk that must have fallen into the aisle. She pressed on it, testing her weight, and then climbed up before turning back and offering her hand.

Jinx met their eyes, and Rat grabbed on, allowing her to help them up and over.

They landed in a half crouch, ready to match her pace, but Jinx didn't move.

All around them, grass pushed up between the floorboards. At the edge of the lantern light, the aisle of abandoned furniture opened into a clearing, and the reedy sprigs of grass turned tall and wild.

Faint traces of gold dust had settled over everything like an early frost. Stalks of mugwort and yarrow sprouted up around the edges of the shelves and drawers at the mouth of the clearing, a burst of yellow mums at the foot of the bookcase.

The weeds didn't stop there. Overgrowth choked the mouth of the next aisle, etched in the dull glow of the dust, and it only grew thicker in the distance.

"Whoa," Jinx said under her breath. "What do you think happened here?"

"Jinx . . ."

"I've been in the tunnels for weeks and I've never seen anything like this." She knelt down and ran her fingers over a bristly patch of grass by her boot. "It's got to be some kind of spell, but I have no idea what sort of working this would be. God. I need a picture so I can show Cromwell and Blakely. How far do you think this goes?"

"It's . . . I'm not sure," Rat said, but they could feel it in the hollow of their chest, like the night before. Something was out there in the weeds.

They glanced over their shoulder, to double-check that everything was still as it should be. The way back hadn't changed. They were still in their own world, still on school grounds. Somehow, though, that unsettled them more.

"I really don't think we should go in any farther," Rat said as Jinx threaded her fingers through the grass. "We don't know what kind of magic is out there, and—"

In a flutter of wingbeats and ruffled feathers, a crow burst out of the grass and touched down on a battered end table.

"Fuck!" Rat leapt back and Jinx whipped around, startled. They clasped their hands to their mouth, lantern clattering down at their feet.

The bird cawed at them.

Biting back a laugh, Jinx grabbed the light off the ground. "Oh, god. Did you—" she started, then broke off.

The bird took off again as a long ripple ran through the grass.

The stalks whispered in a way that made chills break out across Rat's skin.

Jinx's eyes locked on Rat. "We're going," she said, pressing the lantern into their hands. "Get back to the ladder."

"I can't—"

"Back to the ladder! Now!" She turned them around and shoved them back toward the toppled storage trunk. "I'm right behind you!"

Rat dropped the chalk. It clattered behind them as they scrambled over the trunk.

As they came down on the other side, they paused, just for a moment. They glanced back as a long, low form crawled out of the grass on too many legs, feelers sweeping the ground in front of it. Swatches of sky plated its segmented body like armor, star-flecked and deepening blue.

The creature whipped toward Rat as a second one scuttled out behind it, shooting straight for the aisle.

"Fuck," Rat breathed. They broke into a run.

The glow of the lantern swept the ground around them, throwing shadows between the furniture. Rat sprinted from one trail blaze to the next, until they lost all direction. All that mattered was that they were on familiar ground. Their own ragged breath drowned out everything else.

They clipped a broken armoire at the end of an aisle as they passed, smudging the chalk mark. Their lungs burned.

Behind them, a loud crash echoed through the aisle. Rat caught themself on a battered office desk, panting.

Their eyes found Jinx. She scrambled backward up the passage a few feet back, the creatures closing in on her. One scuttling up the narrow aisle, the other just behind it, crawling over the side of the shelves.

Jinx drew her hand through the air, and a heavy sheet of condensation crashed down around her.

The water battered against the creatures' exoskeletons like a breaking wave. The one on the ground reared back. The other wove up the side of the shelf to head her off, the subtle glow of its armored plates bathing the aisle in a dull gray light.

Jinx looked impossibly small.

Rat was unarmed and they couldn't cast. They couldn't help her.

Her hand cut the air again, and another wave of condensation whipped across the aisle, hard and fast as she broke for cover.

She ducked behind a bookcase, breathing hard, and her eyes found Rat's.

"Jinx!" they shouted.

"Go!" she yelled. "I'm okay!"

She pressed a hand to her ribs. Behind her, a thin line of light oozed across one the creatures' backs. Rat hadn't seen the attack land, but Jinx must have hit it between the plates. The creatures were big, though, and she'd barely nicked it.

Rat shot toward her as fast as their feet would carry them.

As they reached her, Jinx shoved against the bookcase. "Come on," Rat said, grabbing her arm.

With a small noise of exertion, Jinx rammed her shoulder into it again, knocking it off-balance. The bookcase rocked back, and a flurry of old papers flew from the shelves, fluttering down around her as the heavy wooden frame toppled into the aisle.

Rat yanked her back, and she scrambled after them, stumbling before she hit her stride.

Without looking to see if the creatures had followed, they both ran.

CHAPTER EIGHTEEN

AS SOON AS THEY GOT TO THE LADDER, RAT CLIMBED up as quickly as they could, Jinx close on their heels.

When they made it to the top, they heaved themself out the trapdoor and dropped onto the floor. Every breath felt like their lungs were trying to turn inside out.

Jinx hauled herself up and slammed the door shut behind her. She stomped it down, latched it, and then collapsed next to them on the floor of the old ballroom.

Rat turned their head. They couldn't see Jinx so much as they sensed her lying there, so close that they could feel the rise and fall of her ragged breaths.

She let out a shaky laugh. "Holy fuck. I was sure we were going to die. What were those things?"

"I have no idea," Rat said, breathing hard.

With a groan, Jinx rolled onto her side and propped herself up. "There's no way I'm staying here and waiting for them to find us. We need to go."

"Ugh." Rat pushed themself off the ground. Their shirt clung to their back, damp with sweat. "If I die, Will is going to find a spell to raise me just so he can kill me again."

"Agreed. Cromwell called dibs on my eulogy, and there's no way I'm letting her have this."

"God forbid." Rat rose unsteadily to their feet and held their hand out to help Jinx up. "Do you need to go straight back to your room after this?"

"I have a bit of time," she said. "What were you thinking?"

It was still early October, but after the damp chill of the tunnels, the night air was a different kind of cold.

Rat gasped down a breath as they shoved through the door to the widow's walk. They'd forgotten how big the sky was over Bellamy Arts, and they wanted to drown in it.

"God," Jinx said, following them out. "I can't believe we're actually on the roof."

"You never came up? I thought—"

"I wasn't after the rooftop, Evans." She spun around, taking everything in. Her curls fell past her shoulders in a tumble of silver and moon shadows, and when she turned back, a breathless grin split her face. "This is incredible," she said, grabbing Rat by the arm. "You're off probation. I declare you officially in. Tell me you're in."

"I'm in," Rat said, stumbling after her as she tugged them toward the edge of the walk. "But, you still have to tell me—"

"Everything." Jinx stopped against the rails and turned her face up to the sky. She drew in one deep breath, and then another. In the moonlight, grit from the tunnels and the faint, luminescent glow of the dust streaked her skin and the soft lines of her leather jacket. "Wow. I really thought we might not make it out for a minute. I never thought I'd be this glad to see campus."

Rat leaned against the rail beside her, and then realized how close they were, enough that they could smell the faint trace of the tunnels still clinging to her.

Before they could shift away, she turned to look at them, the faint glint of moonlight on the rim of her glasses. "Do you still want the end of the story about the school?"

"I . . ." Something in their chest fell.

Rat had been suspicious of Jinx for weeks, but she'd had every chance to leave them in the dark, and she hadn't. They weren't sure that she even knew what the tower was. If anything, Jinx was the one who'd been wrong to trust them.

The worst part was that for a moment, Rat had forgotten themself. They'd wanted whatever delicate, unlikely alliance they'd had with her to be real.

They pushed all of the air out of their lungs. "Tell me."

And, because some secrets were made to be told in a whisper, she leaned in closer, and said, "She sank it."

Rat blinked.

Jinx's mouth curved into another slow grin, sharp with mischief, and they wanted to break all over again. But they'd come too far to be honest now.

"Ingrid," she said. "After she cleared everyone out of the buildings and closed the seal, she sank the campus into the ground. The clock tower is the only part of the original construction left standing."

Rat stared at her.

"After the new campus had been built, the Council of Hours dug access points and sent in a team of earthworkers to do an excavation. They didn't find anything, but every so often they'll go back in and search the place again. They're the ones who built the tunnels and put in all the ladders and hatches down there."

"What are they searching for?"

Her eyes shone. "I told you. Margaret Ingrid was building an archive. What have you heard about the Ingrid Collection?"

"It's full of things?"

"It's *legendary*. Ingrid was one of the most accomplished formalists who ever lived, and that archive was her life's work," Jinx said. "You have to wonder what she must have found that would make her bury it."

"You came to Bellamy Arts looking for this," Rat said, understanding.

"I wouldn't be the first. I pretty much grew up on stories about this place."

Rat looked at her, curious. All over again, they remembered that they knew almost nothing about her. "Your family went here?"

"Almost all of us," she said. "My grandfather was the dean of Magics and High Arts before Fairchild."

Rat furrowed their brow. "Why don't I know about him?"

Jinx paused for a moment like she was trying to decide if she should tell them something. "He isn't a Wilder," she said, leaning in conspiratorially. "He's a Drake."

They blinked at her. "Your name is on the library," they said, and then immediately felt ridiculous, because Jinx obviously knew that.

Her face flushed and they realized that this was probably part of the reason why she didn't tell people.

The Drake family was unrivaled. Once, when Rat was still really young, they'd gone with their parents to the Drake ancestral home on an island off of Maine, but all they remembered was the crash of waves and the sheer rise of the cliffs. Most of the Drake family had an affinity for water spells, but their archives were said to be full of storm workings, and tidal rituals, and spells that summoned titans out of the clouds and salt-scaled creatures from the deepest part of the sea.

"But why doesn't anyone seem to know you?" they asked, and then realized how rude that was. "I—"

"I took private lessons," Jinx said. Idly, she drew a globe of water out of the air as she spoke, the same way they'd seen Harker cast bursts of spellfire when he needed something to do with his hands. "My grandfather offered to teach me, after he retired. I went basically everywhere with him. Actually, I spent a lot of time here growing up." She tilted her head, angling herself toward Rat. "I just can't believe no one's told you anything about the school. You really never knew about the Ingrid Collection?"

"No," they admitted. "I hadn't . . ."

"The sunken campus? The Holbrook Map?"

"Wait—what?"

"The Holbrook Map," Jinx said again, like she wasn't sure if they'd heard her right. "It was one of Alexander Holbrook's last works. I thought you knew. It was turned over to the school after his death, but . . . there's an investigation right now. They haven't disclosed what it's for, but Cromwell's heard whispers that the map disappeared from the private collections right before the year started."

Rat hesitated. "What does that have to do with all this?"

Her eyes lit up, like they'd asked her exactly the question she'd been hoping for. "That's the thing. It's a map of the campus, but rumor has it that it's . . . strange. Difficult to read. No one seems to know where it leads or how it's meant to be followed, except for maybe Fairchild and Holbrook himself. But supposedly?"

Rat watched her, the quiet of the sleeping campus heavy around them.

"He collected sources on the Ingrid Collection while he was working here," she said softly. "Rat, I think he might be the only person who ever found it."

CHAPTER NINETEEN

THE SKY HAD ALREADY STARTED TO FADE BY THE TIME RAT made it back to their room.

Of course Elise didn't tell you, they told themself as they dropped onto their bed. *Why would you need to know that?*

Jinx was chasing a legend. Probably, their father had been, too.

"A personal project," Evening had called it.

Rat slid their phone from their pocket, pulled up Evening's number, and scrolled past the line of panicked text messages they'd sent him before they'd ended up knee-deep in all of this.

Hey, I'm sorry but did my father ever tell you anything about they typed, then remembered what time it was.

With a sigh, they backspaced again and then closed out of the message.

Almost by habit, they swiped back to their thread with Harker.

I know what you're after, they typed, then deleted it.

What does she want with an archive when

They deleted that, too.

You're doing this alone, aren't you?

They shut their eyes and thought of the meadow, slowly creeping through the tunnels, and Jinx on the rooftop, and Harker in the woods, the light fading around him.

They deleted it again. Exhausted, they tossed their phone back onto their bed and reached for their backpack. They didn't want to think about the Holbrook Map anymore, but they couldn't sleep, either.

If they slept, they would dream, and if they dreamt, it would be about the tower.

Rat pulled out the book they'd taken from the War Room. It had been a long time since they'd looked through Harker's notes, but pressed neatly between the cover and the title page was a single sheet of lined paper.

Rat unfolded it and held it up to the light.

History of magic in US northeast—some biographical information on M. Ingrid in ch6 & images of old campus. No, Cromwell, you're not in this one.

Below the header ran a disappointingly sparse index in Harker's spindly handwriting. Usually when he read a book, he outlined exhaustively, copying over quotes and page numbers, and then created an index of any useful spell diagrams.

Rat had no idea what they'd been hoping for, outside of the Holbrook Map itself or maybe a signed confession detailing exactly what Harker was up to. They felt ridiculous. If Jinx and Agatha weren't in on his plans, he wouldn't risk leaving anything in the War Room that might give him away.

It wasn't like Harker had ever made things easy. Rat didn't know why they'd expected any less now.

With a sigh, Rat rolled onto their back and riffled through the pages. "Come at me, Blakely," they muttered under their breath.

They turned to the chapter he'd flagged, thumbing through the pages, then stopped as a photograph flickered past.

Rat flipped back.

The caption read *Ingrid in Profile.*

In the picture, Margaret Ingrid sat hunched over her writing desk, so low that her nose nearly brushed the paper. From the story that Jinx had told them, Rat had imagined that she'd be powerfully built, with waves of wild red hair and maybe a sword slung across her back, but the Ingrid in the drawing was younger than they'd expected, with skin the color of watered-down paste and lank mouse-brown hair.

She didn't look like someone who'd traveled the deep planes and stolen the breath of gods. If anything, she reminded them a bit of Harker after he'd been up studying too many nights in a row.

Something about the picture pricked at them, but they couldn't say why it bothered them so much. They didn't even know what they were looking for.

Furrowing their brow, Rat flipped ahead to the next picture, this one an image of a sunlit lobby. *Cartwright Hall, interior.*

They thumbed through the rest of the chapter, skimming the captions as the images flickered past.

Crows atop the Founder's House.

Benefactors Ms. Westlake and Mr. Cartwright on Carrington Green.

Ms. Ingrid and Ms. Mallorie in North Tower of Linden Bldg.

A corridor in the Sybaris A. Drake Library.

Rat stopped on the last image, taking in the narrow, shelf-lined passageway. For a moment, it looked almost familiar, and then they realized their mistake. The Drake—this version of it—had been buried a long time ago.

They tried to imagine the room in the picture a hundred years in the earth, a century of dust and rubble coating the hardwood floors.

The hairs on the back of Rat's neck stood on end as the realization clicked into place. "Shit," they said under their breath. "No."

Quickly, they flipped back, stopping at *Ingrid in Profile.* Rat hadn't recognized Ingrid. They'd recognized the room.

They'd been there before.

The last time they'd seen that place, the roof was caved in. There had been wisteria spilling through the empty window frames, and the late summer air had been thick with humidity.

This was a drawing of Ingrid's private office, and it was located in Ashwood, overlooking the school.

With a chill, Rat traced their thumb along the edge of the page. They thought of the knight, perched on the same sill, one leg dangling over the ledge, the sheen of moonlight on her battered armor.

"What did she take from you?" Rat murmured to their empty room.

Movement flickered in their dorm window.

Rat jolted up, half expecting to find the knight herself leaning against their dresser as if summoned. But outside, there was only the blackened tree line and dark sprawl of the hills.

They rubbed their eye and reached for their phone again. They opened back to their message with Harker.

The cursor blinked on the screen.

Rat stared back at it, intent.

"Fuck," they breathed. They put their phone back down. They had nothing they could say that would get them an answer.

Sore, tired, and still smelling of the tunnels, they picked up the book again to search the pages for answers they already knew they wouldn't find.

Rat finally caught a few hours of sleep sometime after the sky had started to pale, and they woke up with the tower burnt behind their eyelids, the book from the night before still open on the bed beside them.

Based on their texts, they'd already missed Will, which, given that there was still literal dirt on their face, was probably for the better.

And then, they realized they had another text waiting for them, this one from Jinx. *breakfast*

No punctuation. No explanation.

Rat blinked at it, unsure whether it was an invitation or some kind of imperative.

Blearily, they flipped the book shut and pushed themself to their feet to gather their things.

They'd been lucky enough to get one of the few rooms with an adjoining bathroom, which spared them needing to brave the hall showers, but they were also pretty sure there wasn't enough time in the world to fully scrub the smell of the tunnels out of their skin. In the end, they picked their way across campus with their hoodie pulled on over a pair of sports bras because they didn't have time to find a clean shirt and didn't feel up to binding, their hair still wet in the morning chill.

They found Jinx at a table near the back of the dining hall. Harker had already claimed the spot across from her, his back to Rat so all they could see was his hastily tied-back hair and the stack of library books by his feet.

Books and papers littered the table between the two, like they'd already been up working on something for a while.

Jinx looked and tilted her head slightly, half a question and half an invitation.

Harker followed her gaze, and then immediately looked like he wished that he hadn't.

Heat pricked in Rat's lungs.

Drawing themself up, Rat nodded to Jinx and started across the dining hall.

"Hey." They leaned against the side of the table. "I got your text."

Harker shot a glance at Jinx like he hadn't remotely agreed to this.

"Easy on the charm, Blakely. We need them," she said. She angled herself toward Rat. "We're glad you're here."

Harker offered Rat his most lukewarm customer service smile. "Thrilled. Are you here for the enclosed spaces, or the things with teeth?"

"Jinx caught me up last night," they said, sliding onto the bench next to him. "I knew you were up to something, but I wouldn't have guessed it went so far." They smiled back at him and took a piece of uneaten toast from his plate.

He scowled.

"So," they said, turning back to Jinx. "What is all of this?"

She rubbed her eyes like whatever was going on, she hadn't gotten nearly enough sleep to deal with it. "We went to the library this morning to see if we could figure out what those creatures were. Well, the library, some forums, and basically every book we have in the War Room. It took a few hours, but I think we've finally got a lead. Unless you know any other giant twilight death centipedes."

She picked up a book and passed it across the table to them. The page in front of them had a short entry from a bestiary. An illustration of the creatures from the tunnel snaked below, with long, slinking bodies and spiny legs. One of them reared up, its head angled to show the sharp curve of its mandibles.

"They're commonly called night terrors or terrors," Jinx said.

Rat decidedly did not want to know what kind of person referred to creatures like that commonly.

Jinx leaned across the table and tapped her finger against the page. "If you couldn't guess, they aren't exactly local. I've been trying to figure out a way to ask Frey about them, but I can't really waltz into office hours and tell him what we've been up to."

Rat frowned.

"He's a summoning specialist," she said. "In the Department of Higher Magics. I assumed that was why he wanted you in our class, since he would have been in the same department as—"

"My father," Rat finished. They'd known that. They should have been able to put it together sooner.

Jinx watched them. "Did I get it wrong?"

"No, I just . . . it hadn't occurred to me," Rat said.

Frey knew their father. He would have known about his work. Probably even about the map itself.

Before they could figure out what to say, Agatha swept in and planted herself on the table, paper-wrapped breakfast pastry in hand. She plucked Harker's coffee out of his hands and took a sip. "Blakely, I'm not sure why you insist on punishing yourself like this, but nothing you've done could possibly be this bad," she said, passing it back. "Cream and sugar, dear."

He made a small noise in protest, but she'd already turned to Rat. "I hear you're one of us now, Evans," she said, holding out her pastry. "I dare say that makes us allies."

Unsure of what else to do, Rat ripped off a piece. Then, because they could still feel the subtle heat coming off Harker, they smiled. "Thanks. I'm looking forward to it."

"You'll need to regale me with tales of your adventure later. I'm actually here to steal Jinx." She looked across the table. "My lessons are in the library today. The Council is still at it with the investigation, and I'd really like to avoid a family reunion."

"I'll walk you," Jinx said before Rat could ask, then looked back at the mound of books and papers. "Hey, could you—"

"Go. I'll watch your stuff," Harker told her.

"We'll wait for you to get back," Rat said smoothly.

The second Jinx and Agatha were out of sight, Harker turned to them. "So. Did you get what you were after?"

"What do you think you're doing?" they asked, dropping their voice. "Jinx and Agatha have no idea about the tower. This is all you, isn't it?"

He raised his eyebrows at them. "I thought you already knew that."

"Did you know about the terrors?" they said, leaning in. "You let us go in completely cold. We literally could have died down there. Harker, what's wrong with you?"

"I—" Harker opened his mouth and then closed it again, taken aback.

Suddenly, Rat became hyperaware of the books spread out on the table. Bestiaries and reference texts, but protection charms, too, like he'd grabbed anything he could think of, the way he did whenever he didn't know what else to do. From the amount of material alone, he must have been in the library with Jinx from the moment she'd left the widow's walk, trying to figure out what the terrors were.

He looked like he hadn't slept at all.

"You had no idea," they said, understanding. "The knight never warned you."

Color pricked his cheeks. "They were her creatures. Of course I knew," he said, a moment too late. "I don't remember telling you to follow me."

The wrongness of it settled over them. The knight might not have been kind, but she wasn't careless. Even when she'd been training them, she hadn't ever knowingly sent Rat into danger like that. No matter where she brought them or what she asked them to do, she always told them what might be waiting.

"I've been getting messages from her again," they said. "She found me as soon as I realized you were working with her. Whatever she's after, she doesn't actually think you'll find it. She's just using you to draw me back in."

"You have no idea what you're talking about."

"She's going to throw you aside when she's done."

Heat rolled off of him in a wave. "Right. I forgot that everything has to do with you. There's no way anyone could ever actually choose me."

"Holy shit," Rat said under their breath. "You're jealous."

Harker looked away. "Please."

"You knew, didn't you?" they pressed. "You went back to the tower willingly, but you're still her second choice. No matter what you do, it's never enough, is it?"

His breath hitched like they'd physically hit him.

Rat knew they'd crossed a line. They'd fought with Harker dozens of times, but he'd never looked at them with so much open resentment.

They drew back. "I . . . I know you took the Holbrook Map. Tell me what you did with it, or I'll tell Jinx everything."

"Say whatever you want," he said. His voice ran cold. "Tell her exactly how you know about the tower. You can start with your powers and end with how you were only using her to get to me."

Rat went quiet.

"It doesn't matter if the knight didn't choose me. You didn't go back. I did," he said. "You don't even know what she's after."

Rat opened their mouth to argue, but they couldn't find the words.

A hand clamped down on their shoulder.

"Hey," Will said. His eyes darted from Rat and Harker to the scattered papers on the table. "Am I interrupting something?"

"We're just waiting for Jinx to get back," Rat said weakly. They realized how close they still were to Harker and shifted away from him. The whole table suddenly felt like it had been stationed directly under a heat lamp.

Harker leaned back against the table and calmly adjusted his sleeve, the air around him still rippling. "She asked us to watch her things."

"Yeah, I can see that," Will said. "Rat, we can stop by the dorm on the way back if you need to grab your books before class. I was about to go find you. Ready to head out?" His strained smile told Rat that however they answered, he was prepared to toss them over his shoulder and fireman-carry them back to Mallory Hall if he had to.

"Sure thing," Rat said.

Will grabbed them by the wrist and hauled them to their feet.

"What were you doing over there?" he said as he pulled them through the crowd. "He's the human version of a tire fire. I thought you guys were done."

"Don't worry about it."

"Rat. Seriously. What was that?"

"Nothing. It doesn't matter." They shook Will off and pushed ahead of him, but even as they made their way outside, they couldn't stop thinking about everything Harker had said, and the smell of smoke clung to their sweatshirt the whole walk back to Mallory Hall.

CHAPTER TWENTY

MIDTERMS PASSED IN A BLUR.

Rat spent most of the week trying to piece together a map of the sunken campus and pretending that they didn't have any tests to study for. The rest of the time, they spent in and out of common rooms, listening to Jinx volley her thoughts about the tunnels between casting drills.

For his part, Harker had gone back to avoiding them, turning through theory textbooks and determinedly throwing back cheap dining hall coffee, which might have been less frustrating if Rat wasn't convinced he was deliberately trying to ruin the grading curve for them.

"Some of us have to maintain our GPA to stay here," he said when Agatha finally snapped his book shut.

"And it's not just you, Blakely," she said pointedly. "So whatever this is, please take it out on a class I'm not in."

Rat tried to keep their head down and focus on the paper that they needed to write, since they'd been excused from all of their practical exams. Mostly, though, they found themself thinking about the tunnels and what, exactly, their father must have found there.

They waited until the last day before break to turn in their essay to Frey. It was already late in the day as Rat wound their way up the stairs to his office, and the buildings had begun to empty out.

Frey worked out of a small, sunlit room in the Higher Magics building. Bookshelves lined the walls and the unmistakable tinge of magic hung in the air, like a spell had just been cast.

"Ah. Mx. Evans," he said, sorting through a pile of assignments. "You can just leave your paper on the desk."

They set it down and started to go. Then, steeling themself, they turned back.

"Actually, there was something else I wanted to speak to you about. About my father."

He looked up at them, and then understanding settled across his face. "I suppose you were bound to ask sooner or later." Frey motioned for them to pull up one of the mismatched chairs. "How can I help you?"

"You worked with him," Rat said, before they could lose their resolve.

"Yes. Only for a few years, unfortunately, but he was a brilliant formalist."

"I heard that one of his maps went missing," they said. "From the school's archives. I was wondering if . . ."

"Ah." Frey let out a sigh. "The Holbrook Map."

"I heard it was a map of the campus."

He frowned. "In a sense," he said, then paused. "Elise did tell you what kind of work your father did, didn't she?"

"I . . ." Rat opened their mouth and then closed it again.

Taking their silence as an answer, Frey's frown deepened. "The spellbooks that you inherited with the Holbrook Archives, then?"

Rat shook their head slowly.

They knew on some level that they'd inherited their father's books, but Rat had never accessed any of them. His entire archive had been sealed off along with the rest of the Holbrook family's ancestral home after he passed, now that Rat was the last one.

It was theirs if they wanted it, but they never had.

A heavy silence settled on the air as Frey studied them across the desk.

"I don't cast," they said, hating how weak it sounded.

Finally, Frey rubbed his eyes. "I told Elise this wouldn't help," he said, half to himself.

"She didn't—It was my choice." Rat sank back.

"Oh." He furrowed his brow. "My apologies. I shouldn't have assumed."

Rat fought the urge to look away, since somehow, that was even worse.

"Very well, then. How much do you know?" he asked. When Rat was quiet, he amended, "How much do you want to know?"

"I . . . whatever you can tell me. Please."

Frey paused for a moment, like he was deciding where to begin. "We don't usually teach students about the deep planes until they have a foundation in formal magic, though I would hazard that you might already be familiar with them."

"Deep planes?"

"Other worlds, in a sense. Some of them are easier to cross between than others, but with the right magic, it can be done."

Unease tightened in their chest. They knew this part, even if they hadn't used quite those words for it.

"It's a rare ability, especially for it to manifest like yours, but it isn't wholly unique," he said, choosing his words carefully. "I've encountered a handful of formalists over the years who have become adept at finding crossing points between the planes. It's called wayfinding."

Rat sat forward, but their next question stuck in their throat.

"Your father had a particular talent for it. It runs in the Holbrook family, or so I've been told, though I can't say if it came to him naturally or if he taught himself. Ordinarily, it takes years of study—it's a very advanced type of magic, and a very dangerous one. I can't say I'm surprised that you were never trained," he said. "There are terrible things out in the planes if you know where to look for them, and even more so if you don't."

"Like the tower," Rat said slowly.

Frey let out a breath. "I suppose I should have expected you to ask about that, too, given your case. How much were you told?"

"I . . . not a lot. I just saw it. In some of my father's notes," they lied.

"I know it's the reason I'm at Bellamy Arts. That's what you meant about terrible things, isn't it?"

Frey hesitated, like he was still deciding how much to say. "Among other things. Yes."

"What is she?" Rat asked. It felt dangerous, like they were admitting something just by posing the question.

He thought for a moment. "The tower is home to . . ." he trailed off, searching for the word. "I would say that it has a keeper, but I don't want you to mistake her for human. She isn't. That's just the form that she chooses to take. She's one of Acanthe's seven Honored Rooks, or ravens, depending on who you asked."

"And Acanthe—" Rat started, pronouncing the long *e* the way that Frey had, and the way that once, the knight had, too. They thought of the sky over the tower, hung with strange stars, and how the knight had taught them each one by name. "That's a constellation, isn't it?"

"She's a god, but an old one," Frey said. "Her Lady of Sealed Lips. The Death of Summers. Dusk. Keeper of the Rooks and their Several Secrets. She disappeared into the planes a long time ago, but her Rooks are still out there. Each is a dangerous creature in their own right, but one in particular."

"Iso—" Rat faltered. "The knight."

"Hm?"

"That's what I call her. She looked like a knight, in the notes I saw," Rat said. "I mean, just that she had armor, and . . . you know, came from a tower."

Nervously, they thumbed their compass, her name still hanging unspoken on their lips. She'd told it to them the night that she'd offered them her hand, her voice a curl of smoke over the dry grass. It was the one thing they'd kept back from even Harker.

Again, Frey studied them, and they realized how wholly unconvincing they must have sounded.

"The knight, then," he said after a moment. He gave them a small, sympathetic smile. "I suppose it's as good a name for her as any."

"She knew my father," Rat said before they could stop themself.

"Yes," he said. "She has a long history with the school. Alexander was one of the few people I've known to negotiate with her and come out . . . well, if not ahead, then at least whole. To be honest, I'm still not sure how he managed for as long as he did."

"Did she . . ."

"No," Frey said, shaking his head. He sighed. "Good heavens, no. He was ill. Even the most clever of us can't outwit death forever. To be honest, I always thought she must have been upset that she never had the chance. Elise told me about how her messengers found you. I wish they hadn't, but I suppose it isn't a surprise that she tried to reach you."

"She's taken other students, though."

"Against our best efforts, yes," he said. "Though none of their cases have ever been quite like yours, as I understand it. She finds them from the school. Or, more often, they find her. The wards keep her from setting foot on campus, but there's little we can do when a student goes out searching."

"What happens to them?" Rat asked. "The ones she takes back with her?"

Frey hesitated for a moment too long, like it was a question he'd been hoping to avoid. "You need to understand that her magic isn't like ours," he said, finally. "Her powers have been waning for a long time now. She keeps some of the ones she brings back with her, for a time at least. Trains them, twists their magic into something strange and cruel. But, just as often, she devours them for their gifts."

Rat's throat tightened. "Oh." Their voice came out like a snuffed candle.

They thought of how the knight had once brushed her calloused fingers over their knuckles. Their wrist. Their face.

Rat pushed the memory down. "But—but the others. You said just as often. Do any of them . . ."

"Never for long. Though, to be honest, I'm not sure that to survive by her whims is a much kinder fate." Something in his voice shifted, like he wasn't speaking in the abstract anymore. "The school does what it can, but once something is in her grasp, it's rare for her to let it go."

Quiet settled over the office again.

After a long moment, Frey shifted back. "I understand that you don't have an interest in casting, but if you ever change your mind, even as a defensive measure, I'd be happy to take you on for private lessons. I've found that sometimes, as unpleasant as it is, you can't protect yourself without knowing what you're up against."

"I'll remember that," they said. Then, realizing the conversation had ended, they rose to their feet. "I . . . thanks. I appreciate it."

They started toward the door, but before they could leave, Frey cleared his throat.

"About the map," he said as they turned back to him. "Alexander's work was a puzzle. A beautiful one, to be sure. Fascinating. But I'm sure you'll understand more than most, Rat, that some things are better left unsolved."

Rat made it back outside before they stopped against the side of the building and forced themself to breathe.

They didn't know what kind of answers they'd been expecting. They'd known the knight to be cruel. It shouldn't have surprised them.

"Her powers have been waning for a long time now."

Waning. Like a tide, or a sliver of moon before it winked out. They thought of the way she'd never followed them back through their father's office, like she couldn't set foot there, and how she'd always sent her messengers to find them. How she'd needed them.

It had never occurred to them that she might be weak.

Somehow, though, that wasn't a comfort.

They already knew that some things were better left unsolved. They weren't interested in *better*.

Whatever the knight was after, Rat wasn't leaving Harker to keep searching over break while they were gone. He was far enough ahead of them as it was.

Rat slid their phone from their pocket. They swiped past a new text from Will, without stopping to respond, asking them if they'd made any decisions about their fall break plans.

They pulled up a message to Jinx. *Are you up to anything over the break?* They typed.

They stared at the text.

Are you afraid that Harker's in danger, they asked themself, *or are you just scared he's ahead of you?*

Rat shoved the thought away and hit send.

Immediately, three dots appeared at the bottom of the screen, and then a new message appeared.

But, instead of an answer, it just said, *301 mallory hall, tomorrow noon*

CHAPTER TWENTY-ONE

CAMPUS EMPTIED OUT OVERNIGHT. A NEW KIND OF QUIET settled over Mallory Hall, and in the deserted hush of the building, Rat dreamt about teeth.

The next morning, they didn't need to meet Jinx for a while, but they gathered their things and headed out early.

A storm had rolled through while they slept, and there was a new chill in the air. With so many people gone, a lull had descended over everything. Rat had known that almost everyone would go home for the break, but they hadn't realized exactly how alone they would be.

Damp leaves littered the ground as they picked their way across the lawn, the last of the morning fog clinging low to the path.

They'd brought a sketchbook with them, but as they wound their way through the campus, their mind went back to the knight and the cool touch of her gloved fingers against their cheek.

Rat thought of the way she'd looked at them the first time they'd found their way to her, keen with interest. *"They never told me that Alexander Holbrook had a son. You look just like him."*

They'd hesitated, not because she was wrong but because they'd known that the moment they spoke, the spell would break, and their voice would give them away. Because they'd wanted her to be right. Not a boy, exactly, but their father's son all the same.

"Unless," she'd asked when they hadn't answered, *"I'm mistaken?"*

And Rat, their voice just above a whisper, had said, *"No, you're not."*

They'd flinched, waiting for her to take it back, but when they looked back, she'd still been watching them like they were exactly what she'd hoped to find but hadn't known to ask for until then.

Even now, Rat couldn't help but wonder if she'd meant to devour them, too, or if she'd always had something else in mind.

They still didn't like to think of how close they'd come to returning to the tower with her.

Usually, in the version of the story they tried to tell themself—the way they liked to pretend that things had happened—they'd realized what she was and bolted. But that had never been true.

There was nothing they could have found out about her that would've turned them back, because a part of them had already known. The truth was that they hadn't refused to return to the tower with her because they were brave, or clever, or good. They were just too much of a coward to follow her.

She'd held out her hand to them, and they'd taken it.

A whisper of power had passed through her fingers like a promise of what they could be, and it was dusk, and starlight, and teeth. The knight had met their gaze, her eyes bright and sharp.

Panic had welled in their chest.

She'd been wrong about them. They weren't meant for power. As soon as Rat returned with her, she would see them for the small, frightened thing that they actually were, and she would change her mind about them.

They wouldn't be able to go home. Elise would never trust them again. They'd have to admit what a mistake it had been, to try using their magic in the first place, and they wouldn't be allowed out of her sight.

The knight had pulled them forward, toward the tower in the distance.

It would be their fault, for having ever had the audacity to think they could be what she was.

"*Wait,*" they'd said in a rush.

She'd looked back at them. "*We still have some ways to go, and the stars have already begun to shift. I can tell you everything while we walk.*"

"*I want to go back.*" They'd yanked their hand away. "*This was a mistake. I'm sorry. I have to go home. I—*"

Like she'd realized she was losing them, the knight had grabbed them by the wrist and pulled them back. *"I don't think you understand what I'm offering you,"* she'd said, but a cold edge had slid into her voice. *"What do you think is waiting for you if you go back to that place? Your gifts are wasted there. They'll never see you for what you are."*

"Let go," they'd said, pulling against her. "You're hurting me."

Her fingers had dug into Rat's wrist. *"Why do you think it is, that no one ever taught you to cast? They don't think you're weak. They're afraid of what you could become. You would spend the rest of your days there as a pawn in everyone else's game, but I could make you into something more than that."*

She'd wrenched them toward her, and all their panic had broken over them in a cold wave. Instinctively, Rat had jerked out of her grasp, and before they realized what they'd done, their magic had flared.

They had come down hard in the grass a few feet from where they'd been standing. Something desperate had flickered across the knight's face as they shoved themself to their feet.

They hadn't looked back to see if she was following them. They'd just fled.

They'd made it all the way back home before they allowed themself to stop, and then as soon as they were back in their father's office, they'd crumpled to the ground, shaking. The next morning, there had been a mum on their windowsill and with it, a single human phalange, polished smooth.

One way or another, they'd understood then, she meant for them to go with her. It had never really been a choice.

"What were you after?" Rat said under their breath, but the campus was quiet around them.

They came to a stop as they realized they'd wandered back to the foot of the clock tower.

Not far off, a few Lesser Hours from the Council stood gathered outside the Drake, dressed in evening-gray cloaks like they were still on duty for the investigation. Fog curled around the low form of the library in drifts, already beginning to break apart as the day warmed.

Rat looked past the gathered Hours to the library.

Harker would still be on campus. He'd never gone home for breaks at Highgate, and they were pretty sure he'd lived in the dorms over the summer. With the campus empty and the rest of the break at his disposal, he could be up to anything.

They remembered the knight, tilting Harker's face up to hers where he knelt in the grass, her fingers tight under his jaw, then pushed the thought away.

Suddenly, they didn't want to be out anymore.

They looked back to the clock tower one last time, their eyes traveling over the smooth stretch of bricks where the door had been once. Then, before they could decide otherwise, they turned and started back the way they'd come.

With nowhere else to go, Rat made their way back to the dorms, heading for the room Jinx had written in her text. They knocked, then realized that she probably wasn't expecting them yet.

Before they could turn around, though, Jinx called out, "Let yourself in, Evans."

Rat pushed the door in, and then stopped in the doorway as they caught sight of Harker, leaning against the footpost of Agatha's bed with a to-go cup of dining hall coffee.

Which, at least, answered the question of what he was up to.

He stilled as he met their eyes. "I should head out. I still have some things to get done."

Agatha sighed theatrically from where she sat perched on the bed. "No rest for the wicked?"

He gave her a look, and she flashed her teeth.

"Get some sleep," she called after him as he got to his feet. "Caffeine doesn't count!"

He glanced at Rat as he brushed past, close enough that they could feel the faint heat radiating off of him.

Rat turned after him to say something, but before they knew what, he was already heading down the hallway.

"She devours them."

They shoved the thought away. Harker knew what he was dealing with.

"You're early," Jinx said. Rat turned to her and realized that she had their sketchbook out in front of her on her bed. "We were just finalizing our plans."

"We have plans?" Rat asked, pushing the door shut behind themself.

"As a matter of fact," she said, motioning for them to join her.

Rat walked over, finally taking in the room.

Jinx and Agatha had gotten one of the larger rooms in Mallory Hall, with its own fireplace and a wide bay window overlooking the courtyard below.

They didn't know what they'd expected the room to look like, exactly, but the wall over Jinx's bed was plastered with star charts and spell diagrams and something that looked a lot like a subway map. Open books and papers were spread out on her desk like a storm had breezed through, and pictures cluttered the standing mirror.

"Oh. Before I forget," Jinx said, grabbing something off the night table. "This is for you."

She placed a heavy silver coin in Rat's hand. One side showed a dragon coiled in a field of asters. The other, a sword and crescent moon, etched over with a sigil.

"It's a shield charm," Jinx explained. "Blakely made them—Cromwell and I have one, too. It isn't very strong, but it might buy us some time if we run into anything else in the tunnels."

Rat traced their thumb over the sigil, and something in their chest tightened. They already knew what the coin was. They'd carried one in their pocket all last year, tucked beside their compass. They'd accidentally used up the last of the spell when they tripped on the stairs over the summer, but by then, Harker hadn't been around anymore to make them another one.

"The coins aren't in circulation anymore," Jinx said, and Rat realized they'd been studying it. "It's—"

"A draub," Rat finished, half to themself.

They turned the coin in their hand.

Once, it had been old currency traded among the magic community, but they hadn't been used in a long time. The coins were cast from arcanists' silver, though, and they accepted spellwork easily, which made them perfect for small charms.

Jinx nodded. "They're pretty rare these days. I still can't get Blakely to say how he got ahold of them."

"Right," Rat breathed.

They thought of the stash they'd found in their father's things, tucked away in a cabinet in his office. They'd given a few to Harker. They hadn't realized he'd held on to them.

"He said you'd probably throw it in the lake," Jinx added. "But it's yours if you want it."

"Thanks," Rat said, closing their hand over it.

It wasn't kindness, they reminded themself. It was probably just because he knew that if anything bad happened to Rat, it would take roughly thirty seconds to become his problem.

They slipped the charm into their pocket, hating that they felt safer for having it anyways.

On the bed, Jinx turned back to the sketchbook.

"I already spoke with him about our plans." She flipped the pages open to an aerial map of the campus that Rat had drawn at the beginning of the school year. "I don't want to go that deep into the tunnels again until we know what we're up against. He's going to keep digging in the library and see if he can find anything, about the terrors or otherwise."

"Right," Rat said with a twinge.

"You and I," Jinx went on, "are going to be investigating a few other entrances to the tunnels. There are access points all around campus, but we haven't been able to get to most of them unnoticed while everyone's been around." She tapped the map. A dozen small X's had been penciled in, speckled across the campus. "Once everyone's back, the school's going to start gearing up for the Whisper Ball, so this is probably the quietest it'll be until after the dance."

Rat's chest tightened, but they nodded. "Okay. What's Agatha doing?"

"Traveling, obviously," Agatha said, stretching out on her bed.

Rat turned back to her. Today, she was wearing a long-sleeved dress and the kind of white kidskin gloves that were made for the express purpose of not touching things.

The bed was made up with a dark, floral comforter and a mound of decorative pillows. A violin case was propped against the nightstand, where she'd left out a pile of spellbooks and a small stash of mazapánes, and a lesbian pride flag hung on the wall.

Agatha waved her hand at a suitcase that Rat hadn't noticed before, standing at the foot of her bed. "Just imagine I'll be off doing something vague and perilous."

"She's doing recon," Jinx said.

"Perilously," Agatha said.

Jinx tossed a pillow at her. "Remember about the Holbrook Map?" she asked Rat. "It disappeared at the start of the school year. I was honestly hoping that you'd taken it and we could call it a day."

"What?"

"I told you," Agatha said. "Evans wouldn't have to steal it. They could have asked."

Rat blinked at her.

"Right of succession," she said, like that explained everything.

"I . . . sure?"

Agatha looked at them like they were five. "You're Alexander Holbrook's only direct heir, so you have the strongest claim on his work. If you'd asked the school for it, they would have needed to return the map to you."

"Oh," Rat said.

It was exactly the kind of arcane garbage bylaw that Harker would have known about. He hadn't just taken the Holbrook Map. He was keeping it from them.

"I'd bet money that our thief is after the Ingrid Collection, too," Jinx said. "I just assumed it was you because, you were so . . ." She waved her hand, like their blond hair and sketchbook full of maps explained everything. "Whoever it is, if they have your father's map, they're already a step ahead of us. Which is troubling to say the least."

"Have you asked the Council of Hours?" Rat asked.

Jinx and Agatha traded glances.

"Agatha. Your uncle is in charge of the investigation, right?"

Agatha eyed them warily. "Did he talk to you?"

"Oh." Rat ducked their head. "I just ran into him. Uh, he's a family friend. He told me that the map was missing, but he couldn't say more than that."

A silence that Rat couldn't read settled over the room.

Finally, Agatha said, "No, we haven't asked. I know a few apprentices who might be able to tell me something, but it's better if he doesn't know what we're up to."

On the bed beside her, her phone pinged.

She glanced down at it, then pushed herself back up. "My ride is almost here," she said, then looked back at Rat. "Evans, see me off?"

They hesitated a moment, and then realized that she'd nodded to her luggage.

Without waiting for a reply, Agatha picked up her coat and started for the door, like she expected Rat to follow.

Unsure of what else to do, they grabbed her suitcase and started after her.

As soon as they made it onto the stairs, without turning back to them, she said, "What did Evening actually say to you?"

"Nothing," they said. "He was friends with my dad. I think he just mentioned the investigation as a courtesy."

"We're Cromwells. We don't do good deeds," Agatha said as she took the landing. "Did you tell him anything?"

"No," they said quickly. "I wouldn't. It's probably just some kind of family alliance thing anyway."

She sighed heavily. "You need to be careful around that side of my family. They aren't nice."

"Oh," Rat said weakly, not sure how to respond.

"Evening collects people," she explained. "All of the Cromwells do. Everything is a political maneuver for him. If you haven't noticed it, he's probably trying to collect you, too."

"But I'm—"

"The heir to one of the most powerful bloodlines on this side of the country. Not to mention that you're the only remaining Holbrook. He would love to have you in his pocket," she said. Rat quieted. "It's the same game that all of the oldest families play, Rat. The only reason no one ever catches him is because he's good at what he does."

"I thought he was trying to help," they said. They felt winded.

"Believe me. My parents are still friendly enough with the rest of the family to keep up appearances, but there's a reason we don't have a lot to do with them anymore. They can be valuable allies when they want to, but only if they have something to gain from it."

Before Rat could answer, they reached the bottom of the stairs, and Agatha led them off into the deserted lobby.

She flopped backward onto one of the leather couches as if she was sitting in her own living room. "You know why everyone treats you like that, don't you?"

"Like what?" Rat asked, dragging her suitcase the rest of the way to her.

"Half of them want to protect you, and the other half want to swallow you whole. You can't pretend you haven't noticed," Agatha said.

Vaguely, they wondered which camp she put Harker in.

She propped herself up again. "It's because you act like a frightened animal. It was the same way for me."

"It's not like that. I just, I'm not like you. You're—"

"I'm . . .?"

Agatha Cromwell Rivera was a thing with teeth. Calling her weak or frightened would be like stirring a spoonful of broken glass into a cup of tea and calling it sugar.

In the hush of the empty building, a slow, conspiratorial smile spread across her lips. "Jinx told you, didn't she?"

Rat started to speak and then stopped themself, unsure of how much they were supposed to know. "She said you see things. Glimpses. Of things that have happened and . . . things that haven't yet."

"It runs on my mother's side."

"I didn't know that."

"Not many do. I mean, if you had that kind of advantage, would you tell anyone?" she said. "The Rivera Archives are full of scrying spells, but they haven't had a natural seer in decades. Everyone's furious that it was me."

"Why?"

Agatha pursed her lips like the answer was evident. "No reason."

Even Rat knew that the Riveras were Bay Area royalty, and the Cromwells had one of the oldest bloodlines in New York. Together, they made up two of the most powerful families on either coast. Agatha belonged to both, and she had the kind of power that crowned kings and toppled empires. With the right resources, she could've maneuvered all the Northeast's political players like pieces on a chessboard, already assured of every possible outcome. But instead she was here, stomping through the woods and wearing dresses that looked like nightgowns.

Her eyes glinted.

"Wait. Do you know already?" Rat said. "How this ends?"

"Some of it," she said, propping her chin primly on her knuckles.

"And?"

"Careful, Evans," she said. "You'll ask me that question again, and the next time, I'll tell you."

They made an incredulous noise out of the back of their throat, but Agatha just raised her eyebrows at them, so they couldn't tell if she was joking or not. "But you know where the Holbrook Map is."

She paused, considering.

"Agatha."

"No, I don't." With a sigh, she laid back onto the couch, her dark hair haloing out around her. "Bellamy Arts is different. I don't know if it's something about the school, or the Ingrid Collection, or—I don't know—something else, but half the things I see here don't make sense."

"Oh." Unease tightened in their chest.

"I don't know enough about the map to try anything—I can trigger it sometimes if I have a place or an object—but, even if I could, I don't . . . I already know it wouldn't help. It's like I can't see the way out of the maze, because I'm already in it." She wrinkled her nose. "I just know I'm close to *something*. Powerful magic always throws me off. Anything strong enough to kick up the aether."

Rat frowned.

"Magic," she said, propping herself back up. "Or the physical form of it, I suppose. The stuff of the universe. Sometimes it's left behind by strong enough workings, like a residue. It's a bit like dust, but not everyone can see it very well." She gave them an appraising look. "I've heard stories about arcanists who trained themselves to perceive it, but some of us are more sensitive to it than others. Our abilities interact with it more closely."

Immediately, Rat thought of the dead passages. The veil of dust. They fought the urge to shrink back. "I didn't know that," they managed. "So that's why you couldn't go all the way into the tunnels?"

Agatha tilted her head, like she was listening.

"What's down there?" they asked. "Do you know?"

She paused, considering. Then, when they thought she wouldn't answer, she said, "It's like a well."

Rat faltered. "A well?"

"A well, at the bottom of the ocean," she said. "Every time I go into the tunnels, I feel it pulling at me, and all I can think is that whatever's there, it's a terribly, terribly long way down."

CHAPTER TWENTY-TWO

AFTER AGATHA LEFT, RAT AND JINX HEADED INTO THE woods.

Jinx led the way along the path, the smell of damp earth heavy on the air.

The trees grew tall and close together, and the trail was still muddy from the rain. Rat followed after her, scanning the low branches as they went.

"So," they asked, picking their way through the underbrush. "Do you think there's anything . . . you know. That we should be watching out for?"

Jinx glanced back at them, adjusting her hand on her backpack. "We're not going to run into any terrors out here."

"I know, I just . . ."

She lifted an eyebrow, like they'd forgotten that it was still daylight and they were well above ground.

Rat lowered their head. "You're sure there's nothing else?"

"Here. I can show you a defense spell," she said, stopping between the trees. "Are you able to cast anything?"

"I try pretty hard not to."

Jinx looked skeptical.

"I'm not great at—" Rat waved their hands vaguely in the air. "You know. The whole magic thing."

"This one's simple. It's not that strong, but it doesn't take a lot of power."

They hesitated.

There was a reason they didn't cast. Most of what they'd known, they'd forgotten on purpose, and they weren't sure how much they'd be able to do now, even if they wanted to.

But, at least at one point, they had been able to.

Jinx tilted her head, and Rat realized they hadn't answered.

"Okay. I could try, maybe."

"It's pretty straightforward," she said, tapping their shoulder. "So. With any basic working, there are three parts. Start with gesture."

She drew her hand through the air, like she was pulling an invisible thread.

Rat moved to follow her.

Jinx gave them an incredulous look. "Alright. No."

"What?"

"Your casting stance is an atrocity."

"I'm literally just standing," they protested.

"Yeah, I can see that." She nudged their foot with her shoe. "Shoulder-width apart. And stop locking your knees."

Rat shifted their stance, grinding their heel into the dirt.

She circled behind them and rested her hand on their arm. "Shoulders back. You're slouching."

They huffed a breath. They knew they were slouching. They were always slouching.

Jinx's hand slid to their elbow. "Again, but with more conviction. You're casting a spell, not asking a question."

They raised their arm again and hated that it was so obviously better this time.

"It's a staying spell, which fixes an object in place," Jinx said. "That's your intention. You're going to focus on that, the same way that you would with an ordinary working."

Anxiety knotted in Rat's chest.

They must have looked frightened, because Jinx said, "Alright. Try this. When I was first learning to cast, I said everything aloud."

She stepped out from behind them and drew her hand through the air. "*Stay.*"

A current of magic rolled through the air, followed by an unnatural quiet, like the world was holding its breath around her.

Rat stepped forward, and the spell broke again.

"It's only as strong as your intention. The more specific your target, the better, and the more your target wants to move, the harder it'll be." Jinx knelt down and scooped a handful of leaves off the ground. "Ready?"

Rat let out a shaky breath.

"I promise. It won't be bad."

They nodded.

"Pretend they're terrors," Jinx said, and lobbed the leaves toward them.

Again, Rat drew their hand through the air the way she'd shown them. "*Stay.*"

Their magic rose up to answer. Almost imperceptibly, the air shivered around them, and then they could sense the sprawl of the woods and all of the unseen cracks in the world. They could feel how the pieces fit together, where the world wanted to open, and where it would clamp shut.

Panic washed over them, and Rat choked their power back.

Their voice echoed between the trees as the leaves that Jinx had thrown at them fluttered uselessly to the ground.

Their knees shook.

They looked back to her, apologetic. "I could just use a stick?"

"You're not fighting those things with a stick."

"I mean, I'd definitely get eaten. But you could let me get eaten and run?"

Jinx slung her arm over their shoulder. "Alright, Evans. You're with me. I'm officially covering you. Cromwell's never going to let me live it down if I get the last heir to the Holbrook line killed."

All at once, they realized how close she was standing, the smell of earth and sunlight clinging to her. Their face heated, and they realized they didn't have anything remotely clever to say back to her.

"I'd really like to not die, also," they managed.

Stifling a laugh, Jinx slid away. "Come on. It's this way," she said as she pulled ahead of them.

Rat pushed a hand through their hair, recovering themself. "Hey, can I ask you something?"

"Pretty sure you just did," she said without looking back. Leaves crunched under her boots as she made her way up the path.

"Jinx."

She threw a smug glance over her shoulder, the sun bright on the rim of her glasses.

"I just . . . is there any possibility that one of us stole the map?"

She furrowed her brow.

"I'm not saying we're *close* or anything, but Harker knew some of my father's work, and he works in the library, and . . ." they trailed off as they realized how weak it sounded when they actually laid it out like that. Without the tower to tie it together, they didn't have a case.

"You think he's the thief?"

"No—Just, as a possibility. What I meant—"

"Yeah," Jinx said to their surprise. "I haven't ruled it out."

Rat came up short.

"I haven't ruled anyone out. That map was under lock and key, but Blakely's obsessive enough that if he really wanted a way in, I'm sure he'd find it. Or maybe Cromwell's lying about not knowing where it is. Maybe it's me, and now I'm just keeping you close so you'll stay off my trail."

"But—"

"Or," she said, "maybe it's not an accident that the map went missing right when Alexander Holbrook's only heir arrived on campus. Maybe you just didn't want the school to know what you were up to, so you found another way in."

"Why would I do that? I already have an archive I can't use," they said, then realized that they actually had two archives they couldn't use.

"You tell me. You said you didn't know about the Ingrid Collection, but this obviously isn't a game to you. If it's not about magic, then why are you still looking?"

"Because, I—" they started, except they didn't have a single good answer to that. "What about you? Why do you want it?"

She raised her eyebrows at them. "It's the Ingrid Collection. Why would I need another reason?"

"But if you found it, what then?"

"Then I'd have a legendary archive of forbidden magic."

"What about after that?"

"What else is there?" she asked, but there was something too glib in the way she said it. Rat knew they'd asked the wrong question. It felt like watching a cloud pass over the sun.

They watched her back as she drew ahead of them, off the main path and into the trees. In all that had happened in the past few days, it was easy to forget how little they actually knew her.

It doesn't matter, they reminded themself with a twinge. It hadn't been a fair question to ask.

It wasn't like they'd been up front with Jinx, either.

"Wait," they started, but before Rat could decide what, exactly, they wanted to apologize for, Jinx motioned to them.

"Come on. We're here," she said.

"Where?"

"Where do you think?"

Ahead, the trees gave way to a small clearing. A low brick wall ran across the way, almost like a gate. Past that, a cellar door had been set into the muddy ground, a few stray shoots of grass sprouting up around it.

Farther out, the low *shush* of lake waves drifted through the trees.

"This is . . ."

Jinx's mouth quirked. "Knew it. I did see you out here on Lake Night."

"Shut up," they mumbled. "I already told you that."

"I'm thinking we start here, and then we can make our way around the lake, at least to where the main wards cut through the woods."

"Are we . . ." Rat pantomimed opening the door.

"Not this one. Lucky for you, we've already been down, and—" Jinx stopped as she came to the wall.

Rat slowed beside her, following her gaze.

A line of boot prints tracked through the mud, before vanishing back into the grass.

"You guys didn't already come through here today, right?" they said.

"Weird," she said, half to herself.

Unease prickled through them. Rat glanced around at the trees.

Beside them, Jinx slid her phone from her pocket. "Come on," she said, motioning to them. Before Rat could protest, she climbed over the wall and hopped down on the other side. "Whoever it was, they're gone now."

"Right."

Her phone made an electronic shutter sound as she snapped a picture. "Do you remember what time it stopped raining?"

Rat looked over their shoulder one more time, and then climbed over after her.

"No. But I saw some of the Lesser Hours around this morning. They could be checking the tunnels?" Rat said unconvincingly.

"Let's hope not." She slid her phone back into her pocket and walked to the cellar doors, where the boot prints stopped.

"Wait, are we—"

"This one's sealed. It doesn't go that deep."

She knelt down and pulled the doors open, revealing a set of concrete steps.

"Right," Rat said under their breath. "Not that bad."

Jinx dug her flashlight out of her bag and shined it into the mouth of the passage. The beam jackknifed down the stairs, before tapering out into darkness.

"Would you rather keep watch? I can get you a stick."

Rat ducked their head. "No."

Jinx offered them her arm.

Warily, they peered down the steps. The only thing worse than going down would be sitting up here, alone in woods, with the footprints, knowing that they'd sent Jinx into a dark murder basement by herself.

"I moderately hate you," they said taking her sleeve.

"You're welcome."

Rat tightened their grip as she led them down, the beam of the flashlight sweeping the way ahead. The smell of dust and damp earth hung in the air, like a cellar that had been sealed off for too long. The stairs curved away from the light as they descended.

"You're sure you're good?" Jinx asked.

Rat realized they were clutching her arm, and they eased their grip. Slowly, they nodded.

"Do you want to go back?"

"No," they said, feeling small.

She looked at them like she didn't completely believe that.

"I don't," they insisted, pulling ahead of her.

Someone had been through here—*Harker*, they thought, *it couldn't be anyone else*—and they needed to keep going. Whatever he'd seen or found or figured out, if they turned back now, they were going to fall further behind.

"It doesn't go far. There's a bit of a curve and then . . ." Jinx trailed off as she came around the last curve of the stairs.

Fresh mud flecked the bottom of the steps.

Jinx paused, listening.

Rat held their breath. Silence pressed in around them.

It was a layered silence, made up of the stillness of the woods above them and the hush of the passage, the heavy quiet of the sunken campus, sprawling beneath them in the long-unbroken dark.

The beam of the flashlight washed the ground in pale light.

Chalk sigils sprawled across the floor of the passage in an undecipherable latticework. They curved around each other in a tangle of carefully arced lines, drawn with impossible precision, the chalk bright and fresh.

Suddenly, the air in the tunnel felt charged, the smell of dust too thick. *Not dust,* they realized. *Aether.*

Magic itself.

"Jinx," Rat said under their breath.

"Shit," she whispered. "What is all of this?"

Rat followed the marks with their eyes, but they didn't know anything past the most basic sigilry and the ward marks Harker used to make on their windowsill. It could have been a protective spell of some kind, or an alarm, or something else entirely.

Not all magic was kind.

Beside them, Jinx snapped a picture with her phone.

"Come on, Evans," she said. "We shouldn't be here. For all we know this place is radioactive."

They stole a last look at the net of sigils scrawled across the ground. Then, swallowing their unease, they turned and followed her up the steps.

"Do you know what those were?" Rat asked, once they were back in the clearing.

"Not the ones on the floor," Jinx said, then stopped and looked at them.

"What is it?" they asked.

"Did you see the door? At the back?"

They shook their head. They'd been too focused on the sigils to notice anything else.

"Here. The last time we came here, it was warded." She drew her phone out and swiped back through the pictures of the sigils, then zoomed in on one. The door was just visible at the edge of the light. "That," she said, tapping the screen, "is an opening spell."

CHAPTER TWENTY-THREE

IT RAINED AGAIN THAT NIGHT.

Sometime after Jinx went off on her own, Rat headed back to their room.

Neither one of them had wanted to go back into the tunnels after that, and the whole walk back through the east woods, Rat couldn't shake the prickling, eyes-on-their-neck feeling that they weren't alone.

Once Rat was by themself, they took every spellbook they had and spread them across the floor, before they realized they had no idea where to start trying to identify the sigils they'd found. All that they had were a couple of textbooks and the school history they'd stolen out of the War Room, and the spells in the tunnels had been advanced.

Rat picked up one of the books and riffled the pages. They didn't know what they'd been hoping for, besides maybe that they'd suddenly become good at magic and stumble onto the exact right spell.

They refused to let Harker win.

They were an Evans.

They were a *Holbrook*.

Their father had written the map to the Ingrid Collection. They should be able to figure this out.

They glanced down at their compass, laid across their sketch-book on the floor in front of them. The needle bobbed north, toward the hills.

Rat picked it up and turned it in their hand.

A flicker of power unfurled in their chest, somewhere deeper than bone, and just a little, the room opened up around them.

"*Stay,*" they breathed into the metal.

Carefully, they drew their hand through the air the way Jinx had taught them.

They held their breath, blood hammering in their ears. They released their thumb. Their first finger.

Movement darted in the corner of their eye.

Swearing, Rat jerked up, and the compass thunked into their lap.

A bird peered down at them from the window, watchful.

With a start, Rat realized they'd left it unlocked. Rain flecked the inside the sill, and the bird's feathers were glossy in the half-light, iridescent and slick with aether.

The bird tilted its head.

"What do you want?" Rat asked it softly.

The bird blinked at them, and they felt ridiculous all over again. Then, it shook the rain from its wings and took off again into the dark.

It was still raining when they woke up.

They thought about texting Jinx for breakfast, but it was still early, and they didn't know if she considered them a *let's get breakfast* friend or a *tunnels and intrigue only* friend.

They swung by the dining hall and grabbed a cup of coffee with enough cream and sugar to make sure it didn't actually taste like coffee, before making their way to the Drake.

Rain beat down on the roof of the building as they wandered the aisles. They knew better than to look for books on sigils. If they knew Harker, he'd probably pulled any useful books from the stacks already.

They slowed as they passed a window overlooking the campus. In the haze of weather, the woods in the distance were nothing more than a dark smudge.

Absently, Rat touched their fingers to the glass. The boot print by the cellar doors would be long gone by now. Almost like it hadn't been there at all. It had been the closest thing to evidence they had, without bringing the tower into it.

Harker had the Holbrook Map, even if he wouldn't admit it. And now, for some reason, he'd opened the door in the woods.

"What on earth were you doing out there?" Rat said under their breath.

Like he wasn't far enough ahead of them already.

With a frustrated sigh, Rat pushed off and made for the end of the hallway.

They half expected to find Harker in a reading room, poring over a reference book or sitting in a window or talking to one of the knight's birds, but he wasn't anywhere to be seen.

Probably, they told themself, it was better that they didn't find him.

Finally, they turned and headed out, back toward Mallory Hall.

Jinx sat cross-legged on the couch in the lobby, her jacket draped over her shoulders like a cape. The leather was damp, and she had her boots on like she'd been outside already, but she was dressed in a pair of gym shorts and a faded T-shirt with the words BISEXUAL DISASTER on it, like she'd just shoved her shoes on with her pajamas.

"Evans." She looked up at them. "Where are you coming from?"

They held up their coffee, and her mouth quirked.

"We missed each other," she said, nodding to the paper-wrapped croissant on the table.

"Oh." They opened their mouth to tell her about the library, but they felt strange for being empty-handed. "I just. You know. Wandered. Did you find anything about the sigils?"

She sighed. "Nothing yet. I texted the spells to Cromwell and Blakely, but they don't recognize it, either." She paused. "Rat?"

Something in her voice changed. She sat up, shifting toward them.

"Yeah?" they managed.

"Yesterday," she said hesitantly, "when you asked me what I was looking for. Do you really want to know?"

Rat started to apologize, and then realized that wasn't what she was asking them. "You don't need to tell me. Only if you want me to know. I—You're allowed to have your own reasons. I shouldn't have pried."

She chewed her lip. "What if . . ."

"It's horrible?"

Her mouth pulled into the same wry half-smile they'd seen a dozen times now, but that looked different, too. Less certain.

"Then, I guess," Rat said carefully, "I could probably keep up."

Jinx studied them. A nervous flutter rose in the back of their throat, but they didn't know anymore if it was because they were afraid of what she might say, or because whatever she told them, they already knew that they were past the point of turning back.

Somewhere off in the hills, thunder rolled.

Finally, Jinx pushed herself to her feet. "If you're really doing this, you deserve the full story. What are you doing right now?"

Rat watched her, unsure. "Are we going somewhere?"

"My room first," she said, then looked them over. She reached out and traced a drying spell on their sleeve. "We need to grab a flashlight."

Now that Rat knew the way through the tunnels, the walk down to the War Room seemed shorter than last time.

"It's, um, not a history book, right?" Rat said as Jinx knelt down next to the weathered table in the center of the room.

"For the record, at least some of these are spellbooks." She leaned in, tracing her finger down a stack of books. "Here."

She stopped on a three-ring binder and slid it from the pile. Carefully, she brushed off the cover, then held it out, like she was giving them something fragile.

"Sit anywhere," she said. "Just be warned, the blue chair rocks a bit."

"Thanks." They walked back and dropped into an armchair upholstered in fraying brocade. The mesh of lanterns and fairy lights lit everything from above, but even once Rat's eyes had adjusted, the War Room was dim at best. They riffled the pages, revealing a mix of forum printouts and handwritten notes, and loose pages that had been photocopied out of books. "What is all of this?"

"When I ran into you at the library, you asked about the Breton-Fox room."

Rat stilled. "This is . . ."

"Piper's notes. On the tunnels. And some of the other students, too. The missing ones," she said. "Council of Hours investigative briefs. School records of the tunnels. Everything."

They felt like she'd splashed them with ice water.

"There's another version of the story," Jinx said before they could ask her where she'd gotten the notes from. "About Margaret Ingrid."

"You mean how she sank the school."

She nodded.

For a long moment, she didn't say anything, but Rat knew better than to break the silence.

Finally, she said, "It's an old piece of lore. What do you know about Acanthe? Her Lady of Sealed Lips? Keeper of the Rooks, the Death of Summers?"

Rat's breath stopped. Suddenly, they were wide awake.

Taking their recognition as a sign, Jinx settled against the edge of the table. "Have you heard the story about her seven secrets?"

"No. What are they?"

"No one knows. They're secrets, Evans."

"But—"

"People have speculated. Things like death's one weakness or the true names you'd need to call down the stars. Magic with a capital *M*." Idly, Jinx traced her thumb over a stack of books as she spoke. "Because she was lonely and she needed someone to confide in, Acanthe shaped her seven secrets into seven shadowy hearts, and she gave one to each of her seven Rooks. Because she was clever, she buried her secrets deep in each of their chests, where no one would look. And because she was cruel, she didn't allow her Rooks to know their own hearts. When she'd finished, she sent them deep into the planes and let them scatter, taking her secrets with them."

Rat shifted forward at the mention of the rooks, the binder of notes half forgotten in their lap.

"In time, all seven of the rooks grew to be dangerous," Jinx went on. "They took pleasure in ruin, but they were calculating, too. Any arcanist foolish enough to make a deal with them became a force of destruction. The rooks would topple houses like dominoes and sow wars just to reap the ashes. And one, in particular, set her sights here." She paused. "Enter Ingrid, our magpie queen."

Rat's mouth had gone dry. They'd never heard this story before, but with a horrible kind of certainty, they realized that they knew where it was heading.

"Tensions were already high, but by the time the Rook was done, it was probably the closest thing the Northeast had ever seen to an open war. Half a dozen lesser bloodlines disappeared altogether, and a handful of major ones never fully recovered. After everything had settled, most of the families who were left wanted to move on, but Ingrid had gotten a taste of what the Rooks could do," Jinx said. "In the version I was told, she couldn't let that kind of magic go unchecked, but if I'm being honest, I think there was a part of her that wanted it, too."

"You said it was dangerous."

"It's power," Jinx said, like that answered everything.

With a pang of unease, Rat thought of the knight, even with her magic waning as it was. They didn't need Jinx to tell them that this was different than another spellbook or a vial full of starlight. It was the kind of power that would have tipped the scales between the major families irrevocably, whether Ingrid used it or not. It would have made her untouchable.

"Ingrid was relentless," Jinx went on. "She tracked the Rook to a crumbling tower, in the place where the sky breaks against the earth." She paused. "It's always a rook in the stories but she's not . . . sometimes she's a bird, but she's a person, too. Like a raven knight."

Their chest tightened at the detail. Jinx shouldn't have known any of this.

"Ingrid spent years studying the place. She knew she would only get one chance, and so she was careful. She spent months making simple bargains to earn the Rook's trust. She knew that she couldn't appear to be too easily won, or the Rook might suspect something, so she began by trading for small favors, then bigger ones, until she had methodically built up a debt, which she knew the Rook would need to collect.

"Finally, the day arrived that she was summoned to the tower so that the Rook could call in the sum of all the favors she was owed. As the sun dipped below the trees, a beast made of shadows appeared in her office, with a rope of chrysanthemums around its neck, so there could be no mistaking who'd sent it. That night, at dusk, she rode out. She told no one, and she took nothing with her."

Jinx met their eyes as she said it, and Rat realized that it wasn't just another version. It was the other half of the story she'd told them the first time she'd brought them through the tunnels.

She paused, a question on her face, and Rat realized they'd curled in on themself. Slowly, they nodded for her to go on.

"It's important that she traded favors," Jinx said. "Never things. A possession given freely is a dangerous kind of bond, and Ingrid knew she'd be lucky to escape once.

"She rode for hours, following the seven stars in Acanthe's constellation, until she came into sight of the tower. Sometimes, when the Rook had shown her glimpses of it, the place had been filled with her sworn servants, but when she arrived, the Rook alone flew out to meet her among the fallen stones."

Idly, Jinx riffled the pages of one of the books on the table behind her as she spoke. "Make no mistake, the Rook could be cruel at times. She delighted in cruelty," she said. "But she adored Ingrid. The Rook greeted her like an old friend, and she brought her inside and gave her the most gloriously broken room in the ruin of the building, with a full view of the sky."

An image of the tower rose in Rat's mind, grand and crumbling. They'd never been inside, but they could see it anyways, the way they always imagined it, dusted with rubble, with grass growing up between the cracks in the stone floor and the sweep of unfamiliar stars overhead.

"Ingrid bided her time, waiting for the Rook to call in her favors. Days went by. The Rook played hands of cards with her and invited her to read the spellbooks that she kept in her study and brought back freshly scavenged kills from her hunts. Except, she never asked for anything." Jinx met their eyes. "As it turned out, Ingrid's plan had worked a bit too well, and the favor that the Rook had wanted was nothing more than company. But what she didn't know was that Ingrid had been using her days to search the tower for the secret whenever she was alone." She paused. "You know what happens next. Ingrid is Ingrid."

"She finds it," Rat said softly. A creeping horror rose in their chest as the pieces came together. "Where? How?"

"I don't know," Jinx told them. "In some versions, she cuts the Rook's heart from her chest. Sometimes, she finds it hidden in a drawer, still beating. I found one where she convinces the Rook to give it to her. It changes every time. But once she has it, Ingrid always returns here."

Rat studied her in the warm glow of the fairy lights. "You're after the secret."

"No," she said. "I'm after the tower."

Their mouth went dry. "What?" they asked, but their voice came out strangled and harsh.

Jinx looked back at them, unflinching. And then, something in her face softened. "I can't ever tell if Cromwell and Blakely really believe we're going to find anything, but I know it's out there." She scrubbed her hand over her face. "I know it doesn't mean anything that you're a Holbrook, but I thought, maybe . . ."

"I just—" Rat managed. "Who told you that story?"

"Like I said, my grandfather was the dean of Magics and High Arts before Fairchild." She got to her feet and walked over to where Rat was sitting. "Since the old campus sank, a dozen students have gone missing. The disappearances started out far apart, but they've been getting closer together over the years. Three kids vanished under my grandfather's sight, and he was never able to get them back. Not even their remains. There was one boy who was alive, every time they scried for him, but no one could find him. It went on for years."

Rat suppressed a shudder. "Then you think, maybe . . ."

"I'm certain," Jinx said. She turned back to the binder of notes. "Most of the cases eventually involved the Council of Hours. Cromwell managed to help me get into some of the old records. That's the long story about how I ended up friends with her, if you were wondering. My grandfather stayed on for a while to handle some of the school's business with the Council of Hours after he officially retired, and I ended up spending a lot of time at the Council Chambers with him."

"He brought you along?"

She flashed them a small smile. "I didn't really fit in as a kid. I think he wanted me to feel important. He basically brought me everywhere. And Cromwell was pretty much always up there."

Rat furrowed their brow.

"I guess you wouldn't know. Her mom does a lot of consulting. The Council calls her in whenever they run into trouble with any kind of scrying or predictions," Jinx said. "Cromwell shadowed her a lot, so she took most of her lessons there."

"Oh. She never mentioned it."

"She doesn't talk about it a lot. To be honest, I always got the feeling it had to be kind of lonely for her. There were never that many kids our age, and she spent most of her training by herself because her powers are so rare." Jinx let out a breath. "It's still a bit of a sore point that she left. She's supposed to be doing an exchange program with the London Council right now."

"But, she's here," Rat said.

"Yeah. She is." Jinx paused like she might say something else, then shook her head and gestured to the binder. "We managed to get ahold of some of the Council's notes on the tunnels, since they handled most of the excavation, but we found some papers, too, from the missing students. Most of it had been marked as evidence and sealed. Cromwell basically had to break into her uncle's office to get ahold of them," she said. "Rat. Almost all of the missing students in the last fifty years were looking for the Ingrid Collection."

A chill pricked across their skin. "It's there, isn't it?" they said. "The Rook's heart, I mean. In the collection. That's why Ingrid sealed the school. And the Rook . . ."

Jinx nodded grimly. "I can't tell if she pointed them all toward the collection, or if the stories about Ingrid led them back to the tower. I just know that it's linked. Like, maybe if I can follow their trail far enough, I could finally stop her for good."

Rat hesitated. They thought about the jagged battlements of the tower and the way that the knight had smiled at them, like she wanted to catch the fading daylight by its throat.

"And if it leads you somewhere terrible?" they asked, looking up at her.

"We're looking at a century of disappearances, Rat. Someone needs to put an end to it."

The determination in her voice ripped them open.

That night she'd first taken Rat into the tunnels, Jinx had pulled them into the dark, looking for the same answers they were. If they pointed her toward the tower, she would follow that twisting road as far as it led her. It wouldn't be a question.

They imagined the knight, closing her hand around Jinx the same way she'd taken Harker. They imagined the hiss of the wind over the grass, and black-eyed crows, and ravens, and the rabbit curled at the foot of their bed.

They imagined Harker, cold-eyed and certain, a step ahead of them no matter what they did, the too-familiar scent of smoke clinging to him like a snuffed candle.

Out in the hallway, a low scuffing noise jarred them back.

Rat went still.

"Hey," Jinx said. "Evans, is everything okay?"

They held up a finger for her to wait as their eyes went back to the doors that led deeper into the tunnels.

Holding their breath, they waited for the sound to come again.

The quiet of the tunnels settled heavily around them.

They dropped their voice. "Did you . . ."

She shook her head, but before they could stop her, she pushed herself to her feet and started toward the door.

"Jinx," they said under their breath, following after her.

She stopped, one hand braced against the doorknob, the other raised to cast. Drawing in a breath, she pushed the door open a crack.

Rat tensed behind her, waiting for the flutter of wings or the echo of footsteps retreating up the tunnel.

A sliver of lantern light fell through the open doorway, illuminating the once-grand hallway outside. Debris littered the floor, and the faded wood paneling was spotted with lichens.

There wasn't anyone there.

Jinx let the door close again and waved them back toward the center of the room, but they knew that the discussion of the tower had ended.

"You should look at the notes," she told them, taking up the binder. "There might be something in there for your maps."

Her voice washed over Rat as she flipped through the pages, but the rest of the time that they were in the tunnels, no matter how hard they tried to put it out of their mind, they couldn't stop thinking of the knight, and her messengers, and her still-beating heart, buried somewhere in the sprawl of the old campus.

CHAPTER TWENTY-FOUR

THE REST OF THE BREAK WENT BY QUICKLY.

Rat spent most of their days in the tunnels with Jinx, mapping the shallow parts while she talked them through the rest of her notes. Other days, she sat with them, flipping through one book or another while Rat sketched out parts of the campus, occasionally looking up to throw a theory at them.

Once, they went back by the library with her to sort through reference books, looking for the spells from the woods. She'd led Rat to a sunlit study nook in the stacks, cluttered with books and notes, and they would have known from the faint tinge of smoke on the air that Harker had been working with her even if his handwriting and the pile of books on the floor hadn't given him away.

They'd spent the better part of an hour perched on the edge of the table, riffling through books in case they found anything, but they didn't.

At night, Rat dreamt about doors in the woods, and fields of grass, and the knight, furious and cloaked in raven feathers, her heart cut from her chest.

The morning that classes resumed, they woke up dry-mouthed and already late, sunlight streaming through their window.

By the time they arrived at practicum, Harker was already at his desk, taking notes and studiously ignoring them, but Jinx and Agatha's places in the row ahead were both empty.

"So," Rat said under their breath, "how was your break? Forbidden magic? Stolen books?"

He made a note, like Frey had said something particularly interesting, which Rat was pretty sure he hadn't.

"Hey." They nudged Harker's foot. "Do you know where Jinx is?"

He glanced up at them like he definitely did, and then went back to his notes.

Rat spent the rest of class sitting quietly and drawing black birds in their notebook. At the end of the hour, just when Rat thought they might not hear from her, their phone buzzed. They slid it out under their desk, but all that the message said was, *cromwells back, meeting*

It buzzed again. *e woods, 9*

They looked up to see if Harker had gotten it too, but he was already shoving his books into his backpack, and they knew that he wouldn't tell them if he had.

That night, Rat loaded a camping lantern into their backpack along with their sketchbook and some chalk in case they needed to mark the way. They checked that they still had the shield charm, nestled against their compass, and let themself out into the hall.

"Rat."

Will sat on the narrow staircase just off the hallway, a few steps below, looking like he hadn't expected to see them.

With a pang, they realized they'd missed him after class, and they still hadn't answered any of the messages he'd sent over the break, since they hadn't exactly been able to explain what they'd been up to on campus.

"Oh," they said. "Hey. What are you doing here?"

"I didn't realize you were back already. I texted you," he said. His eyes went to their backpack. "Are you going somewhere?"

"I . . . no. Just the library. I forgot some books," they managed, hating how unconvincing it sounded. "But, can I find you later? You still have to tell me about the break."

"Right. Of course." Will pushed his hand through his hair, but there was something uncertain about it. "I just . . ."

"Will?"

"Are you sure you're okay?" he asked quickly.

The worry in his voice took them off guard, and for a moment they couldn't answer.

"Just, I feel like something's been off with you ever since we got to school here and . . . I don't know." He let out a breath. "You seem really distracted, and it's like I can't find you half the time. And, I know you're going to say it's fine, but, I mean, is it?"

Rat's chest tightened. As soon as he said it, they felt obvious. "It's seriously nothing. I've just been busy with bookwork," they said. They offered him their best attempt at a smile. "I should go before the library locks up. But I can text you tomorrow?"

"Right," he said again.

Hurt flickered across his face as they started down the stairs. A weight of guilt sank in their chest, but the alternative was to explain themself, and that would be worse.

They weren't dragging him into this, they told themself as they made their way out of the building. Will had already had to spend the start of his year walking them between classes and keeping an eye on them. He deserved to do normal student things without worrying about Rat all the time.

It was already dark as they started toward the tree line. Fallen leaves littered the way, and a chill had crept into the air, biting through their sweatshirt. The trail snaked ahead of them, overgrown and streaked with moonlight, but for once, they didn't care what was hiding in the shadows.

They just wanted to get to the east woods, and they wanted to not think about Will.

You're here now, they told themself as they went, one hand on their lantern, the other holding their compass inside of their pocket, the metal cool to the touch.

They slowed as they came to the place where the door was.

Jinx was already perched on the low brick wall, sorting through her backpack by the glow of her own camping lantern. She'd worn her leather jacket, open over a faded band shirt, and a pair of heavy fingerless gloves that Rat guessed meant she hadn't ruled out the possibility of more rusty ladders. Harker and Agatha were discussing something in the clearing behind her.

"Evans," she said, pulling the zipper on her backpack. "You're late."

"Oh. Right." They dropped against the wall next to her. "I mean, I never miss a chance for. You know." They gestured weakly.

"Ticks?" Jinx offered. "Imminent danger?"

"That." Rat flashed their best attempt at a grin, which they were pretty sure came out more like a wince.

"We were just catching Blakely up," she said, and nodded to Agatha, who was fussing with the too-long sleeves of a flannel shirt that looked like she'd stolen it from Harker.

A feeling Rat refused to name twinged in their chest. They weren't friends with him anymore, either, they reminded themself.

Agatha turned toward them. "Unfortunately, there's nothing on the investigation. It looks like Evening is trying to handle things quietly, so if he has anything, he's keeping it to himself. But we did find something else."

"Remember the sigils down there?" Jinx asked.

"Wait. This is where you were today, instead of class. Isn't it?" they said. She met their eyes, her gaze sharp behind her glasses, and they knew they were right. "Jinx. Why are we here?"

"Because," she said. "We figured out what kind of spell it is."

A breeze blew across the clearing. Dried leaves scuttled over the cellar doors that led back to the tunnels.

A small, selfish part of Rat thought of Will. They should have told him and let him convince them to stay back. They should have told him and offered to bring him along.

He's better off, they told themself, feeling hollow.

Jinx nodded for them to follow and started toward the doors.

Behind her, Agatha took her lantern from the wall and motioned to Rat.

"Are you going to be okay?" they asked her. "With the sigils?"

"Don't worry," she said. "If I'm overcome, you and Blakely can carry me."

Harker made a face that could only be described as deeply unamused.

"I'm of a fragile disposition. I might faint."

"Agatha, no."

Agatha huffed a sigh. "Jinx, my love," she said, turning back to the front of the group.

"Absolutely not," Jinx said without looking at her. She knelt by the cellar doors, and something in the woods seemed to still.

Jinx traced a spell on the air and drew her hand back. In the dark, Rat thought they saw her mouth the spell.

As if pulled by an invisible string, the cellar doors swung open.

The familiar smell of stale air and lingering magic rolled up on a cold draft. Below, the stairs led off into the darkness that Rat was coming to know a bit too well.

She started down, the glow of the lantern washing over the steps.

Agatha went after her, leaving Rat alone with Harker.

Instinctively, their eyes flickered to him.

He looked back at them, a challenge on his face.

Before they could think better of it, Rat headed down the steps.

They touched their fingers to the wall, grounding themself against the stones as they followed the curve of the stairs down into the earth. A moment later, Harker started after them, spelling the doors shut behind him.

"None of us were able to find the sigils in any books because we didn't know where to look," Agatha said, her voice echoing back up the steps. "I came back with Jinx to see if I could pick up any traces of who'd been here. As soon as I tried to cast, it was obvious."

Rat slowed as the steps bottomed out.

Agatha had stopped. Ahead of her, the sigils spread across the floor, still crisp against the stone.

"It's a temporal anchor," she said, stepping down onto the web of spellwork. Her footsteps rang out as she paced to the middle of the floor. "It's used to prevent scrying through time. The moment I set foot down here, my powers went quiet. I couldn't pick up anything in either direction. It's like the whole place is frozen in the present."

"It could be a general precaution," Jinx said, "but it feels specific. Whoever we're up against . . ."

"Nobody knows about me," Agatha said. She turned back and glanced around the group.

"Either it's one of us," Jinx said, choosing her words carefully. "Or someone's been paying very close attention."

An uneasy quiet fell over the passage as the implications settled.

Rat looked back at Harker, still standing by the stairs behind them.

"Well," he said, "it's a formal spell, so I guess that rules out Evans."

They started to protest, and he raised his eyebrows at them, like he was daring them to build a case against themself. Blood rushed to their face.

"And I wouldn't bother blocking my own powers," Agatha said. "I'd just lie about what I saw."

"I was with Evans when we found it," Jinx said. She glanced over at Harker.

"You already showed me the pictures of the shoe print," he said. "We're pretty clearly looking for someone taller than me."

"The shoe print doesn't really mean anything," Rat said before they could stop themself. "It might not even belong to whoever unsealed the tunnels. It could have been a groundskeeper or—or one of the Hours just walked by while they were investigating, or something."

Harker leveled his gaze at them, and they realized how weak it sounded. "Evans, if you think I did it, just say so."

Jinx looked over at Rat, too.

Rat *knew*.

They knew that Harker had been there, except they didn't have any evidence, and the moment they said anything, he would match them secret for secret.

They sank back. "Well, we already know it wasn't me."

Another uneasy silence settled over the group.

"The sigils extend farther into the tunnels," Jinx said finally.

Rat's attention snapped back to her.

"We didn't want to go too far alone, but they don't seem interested in concealing the fact that they've been here. Cromwell won't be able to see who drew them, but there might still be a trail."

Her footsteps echoed as she paced across the floor. She traced another spell on the air, and the doorknob turned. The door swung in, opening onto darkness. The glow of her camping lantern spilled out onto the hard-packed earth on the other side, casting a pale arc of light into the passage.

A draft rolled through the open door, cool and damp and still smelling faintly of magic.

"You don't all have to come, but we thought there might be safety in numbers," Jinx said, looking back at the group. "If anyone's with us?"

Rat followed the others into the passageway. The tunnel opened ahead of them as they walked, the ground sloping into the earth and the air cooling as they descended.

They'd gone over their maps during the break and ended up spending more time with the school histories in the War Room than they wanted to admit, trying to piece together a map of the old campus. What they'd learned was that everything had shifted when the school sank, and the tunnels roved haphazardly between the buildings.

Instinctively, Rat slid their compass from their pocket as they went. The needle bobbed and then swung north.

"The door was facing toward campus," Harker said behind them, closer than they'd thought. Rat jumped as he drew even with them, a will-o'-wisp of spellfire trailing after him. "I checked when we came down here on Lake Night."

He looked down at them, and their face heated.

They closed their hand around their compass. "Drop the act," they said under their breath. "I already know it was you."

"What would I want with another entrance to the old campus?"

"I don't know. The same thing you want with the Holbrook Map? This is obviously your work."

He regarded them coolly. "Is it?"

"*Yes.*" Their voice came out harsh and bitten off, just above a whisper in the too-quiet of the tunnels.

Jinx glanced back at them, and Rat realized she'd heard them. They fought a wince.

"Look, Evans." He leaned in, his voice rough and low. "As much as I enjoy being personally responsible for all your problems, have you stopped to consider that I might not be the only one you have to worry about?"

Rat opened their mouth to answer, and then closed it again.

Exasperated, they pulled ahead of him, their footsteps echoing through the passage.

As soon as they were away from him, the cold set in around them again, except it wasn't the biting chill of the woods anymore. It was the clinging damp of the tunnels.

They refused to look back. They weren't playing this game. Harker was trying to get under their skin, because he knew that he could. Probably, he'd been using the door in the woods to sneak into the old campus without being seen, so he could search for the Ingrid Collection or practice horrible tower magic or speak to black birds or something.

With a pang of unease, they shoved the thought away.

Something scurried past them in the dark. Rat flinched back.

"Fuck," they said under their breath as they hurried to close the rest of the distance to Jinx and Agatha.

Jinx glanced back at them. "Are you good?"

"Maybe," they mumbled, taking her sleeve.

Up ahead, the tunnel narrowed, the ground leveling off. Rat wasn't sure how far they'd walked or how deep they were beneath the school, but if they had to guess, they'd say they were back below the campus proper, if the path had curved the way they thought it did.

Rat slowed. They knew this place. They didn't know if it was the passageway itself or the series of turns, but they'd been here before.

Jinx had taken them, they realized with a start. They'd come through this way their first night in the tunnels, while they were heading toward the old ballroom. Suddenly, they were sure of it.

They pulled ahead.

"Rat?" Jinx started as they slipped past her.

Their lantern flickered over the walls, searching.

They stopped as they found one of their trail blazes, marked in chalk just below eye level.

An anchor sigil marked the wall beside it. Aether dusted the bricks around it, the marking still fresh.

A sick feeling surged through them.

Rat shoved off, down the passageway, searching for the next blaze. Someone shouted after them, but they couldn't stop.

Blood pounded in their ears.

Ahead, a glint of aether caught their eye. The glow of their lantern washed over it, but they already knew.

Another sigil. Another trail blaze.

Except.

Jinx caught them by the shoulder. "Rat," she said, breathless, and they realized they'd been running. "What's going on?"

"They're going the wrong way," Rat said in a rush.

"What?"

"Whoever was down here. Once they picked up our path, they started following my trail markers, but we're heading away from the ballroom right now. If they were following our route toward the underground meadow, they would have forked in the other direction and doubled back, but they're taking the markers back toward . . ." they trailed off.

"Rat?"

"Shit," they breathed.

Jinx's brow furrowed, and then understanding broke over her face. "The War Room."

They looked back. Behind them, Harker and Agatha had both come up short.

"This way," Rat said, pushing down a wave of dread.

They turned at the next fork, over a threshold where there might have once been a doorway. Then the rough earthwork of the tunnels turned back to broken hallways and crumbling masonry, and they were back on familiar ground.

Footsteps pounded after them.

Rat skidded to a stop as they came back to the doors on the far side of the War Room.

Aether streaked the age-worn wood, lighting the edges of an anchor sigil slashed across the back of the door. Rat stared at it, breathing hard. They tasted metal.

Jinx pushed the doors in, and everything inside of them stopped.

The War Room lay in shambles. The books from the coffee table littered the floor, left open amid the mess of crumpled notes and spell diagrams, the table broken on its side like a storm had blown through.

Rat stepped past her, their footsteps echoing through the expanse. Without the lights, the room seemed bigger, its ceiling rising cavernously overhead. Their flashlight swept across the circle of overturned chairs, stopping on the blue one, a sharp X slashed across the upholstery.

Every inch of the room had been thoroughly ransacked.

They scanned the dark for the glint of aether, or mums, or feathers, or something, but there wasn't anything there.

Instinctively, their eyes went to Harker, surveying the wreckage from the doorway. The spellfire in his hands had gone out.

Like he didn't even realize he was doing it, he traced the line of a fresh burn on his wrist where his bracelets had been. An old nervous habit.

More than anything, Rat realized, he looked shaken.

Suddenly, they felt cold all over.

This wasn't the tower's work.

"I want to know who did this," Jinx said. "Whoever was here. I want to know why."

Behind her, Harker finally let out a breath. "They were looking for something."

And even as he said it, Rat already knew what. The first time they'd come to the War Room, they'd been looking for the same thing.

"The Holbrook Map," they said softly. From the grim way Harker looked back at them, they knew they were right.

CHAPTER TWENTY-FIVE

THE WALK BACK UP THE STAIRS WAS LONG AND QUIET.

Jinx and Agatha split off to the third floor, and then Rat was alone in the stairwell with Harker.

Rat looked at him for a moment, unsure of whether or not they should say something, and then, they turned and started back toward the second floor.

As soon as Rat made it off the stairs, they cut back through the building. They didn't stop to think about where they were going until they'd made it to the widow's walk.

The late-night chill broke over them as they let themself out onto the roof. Overhead, the stars pricked against the sky, too crisp after the dark of the tunnels.

Rat shut their eyes and drew in one deep breath, and then another.

Until tonight, they'd assumed that Harker was their only problem. They didn't know what to do with the fact that there was someone else now. Someone with enough power to break the wards on the tunnels. Someone who knew to search the War Room.

Rat didn't know if they should be relieved or not that whoever they were dealing with was a step behind him, too.

They leaned out over the rails, steadying themself.

They wanted to push Harker in the lake. They wanted to grab him by the shoulders and ask how he'd even pulled it off, stealing the Holbrook Map in the first place.

They wanted to know what he'd found.

Behind them, there was the low rush of air as the door swung in.

They tipped their face up at the sky. "Friend or foe?" they said, half expecting Jinx's footsteps on the walk behind them.

In answer came the quiet rush of wings.

Rat's pulse skipped. They turned back to see a bird, a square of paper clutched in its talons.

Behind it, where the entrance to the widow's walk had been, a new dead passage had opened like a slash across a veil. Flecks of light drifted through the air, curling away from it in shifting currents. Beyond, where the staircase should have been, lay the mouth of a narrow stone passageway, the air damp and stale with the smell of magic.

Like remembering a dream, Rat knew that it would take them back into the tunnels, even if they couldn't say where.

The bird blinked up at them, and Rat realized they'd taken a step forward without meaning to.

Holding themself steady, they knelt down. "What do you want?"

They bird tilted its head as Rat reached down to take the piece of paper from it. The page was stiff, like it had been torn from an old book, the edges dusted with aether.

Something slid out as Rat unfolded the paper, revealing a spell diagram too complicated for them to read, let alone use. They didn't need to read it to understand though. It was a taunt.

The knight could send them a thousand spells. Rat wouldn't be able to cast a single one on their own.

They glanced down to see what they'd dropped, and their hand tightened on the page.

A bracelet. One of a set.

Harker's.

Rat picked it up and ran their fingers over the blackened, tooth-marked leather. They remembered the story Jinx had told them in the War Room. *"A possession given freely is a dangerous kind of bond."*

They didn't know why they'd thought the knight would ever allow them to ignore her.

They didn't know if the bracelet was an offer or a threat.

She had Harker.

She could have them instead.

The bird cawed at them and leapt back up, its wings catching the air.

"Wait—" Rat reached after it as it flew back toward the dead passage. It touched down in the mouth of the tunnel, watching them.

Shakily, they pushed themself to their feet.

They slid their phone from their pocket and turned on its flashlight. The beam quivered over the aging stonework, lighting a small crescent of floor. Beyond that, the passage vanished into a deep, unbroken darkness.

"Hello?" Rat called into the dark. Their voice came out chalky and small. "Is anyone there?"

The bird blinked up at them, and they realized that it was not the kind of question they wanted an answer to.

They knotted their fingers around the bracelet. All of their convictions from the morning felt far away now.

They took a step toward the passage.

They could follow where the knight led them. Accept this lead, and see what she wanted to show them. Play this game, and stay her hand a little longer. It didn't mean they were promising her anything.

Movement caught their eye in the windows below. A light, heading along the hallway. Toward them.

"Fuck," Rat breathed.

Their knees shook, and they hated themself for it. They hated her.

The bird looked up at them, its eyes glassy in the dark.

Somewhere below, past the dead passage, they heard footsteps on the stairs.

In the passage, the bird blinked at them. Then it took off, disappearing down the tunnel.

Rat slid the bracelet on over their wrist and took off after it. The aether broke around them as they crossed the mouth of the passageway, dust spinning in their wake. The boards of the widow's walk gave way to stone. All at once, the air had turned cool around them, heavy with the damp taste of deep earth.

Without stopping, they took the chalk from their pocket and marked an uneven dash on the wall.

They were going to find the knight's heart themself and unravel it, sinew by sinew. They would pry whatever hold she had over Harker from her grasp and destroy him themself.

Ahead, the hallway ended, and the bird swept through a wooden archway, veiled in dust. Another dead passage.

Rat rushed after, their breath ragged.

Their chalk glanced off the arch and flew out of their hand. They stumbled as the room opened up around them, barely catching themself.

All around them, the tiled floor had given way to tall, dry grass.

It took Rat a moment to realize they were still indoors. Thick drifts of aether covered everything, and gold dust blew through the air in heavy sheets, like a flurry of daylight.

They stood in a clearing in what could have once been a library or another junk room. Now, the aisle behind them was so choked with weeds that it was nearly impassable.

Ahead of them, the grass grew higher and higher, until it gave way to an overgrowth of wild chrysanthemums and shoots of mugwort and frothy bunches of yarrow.

At the center of it all, a thin, gold line split the air, like a crack in a mirror.

The bird cawed, circling low over the strange meadow, and then it slipped through the crack, vanishing from sight.

"Wait! You can't—" Rat took a deep breath through their teeth and rushed after it, beating their way through the grass.

They shoved into a patch of mugwort, snapping stalks as they forced their way through. Aether streaked their skin.

The crack ran from the floor to the ceiling, in a long and crooked line. The plants grew tallest around it, almost as if the mass of overgrowth had spilled through from the other side, and the aether fell thickest there.

And then Rat understood where they were.

"No," they said softly.

This was at the heart of the underground meadow. When Rat was with Jinx, they'd stumbled onto the edge of it. Now they were at the center.

What Agatha had felt down here wasn't a well. It was a tear.

There was a break in the ward.

They'd been thinking of the school's wards all wrong, they realized. It wasn't just the ring of protections at the edge of campus. This was an older, deeper magic, stretched thin between the planes like a film or a bubble of soap, closing the school in against the world of the tower. Maybe against all of the other worlds outside of it.

But slowly, it was wearing down.

Rat reached up to thread their fingers along the crack and gasped. The edge of it sliced into them. They yanked their hand back and clutched it against their chest, blood beading on their fingertips.

For a split second, they caught a glimpse of the tower on the other side. Crumbling stone and evening stars.

Then the light shifted, and the crack was just a thin gold line again.

They couldn't pass through the break without cutting themself apart. They didn't think the knight could, either.

But, in the chill of the underground meadow and the low, impossible whisper through the weeds, hung an unspoken *yet*.

Something rustled in the grass behind them.

Rat spun around.

Nothing.

They stared out at the expanse of the clearing. Drifts of aether turned through the air, but the overgrowth below was still.

Slowly, it dawned on Rat that they didn't know this place. The beam from their phone's flashlight fell weakly over the grass, but it didn't reach far before it was swallowed up by the dark.

Suddenly, they could feel the aisles of the ballroom branching out around them, not the direction so much as the sheer size of where they were.

Their throat tightened. They shouldn't have come here. Nobody knew where they'd gone, and the path they'd taken had already closed behind them.

They were lost.

Movement flickered in the corner of their eye. Frantic, Rat spun as a long ripple snaked through the grass toward them.

Terrors.

"Fuck," Rat said under their breath.

A second ripple followed, a little bit behind. Then a third.

Rat launched themself away from the break and shot toward the edge of the clearing, the overgrown grass grabbing at them as they ran. The rustling grew louder behind them, but they didn't look back.

They couldn't.

Last time, Rat had only made it out because Jinx hung back to slow down the terrors. If they'd been alone, they doubted that things would have ended the same way.

If they died, nobody would find them. Their body would stay here in this lost, dark place, rotting among the weeds, and everyone would be left to wonder how they'd vanished.

Rat shoved themself forward and barreled into one of the aisles, breaking through the overgrowth.

Behind them, one of the terrors let out a rattling hiss.

Rat pushed themself faster. Lungs on fire, they finally stole a glance over their shoulder. One of the terrors scurried into the aisle close behind them, cutting easily through the grass that sprouted up between the floorboards. The other two crowded in after it, crawling up the sides of the shelves.

The closest one lunged forward.

Rat veered away, knocking against a shelf. It rocked, scattering odds and ends across the ground. Something shattered behind them, dangerously close to where they'd been standing.

They spun down a fork in the aisle into a narrow pass between a stack of boxes and storage trunks, the first terror careening after them. Behind it, the others scuttled effortlessly up to the top of the aisles, slinking over the uneven heaps of castoffs.

Rat's pulse beat hard against their ribs as they realized what was about to happen.

One of the terrors crawled past them overhead and curved back down into the aisle to block their path.

"Shit," they breathed.

Jinx might have been able to stand and fight, but Rat was surrounded, and all they knew how to do was hide.

The terror shot toward them. Rat flinched back, bracing themself.

A wall of force shuddered through the air, curving away from them. With a jolt, the terror was thrown back. Rat drew a ragged gasp of air as it smashed into a row of shelves, curling in on itself.

The shield charm, they thought, breathless.

Instinctively, their hand went to the draub in their pocket, still warm from the spell. They hated Harker a little bit more for the fact that it had worked.

The terror twisted over itself, its many legs finding the ground.

Without waiting for it to pick itself up, Rat turned hard on their heel and ran.

Just ahead of them, a narrow gap opened in the wall of cast-off furniture, and they locked onto it. Lungs burning, they shoved themself forward.

Another terror snaked its long, plated body down from the shelves, heading off the mouth of the aisle ahead of them. Rat shot for the crevice, wedging themself into the jumble of old furniture. They struggled between an end table and a stack of trunks, fighting their way toward the other side.

The terrors hissed behind them, and Rat slipped free, the castoffs shifting beneath them as they fell through on the far side of the aisle.

They slammed against the ground hard enough that the air went out of their lungs, and they felt what little was left of the shield charm give way. The taste of blood and aether coated their mouth.

Pain rolled over them in a wave. They grabbed for their phone, snatching it out of the grass. Weeds sprouted up around them, creeping out between the mounds of old furniture, and the air burned cold and fresh in the back of their throat.

Behind them, the wall of castoffs creaked.

Rat propped themself up on one arm as one of the terrors poked its head over the top of the aisle, antennae flicking at the air.

Their pulse skipped.

The other two appeared behind it, cresting the mound of furniture as they crawled past it, spooling their segmented bodies onto the other side.

Rat shoved themself up, scrambling to one knee.

A hand caught them from behind, and then someone was hauling them to their feet. Before Rat could think of what they were doing, they stumbled backward, colliding with their rescuer.

"You're welcome," Harker said. His hands were feverish against them like he'd just been casting and had forgotten that he needed to be careful.

Ragged will-o'-wisps of spellfire hung in the air around him, throwing pale light across the aisle.

"You're—"

They bit back a startled breath as he pulled them to him. His other hand shot out to cast, drawing another burst of spellfire from the dark.

The terror reared back.

"Rat, let's go," he said, dragging them toward the edge of the grass.

They hurried after him, the weeds whipping at their legs as they sprinted for the mouth of an aisle.

The ground turned hard beneath their feet, the meadow giving way to the sprawl of the storage room.

"Open a passage," Harker said, his arm tight around their waist.

"I can't—"

"You have to."

Rat drew in a ragged breath. Too close, a terror scuttled up the aisle after them.

"Do it," Harker said.

A familiar whisper of power flickered in their chest. Before Rat could stop themself, they reached for it.

Something in them unhinged, and they felt the world open slightly, like a puzzle with just a bit too much space between the pieces. All at once, they could breathe again. Really breathe, like they'd spent so long underwater they'd almost forgotten what it was like.

"This way," Rat said, pulling him to the left, before they could think about where they were going. The aisle ahead of them opened where it shouldn't have, giving way to a narrow row of bookshelves.

Rat led Harker through, one of his arms around them, his other hand raised to cast.

The aisle spit them out in a small clearing, surrounded by old furniture, the air thick with the smell of dust and cedar oil. Harker pulled them against another wall of shelves, breathing hard, and Rat knew without looking that the passage had closed behind them.

Heat from the spell rolled off of Harker in waves. In the light of the spellfire, color ran high on his cheekbones. Ash smudged his cheek, and his too-long hair had slipped free again, falling into his face.

They looked up at him, still unsteady on their feet. "You know that everything here is made out of wood, right?"

He looked like he was seriously considering letting them fall.

Rat flashed him a shaky attempt at a smile.

Finally, he let out a breath, and something in his face softened. "Are you okay?"

"Yes." Their knees buckled, and he steadied them, pulling them against his side. Now that the adrenaline had gone out of them, Rat realized how badly they were shaking. "Maybe," they said weakly.

His arm tightened around them. "You're trembling."

Heat crept up the back of their neck. "Don't flatter yourself. I do that a lot," Rat said. "What are you even doing here?"

"Nothing. I—"

"It was you, upstairs," they said, putting it together. "You came after me." They stopped. "I thought you went back to your dorm. Were you looking for me?"

He looked away. "No."

"You were."

His skin heated, and they remembered how rattled he'd looked in the War Room. He'd sought them out, they realized. He must have known there was someone else in the tunnels since they'd first found the sigils, and Rat had to be the only other person who felt as thrown off as he did.

"Don't worry," he said, before they could follow that train of thought any further. "Jinx is looking for you, too. She's probably right behind me."

Rat raised their eyebrows in a question.

He drew a nub of casting chalk out of his pocket. "I cheated."

"You know a wayfinding spell," Rat said under their breath.

For a moment, in the flickering light of the spellfire, Harker looked almost smug about it, that he'd managed to rescue them with their own magic.

Rat's chest tightened. All over again, they remembered that he wasn't on their side anymore.

As if he'd realized it too, something in his face shifted. "Come on," he said, adjusting his grip. "We should get you back to the ladder. Are you hurt?"

"Harker." Rat grabbed on to his shirt. "I know what you're after. I . . . what kind of deal did you make with her?"

"I told you—"

"What kind of deal?"

He moved to peel their hand away, and then stopped as his fingers found the bracelet, still around their wrist. "Where did you get this?"

They lifted their chin, forcing themself to hold his gaze.

"Rat."

"You know where. She doesn't plan to keep you. The knight—"

"Isola," he said.

All of the heat on his skin died, and a sharp chill stole through the passage. Rat stared up at him, her name strange on his lips.

Isola. A raven knight in a field of grass. A cruel and distant star.

He drew his thumb over the inside of Rat's wrist, his fingers suddenly cool on their skin. "That bracelet is part of a binding spell. There are four more of them. I'm sworn to her service, and she isn't far behind me."

Harker's voice ran over them like ice water. They suppressed a shiver. "I'll stop you."

"Please. If you were going to end this, you would have already."

They looked up at him, but they didn't have an answer for that.

"I'm right, aren't I?" he asked. "You could have told the Council of Hours and walked away, but you're here instead. You know as well as I do that as soon as this ends, this world closes behind you." He studied them. "The school would never actually let you have the Holbrook Map. The moment you return it, you'll have to forget about the old campus and go back to being the perfect heir to an archive of spellbooks you'll never touch."

"Stop it."

"It took me the longest time to figure out why you never cast when it came so easily to you, but I think I get it now. You're not afraid of your magic at all, are you?"

Rat's jaw tightened as he drew in, the damp chill of the passage clinging to him, and they caught the faint scent of mugwort and ash on his skin.

"I think," he said, "you're afraid of the things you want. I think you're afraid that if you asked, you might actually get them."

They looked up at him, holding his gaze. Their knees trembled, and they hated him for it. They wanted to shove him away, and they wanted to lean in just to prove that they wouldn't flinch.

"Blakely, what the actual fuck do you think you're doing casting down here?" Jinx appeared at the mouth of the aisle, flashlight in hand. "You can't just run off like that. You could literally set this place on—" she stopped short. "Rat. You're okay."

"I . . ."

"They're fine," Harker said smoothly. "Just shaken. They thought they had a lead and came back down to investigate."

Unsure, Jinx looked from him, back to Rat, and they realized that they were still holding on to him.

They loosened their grip on his shirt. "I'm sorry. I wasn't thinking."

Jinx hesitated a moment, and then started toward them. "You could have told me. I would have—" she let out a sigh, and then like she was suddenly seeing them, something in her face softened. "Here," she said, shrugging out of her jacket. Rat opened their mouth to argue, but she held it out to them. "Take it. You're shivering."

"Thanks." They ducked their head and pulled the jacket over their shoulders. It draped heavily around them, warm against the chill of the tunnels and still smelling faintly of earth.

"Agatha's waiting at the top of the ladder. We should get back." Jinx extended her arm to them, and then her eyes ticked back to Harker. "Unless you'd rather . . ."

"No. I wouldn't." Fighting the urge to look back, Rat allowed her to wrap her arm around them and lead them back through the dark.

CHAPTER TWENTY-SIX

JINX WALKED RAT THE REST OF THE WAY BACK TO THEIR dorm room, her hands not leaving them the whole time.

The hall lights had gone out, and moonlight striped the hallway behind her.

"You're going to be alright?" she asked.

They opened their mouth to answer honestly, but then they just nodded.

"Cromwell and I will probably be awake for a while, if you need us," she told them.

Then, leaving them with her jacket still draped over their shoulders, she headed back up the hall.

Rat stood for a long moment with their back pressed to the door, listening to her footsteps recede.

When they were certain they were alone, they crossed back to their desk and pulled out their spare sketchbook.

They touched the bracelet, their fingers trailing onto their wrist where Harker's hand had been. They wanted his voice out of their head and the chill off of their skin.

They flipped open to a map of the campus they'd done. Steadying their hands, Rat tore the page out and folded it over.

They crossed the room and unlatched the window. The hinges creaked as they pushed it open, letting in the cool night air.

Rat pursed their lips and whistled three high, airy notes the way the knight had taught them once, in another lifetime.

Outside, the campus lay still below them. Their eyes flickered from the darkened line of the rooftops out to the rise of the hills in the distance, long and low like sleeping giants.

Maybe, they thought, they'd forgotten how, after all.

Then, the familiar sound of wingbeats broke the quiet.

A black bird lit on the sill beside them and canted its head.

Rat held up the paper. "Tell her I want to know where he's keeping the Holbrook Map. As a . . . tell her I'd consider it a favor."

Slowly, half expecting the bird to take off, Rat lowered their hand. "And, say that I expect this back," they added softly.

Again, the quiet set in around them.

Then the bird leapt up, catching the map in its talons, and took to the air.

It wasn't a promise, they reminded themself. She didn't have to answer. They didn't have to give her anything in return.

A cold draft rolled in over the trees. The chill had crept in under the leather jacket, and goosebumps pricked up their arms.

Finally, Rat shut the window and went to bed.

As the sky started to fade outside, they pulled the covers over their head and tried to sleep, but even though they were exhausted they lay awake for a long time after, thinking of Jinx's arm around their waist, and the dark sprawl of the tunnels, and the whisper of Harker's breath against their skin.

CHAPTER TWENTY-SEVEN

RAT DIDN'T KNOW WHEN THEY DRIFTED OFF, BUT WHEN they did, they were back at the tower, and it was cool, and dark, and waiting for them all along. Rat had never set foot past its doors, but in their dreams, the ones about the tower itself, they knew every room and corridor, and where the crumbling ceiling gave way to sky they could call every star by name.

In those dreams—the worst ones—they had always gone willingly.

Rat woke up to the sound of the clock tower, their lungs still tight in their chest and their heart beating hard.

They pushed themself upright, then stopped when they caught sight of the leather bracelet still wound around their wrist.

Their chest ached. Rat traced the line of the bracelet with their thumb. For a moment, they'd nearly forgotten that the night before hadn't been another part of the tower dream.

Nearly.

If Harker wanted to belong to the tower, that wasn't their problem anymore. They'd get the Holbrook Map back from him, and when they had it, they'd find the knight's heart and put an end to this somehow.

Forcing out a breath, Rat set the bracelet on the nightstand and grabbed their phone to check the time. Their pulse skipped as they caught sight of a text from Will.

Rat swiped it open, and then realized he'd sent it yesterday, while he was on the way over to their dorm. Their chest sank.

They hadn't wanted him to reach out, anyways. It was better this way.

They flipped past it, to a message from Jinx sent half an hour ago that just said, *library*

Rat stopped. They stared at their phone for a long moment, then went to find a shirt that didn't smell like a doused campfire.

By the time Rat arrived, Jinx was already set up in one of the upstairs reading rooms with a pile of reference books. She had a colorful windbreaker, which looked like she'd stolen it out of the nineties, folded beneath her, and Rat remembered that her leather jacket was still in their room.

Agatha sprawled in one of the reading chairs beside her, holding a book over her head at an angle that suggested she couldn't possibly be reading it.

"Oh," Agatha said, looking up at them. "You're alive."

Jinx gave her a look. "We weren't sure if you were on your way. I knocked on your door earlier, but you weren't up." She hesitated a moment. "How are you?"

"Great," they said, by which they meant they felt like they'd swallowed a handful of hot ashes.

The faint trace of smoke hung in the air, like Harker had already been there. If Rat knew him at all, he was searching the stacks for a counter spell to the anchors, or off somewhere whispering with the knight's messengers.

Probably, he'd already turned his attention to whoever had been in the War Room, now that he'd established that Rat wasn't a threat to anyone but themself.

They settled onto the couch next to Jinx.

"Last night—" she started.

"I made a mistake. I . . . thanks. Again. For coming to find me." They looked back at the books. "Did you figure anything out?" they asked, before she could ask any questions they didn't have answers to.

She rubbed her eyes behind her glasses. "Nothing yet. I just wish I knew who it was. I don't like that someone knows so much about us, and we have no idea who they are."

Agatha set her book down. "Even if we broke the spells on the tunnels, all of that time is still lost," she said, pushing herself upright. "I honestly don't see us getting anywhere before the Whisper Ball."

"What are we doing?"

They looked up to see Harker, standing in the doorway with a cup of dining hall coffee. He'd changed his clothes from last night, but he looked like he hadn't slept at all. Fresh burns marked his hands, and there was still a smudge of ash on his cheek, which could have been new or old.

"The Whisper Ball," Agatha said as he started across the room. "Keep up, Blakely."

He raised his eyebrows at Rat, and they realized he'd been sitting where their feet were, judging by how the books were splayed out.

They shifted over. "Satisfied?" they said under their breath.

Harker settled against the arm of the couch beside them and looked at them like he had never in his life been satisfied with anything.

Agatha clapped her hands, jarring them back. "Evans. Blakely. Are you done making eyes at each other, or should I wait?"

Blood rushed to Rat's face. Harker ducked his head as Rat turned back to the group, in time to see Jinx shoot Agatha a look.

She folded her hands. "It's a dance. The school holds one every year around Halloween. It runs until dawn, to keep the spirits busy so they can't get up to any mischief."

"Spirits," Harker repeated.

"And anything else that might slip through."

He looked skeptical, but there was something sharp and attentive underneath it. Agatha was explaining this for his benefit, Rat realized. He hadn't grown up around magic, and no matter how good he was at casting, he'd never been a part of blooded society. The whole time they were at Highgate, Rat wasn't sure he'd ever received an invitation to anything.

Agatha turned to them, and Rat realized they'd leaned in, too.

"I thought you knew all of this, Evans," she said, eyeing them. "You've never been to one?"

"I . . . no," they said, embarrassed. "I'm not really a fan of parties."

Their parents had thrown one once, years ago, but they'd been sent to stay with their grandparents that night. Mostly, Rat remembered their father setting out bursts of autumn flowers around the great room, and the way the house had smelled the morning after, like candle smoke and dust.

There were always rumors of a few seniors at Highgate who managed to snag invitations to the ball at Bellamy Arts, but by then, Rat hadn't seen the point in tempting fate.

"It's lucky you have me, then," Agatha said. She waved her hand, and they realized she was officially done with sigils for now.

They nodded and tried not to look too nervous as she went on.

"Whisper balls were made to provide cover for powerful workings. They're usually associated with necromancy, but sometimes advanced summoning spells, too—the kind of magic that has a way of drawing unwanted attention. The ball is a sort of distraction to keep any uninvited guests, so to speak, from interfering with the casters or escaping into the world. The idea is to keep them trapped, so that nothing gets in or out before sunrise." She paused. "Bellamy Arts doesn't use theirs to cast anything anymore. It's usually just for show these days, though they still follow the same rules. You might have guessed, but real whisper balls have a tendency to end badly."

Beside them, Jinx's eyes lit up, like for a moment, she'd forgotten about everything that had happened last night. "We're going, obviously."

In spite of themself, Rat smiled back. "Obviously."

"We'll all need to meet inside," Agatha told them. "It's bad luck to arrive together."

They looked up at her, and her eyes glinted.

"There isn't much telling what might follow you in," she said. "It's a good night for caution."

It was a night when everyone would be in one place, and the campus would be empty. The kind of night Rat knew it would be easy for someone else to take advantage of, if they didn't move first.

Outside, movement flickered in the trees.

Rat looked out the window, but whatever they'd seen in the high branches was already gone.

It took three days for Rat to receive an answer from the tower.

In the time that passed, they spent most of their free moments helping put the War Room back together and sitting in the library while the others thumbed through spellbooks for a way to untangle the anchor spells. The rest, they spent pacing restlessly around the dorm while the school slowly began to set up for the Whisper Ball.

Then, when they'd nearly convinced themself they wouldn't get a reply, Rat opened their bedroom door to the unmistakable scent of mugwort and aether, and they found their map tucked neatly beneath the window latch.

Their breath hitched. They never got used to hearing from the tower, but this time felt different from the others, maybe because this time, they had asked.

They stepped into the room, pushing the door shut behind them. They could still tear the note apart and pretend they hadn't seen it, or burn it, or call Evening and turn it over to the Council of Hours, but they already knew they would do none of those things.

Rat slid the note free and carefully unfolded it, brushing away the traces of aether.

Over Armitage Hall, in a corner of the building where Harker's room must have been, an *X* marked the map in crisp, dark ink.

A bird peered down from the high branches of the tree outside.

Rat met its eyes, refolding the map neatly in their hands, and nodded.

CHAPTER TWENTY-EIGHT

THE NIGHT OF THE WHISPER BALL CAME ON COOL AND unexpectedly crisp, the first hint of frost already on the air.

Rat looked down at the map on their desk for the twelfth time since they'd gone back to their room to gather their things for the dance.

They'd spent the last few days trying to figure out a next move. A part of them had hoped that Harker would have done the reasonable thing and stashed the Holbrook Map somewhere in the tunnels, or maybe a reading room in the library. They didn't have a plan for breaking into his room in the boys' dorm.

He had chosen the most obvious hiding place, almost like he'd wanted them to figure it out. Probably, the Holbrook Map was on his nightstand right now.

They hadn't realized it was possible to hate him any more than they already did.

Their phone buzzed. Rat glanced down to see a new text from Elise to say she was almost to campus.

"It's fine," they said under their breath. "You're literally fine."

Rat looked to the map one more time, but they still didn't have any ideas. Frustrated, they slid the paper away and crossed back to their closet.

They needed to be at Galison Hall in less than an hour, and Elise would probably disinherit them if they showed up in their sweatshirt, which still smelled vaguely like it had been set on fire a couple of times.

Rat thumbed through their clothes. They'd packed a few of their nicer dresses when they'd left for Bellamy Arts, just in case. There were even a few that they still liked, though if Rat was honest, they hardly wore them anymore. It had just felt like too much of a statement to leave half of their closet behind when they left for school, and it was hard to throw away things they knew looked good on them, even if it wasn't in the way they wanted.

They paused on a suit, then pushed past it to a black floor-length dress stitched with vines of climbing ivy. A burst of embroidered wildflowers sprouted rampant over the bodice and spilled onto the sheer length of the sleeves. Rat traced their fingers over the stitching. It was probably one of the most beautiful things they owned, and they hadn't had a chance to wear it, since they'd skipped the party that Elise had gotten it for.

For a few hours at an alumni event, it was probably the easiest thing.

Rat drew in a breath and took it down from the hanger. They changed quickly, working the laces behind their back as well as they could, until the spellwork kicked in and it tightened the rest of the way on its own, then did the buttons where the long sleeves cinched around their wrists. When they'd finished, they rolled on two pairs of stockings over their boxers, one opaque, the other one patterned with dark lace so no one would be able to tell that they hadn't shaved their legs since the beginning of senior year.

When they'd finished, they turned back to the mirror.

They looked nice. Rat had never really thought of themself as pretty, but to someone who didn't know what else to call them, they felt like they might be described that way.

They drew themself up, trying to ignore the tightness in their chest, and gave their best smile as Miranda Holbrook Evans, Technical Heir to an Archive of Spellbooks They Will Never Touch.

"Fuck," they muttered.

They undid the buttons on the cuffs and then reached around to loosen the laces on the back of the dress.

"No," they said under their breath. "No. Nope. No. Absolutely not."

They slipped the dress down over their shoulders and let it slide to the floor, pooling around their feet.

Before they could let themself think too hard about what they were doing, they dug a binder out of their dresser and pulled it on over their head. Then an undershirt from the drawer below.

Stepping over the dress, they went to the closet and took down the suit at the back.

It was a deep shade of blue and one of the few things they'd had tailored to fit them, meaning that last year they'd offered to buy Harker breakfast if he could stitch a tailoring spell into the lining. It was one of the few pieces of menswear they'd ever found that hadn't taken a lot of alteration to begin with, and on the days they felt comfortable enough to wear it, it was probably one of their favorite items of clothing that they hadn't stolen out of someone else's closet.

They worked the buttons up the front of their waistcoat, then knotted their tie the way that they'd practiced but rarely got to do.

When they'd finished, they tucked their compass into one of the inner pockets of the jacket and their phone into the other.

Rat glanced back at the mirror.

Their eyes tracked over their reflection, taking it in from the sharp lines of their suit to the buzzed sides of their head where their haircut from before the start of the year had begun to grow out. They didn't know how to explain it, except that they recognized themself.

If they had to be seen, if they let themself admit it, they wanted to be seen like this.

In the glass, their eyes went to the trunk on the floor behind them.

Drawing themself up, they paced back to the foot of their bed and undid the clasps on the trunk. Inside, they found their cloak still folded on the top where they'd left it on Lake Night.

A familiar want pulled at them. Carefully, they traced their hands over the fabric. The Whisper Ball was a formal event, and they wouldn't be the only person wearing one, even if it was just to the doors.

Magic flickered in their chest, and for a moment, they could sense the campus around them, opening into the far-off sprawl of the hills.

Rat looked across at the standing mirror, their reflection still kneeling in front of the trunk with the cloak folded across their lap.

Before they could stop themself, Rat pushed themself to their feet and drew the cloak around their shoulders. Then they let themself out into the hall and headed for the stairs, fastening the clasp as they went.

Rat crossed the campus alone.

Lanterns drifted over the path ahead of them as other students made their way through the dark toward Galison Hall. A chill had crept into the air even though it was still early in the night, and Rat knew from the low, flickering lights in the windows that the Whisper Ball was already underway.

They drew their cloak tighter around themself as they slipped in through the main doors.

Inside, Galison Hall had changed. Garlands of autumn flowers draped the walls and candles lined the wide throughfare, wax melted on the marble floor of the main entrance, though Rat knew that by morning, all of it would be cleaned away. A droning waltz drifted from somewhere deeper inside the building, and the air smelled faintly of smoke and fresh-cut marigolds.

Instinctively, Rat's hand found their compass in the pocket of their jacket as a pair of girls slipped past them, giggling as they raced up the hall before disappearing into the crowd.

You're fine, Rat told themself. *You're here.*

They closed their hand around their compass, steeling themself, and started up the hall.

They followed the music farther into the building, unclasping their cloak as they went. Neatly, they folded it over their arm, unsure of where to leave it. They'd walked through Galison Hall more times than they could count, but now, it felt like they'd stepped through a mirror. A small part of them didn't trust that all of the rooms would still be in their places. Like maybe, in the candlelight, everything had shifted a little.

Rat slowed as they came to the ballroom.

Once, while they'd been working on their maps, they'd paced around the wooden floors and counted floor-to-ceiling windows overlooking the woods behind Galison Hall.

Now, heavy velvet curtains hung along the back wall, and candles cluttered the edges of the room, casting everything in a flickering light. A low dais had been raised at the front of the room, empty and draped in flowers. The crowd had already gathered, scattered about the floor like they were waiting for something, and even though the music had gotten louder, Rat couldn't tell where it was coming from.

"It's quite something, isn't it?" Rat looked up to see that Frey had appeared beside them, his hands folded one over the other.

"Sir. Hi."

"I thought I saw Elise around here. I take it she's joining us tonight?"

"I'm supposed to meet her," Rat said. "I bet she'd love to say hello."

"Ah," he said. "In fact." He looked over their shoulder.

Rat moved to follow his gaze, but before they could, a hand took them by the arm. "Miranda, there you are!"

They spun as Elise pulled them into a hug.

"I was looking for you," she said, drawing back. She was wearing a floor-length black gown, and her dark hair was pinned up in an elaborate twist. Rat was so used to how she was at home that they sometimes forgot she was also the keeper of the Evans Archives and head of one of the most powerful families in the Northeast. Even when she wasn't trying, she exuded a quiet kind of power that had nothing to do with magic.

She beamed at them.

"Hi," Rat managed.

"How have you been? You'll need to tell me everything you've been up to." Her eyes flicked over them, and she paused, frowning as she noticed their cloak. "This isn't the one I had fitted for you," she said, taking the hem. "Where did you even . . ."

She trailed off as she recognized it.

"I found it," Rat said. "In Dad's things. It has a tailoring spell already. And pockets."

"I thought I recognized it from somewhere," Frey said.

Elise turned to him, brightening. "I hope this one hasn't been giving you too much trouble?"

"No more than you'd expect," he said. "But I was meaning to ask . . ."

Rat scanned the crowd as he and Elise chatted. In the few minutes since they'd arrived, more people had made their way in, drifting around the dance floor in clusters. From what Agatha had told them, almost the entire school turned out, students and faculty alike.

With a small thrill of unease, they realized that whoever had trashed the War Room was probably here, too. The only alternative was that they hadn't come and had free rein of the campus instead.

Rat pushed their anxiety back down. It wasn't something they wanted to think about.

"Evans!" They turned as Jinx made her way through the crowd in a long, gray dress made from layers of chiffon that floated over the soft lines of her curves like fog. A crown of delicate glass beads glinted in her hair like morning dew, and her eyes were bright behind her glasses.

Before they could say anything, she turned to Frey. "Professor."

"Miss Wilder," he said with a small nod.

"Mom," Rat started. "This is—"

"Jinx Wilder," Jinx finished, putting her hand out.

"Of course." Elise shook her hand, beaming. "I remember when your grandfather used to bring you to the alumni events. I was sad to hear he wouldn't be here tonight, but it's wonderful to see you again."

Jinx flashed her a polite smile that Rat didn't think they'd ever seen before, but in the candlelight, they could swear that her face flushed. "He was hoping to make it, too. I can tell him you said hello."

"Actually," Rat said quickly, turning back to Elise. "Would it be alright if me and Jinx . . ."

"Go on," Elise said. "I'll be here all night. I can catch up with you after I've made some rounds."

They nodded, grateful.

"And Miranda," she said, drawing them back. "I have my phone. Text me if you can't find me."

Their chest tightened. "Oh. Right," they said. Suddenly, they felt self-conscious. They'd forgotten that Jinx had probably never known them as anything other than Rat.

Quickly, they turned, letting Jinx lead them into the crowd. "So," they said, not meeting her eyes. "Were you heading anywhere?"

"This way." She motioned to them as she slipped back toward the doors. As she went, she glanced back at them like she was trying to ask a question and wasn't sure how.

"It's not a deadname," Rat said, reading the silence. "It just isn't what I go by, and basically no one under fifty ever calls me that."

They didn't have a better way to explain it. Maybe because it was still theirs, and they weren't sure they wanted to put it to rest completely. Maybe because there was a certain gravity to making it a deadname, like once they let themself care about it, they'd never get to stop correcting people, and *Rat* never felt quite name enough to replace it.

"Then I won't be calling you that," Jinx said. "Where are you watching the opening remarks from?"

"What?"

She glanced back at them. "Trust me?"

"No?"

Her mouth quirked. "Alright, then, Evans. Follow at your own peril, I guess."

"But—"

She raised her eyebrows at them, daring them to turn back.

"I already regret this," they said, taking her arm.

"As you should." She pulled them in and took off, weaving through the crowd.

She motioned to them as she stepped over a length of velvet rope, onto a narrow side staircase.

Rat stole a glance over their shoulder, then followed after her. They'd lost track of where they were in the building, but for once, it wasn't a bad kind of lost.

They'd been to parties before, but they never really participated in anything. Usually, within the first half hour, they'd be sitting on a back staircase somewhere with a plate of hors d'oeuvres, texting Harker updates about social intricacies of old blood social politics and not talking to anyone.

"Up here," Jinx said, catching their wrist to pull them up a bend in the staircase.

At the top, she pushed through a heavy velvet curtain, revealing a small balcony, and then Rat realized they'd been here before, too.

"I mapped this," they said, allowing Jinx to pull them out.

She chewed her lip. "I might have used your notes. For reference purposes."

The ballroom spread out below, awash with candlelight. It was still early in the night, and a crush of people milled about the edges of the floor below, the music drifting up from somewhere in the ballroom, although Rat still couldn't tell where it came from.

In the candlelight, it all looked a little unreal, like something that belonged in a dream, or at the end of a dead passage.

"And," she said, "I thought I should probably find at least one place to take you that wasn't entirely cursed."

They bit back the edge of a smile. "I mean, I could try to cast something."

"Absolutely don't." She grinned. Up close, she looked like daybreak after a storm, and the faint smell of turned earth and freshly cut forest growth clung to her, like she'd cut a path through the woods on her way here.

She met their eyes, like a question, and all at once Rat realized how close they were standing. If they leaned in, they could have kissed her.

Suddenly, they couldn't breathe.

"I think you're afraid of the things you want."

Rat shoved the thought away. Maybe they wanted this, too.

Jinx was beautiful, and recklessly good, and she actually *liked* them. She was a Drake, and she hadn't sworn an oath to the tower or stolen their father's work, and she didn't know about their magic at all.

As far as Jinx was concerned, Rat had never successfully cast a spell in their life. They were the all-but-powerless heir to a prominent family, who happened to be good at making maps and occasionally had to be saved. Someone ordinary and easy to care about.

There wasn't any reason they couldn't want something like that.

Her brows drew together, and Rat realized they hadn't moved. Blood rushed to their face.

"Evans?"

"Sorry, I just—"

Below, the lights flickered as if a draft had swept the room, and the candles along the balcony dimmed.

"I think the speeches are starting," they said quickly.

"Oh. Right," Jinx said uncertainly, settling back against the balcony.

Rat turned back to the front, fighting the urge to sink to the ground and burrow into their cloak. Their whole face burned, and their pulse still hadn't slowed down.

They'd been close enough to kiss her, and Jinx Wilder had looked at them like she maybe wanted them to ask, or say yes, or *something*.

They didn't know what was wrong with them.

Furiously, they focused their attention on the ballroom, their heart still in their mouth as Fairchild made her way onto the dais at the front of the room.

She'd traded her usual businesslike suits for a long black robe that trailed dramatically over the floor, her hair hanging loose down her back in pale gray waves. Candles drifted after her, bobbing on the air.

A silence settled over the room.

Rat stole another glance at Jinx, but she was looking ahead, her expression hard to read.

Rat wanted to vanish.

They wanted to find Harker and hide in a stairwell somewhere, and they hated the small part of themself that still hadn't gotten the message that he wasn't their friend anymore.

"I'd like to thank you all for coming out tonight," Fairchild said below, her voice crisp and clear. "I am aware that many of you have traveled a long way to get here, and some of you may have a long way to travel, yet, before morning.

"For those of you who are joining us for the first time, I'd like to remind you all of the rules. Although we will not be casting tonight, fate is not a thing to be tempted." It might have been a flicker of the light, but something that might have been mischief tugged at the corner of her mouth. "As soon as the clock strikes nine, the main doors will be closed through the deepest part of the night. For anyone who does not wish to stay, our staff will be waiting by the doors with lanterns to see you safely off the premises. I ask that you begin making your way to the doors now and take all of your belongings with you, as you will not be allowed back in to get them."

A beat of silence followed. Rat glanced around as a few people slipped back toward the doors, weaving through the crush.

After a moment, Fairchild continued, "Refreshments will be served in the dining hall throughout the night. Doors will reopen the hour after midnight, and the ball will run until sunrise for all who wish to stay. For any students who choose to leave before morning, you are to find a group of hallmates to return with and keep to the paths. No one will be allowed past the doors in groups smaller than three."

Rat thought of what Agatha had said, about whisper balls creating a cover for spells that drew the wrong kind of attention. In their mind, they could see the winding path back to the dorms shadowed by the trees, and they knew how frighteningly easy it would be to vanish between Galison Hall and the edge of campus, spell or not.

From farther off, the clock tower struck, the bells hollow and low in the still of the ballroom.

"And so," Fairchild said with a small flourish, "we begin."

CHAPTER TWENTY-NINE

BY THE TIME THAT RAT AND JINX MADE IT BACK DOWN the stairs to the ballroom, the night had started in earnest. The candles had flared back to life, throwing shadows around the ballroom, and music drifted over the dance floor.

For a moment, they hesitated, and then Agatha appeared out of the crowd in a long, white slip dress that trailed across the floor like starlight, her hair braided with lilies and moonstones.

"Jinx, I need you," she said. "Camilla Van Sandt is here, and I will actually perish if I don't ask her to dance with me."

Jinx glanced back at Rat, like a question.

"I—You guys go," they said quickly. "I might get some water."

Disappointment flickered over her face. "Only for you, Cromwell," she said, taking Agatha by the arm.

She gave Rat a last look over her shoulder as Agatha led her off, and then they were both swallowed up by the crowd.

As soon as Rat was alone, they sank back against the wall at the edge of the crowd. Elise had already left the main room, although they weren't sure where she'd gone, and they weren't eager to find Will, since they still hadn't answered any of his texts from the last few days.

They ran through everything that had happened on the balcony again, but their thoughts kept turning back to the night in the tunnels, Harker's breath gone cool against their skin.

"I think you're afraid of the things you want. I think you're afraid that if you asked, you might actually get them."

They did want this, they told themself. They didn't know why they were making such a mess out of everything.

Across the room, they caught sight of Harker watching the crowd.

He wore a suit, fitted meticulously like he'd worked the tailoring spells himself. His hair was tied back at the nape of his neck with a length of dark ribbon, and he'd worn a pair of leather gloves that Rat knew had come from a secondhand shop next to Highgate, since they'd seen him stitch in the fireproofing wards last winter so he'd still be able to cast.

He looked up as he noticed them watching and gave a small, smug tilt of his head, like he somehow knew he'd already managed to ruin their night.

He wasn't their problem tonight, they reminded themself. As long as he was at the Whisper Ball, at least for the next few hours, he couldn't go anywhere.

His mouth tugged. Like he knew he had their attention, he started into the crowd.

"Fuck," Rat breathed.

Without thinking about what they were doing, they took off after him.

"Harker." They caught him as he passed an alcove at the back of the room, the candle flames listing toward him like a tidal pull.

He glanced back at them. "Lost, Evans?"

They opened their mouth, and then closed it again as they realized they hadn't planned this far ahead. "Where are you going?"

"I thought I'd look around," he said coolly. "I've never been to something like this. I'm kind of enjoying it."

"You're planning something."

He gave them a look like he definitely was. "I do occasionally take breaks."

"When?"

His eyes glinted. "Occasionally."

In the center of the room, the couples on the dance floor began to break apart as the song came to an end.

He met Rat's gaze, a question on his face, then paused like he'd remembered something. Carefully, he peeled his gloves off and tucked them into his pocket.

He held his hand out to them.

Rat eyed him warily.

"You're obviously not letting me out of your sight," he said. His eyes flickered back to the floor behind them, where Jinx and Agatha must have been. "Unless you're waiting for someone else?"

They wanted to ask what he thought he was really after, but they weren't sure it mattered. Whatever it was, he must have known it would bother them for the rest of the night.

They could play that game, too.

Rat set their cloak down and laid their hand over his. "I assume you're leading."

"If that's okay?" he asked, taking them out to the dance floor.

"By all means," they said. In spite of themself, something twinged in their chest. If they knew him at all, they doubted he would have given anyone else the option.

Harker stopped as he found a place among the couples. The low drone of a violin cut the air, and he dipped into a bow. His lips brushed their knuckles, sending a chill up Rat's spine as the music began anew.

A soft, tilting melody drifted in, as if carried on the wind from some-where far away. There was something hollow and airy about it, like the breath and bones of a waltz.

Rat let him draw them in, following him into the first turn.

It had been a long time since they'd taken lessons, enough that for a moment Rat thought they might not remember, but the steps came back to them like muscle memory.

"I half expected you'd be gone by now," Harker said, his hand pressed to the small of their back. "Obviously, you think there's a chance you could win or you would've taken your maps and been out of the sunken campus already."

"And you showed up tonight, when you could have had the entire school to yourself," they said. "If you knew where the Ingrid Collection was, you would have moved to take it already."

"Maybe I didn't want to be too obvious."

"You've been obvious the whole time," Rat said, stepping in to be heard over the music. The familiar whisper of smoke and magic clung to him like a struck match, but up close there was something else warm and human underneath. "I don't think you actually want to get away with it."

He inclined his head. "No?"

"You could have lied when I asked you on Lake Night, and you dared me to follow you. You knew I wouldn't have put it together on my own."

"You already had."

"Not fast enough," they said. "Like how you could have left Jinx and Agatha out of it."

"They approached me."

"There are other entrances to the tunnels," Rat said, then paused. "You're actually friends with them."

"Please. We're allies." Harker drew them into another turn, dropping his gaze as he led them through the next set of steps. "Believe me, I've learned the difference."

Heat flickered in their chest. Since they'd gotten to Bellamy Arts, it wasn't like he'd stayed his hand, either.

"I'm still right. Admit it." Rat touched his cheek, and he looked back at them. "The moment you find the Ingrid Collection, the game ends and this world closes behind you, too, doesn't it? Even if you pull it off, you'll be out of excuses to keep up the act. You'll have the tower and nothing else." Something like resentment flickered over his face, and they knew they were dangerously close to the mark. They trailed their fingers along his jaw, and for one satisfying moment, they felt his breath catch. "Then again. Maybe I'm wrong. You always wanted power."

"I somehow don't think you're the best judge of what I want," he said, half to himself.

His breath whispered over their skin, warm in the cool ballroom. Goosebumps raced up their arms as he pulled them to a stop. "You're missing a piece, though."

The song ended, and Rat realized how close he was still standing, his hand still pressed to the small of their back.

He drew in, close enough that they could feel the subtle heat rolling off his skin. "I'm still a step ahead of you," he whispered.

Rat's jaw tightened.

They stared up at him as he pulled back again, their heart beating hard. He lifted his chin, daring them to say otherwise, but they couldn't.

Then, he released their hand and turned to go, leaving them alone on the floor.

Rat grabbed their cloak and made their way up the stairs to the second floor before they thought about where they were going. They just needed to be away from the ballroom.

They wished they hadn't come to the Whisper Ball to begin with. They didn't know what they'd been thinking.

Rat made their way down one hallway, then turned into the next, the building unfamiliar in the candlelight. Elise had to be wondering where they were by now. They hadn't seen her downstairs in any of the main rooms, which meant she had to be upstairs somewhere. The faster they found her, the quicker they could leave at the end of the night.

They finally caught her voice as they made their way down a wing of reading rooms, the noise of the party growing fainter behind them.

"Thank god," they breathed, starting toward it.

". . . that something like this would happen—and the week they arrived here," she was saying, but the words came out tense, her usual polish gone. With a creeping unease, Rat realized this wasn't a conversation they were meant to overhear.

They stopped, inches from the door.

It had been left open a crack, to a room with a large set of windows overlooking the lawn. Elise leaned against the side of a high-backed chair, a glass of scotch in her hand.

"The investigation is ongoing," they heard Evening say from somewhere deeper in the room. "We'll find it, I promise."

"I should have just had it burned," she said, letting out a breath. She dropped back, settling a bit. "I should have had the entire archive burned before it could pass to them. There's nothing good in there."

Rat's pulse dropped into their stomach. She was speaking about the Holbrook Archives.

Elise barely acknowledged that the Holbrook Archives existed most of the time. The only thing Rat knew for certain was that she'd sealed the doors after their father died, and that was how things had stayed.

They didn't know what to make of the hard edge in her voice now.

They stilled, waiting for her to go on, but instead of speaking again, Elise turned to the doorway. Her eyes went to them. "Miranda?"

Rat shrunk back. "I was looking for you. I'm sorry. I can come back."

"We were just finishing up," she said, her tone easy again. She set her glass on the end table, then rose from the arm of the chair. "I'll join you."

Rat followed after as Elise moved past them into the hallway. For a long moment, they didn't say anything, not sure how to approach it.

"Was that about the investigation?" they asked finally, choosing their words with care.

"You don't need to worry about it."

"But was it?"

Elise let out a breath. "Your father did important work here, but it isn't a kind of magic that I want you getting involved in. I would appreciate it if we could leave it at that."

Something about the way she said it raised the hairs on the back of their neck. "Did you not tell me on purpose?"

"It's more complicated than that. I just don't want you getting swept up in this," she said.

Rat knew that this was where they were supposed to drop it, but they couldn't let it go. "What did you mean about the Holbrook Archives?"

Elise quieted, and for a moment, they thought that they weren't going to get an answer.

"The Holbrook family practiced a dangerous type of magic," she said finally, a sharpness they hadn't heard before creeping into her voice. "Maybe your father was good, but not all of them turned out that way. They consorted with terrible creatures and paid a horrible price for it. You don't understand what's out there."

"What if I do?"

"You think you do," Elise told them, but then something in her face softened again. "I know you don't see this now, but some things are kept locked away for a reason."

Rat opened their mouth to argue, but Elise put her hand on their shoulder.

"The situation with the map is already being handled. As soon as it's found, I'll make sure it's returned somewhere safe, where we won't have to think about it again. I don't want you to worry about this."

"But . . ." they started.

Before they could finish, Elise gave them a small smile, and they realized that the conversation had ended. "Let's get back downstairs," she said. "There are some people I want you to meet."

"I . . . can I get some air first?"

"Of course. I'll be in the main room. Text me if you can't find me."

Rat nodded, and then, without waiting to see if she was behind them, they started back down the hall.

They made it around the corner and stopped in one of the windows where a few candles had been left burning. Outside, the moon had risen over the high branches of the trees.

They looked out, half expecting a black bird to come and find them with another message, but nothing did.

The knight had already delivered what she wanted them to know.

They were the one who hadn't used it yet.

"You're not afraid of your magic at all, are you?"

Their hand knotted in their cloak. They already had all of the pieces, even if no one else thought they were capable of handling this for themself.

Their mind flickered back to Harker in the ballroom, and the warm brush of his breath against their skin.

If he wasn't going to move first, then they would.

Rat took off toward the back staircase, pulling their cloak over their shoulders while they walked. The candles along the hallway flickered as they passed. If the back doors weren't attended, they could be across campus before anyone even realized they were gone.

"Rat!"

Will's voice stopped them.

They turned to see him standing in the hallway behind them. He'd left his suit jacket somewhere in the party, and his sleeves were rolled up, his hair mussed like he'd been dancing.

He rushed to close the distance. "I was looking for you. Elise said I'd find you up here," he said, a bit breathless. He stopped as he registered the fact that they were wearing their cloak. "Are you leaving?"

They stiffened, caught off guard.

"Is anyone taking you back?" he said. "I thought the doors were still locked."

"It's fine. I don't want to bother anyone. I just—"

"I can go with you."

"Will—"

"Hold on. I'll get my coat," he said.

"I said it's fine," they snapped.

He drew back. His voice softened. "Rat. What's going on with you?"

They forced out a breath. "Nothing. Please just tell Elise I went back early."

They started down the stairs. Their chest felt tight, and the hallway was too warm around them. They just needed to leave.

"It's the tower," Will said behind them. "Isn't it?"

Rat froze.

They'd never actually spoken about it with him. When everything had first happened with the tower, they'd kept it hidden from everyone until they'd finally gone to Harker for help. Once it was over, Will had just seemed relieved to let things go back to normal and he hadn't pried.

They'd assumed he'd picked up the bits and pieces of the story from Elise, with how much time he spent in and out of the Evans house over the summer, but he'd always acted like he didn't know.

Heat flashed across their skin. They wanted to run, but they couldn't move.

"I saw the chess piece. At your door. You had a drawer of things just like it at your house," he said. "Whatever happened last year, I know it was worse that you let on. I'm just really worried about you. If you're in actual trouble, we need to tell someone."

"Will. You can't." Rat spun toward him, dropping their voice. "Elise would pull me out of school."

"Then let me help," he said. Rat stared at him, and the most painful kind of hope flickered across his face. "You're doing something in the tunnels, aren't you? That's where you snuck off to on Lake Night."

"You . . ."

"Rat. What do I cast?"

They opened their mouth and then closed it again.

Will had always had a talent for earthworking. Rat had seen him raise small kingdoms out of rock, just to put them back again when he was finished. It was one of the reasons why Elise had taken a liking to him, since her magic tended in the same direction.

And there were miles of tunnels carved into the ground beneath their feet. Suddenly, Rat couldn't imagine that he hadn't known that from the beginning.

"I could go with you," he pressed. "I'm good with defense spells. I could be like the team tank. Or you know, the only person over five foot six."

Their heart dropped.

They couldn't pull Will into this.

The knight would close her hand around him, like she'd done with Harker. Like she was going to do with Jinx.

Like always.

As soon as she saw that Will was a part of this, she'd sweep in and take him, to remind them that she could. One way or another, she would pare away everyone until Rat was the only one left, and then she would close her hand around them, too, and the game would end.

"No," they said before they could stop themself. Their voice came out harsher than they'd meant, and he flinched back.

"But—" he started.

"Everything that happened last year was because I made it happen. I wanted it to." The words came out awful and ragged, but they didn't stop. "Nothing *found* me. I went looking."

"Rat?"

"We aren't friends, Will." They drew as much ice into their voice as they could. "You're a political ally, and I didn't ask you to protect me."

He stared at them, wounded.

Something in them threatened to crack.

If they were going to lose him, they refused to lose him to the tower.

"Don't follow me," they said. They turned before they could take it back and took off down the steps, away from the party altogether.

CHAPTER THIRTY

RAT LEFT THROUGH THE BACK DOORS. THEY HALF
expected someone to stop them, but no one else did, and they made their
way back across campus alone. The night had grown colder around them,
but they barely felt the chill.

Harker's room was wedged behind a flight of stairs near the back
of the building. Rat would have missed it entirely if they hadn't known
where to go.

When they made it to his door, the same whisper of power they'd felt
in the tunnels flickered between their ribs, and for a moment they could
feel all of the seams and edges of the world.

A small, vestigial *don't* tugged at them.

They shoved past it.

Harker had been taunting them this entire time because he still
thought they'd never actually stop him. They were done with that.

Rat pressed their hand flat against the door, and somewhere in the
hollow of their chest, they felt the world around them expand a little.

The door swung open.

With a twinge of cold satisfaction, Rat stepped in and eased the door
shut behind themself.

They weren't sure what they'd expected, but the room was clearly
his. Unlike Rat's room, which was technically a double, he had a
narrow shoebox of a single, with one long window overlooking the
trees. The faded trans pride flag from his dorm room at Highgate hung
on the opposite wall, and stacks of library books cluttered the floor by
the neatly made bed, the twin scents of magic and candle smoke still
lingering on the air.

Rat went for the books first. It would be exactly like Harker to hide a needle in a stack of other needles. They dropped to the floor next to the first pile and ran their finger along the spines, their eyes flicking across the titles.

Nothing.

They turned to a stack of formal references he'd probably smuggled out of the library. Rat lifted one off the top and riffled through the pages, but it was just spell diagrams.

Frustrated, they pushed themself back to their feet.

Their phone buzzed as they moved to the dresser. They ignored it, scanning the surface. Practice votive candles and nubs of casting chalk had been left out on top of the dresser, their image doubled back at Rat in a tarnished folding mirror that was almost definitely haunted.

Rat reached for the first drawer and then hesitated.

The wrongness of it twisted in their gut. Even when they'd had a free pass to show up at Harker's room unannounced, they hadn't dug through his clothes.

Rat looked back at their reflection and then stopped as something on the dresser caught their eye.

In the corner of the mirror, almost out of view, was the barest edge of a *something* that shouldn't have been there.

The strangeness of it brought them up short. "Of course," they said under their breath.

Carefully, they tilted the mirror, angling it away from the wall. There, in the glass, was another pile of books that looked like holdovers from the Evans Archives, stacked neatly in the reflection of the dresser, but not on the actual thing.

On top of them, there rested a simple leather tube no longer than their forearm, banded with spellwork.

Rat pressed their fingers to the surface of the mirror. The glass pushed back against them at first, but then, with the uncanny ease of dipping their hand into a pool of standing water, it gave way.

They drew out the map, aether curling around their hand in lazy drifts.

As they set it down, they caught sight of a packet of papers tucked beneath the books. Rat grabbed those, too, almost dropping them.

Swearing, they fumbled to catch what they could and mostly got it. A handful of scraps fluttered down around them, and then they realized what they were looking at.

Notes.

Some in Harker's handwriting. Some documents and illustrations of the campus he'd no doubt stolen from somewhere else. A smudgy pencil sketch of the clock tower in Rat's own hand.

Heat flickered in their chest. They hated him for using their own work against them, and they hated him more for having kept it all this time in the first place.

Rat shoved the notes into the inside pocket of their cloak, then turned back to the leather document tube.

They expected resistance, but if it had been sealed, Harker had already broken the protective spells before them, and a sheet of heavy, cream-colored paper slid easily into their hand.

Rat's pulse jumped. Carefully, they unrolled it.

It was blank.

Frowning, they traced their finger over the page, and their magic flickered as if in answer.

They let out a small, surprised gasp, yanking their hand back.

Ink seeped across the page, etching itself into a thicket of tight, architectural lines, marked out in their father's hand. The lines spread outward, swallowing the white space in a maze of twisting corridors.

A pathway snaked across the page, but there wasn't any telling where it had started and where it led, or if the rooms on the map were even a real place.

Cautiously, Rat reached out again, tracing their finger over the path, and the map shifted, revealing an open field. The same path slicing through it in a clean arc, but it started from somewhere else on the page, so they couldn't follow it.

Then, to a forest, cut through by the same path.

They watched as it changed again, the lines redrawing themselves once more.

The pathway had vanished, but it took Rat a moment to understand what they were looking at. Then they caught sight of a long, sprawling shape near the middle of the page, and realization pricked through them. The Drake.

Rat traced their finger over the map, where the infirmary and chapel were drawn in across the main lawn. Galison Hall. The dorms in the outlying circle. The clock tower, like a fulcrum at the center of all of it.

They were looking at the campus.

Even though Rat couldn't say why, a shiver tracked down their spine.

Something about it pricked at them, like even though they didn't understand what they were seeing, they could almost feel the shape of it.

It was a riddle, maybe, but a riddle that had been written for them.

From the hallway, there was the distinct click of a lock.

Rat stilled as everything inside of them turned to ice. Quickly, they grabbed the document tube from the dresser and rushed for the sliver of space beneath the bed.

The doorknob rattled as they pressed themself to the floor, and then the door swung in.

Rat's breath caught.

Harker's footsteps tracked across the hardwood floor, the telltale whisper of magic following him in. He pushed the door shut and stopped in the threshold.

Rat held their breath as he paced toward the bed.

The clock hadn't even struck twelve yet. He should have been at Galison Hall for at least a few more hours.

They watched as Harker stopped in front of the mirror, the faded black cloak from Lake Night draped loosely across his shoulders. His hair fell loose around his face where it had escaped from its tie, and he looked pale in the light.

He braced himself against the dresser, and something in his posture seemed to give. All of his self-assurance from the Whisper Ball had disappeared, replaced by something Rat didn't recognize.

His reflection looked back at him from the glass, his eyes shadowed like he hadn't been sleeping much. Suddenly, Rat was sure that he hadn't.

"Fuck," he muttered. He smudged his hand over his cheek like he was still trying to get their touch off of his skin, and then stilled.

A chill slid through the room, too sharp to be a draft. Faintly, the scent of mugwort and aether cut the air, raising goosebumps along Rat's arms.

Their breath caught.

They didn't know what it was, like a sudden drop in the air pressure, but all at once, they realized that he wasn't alone in the room.

"You're back early," said a voice that Rat still heard in their tower dreams, cold and clear like ice water.

Their mouth went dry, and for a moment they were back in the field of fallen stones.

Harker dropped his hand, still facing the mirror, but his gaze flickered to something deeper in the glass. "What do you want?" he asked stiffly.

"Maybe I was bored," Isola said, drawing it out.

"I know what this spell costs you. You wouldn't be here without a reason."

"Fascinating," she said. "I don't remember that being your concern." Rat curled into themself as she strode past them, carrying the faint, sharp scent of autumn air in with her. They caught a flash of her worn leather boots, but something about her didn't seem quite *real*. Like if they reached out and touched her, she might dissolve back into the shadows.

It's just a spell, they told themself.

She couldn't set foot on the school grounds, even now. She had cast this from somewhere far away, where she couldn't get to them.

Smoke curled away from her in thin, gray tendrils, like it was an effort to hold her form.

"You're falling behind," she said to Harker.

He tensed. "You gave me the year."

"And you've had the map for almost two months. Tell me. How many other people are looking now?" she asked, but she didn't sound like she wanted an answer. She sounded like she'd already dismissed him. "If I didn't know what was at stake, I might think you weren't really trying."

He clenched his teeth. "I've made it further in two months than anyone you've sent in the last hundred years. I told you I could do it, and I'm going to."

"Will you?"

Heat pricked the air around him. "You don't need to be here," he said. "You already got what you wanted."

Rat caught a flicker in the mirror as Isola stepped in, smoke trailing from her fingertips. She reached out and tucked a strand of hair behind his ear. "Oh, Harker," she said with a sigh. "I think we both know that's not true."

His jaw trembled.

Then, without another word, the spell broke, and he was alone again. A lingering trace of smoke curled through the air where she'd been standing a moment before, and then that was gone, too, as if she'd never been there at all.

He stared at the place where she'd been, and for a moment Rat thought he might set the air itself on fire.

Finally, the tension went out of him and he slumped back to the dresser. Shakily, he pushed his hair back.

Then, he froze.

Frowning, he touched one of the candles, nudging it back into place.

Rat's pulse rose into their throat as he turned back from the dresser. His gaze swept the room.

Intently, he knelt down and lifted a scrap of paper from the floor. His face iced over.

All at once, Rat realized what was about to happen. They reached for their magic, but they'd already lost the thread of the spell that had opened the door, and then Harker's eyes found theirs.

They shot out from under the bed, still clutching the map.

Harker whipped after them as they rushed for the door, but they ducked low, out of his reach. He lunged after them, catching the back of their cloak.

Rat jerked back, off-balance, and then before they realized what they'd done, the wall gave way, opening into woods. They stumbled forward, pulling Harker after them as they came down hard in the mulch. Underbrush crunched beneath them as Rat shoved away from him, scrambling for purchase on the uneven ground.

The smell of dirt and lake water hung heavy in the air. Trees rose up around them, dark except for the distant glow of the wards.

A bolt of recognition hit them as they stumbled to their feet. They were back in the east woods.

They turned hard on their heel back toward the school, but a blaze of spellfire swept ahead of them, blocking off the trail.

Rat whipped back.

Harker stood with his hand outstretched. Will-o'-wisps of spellfire drifted between the trees behind him, crackling against the quiet of the woods. The air around him rippled with heat.

He looked across the narrow strip of moon-striped trail, daring them to move. "Give it back."

Rat let out an incredulous laugh, but it came out broken and wrong. "You didn't think that I could. You've been baiting me this entire time, and you can't stand the fact that I actually did it!"

The spellfire around him flared a warning. "Rat, I swear—"

"I was right, wasn't I?" they asked. "You don't care if you get caught, you just wanted me to know that I couldn't beat you."

"You have no idea—"

"No. Everyone was right about you," they said. Something in them broke. "You saw that I was in trouble, and you used me to get ahead. Were you ever actually friends with me, or did you just like that I was so powerless?"

"Stop it," he snapped. There was a bite in his voice that they hadn't heard before.

"Please. How long did it take for you to go back to her after I was gone? Was it a day? A week?"

"You threw me aside the second I wasn't useful to you! I don't owe you an answer!"

"She told me where to look for the map," they said, pushing on. Their voice came out harsh and burnt in the night air. "You know that, right?"

"I—"

"What did you need to offer her to convince her to take you on? That's what happened, isn't it? You knew what she was, and you knew you were opening the door for her to come back, and you still went to her!"

"She would have killed me!" he shouted, then froze, like he was startled by the sound of his own voice.

Rat came up short as everything inside them guttered out. Their arms tightened around the map, pulling it to their chest as they stared at him through the trees. "What?"

"You didn't actually think she'd let me leave," Harker said, but the words came out too fast, and his voice pitched in a way they knew he hated, sharp and frantic. Color streaked his face, heat still wavering off him. "She found me again as soon as you were gone. She was going to take me back to the tower with her—she wanted to make a bet. If you came back for me, I was free to go, and otherwise, I was hers to keep."

The words hit them like a physical blow. "But you said—"

"I had to beg her to let me swear myself to her instead so I wouldn't die waiting for you."

Rat stared at him. His hand was still raised to cast, but his lip trembled. A gust of hot air blew past, tugging the hem of his cloak, and the will-o'-wisps of spellfire burned dangerously bright on the air around him.

"I would have gone," they said, feeling small. "I can still—"

"I don't want you to," he snapped, his voice ragged. The spellfire flared, but he didn't look powerful anymore. He looked like he was trying not to break. "I don't care how it ends. I'd rather spend the rest of my life bound to that place than ever need you again."

Their face softened. "Harker."

He leveled his gaze at them and raised his hand to cast. "We're done here. Give back the map."

"We can find another way out of this."

"Give it back or—"

"Go ahead! Fucking burn me, Harker. You couldn't hurt me if you wanted to." Rat drew themself up. "I'm not letting you do this."

His jaw tightened. He traced a spell, and a wisp of spellfire sparked beside them. Rat feinted out of the way, but before they realized what he was doing, Harker raised his hand to cast again.

They moved to dodge, but it wasn't an attack.

It was the retrieval spell.

The map pulled out of their grasp and shot toward him. Rat reached after it and lost their footing, already off-balance. Their hand closed on nothing, and they came down hard on the forest floor.

Harker caught it out of the air. He looked down at them, then turned hard on his heel, spellfire closing in after him to block the path.

Rat moved on instinct, shoving themself to their feet. Their hand cut the air in the only spell they knew. *"Stop!"*

The spell ripped from their throat, and then their magic rose to meet it. Power prickled across their skin like lightning.

With a horrible, bone-deep crack, Harker jerked to a stop, his arm wrenched back at an unnatural angle. He cried out, and then his voice choked off in a ragged, pained gasp as the spell forced his hand open, and the map dropped to the dirt.

Rat stared at him, frozen.

Moonlight shifted across the pathway, etching everything in silver. All around them, the woods had changed to something else, strange and overgrown. Weeds sprouted up between the trees, wild with night-blooming things, and the stars above them had changed.

A faint shimmer glinted on the air in the distance, but the steady glow of the school's main wards had vanished, replaced by something older and more subtle, like they'd seen in the tunnels. They weren't in the east woods anymore.

"I don't—I didn't—" they said softly.

They didn't know how to fix this.

Harker looked back at them, wide-eyed. His hair had come untied during the fight, and bits of forest stuck to the edges of his cloak, his arm still pinned by the spell.

"I—" They cut their hand uselessly through the air. *"Release him! Let him go!"* Their voice came out high and panicked, echoing through the woods.

Nothing happened.

"Rat—"

"I'm trying!" they shouted.

All at once, they felt something snap, like cutting a violin string. The spell broke, and Harker collapsed in a heap on the ground.

Rat rushed to him.

"Shit," they breathed, dropping to their knees as he tried to force himself back up. Even in the moonlight, they could tell that something was wrong, like all of the bones between his wrist and his shoulder had twisted in a way they shouldn't have. "I'm sorry. I'm so sorry."

Out past the edges of the trail, something scraped in the underbrush.

Rat jumped, and Harker tensed beside them. Before they could move, he grabbed their cloak with his good hand. "Rat. Take us back."

"I can't—"

Desperation flickered across his face "Just get us back to campus. I don't care what you did."

"I don't know where we are! I—I don't know how!" they shouted. This had never happened to them before, and they didn't know how to undo it.

"*Rat.*" His hand tightened on their cloak. Heat bled off of him, feverish in the sharp chill of the woods.

"I can't! I'll make things worse!"

Wind rustled through the underbrush, and the shadows shifted over the ground. Before they could move, a creature like a wolf covered in dark raven feathers stepped out into the clearing, its body sleek and oil-black in the moonlight.

Harker jolted.

Instinctively, Rat pulled him back, even though there wasn't anything they could do to protect him.

Their arm tightened uselessly around him as he raised his good hand to cast, biting back a wince. Spellfire flickered weakly in his palm.

His control was spent, they realized. If he tried anything more than that, he'd be just as likely to lose the spark altogether as he was to set the woods on fire.

Dread sank in the pit of their stomach. They'd never seen him struggle to cast before. They'd counted on the fact that it was second nature to him.

A second not-wolf emerged from the shadow of the trees, circling the edge of the clearing.

Rat ducked their head, fighting the urge to bury their face in Harker's shoulder. Their magic surged back up in answer, but they couldn't focus. The woods opened up huge and sprawling around them, and they didn't know how to find their way back.

The not-wolves drew closer.

Harker pressed himself into them, heat rolling off him in ragged waves. The spellfire guttered in his hand, throwing shadows across the clearing. Rat's pulse beat hard and fast against their ribs, and they couldn't breathe.

They squeezed their eyes, panic welling in their chest.

Then, with a sharp snap, they felt the spell break.

The world crashed in around them, and then they were back in sight of the campus, on a path in the east woods with moonlight spilling through the trees, their arm still tight around Harker's waist.

"I—" they started.

He shoved away from them. "Let go of me."

Instinctively Rat reached after him, and he flinched back.

They froze, their hand still hanging in the air. They knew the look on his face. They'd seen Harker afraid before, but he'd never been afraid of them.

"That's quite enough," a voice said from the pathway.

They looked up to see Vivian Fairchild standing over them, her hand raised in a casting position, still dressed for the dance. Slowly, Rat realized they hadn't been the one who'd broken the spell. She had.

A small crowd had gathered behind her. They picked out Jinx, her mouth parted like she didn't quite understand, but also did. Agatha, beside her, her white cloak almost luminescent in the dark. Will, worried and more lost than they'd ever seen him, watching them like he wasn't certain if he should be there.

Rat lowered their gaze. Fairchild said something about calling the infirmary, but they'd stopped listening.

Suddenly, the clearing felt too crowded, their skin too warm. They needed to be anywhere else.

Before Rat could think of what they were doing, they backed toward the trees. Then they took off, the undergrowth growing thicker around them as they went, and they didn't look back.

CHAPTER THIRTY-ONE

RAT DIDN'T STOP UNTIL THEY RAN OUT OF TRAIL AND THE path ahead of them had become too overgrown to follow.

The woods opened into sky and stars, but wherever they were, it wasn't somewhere they knew. They sank down at the edge of a clearing, hugging their knees to their chest.

They didn't want to be found.

Their cloak pooled around them on the forest floor. Underbrush clung to the hem, and their legs were covered in scratches from the woods, but they didn't care anymore. They'd left the Holbrook Map behind. Probably, someone had already picked it up by now.

The impossible quiet of the woods settled around them, and they thought again about the frightened way that Harker had looked at them and the visceral crack of bone.

They felt hollow.

Rat curled against the base of a tree, drawing their cloak against the cold of the deep woods. When they finally drifted off, their sleep was fitful and shallow, and for the first time in weeks, they didn't dream of anything.

CHAPTER THIRTY-TWO

MORNING FOUND RAT SORE AND EXHAUSTED. AT SOME point in the night, dew had seeped into their things, which had somehow made the damp weight of their cloak feel colder than the air around them.

They forced themself off the ground and worked the feeling back into their shoulders. Everything ached.

They looked out across the clearing. Where the foothills should have been, miles of weeds and old stone sprawled out beneath the fading sky, flat and endless.

Rat hadn't been thinking last night, and they'd left the campus farther behind than they should have.

With a chill, they thought of the not-wolves. If anything found them out here, they wouldn't have help this time.

The underbrush rustled behind them.

Rat whipped back as a black bird leapt up from the grass, taking flight. It swept past them and landed on the low branch of a tree, watching them.

They let out a breath, their heart still beating hard.

The bird blinked at them.

"I don't have anything for you," they told it.

It tilted its head thoughtfully. Then, it took off again.

They stared after it, a stale taste stuck in the back of their throat.

This should have been a victory. They might have lost the Holbrook Map, but they'd at least gotten it away from Harker. They already had everything they needed to beat him at his own game if they could just put the pieces together.

Mostly, though, they felt spent. They took a last look out at the field, past the thin veil of the wards, and then, with nowhere else to go, they drew their cloak around themself and started back the way they'd come.

💀

Rat walked until their feet were sore, the wild overgrowth of the woods slowly retreating as the morning broke pale and gray around them.

They didn't know when they crossed back into the campus proper, exactly, but little by little, the smell of lake water overtook the bite of mugwort and frost, and the grounds became familiar again. Then, farther out, they caught sight of the jagged sweep of the school rising up against the sky, which told them that they'd made it back, even if they weren't sure how.

Up ahead, a light flickered between the trees, cutting the early morning dim.

Rat's breath hitched. For a moment, they thought it might be spell-fire, and then they realized it was the beam of a flashlight.

Everything in them sank, and they knew the moment before it found them that this morning was about to be much, much worse than they'd anticipated.

"Rat?"

Will jogged toward them, a few of his friends trailing after. Something that might have been relief flickered across his face, and then he slowed a few feet from them, like he wasn't sure how close he was allowed to get.

His breath hung in the morning air. At some point in the night, he'd changed into running shoes and a pair of sweats, but he didn't look like he'd slept.

"Everyone's looking for you." His voice came out soft in the still of the woods, like he thought they might bolt if he moved too fast or spoke too loudly.

Rat opened their mouth to speak, but they didn't have anything left.

Finally, they ducked their head and started past him, the muddied hem of their cloak flapping after them. "Let's just go."

"Right," he said, winded.

The walk back to campus was long and quiet. The ground had frozen over the night before, and the only sound was the crunch of the undergrowth as they picked their way back up the trail.

A makeshift search station had been set up on a few aging picnic tables on the grass, and a handful of faculty members and Lesser Hours milled about the grounds, some with maps and flashlights, others with paper cups of coffee and wakefulness spells, their faces grim.

Fog rolled low over the grass as Rat started toward the tables, everyone stilling around them as they passed.

Ahead, they caught sight of Fairchild and made for her, Will and the others still trailing after.

Fairchild straightened when she saw them.

Rat braced themself for a lecture, but after a long moment, she just looked to Will and the small search party behind him and said, "I'll have the Hours call everyone else in," and then, to a group of faculty at a nearby table, "Someone please find Elise."

Rat stood quietly, the conversation washing over them as Will was handed off to speak with one of the Hours, and the group began to disperse.

Once Will was gone, Fairchild looked Rat over, like she was determining how many pieces they were in, and then said, "Come with me."

They followed her to a table at the center of the search station, strewn with spell diagrams and abandoned paper cups.

Dawn of the Council of Hours looked up as they approached and turned toward them.

Rat had met Dawn a handful of times, usually on the rare occasion that their paths had crossed at the Council Chambers. Their full name and title was Morgan J. Taylor, liege of all things made bright, their pronouns were they and them unless otherwise noted, and they were basically the human equivalent of a genderfluid sunrise, in case sunrises were somehow not implicitly genderfluid.

Rat had no idea what Dawn did, officially, but they were a full decade younger than the rest of the Greater Hours, so whatever it was, they must have been unspeakably good at it.

They wore a pale mint suit, a pair of tinted glasses clipped neatly to the pocket. A sweep of pastel lipstick showed bright against their cool, dark skin, their makeup still fresh like they'd just arrived.

"We're calling everyone back," Fairchild said. "Morgan, if you would—"

"I've already let the rest of the Hours know," they said.

Fairchild said something else, but Rat stopped listening as they caught sight of Elise across the clearing.

She'd changed into long pants and hiking boots, and her long hair was now braided back away from her face. For a moment, they thought that she might run at them. But then, like she was really seeing them, she stopped where she stood.

Rat held her gaze for a too-long moment, and then they looked back to Fairchild. "I'd like to go back to my dorm."

She paused.

"So I can change," they said, their voice still ashy. "Please."

Before she could respond, Dawn gave her a placating look. "I'll take them," they said.

Fairchild studied Rat for a moment, then looked back to Dawn. "My office. As soon as you're done."

Dew had seeped into Rat's shoes, and they were sure they were going to be expelled.

They stole a glance at Dawn as they walked back to the dorm.

"I'm not going to ask," Dawn said, their eyes fixed on the path ahead.

Rat sank into themself. "You should."

"Would you tell me if I did?"

Heat rose in their cheeks. They wondered if it was too late to run back into the woods. "What did Harker say?"

Dawn exhaled. "Nothing. He's still in the infirmary."

"What?"

This time, Dawn did look back at them, like they were surprised Rat didn't know. All over again, Rat thought of the visceral crunch of bone giving way.

"There's a spell though? Right? For his arm?"

"Yeah," Dawn said, rubbing their eyes. "We managed to put him back together. I don't know what you did, Evans, but you broke a lot of bones."

Rat flinched.

That really wasn't what they'd meant to do.

Dawn sighed like they knew that and turned back to the path.

The rest of the walk was mercifully quiet. Most of the campus still hadn't woken up yet, but enough people had been in the woods last night that the whole school would know by breakfast.

When Rat got to their room, their window was open, a pile of crumpled mums and leaves and the broken length of what might have once been a silver necklace left waiting for them on the sill.

Feeling hollow, they swept it inside and pulled the window shut again.

CHAPTER THIRTY-THREE

WHEN THEY FINISHED GETTING CHANGED, DAWN WAS waiting downstairs with a paper bag of breakfast pastries.

"One of the Lesser Hours came by," they said, holding it out. "I wasn't sure what you wanted."

Rat mumbled a thank you, even though the thought of food turned their stomach.

They walked most of the way to the Founder's House in silence.

"You can go up," Dawn told them once they'd made it to the lobby.

Fighting the urge to duck their head, Rat made for the stairs. Elise would have already spoken to Fairchild. She was probably waiting to drive them back home and lock them in a box somewhere.

When they got to Fairchild's office, they froze.

Harker was there.

He'd already taken one of the chairs across from the desk, like he'd been politely waiting for them to arrive and not lobbying to have them expelled.

He'd changed into an old pair of sweatpants and a loose black T-shirt, nearly concealing the added bulk of what Rat guessed was a compression bandage, which had to be holding most of his shoulder in place. The neck of his shirt hit just low enough to show the strap of his binder, and Rat distinctly didn't want to know what unholy combination of spite and arcane magic he'd needed to get it back on over his shoulder.

His hair hung loose past his jaw, and when he turned to meet their gaze, Rat knew from the shadows under his eyes that he hadn't slept at all.

"Mx. Evans," Fairchild said, motioning to the open chair. "If you would."

Uneasy, Rat tracked across the office and took a seat.

"I'm going to say this once," she went on. "We have a very strict policy here regarding the use of magic against other students. I don't know what the two of you were up to last night, but you are both incredibly lucky that things didn't turn out much worse."

Rat ducked their head, and Fairchild's gaze settled on them, her eyes steely behind her glasses.

"If it was up to Elise, you'd be on your way home right now. I've convinced her to give me a chance to speak with you, but I haven't decided yet whether it's wise or even safe for me to vouch for your continued enrollment here."

"I understand," they said weakly.

Her attention shifted to Harker. "Don't think you're in the clear, either, Mr. Blakely. Your spellfire alerted us to your location."

Harker sank down in his chair.

Fairchild reached into her desk and drew out the Holbrook Map. "If either of you has any intentions of remaining on campus, I expect a full explanation of what you were doing in the woods last night and where you came by this."

Her gaze shifted between them.

Quiet settled over the office.

"It was me," Rat said quickly, at the same time that Harker said, "It's my fault."

He eyed them warily.

"It was mostly me," Rat started, and then realized they hadn't thought through what was supposed to come next. "I . . ."

Fairchild folded her hands on the desk, waiting for an explanation that Rat didn't have.

They shot Harker a pleading look.

"It was mostly Rat," he said, and they immediately stopped feeling bad for him.

A too-long moment passed.

Finally, Harker let out a breath. "We found it by the entrance to one of the old service tunnels," he lied smoothly. Rat bit back a noise of disbelief. Harker had a story already. This was what he'd done in the infirmary, while the school's healer was puzzling his bones back together. "Rat saw footprints around the one in the east woods a few days ago and wanted to investigate. I told them it was a bad idea, but they were going to leave the dance early and I didn't want to let them go by themself."

"Right," they said.

"We thought we heard something in the trees. They tried to cast a defense spell."

"I really didn't mean for this to happen," Rat added.

Fairchild looked between the two of them, like she wasn't sure if she should believe them or not. Finally, she said, "I see."

Rat hesitated, waiting for more questions, but she just reached for the stack of papers on the desk.

"There was something else." Fairchild slid a photograph of a spell diagram across the desk, chalked onto polished wooden floors. The same temporal anchors they'd seen in the woods etched the ground around it, precisely drawn and evenly spaced. "Are either of you familiar with this?"

Rat furrowed their brow. They had no idea what they were looking at, but something about it set their teeth on edge. Their eyes went back to the room in the photograph, skimming over the bookshelves lining the wall, the tall windows, the heavy curtains.

Beside them, Harker leaned in, frowning.

"It's a lesser summoning spell," he said, like he was answering a question on a test at the same time that Rat said, "That's Galison Hall."

They traded glances.

"It was found upstairs during the dance last night, uncast."

Rat's eyes flickered from the paper back to Fairchild. "You mean someone was trying to . . ."

"Let something into the campus. Yes," she said. "Frey has been studying it to see if he can identify what kind of creature it was for. This is serious magic."

Harker's frown deepened. "Why would someone do that?"

"I can't say," Fairchild said, taking back the photograph. "But if I had to hazard a guess, your stunt in the woods last night might have been what distracted them."

An uneasy silence fell over the room.

After a long moment, Fairchild pushed the photo aside. "I understand this is troubling, but I don't want either of you taking matters into your own hands again. For as long as you're students here, it's the school's job to protect you and not the other way around. I'm handling the investigation. In the meantime, you are to come directly to me if you see anything else. Am I clear?"

"Yes, ma'am," Harker said, ducking his head.

"Sorry," Rat mumbled.

"We're far from finished here. You'll both hear from me as soon as I figure out an appropriate course of action. In the meantime, I don't want to hear a word about either of you." She folded her hands. "Now. It's been a long night for all of us. Mx. Evans, I'll have one of the Hours escort you back to your dormitory. Mr. Blakely, you will report back to the infirmary so we can see if there's anything else to be done."

"So," Rat said as soon as they were alone in the hallway. "How many plastic shoulder braces did you melt before they figured it out?"

Harker glared at them, in a way that definitely meant more than one.

Something in them fell. "Wait," they said. They reached for his sleeve, but he flinched away. Slowly, they lowered their hand. "Last night, I didn't—I mean, I would never—" Except, they *had*.

"That's great for you, Evans."

"Hey—I was trying to stop you. I wouldn't have been in your room in the first place if you hadn't—"

"Hadn't what?" He raised his eyebrows at them, and Rat remembered where they were.

Even now, he knew they wouldn't say it out loud.

They opened their mouth to argue, but they didn't have anything. "I'm really sorry," they said, even though they weren't sure anymore which thing they were sorry for.

"You can have the map." Harker's voice ran cold and flat. "I already solved it. You gave me the last piece."

"What?"

He regarded them evenly, like the answer should have been obvious.

Then, without answering, he turned toward the stairs and headed down to the first floor, leaving them behind.

Harker was gone by the time Rat made it down to the lobby, which figured.

They dropped into one of the empty chairs lining the wall. They wanted to go back to Mallory Hall and sleep for the next thousand years, but they were also pretty sure that if they so much as breathed without Fairchild's sign-off, they'd be shipped home immediately.

"I already solved it."

"Fuck," they muttered. "Of course you did."

"Rat. I thought I might find you here."

They snapped up as Evening appeared in the doorway. His white-blond hair was parted immaculately to the side, the lines of his coat still neatly pressed.

"Sir," they said. "Um. Hi." Rat fought the urge to draw into themself, suddenly aware of the fact that they'd slept on the ground last night and probably looked like it.

"I just saw that boy leaving. Are you alright?"

"I . . ." Their mind flickered back to what Agatha had told them about Evening wanting to collect them, and they hesitated. They'd always assumed he'd helped them as a favor to their father. After last night, Rat couldn't imagine they had much political value left. "Yeah," they said cautiously. "I think he's worse off than I am. I've just got a couple of scratches."

Evening frowned.

"I'm fine," they said. "I didn't go that far from the school."

"I know. But the wards are old, and there are places where they aren't as strong," he said. "I'm just glad you're alright."

"Oh," Rat said, pushing down a pang of unease.

All over again, it dawned on them how much worse the night could have gone, if Fairchild had found them a bit later or their spell had hit Harker somewhere he wouldn't have recovered from.

Evening exhaled deeply. "I'm going to be honest. I'm not convinced the investigation is over. I don't know if Fairchild showed you the spell diagrams that were found last night, but whoever did this is still on campus somewhere." He put his hand on their shoulder. "Elise spoke with me about the possibility of having you come stay at the Council Chambers until all of this dies down. I know it probably isn't what you'd choose, but I hope you'll at least think about it. I've seen enough things happen at Bellamy Arts over the years, and I have a feeling this is going to get worse before it gets better."

As he finished, Dawn appeared behind him. "Cromwell."

He turned around. "We were just having a word."

"I see that," they said. "I'm here to bring Rat back to the dorms. You can tell Fairchild I'll be up to see her as soon as we're finished."

"Of course," he said, then turned back to Rat. "I'll be on campus for the rest of the day if you need anything."

"Right. I'll remember that." Rat offered a weak smile in return.

They weren't sure if he was genuinely being kind or if this was just a political game, but at least they had someone on their side. If they were expelled, the knight would be after them as soon as they were outside of the wards, and they would need a place to hide. Rat didn't need kindness right now. They needed allies.

Outside, the sky had deepened into the kind of crisp, perfect blue that could only mean a storm was on the way.

"Fairchild asked me to send someone back with you to the dorms," Dawn said, leading the way. "Ordinarily I'd just let you go, but after last night, it's better to be safe."

Rat rubbed their eyes. "Thanks."

They followed Dawn across the grass, the morning quiet of the campus settling around them.

"Dawn," they started.

Dawn glanced back at them.

"I just—how bad is it really?"

Dawn tipped their face up to the sky like they were looking for a better answer. "Bad," they said finally. "The school is still debating what to do. You put another student at risk."

"I didn't mean to—"

"Which some would argue is evidence of how ill-equipped you are to continue your studies here." Dawn let out a breath, and something in their face softened. "There's also the matter of your own safety. Between your history with the tower and the Holbrook Map turning up near the tunnels, there are broader concerns we need to account for. There's been talk of having you stay on at the Council Chambers until this all blows over."

"Right," they said, winded. "Evening mentioned that."

"He's offered to take you on. There's already been some discussion about setting you up with classes while you're there," Dawn said, but it sounded like an apology. "It would be more like an apprenticeship."

"Wait but—" Rat said. "I just . . . I thought it was still up for debate. It's happening, isn't it?"

"Nothing's official yet," Dawn said, but Rat could hear in their voice that it might as well be. "If it was up to Elise, you would have left with her as soon as you were found. Fairchild convinced her to give it another day to let the dust settle, but arrangements have already been discussed."

"But, I'd still have to agree to it. I'm an adult," Rat said, and then immediately realized that no one who was actually accustomed to being treated like an adult ever had to say those words. "Elise can't actually do that, can she?"

"Withdraw your admission? No. Not on her own," Dawn said. "But Fairchild could. Ordinarily, I haven't known her to bow to pressure, but she takes the safety of her students seriously. I can't imagine she'd allow you to stay on if she thought that you were in harm's way."

Everything inside of Rat sank. "How long do I have?"

"Tomorrow morning. Maybe until the end of the weekend so you have time to pack your things."

That wouldn't happen. When Rat had been withdrawn from High-gate, they hadn't even been allowed to say goodbye to anyone before the wards had gone up on the Evans House. Elise would take them off campus as soon as she could and have everything shipped to them later.

"Oh," Rat said, feeling small.

They couldn't even say that it was the wrong choice. Bellamy Arts wasn't safe for them. They hadn't even wanted to be there.

They weren't prepared for how much the thought of leaving stung.

They were quiet after that.

By the time they made it back to the dorms, the building had started to wake up and a handful of students were about. Rat said goodbye to Dawn and made their way through the lobby, trying to ignore everyone's flickering glances as they passed.

They ducked into the stairwell, determined to make it back without speaking to anyone, then stopped.

Jinx peered down from the landing above them, looking like she'd gotten about as much sleep as they had, her windbreaker draped over her shoulders.

She stared at them, stricken, and then her face steeled over like she didn't want an explanation for last night, after all.

Before Rat could think of something to say to her, she was already past them, cutting toward the lobby.

"Wait," they started, but she didn't turn back, and then they were alone on the stairs again. Something in them sank a little further.

Finally, with nowhere else to go, they started up the steps, and they didn't stop until they'd reached their room.

CHAPTER THIRTY-FOUR

AS SOON AS RAT MADE IT BACK, THEY COLLAPSED ONTO their bed.

Whatever mixture of guilt and adrenaline they'd been running on since the night before had finally run out, and the last twelve hours came crashing back down on them.

They should have realized the moment they first saw Harker on campus that they'd never be able to win. Even when they'd gotten the map away from him, he'd still come out a step ahead of them, and they'd somehow managed to make an enemy out of everyone at the school.

Rat thought how Jinx had looked at them, like they were someone she didn't know. They felt sick.

Their stomach knotted, and they realized that aside from half a croissant they'd managed to get down on their way to the Founder's House, they hadn't eaten since before the Whisper Ball.

Rat pushed themself to their feet and grabbed an energy bar from the box on their bookshelf. Then, unsure of what else to do, they pulled their cloak from the bedpost and rooted through the pockets. They gathered all the papers they'd managed to hold on to from Harker's room and dumped everything in a heap.

Aether dusted everything, though Rat wasn't sure anymore if it was from their own magic or Harker's. Scattered on their bed, the pile of papers looked almost like something Isola might leave them.

Rat shoved the thought away and reached for a sheet of notes.

A web of complicated lines wove across the page, like a chart of the stars in motion. It had to be a spell diagram, but Rat couldn't begin to guess at what it did.

"I get it, you're smart," they muttered. They crumpled the page and threw it back on the bed. Harker was welcome to bite them.

They reached for the next page and then stopped as they caught sight of one of their tower sketches mixed in with his papers.

They looked out the window at the hills. Unbidden, they thought of Isola the night she'd offered them her hand, the grass whispering around her in the always-dusk of the tower.

Would it be so bad? Something in them wondered. *Never coming back?*

If they went, she'd be waiting for them. They knew that, even now.

They could be awful and magnificent and *hers*. Maybe it wouldn't be awful at all.

Maybe they still wanted it, even if it was.

Rat shoved the thought away and dropped back onto the mattress, burying their face in their pillow.

"You gave me the last piece."

They'd been with Harker when he figured it out. They had all the same information. They should be able to solve this, but they felt further behind than they'd been before.

They lay like that for a long time, trying to hold the image of the Holbrook Map in their mind like somehow, if they thought about it for long enough, something would come to them.

But nothing did, and eventually, sleep pulled them under.

In their dreams, they were back at the tower, except this time, Harker was with them, and they were hiding in the bend of a ruined stairway, the steps weathered and dusted with rubble.

Footsteps echoed from somewhere above them.

"Come on." Rat took his sleeve. "We have to go."

They pulled him forward, but he didn't move.

"Rat," he said softly, close enough on the narrow landing that they could smell the familiar, struck-match scent of his magic. "I can't. You left me here."

Before they could argue, he tugged his arm away from them, and then the shadows of the stairwell closed over him.

Rat jolted awake.

They shoved themself upright, and then remembered they were still in their dorm room and still alone.

Unsteadily, Rat reached for their compass, and then realized they'd fallen asleep in their clothes. At some point while they were sleeping, it had gotten dark again, and the fall chill had crept back in through the walls.

You're fine, they thought, touching their fingers to the metal casing to ground themself. *You're here.*

The needle of their compass bobbed over north. Rat let out a staggered breath.

"Fuck," they said under their breath. They smudged their hand over their eyes and realized they were shaking.

They shoved the compass back into their pocket and grabbed their phone. Before they realized where they were going, they were halfway to the door.

Outside, the hall lights were already off, which meant it had to be even later than they'd thought. Their heart was still beating too hard as they made for the stairwell, but they didn't allow themself to stop until they'd reached the third floor.

When they knocked, they'd been half hoping, half afraid they'd get Jinx, but Agatha answered the door, wearing a long silk bathrobe that might actually have been a dress.

She looked them over, head to toe, and said, "Oh. You."

"I'm sorry. I know you don't want to see me, and I can explain everything," they said quickly. "I just need your help."

"More's the pity, I guess."

"Agatha."

She huffed and leaned into the doorframe. "Jinx isn't here. She doesn't want to talk to you and you should stop looking for her."

"But—"

"Good night, Rat."

She tried to close the door but Rat stopped it with their foot.

"Wait. Just—You said you'd tell me what happens the next time I asked. Agatha, what happens?"

She looked back at them, deeply unamused.

"Something bad is coming. I know you can feel it, too," they said in a rush. "I don't know what it looked like last night, but I wasn't the one who had the Holbrook Map. I found it in Harker's room. He was—"

Agatha let out a broken laugh. "Please. You think I care about some map?"

Rat shrunk back. "No. I just—I'm sorry, I . . ."

"No. You're not. What you are is a coward." The singsong lilt had gone out of her voice, and it was only now that Rat realized how put on it had always sounded. Her voice came out a sharp, scissor-blade rasp. "You know all your secrets come out at some point, don't you? I didn't have all the pieces, but I knew there was something. I kept telling myself it wouldn't go this way, but I've been *waiting* for this to happen." She looked up at them. "Do you actually have any friends, Evans, or is everyone a means to an end for you?"

"I didn't . . ."

"You're only here now because you need something," she said. "You wouldn't even be apologizing if I hadn't said no to you."

"I would have made things worse," they said, hating how small they sounded.

"Because I want you to leave, I'm not even going to dignify that with a response." She folded her arms. Her eyes slid over them again, her face stony. "Do you really want to know where this ends?"

"I . . ." Something in the way she looked at them made them wish they hadn't asked, but they'd come this far. It wasn't like Agatha could think any less of them. "Tell me."

She paused, considering. "No."

"But you said—"

"I changed my mind," she said. "I don't think I need to tell you. I think you already know."

"Agatha."

She touched their cheek. "Leave."

With that, she stepped back into the room and shut the door.

CHAPTER THIRTY-FIVE

RAT ENDED UP BACK ON THE WIDOW'S WALK, MAYBE because they always ended up there.

The darkened campus sprawled out below them, and the air already smelled faintly of rain, the clouds heavy overhead.

If Harker hadn't acted yet, he would soon.

They settled back against the door, letting themself slide to the ground. Even that night in the tunnels, they'd never asked him what Isola meant to do once she had her heart back.

Rat thought of the way she'd looked at them when they'd first found her in the field of grass, her eyes bright and cold in the tower's fading light.

It wouldn't matter if they let her have this. If they let her have everything. She would still come after them.

They knew her too well to think she'd ever actually let them go.

They rubbed their hand over their eyes. They needed a move, but they didn't have one.

They slid their phone out of their pocket and opened to their message thread with Harker. *She'll still destroy you, even if you find it for her,* they typed, and then, realizing he must have known that from the beginning, they deleted it.

Whatever you think you figured out, they started, and then deleted that.

You burning wreckage, I would have come for you.

They stared down at the screen for a long moment. Then, they deleted that, too, and put their phone down.

"Fuck," they muttered.

Behind them, someone knocked on the door.

Rat jumped.

"I know you're out there, Evans," Jinx called. "I can hear you cursing."

"Fuck," they said under their breath, a bit louder.

They shoved themself to their feet, their legs still stiff, and pulled the door open to find Jinx waiting on the other side in her windbreaker. All the air went out of their lungs.

Before they could get out a word, she brushed past them onto the roof. "I still haven't decided if we're on speaking terms yet."

Rat stared after her as she paced to the rails.

"What are you doing out here?" they said after a moment.

"I'm brooding on a rooftop," she said, her back to them.

"It's probably going to rain soon," they said weakly.

"Then I guess you're going to get wet." She traced her fingers through the air, drawing out the humidity as if to remind them that someone on the rooftop could weatherwork, and it wasn't them.

Without looking back, Jinx let the droplet splash down on the rails, and they lapsed into silence again.

Rat watched her across the distance, uncertain. "Jinx—"

"What really happened last night?"

"I . . ." Their voice stuck in their throat.

"I think Cromwell has more of the pieces than I do, but I don't want to make her explain it to me. I can't tell if she already knew it or not." Jinx folded her arms, her shoulders hunched. "Sometimes I think she lies about how much she's seen because she doesn't want to ruin things while they're good."

Rat was quiet.

A breeze blew across the rooftop, tugging at her curls.

"You had the Holbrook Map," Jinx said finally.

"I did," they said softly. "I found it in Harker's room."

"How long did you know he had it?"

"Since the night in the tunnels," Rat said, and then, because it felt like half a lie, "but I suspected before that. From the beginning."

Jinx was quiet, and they braced for her to ask them about their magic, or the tower, or what they'd done, but she just said, "Were you using us to get to him?"

"No," Rat said quickly, but that wasn't all true, either. "I mean, a little. At first."

She let out a breath. "God, I don't know why I care. It's not like I didn't want something from you, too."

"I am sorry. I . . . you don't have to forgive me." Rat sank back, hating how inadequate it sounded. They owed Jinx a dozen apologies, and probably a lifetime of never speaking to her again.

Jinx didn't respond.

Hesitantly, they paced to the railing. When she didn't shove them away, they settled beside her, as close as they dared. "I could tell you. All of it. If you really want to know."

She looked up at them, holding their gaze. "All of it."

Rat nodded, but when they opened their mouth, their voice caught.

She would hate them.

"What if I already knew about the tower?" they said before they could stop themself. "Before you told me?"

Beside them, Jinx went still. "What?" she breathed, something that was shock and anger and desperation all in one sliding into her voice.

Shame rolled over Rat in waves.

They folded their arms around themself. They couldn't meet her eyes. "What if I've seen it? What if I knew exactly what lived there?"

Something in Jinx's face softened. "Rat?"

"What if—"

"Hey. Breathe," she said, and Rat realized they were shaking. Their breath came in shallow gasps.

Their legs trembled. Before they could think about what they were doing, they sank to the ground, drawing their knees to their chest.

Jinx knelt down beside them. "You can tell me."

"You won't like it."

"I don't have to." Firmly, she laid her hand over theirs. She met their eyes, determined. "If you know something about the tower, I want to know."

They swallowed hard. "I don't know where to start."

"From the beginning. Start with the tower."

"Okay," they said, their voice hoarse. They were quiet for a long moment, collecting themself. "You were right about the Holbrook Map. I . . . my father was looking for the Ingrid Collection. I think he dealt with the tower a lot when he worked for the school. He did something called wayfinding. It's—" Rat reached for a way to explain, then remembered what Frey had told them. "It's a school of Higher Magic. It isn't used a lot anymore, but it's for moving between the planes. The tower is another world, but it's like . . . some places are closer together than others. It's far away in some ways, but it's also close to Bellamy Arts."

Slowly, Jinx nodded.

"I found it. In his notes first, I mean, and then, I actually found the tower itself." They hesitated. They could see the unspoken *How?* forming on Jinx's lips, but they didn't feel ready to answer that question yet, so they just said, "It was like you said. In the story."

"The Rook."

"Her name is Isola," Rat said softly.

Jinx watched them, waiting for them to go on.

"She knew him. My father. I think she wanted me to get her heart back, or—or maybe because that's just how she is." Rat's arms wound tighter around their knees. "Harker helped me with protection spells so she wouldn't find me, since I'm not very good at magic. That's how I know him."

"What happened?"

A fresh wave of shame broke over them. "He didn't tell you?"

She shook her head. "He wouldn't talk about it."

"My family found out about everything, and I didn't . . . he'd been in our archives, and Elise thought he was taking advantage of me. He got blamed for pretty much everything." They looked away, unable to say the rest. "Isola found him again after we stopped talking. She wanted to take him back with her, but he made a bargain instead."

Jinx's breath caught. "But he wouldn't—"

"Why did he tell you he was searching for the Ingrid Collection?"

She quieted.

"She put a binding spell on him," Rat said. "I don't know how it works, but he's sworn to her. I don't think he had a choice."

"Why wouldn't he tell me that?"

"I—"

"The story about Isola looking for her heart—she is, isn't she?" she said. "What if we found it first? All of us. If we could make sure that she never hurts anyone again?"

Rat hesitated.

"What?" she said.

"I don't think he'd let us," they said, feeling small. "He's convinced himself it's better this way, and I think he intends to see it through."

"But . . ." she started, and then, like she'd finally understood, hurt flickered across her face. "And then what? Once he finds it and gives it back to her, what happens?"

"Then I guess," they said, "he'll have outlasted his usefulness, and she'll tear through whatever defenses are left and find me."

For a long moment, neither one said anything. Another gust of wind blew in, stronger than the last and heavy with the smell of rain.

Finally, Jinx said, "That won't happen," and they badly wanted to believe her, maybe because they'd been telling themself the same thing for weeks. "You said he had the Holbrook Map. Has he been working on it the whole year?"

"I think so."

"And I gave him my notes on the tunnels. Fuck." Jinx tensed. "The War Room—was he . . ."

"That wasn't him," Rat said. "There's someone else. I don't know who, but they're the one who drew the sigils in the tunnel in the east woods. They must have thought one of us had the map, or maybe they knew Harker had it and thought he'd hidden it there. It was my first guess, too."

"And, at the Whisper Ball?"

"You saw the summoning spell," Rat said, understanding.

"Agatha and I found it. That's why we went to look for you."

They sighed. "I'm not sure how much of a difference it makes, anyway. Harker's already figured it out."

"The Ingrid Collection," Jinx said, understanding. "You think . . ."

"He knows where it is. He said I gave him the answer, but . . ." Rat leaned forward, resting their chin on their knees. "I feel like I'm so close to getting it, but I only had the map for a few minutes. It's back with Fairchild now."

"But it's technically yours," Jinx said.

"I don't think the school would let me have it. Besides, Harker's probably halfway there already."

"We're not letting this happen," Jinx said. "There has to be something else. We need . . ."

Rat looked up at her through their fingers. Her eyes traveled over them like she was trying to decide something.

"What?" they asked.

"There's still one thing you haven't told me." She closed her eyes. "I'm going to ask you something. You can say no, and I'll never ask you again. But I still need to ask."

There was a catch in her voice that Rat didn't like. "Ask me."

"That night, when you ended up alone in the tunnels," Jinx said. "You went back up to the roof after we left the War Room."

"I did."

"But there isn't a way from the widow's walk back into the tunnels without passing my room."

Rat hesitated. "There isn't." Their voice barely came out a whisper.

"I would have heard you. You never came back through."

A drop of rain splattered on the ground by Rat's shoe, and a gust of wind blew in from the campus, cold and damp.

They took a staggering breath. It shouldn't have mattered if Jinx knew this, too, or what she thought about them now. As soon as they left the roof, whatever this was would end, and she wouldn't want to speak with them anymore. They'd probably never even see her again.

"I didn't," they said. They wanted to say more, except, they didn't know where to start.

Jinx was quiet for a long moment, but they couldn't meet her eyes to figure out what kind of silence it was.

"I'm going to show you two things," she said finally. She held her hand out, but all Rat could do was stare at her. "Promise you won't hate me."

Jinx pulled Rat to their feet, and as soon as she touched them, whatever working she'd been using to keep the weather off slipped over them, too. The rain speckled the sidewalk around them as they followed after her across the widow's walk.

When Jinx got to the rail, she leaned out and pointed across the building to a bay window on the other side of the courtyard. "See the one with the light on?"

"It's yours, isn't it?"

"I wasn't sleeping that well when I first got here. If I was up early in the morning, I'd sit in the window and catch up on reading. But sometimes I'd look up, and every time I did, there would be this light out on the roof."

Rat swallowed the tightness in their throat. "What does this have to do with my powers?"

"I lied when I said I hadn't tried to come up here," Jinx said, pulling them away from the railing. "Except—" She stopped in front of the door and took the handle. It rattled and stuck. "This door locks."

Rat sniffled, then laughed. "No it doesn't." Jinx raised her eyebrows and they nudged her out of the way. They turned the knob, and it twisted smoothly one way, then the other. "It's literally always open. You just came up here."

"After you let me out," she said. "Move."

They stepped back. "I don't know what you think my powers are, but that door doesn't lock."

Again, she turned the doorknob.

Again, it rattled and stuck.

"It doesn't lock *for you*," she said. "Like that service passage. Impressive sketches, by the way, especially since you drew them before I took you inside."

Rat shoved their rain-damp bangs out of their eyes. "Yeah, because that door never actually locked. You were the one who said it didn't work."

She studied them. "When's the last time you came across a door you couldn't open?"

"What kind of question is that?" They took the doorknob from her. "I run into closed doors all the time. Literally every other door in this building is probably locked right now."

"Did you ever try to go through any of them?"

"Why would I do that? They're locked—" Rat ground their heel into the rain-slicked boards. "That's a bad example! You can't—"

Jinx pushed their hand off the doorknob. Pointedly, she tried to turn it.

It stuck.

"You don't get it. That's not what I do," Rat said, frustrated. Their chest tightened. "I see . . . I think of them as dead passages. I'm surrounded by hallways that no one else can see, and there could be terrible things waiting at the end of any one of them. I've spent so long avoiding them that I barely have any control over it anymore. Half the time I'm scared I'll wander off the map or—or let something through by accident, and the rest I'm afraid that I—" They broke off.

That I'll go looking for something on purpose.

"Rat?"

"I don't want it," they said, the words tumbling out in a panicked wave. "I just want all of this to stop so I can take over my family's archives like I'm supposed to, without everyone trying to figure out what I am or, or if there's secretly something wrong with me. I'm so tired of it, and so sick of being scared all the time, and I just want it to go away."

Across from them, Jinx had gotten quiet again.

"And—and I want to never do magic again, and I want to be cis."

Jinx frowned, but something in her face had softened. "Do you really want that?"

"No," they said, just above a whisper. "I just feel like I'm drowning all the time."

Deep down, they wanted all of it—their powers, and the keys to the Holbrook Archives, and every horrible secret they'd never asked for, even if there were monsters around every corner. They wanted to *be* monstrous, to make themself so powerful that nothing would ever touch them again and no one would be able to pretend they were anything other than what they were.

A damp wind blew across the widow's walk.

"Last night, at the Whisper Ball," Jinx said slowly. "It's not me, is it?"

"I . . ." Something in Rat's chest sank. "I'm really sorry."

Jinx exhaled deeply. "Don't be. I had a feeling. I think I just needed to be sure."

She settled heavily against the railing, her shoulders drawn up. Rat opened their mouth to say something, but they didn't know how to make this better. Uselessly, they closed it again.

"To be honest, a part of me already knew," Jinx said. "I just . . . I don't know. I've been accused of getting swept up in things. I think I didn't want to admit it to myself." She gave them a small, half-hearted smile. "I've seen the way you look at him. You followed me into the tunnels for a reason, and I think we both know I'm not it."

Their face heated. "What? No," they sputtered. "It's not like that."

She gave them a pointed look, and they realized she hadn't even needed to say who she'd meant.

"Jinx. No. He's literally the worst person I know. He's mean, and like actually my sworn enemy, and he lights things on fire!"

"Rat," she said.

"He hates me." Their voice came out small and ragged.

Rat thought about the way Harker had looked at them in the woods, desperate and crumbling and furious they'd seen him that way.

A dull ache settled in their chest. He should hate them. They didn't have a right to want anything else.

They folded their arms around themself. "Please don't make me say it out loud."

Jinx put her hand on their shoulder.

Rat curled in on themself. They hated that this couldn't be simple, and they hated that Jinx was somehow still trying to make them feel better when she probably felt just as badly as they did.

"I'm sorry," they said again. "You deserve someone who'd choose you without a second thought. It shouldn't even be a question."

"I am pretty great," she said with a sigh. "It's a shame though. We would have looked really good together."

They sniffled. "I know. I'm honestly kind of mad about it."

"God, my siblings would have lost it if I brought home an Evans. Absolute power-couple material. We could have literally taken over New York." She huffed a breath. "I just can't believe I lost to *Blakely*. God, Cromwell is never going to let me live this down."

Rat let out a weak laugh. "Shut up."

"Is it the way he scowls at you, or the hoard of overdue library books?"

"Shut *up*," they said again, laughing. "I don't like him."

Jinx raised her eyebrows, and Rat felt like they were sinking all over again. It didn't even matter what they felt. Harker was the tower's now, and Rat would probably be gone from the school as soon as the sun came up.

"Hey," Jinx said softly, nudging their arm. "He's my friend, too. We'll get him back."

They swallowed hard and nodded, because they weren't about to start crying again.

Rain pattered down on the widow's walk. At some point, it had built to a steady drizzle; the campus below them looked like paper cutouts rising out of the fog.

Jinx looked up at the sky. "Okay. So what's next?"

Rat sighed. "I don't know. I don't have the Holbrook Map anymore and Harker could be anywhere."

"If you had the map, do you think you could figure it out?"

"Maybe. But Fairchild's keeping it in her office, and unless . . ."

They looked back as they realized that Jinx was watching them. "Unless?"

Before they could answer that, thunder rolled in the distance.

Jinx glanced up again. "I think it's time to get off the roof. We can finish talking inside. I still have your sketchbook in my room."

"I can't ask you to—"

"You didn't have to," she said. "I'm in."

Rat looked out at the campus one last time and then nodded. "There's one more thing I need to do. I'll meet you there."

CHAPTER THIRTY-SIX

THE RAIN PICKED UP AFTER JINX LEFT. RAT STAYED ON the stairs a moment, trying to gather themself.

They already knew where the Holbrook Map was. It was theirs by right, and their powers had gotten them through locked doors and protection spells before.

Harker might have solved it first, but they could still get ahead of him and end this game.

They could find Isola's heart, maybe to slay her or maybe just to keep.

A shiver ran through them, but it wasn't from fear.

They wanted to take something from her. They wanted to kick up the tall grass and turn the battlements to rubble. They didn't even want to win. They just wanted Isola to lose.

It terrified them to put words to it.

They let out a breath. Steeling themself, they slid their phone from their pocket and swiped back to their message thread with Will.

A dozen new messages from the night before had appeared at the bottom of the chain, probably sent while he'd been combing the woods for them.

I'm sorry, they typed. *I know that you don't want to hear from me, but*

Rat stared down at the screen. They moved to delete it, then realized that their hands were shaking.

They tightened their grip, grounding themself.

They owed Will at least this much.

You're one of my best friends and I was scared and I shouldn't have kept you in the dark, they started, feeling their way through the story, the chain of events still sharp in their mind from explaining it to Jinx.

Their fingers skated over the screen as they typed out the rest, sending each message as they went.

When Rat finished, they pressed their lips to the top of their phone. "Whatever you do, please be safe," they breathed.

As they drew back, a small *read* appeared on the screen.

Their chest knotted, but they'd taken too long already. They watched the screen for a moment, anyways, but there was no response.

Finally, Rat slid their phone back into their pocket and headed down the stairs.

Before they went to find Jinx, Rat snuck back to their room for their things. They grabbed their sketchbook from the bed and a fresh pack of chalk from the desk in case they needed it.

Rat took a few of the spell diagrams they'd stolen from Harker for good measure, too, then stopped as they caught sight of his bracelet, left out on their bedside table.

He was still bound to the tower. If he lost and Isola was left standing at the end of the night, he would be punished for it.

They closed their hand over the bracelet, running their thumb along the pitted leather.

Ingrid had stolen from the tower once, and it had taken her seven years.

They couldn't help him right now. Not while he was still a danger to everyone else. They needed to fix this first, before they could come back for him.

As soon as I can, they promised themself.

Rat set the bracelet back down and finished throwing everything they needed into a backpack.

Then they went to the closet and took down Jinx's leather jacket. Neatly, they folded it over their arm and stepped out into the darkened hall.

Rat knocked on Jinx's door, even though they knew she was waiting for them.

Inside, they heard her get up off her bed. She padded across the room, and then the lock clicked.

"For all the difference it makes," she said, letting them in. She tilted her head toward the leather jacket. "Are we going somewhere? I thought you said we didn't have a plan."

"We might have a plan," they said, handing it back to her.

Her eyes glinted. "Talk."

Rat started to speak as she pushed the door shut behind them, then stopped.

Agatha sat cross-legged on her bed, her head propped in her hands. She'd changed out of her robe into a dark, long-sleeved dress, and her hair was braided back.

She looked up at Rat, impassive, then stretched. "I'm on my way out. I have business to attend to elsewhere."

"Wait," Rat said. "I should—I'm sorry. Again. Has Jinx told you—"

"She's caught up on what matters," Jinx said.

"Honestly, it's disgusting how surprised I was," Agatha said. She pushed herself off the bed and slid her feet into her hiking boots. "You can consider this a cease-fire between us, at least until this has all been sorted out. But right now, I'm off to find a certain friend of ours before anyone else comes to harm."

"You're not seriously going to fight Harker, are you?" Rat asked.

Agatha grabbed her coat from the bedpost. "That boy died thirty minutes ago, dear," she said, draping it over her shoulders. "He just doesn't know it yet."

With a toss of her braid, Agatha picked up a lantern and headed out.

"Cromwell isn't going to confront him yet," Jinx said, once the door clicked shut. "She's just hoping she can get a lead on his plans."

"No, that's good," Rat said quickly. "We need to keep Harker from moving. If he finds the Ingrid Collection while we're distracted, we still lose. And, if it comes to a fight, then, okay."

Jinx gave them a long, appraising look. "You know, he refused to say a word about your magic. At one point he tried to tell me you were so embarrassingly bad that you just pretended you couldn't cast. Even after I knew it was garbage, he kept insisting."

"What?" Their pulse skipped. "Why would he do that?"

"You tell me." She dropped onto the floor, draping her jacket over her shoulders. Printouts and maps were spread across the floorboards in front of her. "I'm not going to pretend I understand what's going on between you two, but if you need to sit that part out, I'm not going to ask you to fight him."

"It's fine," Rat said. "Whatever he's playing at, he stopped pulling his punches a while ago. Nothing changes the fact that we still need to stop him." They squared their shoulders and sat down on the floor across from Jinx. "Anyways. You haven't even heard the plan yet."

"So, there is a plan?"

"Well, half of one," Rat said. "Hypothetically, how do you feel about breaking into the Founder's House?"

Mischief tugged at the corner of her mouth. "Go on."

Over the steady patter of the rain, Rat began.

CHAPTER THIRTY-SEVEN

THEY MADE THEIR WAY BACK THROUGH THE LOBBY OF Mallory Hall sometime after the clock struck.

It was already past midnight, and the empty couches and unused chairs seemed even more deserted than they had during the day, the quiet heavier around them.

Jinx made her way toward the entrance, her footsteps soft in spite of her boots. The gray storm light caught on her leather jacket as she stopped to wait for Rat, the rain coming down hard on the other side of the doors.

Rat hurried to keep pace. This needed to be quick.

Their fingers brushed their compass and they tried not to think about what would happen once they had the Holbrook Map.

Ahead of them, Jinx shouldered the front door open and waved them through.

Rat stepped out over the threshold, and cold rain poured down on them.

"You really need a better coat, Evans," Jinx said, catching them by the sleeve. She extended her working to cover them as she started down the pathway, rain beating down on the gravel all around her.

Rat followed after her between the darkened buildings, the wind blowing leaves around them, thick with the smell of frost and mulch.

"Left at the fork," they told her, before she could point out how they owned two archives and zero of their own jackets. "Toward Galison Hall."

Her hand tightened on their sleeve, and she turned, pulling them up the path.

All of the lights in the Historic Founder's House were off, but the door wards had been left down.

Jinx rattled the doorknob. "This one's you."

"God. That's never going to be normal," they said, pulling it open.

She started past them, but they stopped her.

"Wait," they said. They drew in a breath. "I've pretty much been expelled already, but you could still get in trouble. If anything happens, you have to run."

"I'm not ditching you."

"Jinx—" they caught her sleeve as she pulled ahead of them, and a note of desperation crept into their voice.

She turned back to them, and they realized how hard their heart was beating. This whole thing was their fault. Jinx couldn't get caught because of them.

Her face softened. "I'll leave at the first sign of danger," she said. "I promise."

Rat stepped over the threshold, leading her into the deserted lobby. A gust of wind howled past outside, but all around them, the darkened halls of the Founder's House were perfectly still.

Ducking their head, they motioned for Jinx to follow them up the stairs, and then toward the office.

They pressed their hand flat against the door. No light seeped under the cracks. No sound came from behind it.

Rat took a deep breath and turned the knob. Smoothly, the door opened.

The office was exactly as it had been before. Books and papers cluttered the desk in orderly stacks, and the extra chairs had been lined neatly against the wall.

"The map was in one of the drawers," Rat said, circling behind the desk. "I just need to figure out which one." They started at the top.

Office supplies.

As they pushed the first drawer shut, Jinx cast a searching look over the desk.

They tried the next drawer, but it was more of the same.

Rat moved to the last one, revealing a row of neat files. They skimmed their thumb along the tops of the folders, but there was nothing there.

Jinx craned her neck. "No?"

Rat opened the drawer above it again. They took out a stack of papers, but there wasn't anything underneath it. They slid it shut and went back to the first one. "It has to be here. I saw it a few hours ago."

Or it could have been back in the library already, shut away somewhere deep in the building. Fairchild could have sent it back to the Council of Chambers.

"Fuck," they breathed.

And then, in the dark, they caught a glint of aether.

"What?" Jinx asked as they went still, and Rat remembered she couldn't see it.

The same uncanny feeling they'd gotten in Harker's room when they found the mirror came over them. Like there was something there that shouldn't be.

"Here," they said.

"Here?"

They glanced back at Jinx. "It is here. It's just . . ." they trailed off, suddenly less sure of what they were about to do. She gave them the smallest of nods.

Rat exhaled deeply.

They reached for their magic, and the woods flickered through their mind.

Not like last time, they told themself.

Their chest tightened as the edges of the world came into focus, and then, before they could release the spell, the subtle offness of the desk caught them.

Rat reached back into the drawer, where they knew that the map would be, and they felt the world give just a little, like reaching through a gap.

Their hand closed around the map, and they drew it out.

The original holder was gone now, replaced by a plain aluminum document tube that must have been sent over from the school's archives. They looked up at Jinx, who was staring down at the map with a look of open wonder.

"This is really it," she said half to herself, and Rat remembered she'd grown up on stories about this. The Holbrook Map was half a legend to her, and now it was here.

She dropped down on the carpet next to them as they slid the map free and unrolled it on the floor.

Rat drew in a breath and traced their finger over the paper, letting their magic rise to the map's spellwork as they did.

Ink seeped across the page, forming into the familiar shape of the Founder's House.

"That's us," Jinx said, then looked at them. "Did you . . ."

They nodded and turned back to the map, willing it to shift.

Slowly, it changed in front of them. The campus, both new and old. The hills. A pathway twisting through miles of woods.

"How many are there?" Jinx asked.

"I don't know. It might literally go on forever," they said. "I'm not sure how it works. There's a route, but as far as I can tell it doesn't start anywhere and it doesn't have an ending," Rat said, tracing their finger along the page, the map rearranging itself as they did. "I don't even know if it connects."

It pulled at them. These maps had all been drawn for someone like them. Rat had tracked across whole worlds without even meaning to. They should have been able to piece it together.

Harker had solved it already.

"What if it isn't?" Jinx asked.

Rat looked up to see her studying the map, her brow furrowed.

"A route, I mean. What if this line is something else?" She touched her fingers to the page. "Can you show me the campus again?"

"There's no path there. Maybe . . ." They stared down as the campus etched itself across the page, sprawling out from the clock tower.

All of the hairs on the back of their neck stood up as it clicked. "It's the wards."

Jinx looked up.

"My father was mapping the wards. That's what the line is. Not the main wards, but the old ones, the ones that keep the school away from the tower. Maybe from all other planes," they said. "When I was with Harker last night, I accidentally took us somewhere else, to the edge of the grounds. That's what he must have seen."

"Why, though?" Jinx asked. "What does that have to do with the collection?"

Rat brushed their thumb over the clock tower, and the map shifted again, a wide, circular room forming around the center of the map. They stared down at it for a moment before they realized they were looking at the only building on campus they hadn't been able to set foot in.

A net of interlocking lines wove over the map before they curved off the page.

They were looking at the inside of clock tower.

Not just the clock tower, they thought. They were looking at the seal, where the wards came together.

Outside, the clock struck the hour.

Then again. And again.

The strangeness of it brought Rat up short before they could answer Jinx. They'd left after midnight, but it couldn't have been later than one o'clock.

"Shouldn't it . . ." they started.

The clock chimed again.

And again.

And again.

Jinx tensed beside them. "What's happening?" she asked, over the sound of the bells.

"I don't know . . . I never—"

Jinx went to the window and pushed back the heavy curtains. Outside, the shape of the clock tower rose against the sky, jutting over the rooftops. Beneath it, the rest of the campus was dark. Rain came down in sheets.

Dull and clanging, the bells tolled on.

Rat traded glances with Jinx, but she shook her head like she didn't have an answer.

Harker, they thought.

Quickly, they rolled up the map and slid it back into the metal tube.

They scrambled to their feet as Jinx started toward the doors. "Come on," she said under her breath.

She shouldered through the doors and shot toward the stairs. Rat followed after her, careening down the dark, narrow hallway of the Founder's House, the toll of the bells still crashing around them.

As they bounded onto the top steps, glass shattered on the floor below.

Jinx stopped, and Rat came up short behind her, barely catching themself.

"Jinx."

"Shh." She went very, very still.

Below them, something scuttled over the floor.

A dull thud sounded at the bottom of the stairs. Then a hiss.

Rat's breath came in short, shallow waves. They knew that sound.

Jinx pulled on their arm as a terror appeared around the bend in the stairs, antennae sweeping the ground before it. Its body rippled as it slinked over the landing, a second one close behind.

"Shit," Jinx said, tugging Rat around. They stumbled as she launched herself back up the steps.

Jinx's momentum carried her up into the hallway, away from Rat. She spun around, but the terrors were close. The handful of steps between her and Rat might as well have been a mile.

Rat scrambled back to their feet, but they knew they wouldn't be fast enough.

They raised their hand to cast. Their magic flared in their core, rising to meet them, and they tasted metal.

Their mind flickered back to Harker in the woods, with his arm wrenched back and the forest gone strange around them.

Panic crashed over them, and the spell slipped away. Uselessly, they cut their hand through the air as the terror closed in on them.

A line of water snapped through the air, slashing over their head.

Before Rat could move, the terror behind them curved up onto the wall. They flinched as it scurried by, so close that they could have reached out and touched the chitinous plates of its back.

It snaked past them. Toward Jinx.

She traced her fingers through the damp air, and a wall of water crashed down in front of her, stopping the terror in its tracks.

"Rat! Go!" Jinx shouted, her hand already raised to cast again.

The look on her face was a warning, and something in their chest clenched.

"Get back to the office!" they shouted to her.

Behind her, the terror reared back, hissing.

"*Stay!*" Their hand sliced the air before they could think about what they were doing, and the spell spilled out of them in a panicked burst.

The terror jerked to a stop. Its antennae flicked the air, and then the spell gave way as Jinx shot past it, back toward the office.

The terror whipped after her as she threw herself over the threshold and shoved the heavy wooden door shut.

With a resounding thud, the terror crashed against the door. It glanced off and then turned toward Rat, hissing.

Rat grabbed the railing and shot up the stairs. At the landing, they scampered around the bend, onto the next flight. Their sneakers pounded on the steps as they ran.

The terror bolted after them. Rat glanced back to see another one scuttling up the stairs behind it and hauled themself around the next bend.

You know this place, they told themself. They'd drawn floor plans and studied maps of this building. They'd marked all the windows and counted the doorways.

They charged off the steps, onto the third floor. With the terrors close at their heels, Rat shouldered through a half-open door, into a storage room full of boxes and filing cabinets.

As they slammed the door shut behind them, they caught a last glimpse of the terrors, their segmented bodies glinting faintly against the dark, armored in swatches of sky.

Rat scrambled over a stack of cardboard boxes, toward a smaller door in the back, painted to blend into the wall. If they hadn't mapped the building, they would have taken it for a closet. But when they nudged a box out of the way and pushed the panel open, they found a narrow staircase, barely wide enough for a single person.

Out in the hall, one of the terrors made a rattling hiss.

Rat pulled the door to the service staircase shut, and darkness rushed in around them.

CHAPTER THIRTY-EIGHT

THE STAIRS LED UP TO A CRAWL SPACE WITH A LOW, SLOP-
ing ceiling. Aside from the glow of Rat's phone, the only light came from
a single round window at the back of the room, half hidden in the clutter.

Rain pounded on the roof as Rat dropped down among the stacks of
boxes and old furniture, breathing hard. They hadn't been able to map all
of the service passages of the Founder's House, but if they guessed cor-
rectly, there would be another staircase down, somewhere in the clutter.
Craning their neck, they swept their gaze around the room.

"Rat?" a voice whispered in the dark.

They whipped around.

A few feet away, Jinx sat on an antique fainting couch, her boots
pulled up on the faded upholstery.

"Jinx. You're here. How—" Rat started. Her mouth pulled into a grin.
"You found it."

"The wall panel, behind Fairchild's desk," Jinx said as she slid down to
join them on the floor. "You know, I always wanted to know where that
door led, but I was kind of imagining different circumstances."

"I wasn't sure if you'd try to escape the building, once the terrors
were gone."

"There are more of them." The humor went out of her voice. "I just
got a message from Cromwell, and they're all over campus. She's headed
our way."

"Did she find Harker?"

"Rat—"

"He's up to something. We need to find him before—"

"She did."

Rat came up short.

"Cromwell found him right after we left," she said. "This wasn't him."

"But . . ."

Silence stretched between them, and for a long moment, there was nothing but the steady sound of the rain.

"The boot print," Jinx said softly.

All over again, Rat thought of the War Room, and the summoning spell, and the possibility that there was someone much more dangerous out there.

"And now that the Holbrook Map is here and . . ." they started.

"And we have it," Jinx said, looking back at them.

"They're going to come after us, aren't they? Jinx—"

Lightly, she put her hand on their shoulder. "You said you can find passages, right?"

Their pulse jumped. This wasn't like opening a drawer or throwing a wisp of power at one of the terrors. "I—I wasn't trying then. I can't—"

"Can you try now?"

If Rat said no, they already knew she wouldn't push. They thought of Harker in the tunnels, telling them to open a passageway, but they hadn't had time to think then, and he already knew their powers almost as well as they did.

"Okay," Rat said, so softly that they weren't certain they'd spoken at all.

They shut their eyes and drew in a breath.

The world around them unhinged, just a little, and for a moment they could feel the shape of the Founder's House spread out below them, and all of the strange halfway spaces between.

Electricity prickled under their skin. It felt dangerous, and it felt like home.

Before they could stop themself, they took Jinx by the wrist. "This way," they said, pulling her forward.

Half hidden among the old furniture, Rat caught sight of the second stairway, not as far as they'd thought. Quickly, they slipped down the narrow path between a pair of armchairs and climbed onto the steps.

"Wait," Jinx said. "Are we going back through Fairchild's office?"

"I—" Rat opened their mouth to explain the route, but they couldn't. They'd never been able to explain it to Harker, either, no matter how hard they'd tried. "Yes. We are."

They half expected her to argue, but instead, her mouth pulled. "Lead the way, Evans," she said, following them onto the steps.

At some point, the bells had stopped, though Rat couldn't say when. There was no sound but the rain.

They slowed as they let themself back out into the office. Jinx tipped her head toward the door, a question on her face.

They paused, listening for the terrors, but there was nothing. The quiet pricked at them.

All at once, Rat realized where they were going. There were shortcuts through the building, where they could sense the path to the door pinching in on itself, but that wasn't what had pulled them.

They'd been searching for a route without terrors, but they were just retracing their steps toward the main staircase.

All around them, the building had turned eerily still.

Jinx's brow knit together, like she'd noticed, too.

"Just stay close to me," they whispered. "Okay?"

"Right behind you." She curled her fingers through the air. Drops of water drifted into orbit, condensing over her fingertips.

Rat crept across the room. They stopped, one hand to the door.

A low creak came from the floorboards, somewhere out in the hall.

Then silence.

Rat took a deep breath. Either they were doing this, or they weren't. They pushed the door open and froze.

On the other side stood Evening, a lantern in one hand, the other raised in what Rat guessed had to be a protection spell. Aether dusted his gloves, and the scent of magic clung to him, the air in the hallway suddenly cool.

"Rat," Evening said, looking down at them. "How did you get here?"

His eyes went to the map, and they realized they were still clutching it. Rat pulled it to their chest. "I . . . it's mine by right."

Evening let out a breath. "We can sort that out later. Everyone is looking for you. Is it just you here?"

Rat opened their mouth to answer, and then stopped as they realized Jinx hadn't come out. They wanted to tell her that Evening was on their side, or could at least get them safely out of the building, but if she showed herself, then the night was over for her. There would be no one left to stop this.

Something twinged in their chest. They knew Jinx too well to think she would ever agree to that.

They nodded. "It's just me."

"Good," he said, taking them by the shoulder. "You need to come with me. The other students have already been evacuated to Galison Hall, but we need to get you off campus."

Rat drew themself up, blocking the doorway. "Wait—but—"

"We're doing everything we can." Evening traced a spell on the air, which might have been another protection working. "There's a travel spell waiting to get you back to the Council Chambers. I'll explain on the way, but we have to go. It isn't safe for you here."

Panic kicked in their ribs. If they left campus with him now, they'd never be allowed back. Elise would make sure of it.

Evening pulled them forward. "Quickly, Rat."

They tugged away from him. "I'm not going anywhere."

The door swung inward as Rat stumbled back into it. Their heart dropped. *Jinx.*

They fought the urge to look back.

Coolly, Evening swept the surroundings, surveying the mess of the desk, the papers on the floor, the open drawers. Rat followed his gaze. Behind them, the wall panel had closed again.

They were alone.

Rat backed into the room. All over again, they remembered what Agatha had said about him collecting people—wanting to collect them—and they realized this would cost them.

But if it bought them a few more hours on campus and a clear way out of the building for Jinx, they'd pay it.

"I'm not leaving," Rat said again. "I . . . you were right about the tower finding its way onto campus. She's sending someone after the Ingrid Collection. There's a path through the clock tower, and I know that I can get there first, but I need you to let me go." They forced themself to hold his gaze. "I'm asking you as my family's ally."

"I don't think Elise would forgive me for that."

"Then I'm asking as a Holbrook."

Evening sharpened and considered them. All over again, Rat fought the urge to shrink back as they realized how they must look to him.

They leveled their gaze at him. "There's someone else searching for the Holbrook Map now. It's the same person who cast the summoning spell. If you let me go, you could still catch them," Rat said, fighting to keep their voice even. "They've been accessing the tunnels under the school through a door in the east woods, and I think that they were in the search party last night. That had to be what interrupted their casting. It's going to be someone who's . . ."

Rat stopped a moment before the words left their mouth.

Someone who's close to the case.

Someone who knew them and knew Agatha's powers.

Someone who'd been trying to get ahold of the Holbrook Map.

A kind of cold amusement flickered across his face as he saw them put it together.

"You know, I think it's quite admirable, you taking things into your own hands," he said, stepping deeper into the room. "Dangerous, surely. But admirable."

Something in his voice sent a shiver down their back. "Why were you here?"

"Quick, but not quick enough," Evening said, considering them. "You really are your father's child."

Their eyes flickered to the dark stretch of hallway behind him, but before they could decide whether or not to run for it, he paced past them to the desk. Effortlessly, he traced another sign on the air and the door slammed shut.

"Let's speak like adults," he said, leaning against the desk. "Right now, the campus is overrun with creatures. Fairchild will have no choice but to withdraw you, if Elise doesn't see to it herself. Even if you run, by the time the sun comes up, your safety will be entrusted to the Council of Hours, and the Holbrook Map will be collected as evidence."

Their stomach dropped. "Why are you doing this?"

He regarded them coolly. "Why don't you tell me?"

"I don't know," they said.

Except, they did. There wasn't anything else.

"I'm sure you'll understand more than most, Rat, that some things are better left unsolved."

"The Ingrid Collection," they said. "That's why you took my case last year, isn't it? To get close to me and Elise. And the investigation, when the map went missing."

They waited for him to stop them, but he didn't.

"And the tunnels. You went through our things," they said,

remembering the state of the War Room. They suppressed a shiver. He hadn't bothered to hide his work. He'd wanted them to know they weren't alone in the sunken campus. "And it was you, at the Whisper Ball. The summoning spells were yours. But . . ."

He gave them a knowing look.

"It was going to look like an attack from the tower, wasn't it? When I didn't leave the school on my own, Elise would have to pull me out."

"But then," he said, "you and your friend beat me to it. I couldn't have asked for a better reason if I'd tried."

Blood pounded in their ears. "But our families are allies. My father—" they started, and then realized how weak it sounded.

Evening's mouth tugged into a small, cruel smile. "You still have no idea how this works, do you?"

They fought the urge to shrink back.

"Alexander was always too softhearted for this world, too," he said. "You know, he planned to dismantle the Ingrid Collection one day, before he decided it was safer left hidden. It's a shame he was the last heir to the Holbrook line. He was never cut out for it." Evening tilted his head. "Though, I suppose he served his purpose in the end."

Rat forced themself to hold his gaze. "You won't find it."

"You don't really believe that," he said. "I've been at this for a very long time, Rat. Maybe no one has managed to recover it before, but look around you. Things have already changed."

As much as they hated it, they knew that he was right. Everything was already in motion. Others might have tried in the past, but the game was different now, because they were on the board. Because Harker was, too.

This wouldn't be like the other times.

This time, one way or another, it would end.

"In fact, I already have the location," he said, tracing another spell on the air. Before Rat could stop it, the map flew out of their grasp and landed in his open palm. "There's a theory about the old campus, you know. In most versions of the story, Ingrid sank it to hide the collection, but some think the school was swallowed up by the spell that made the wards. I've heard that it was recklessness, but I always wondered if the school was just another cost of the working. Her life and her life's work, traded away to keep the real entrance sealed." His mouth curved. "I'd long suspected there might be a way through the clock tower. Fairchild all but confirmed it for the investigation, and clearly, you've drawn the same conclusion."

"You—"

"I was hoping to wait until I had your cooperation, but I don't see the point now," he said, turning the map in his hands. "The collection is in a pocket of the campus, one that Ingrid sealed from both sides when she put up the school's wards." He glanced up at them. "It's clever, really. Impossible to reach from outside the school's grounds. Impossible to reach from within."

"But she left a way through, didn't she?" Rat said. "That's what you were looking for."

He gave them a small, strange smile that they couldn't read. "In a sense."

They suppressed a shiver. "And you think I can get you there."

"I'd hoped you'd come willingly, but I guess this will have to do." His eyes glinted as his hand tightened around the map. "Here's what's going to happen. You're going to open the way. Then, after tonight, you'll take a position as an apprentice at the Council of Hours, where we'll leverage tonight's attack to establish a presence on campus and work to recover the collection—for safekeeping, naturally. Maybe eventually, you'll even be allowed to resume your studies here."

"You can't do that," Rat said.

"As far as I'm concerned, I already have," he said. "This doesn't have to be a bad thing. You jump at your own shadow, but you have an extraordinary gift. If anything, people should be afraid of you." His voice was slick like oiled steel. "Think of it as an opportunity."

Rat edged back. "And—and, if I say no?"

"Of course. You're going back to the Council Chambers regardless, but it's your choice whether you'll be spending that time as a prisoner or a guest," he said, raising an eyebrow. "I suppose it's also your choice who else will return with you. Did you know, we already have a suspect for tonight's attack?"

Dread slithered through them.

"I think you know him, actually. I have to admit, I was surprised you didn't turn him in sooner."

"Leave Harker out of this," Rat said, their throat tight.

"It always struck me as an oversight that he was allowed into a place like this with his lack of standing. I wouldn't be surprised if there was a case to seal his powers altogether."

"You can't—"

Evening tipped his head. "Then again, since he's obviously the tower's now, I wonder if she'll call him back before the Council can bring him in."

"Stop it."

"I'm sure I could always find someone else to do the trick. You're good friends with the Drake girl, aren't you? There have been so many missing students over the years, do you think anyone would find it hard to believe she followed them down the same path?"

Rat's lip trembled, and they hated themself for it. They wished they could open a dead passage under his feet and let the earth swallow him.

They didn't even trust themself to speak.

Behind the wall panel, Jinx's phone buzzed, cutting the silence.

Rat's heart plummeted.

It buzzed again.

Evening's lip curled. "And here, I thought that we were alone."

"That was mine," Rat said as he stepped around them. "My friends are looking for me. We should get to Galison Hall before they realize something's wrong."

"I'm sure."

"Wait." Their voice broke. "I'll go with you. I won't say anything. I'll help." They grabbed at his sleeve, but he brushed them away and stalked toward the wall.

Lightly, he touched his fingers to the panel, searching for the opening. His hand found the latch.

Before Rat could move, light burst outside the window.

Evening pulled back, startled, and the wall panel swung inward. Jinx shot out, shoving past him as she ran into the office.

She grabbed Rat by the wrist and yanked them forward. "Cavalry's here! Let's go!"

Rat stumbled after her. She wrenched the door open and dragged them into the hall.

Outside, a pair of terrors thrashed against the walls, disoriented by the light. Jinx pivoted away toward the staircase.

Rat raced to keep up with her, their breath ragged. "Holy shit. I thought he had you."

"I swear to god, Evans," Jinx gasped. "If we get out of here, we're doing something fun."

Rat's shoulder glanced off the wall, sending bits of plaster crumbling down from the ceiling. "This isn't fun?"

Jinx bounded down onto the steps, pulling Rat behind her. They took the stairs two at a time, not daring to look back.

Then Jinx stopped, bringing them up short.

A terror writhed on the landing. Its body twisted and curled in on itself, spiny legs flailing at the air.

"Shit," she said under her breath.

"This way." Rat grabbed on to the railing and scrambled over. They dropped onto the stairs on the other side, barely catching themself.

As they spun back, they caught sight of Evening sprinting down the hall, coat billowing behind him.

"Go! Go!" Jinx shouted. She sliced her hand through the air, sending a wave of condensation crashing down.

Evening drew back his hand without breaking stride. A wall of force rolled through the hall to meet her spell and the wave crashed back on itself, splashing uselessly to the ground.

Cursing, Jinx pulled herself onto the rail and swung her legs over. Rat took off as she touched down behind them.

They charged onto the first floor. In the lobby, the front doors had been knocked open. Rain blew into the foyer, and the wind that carried it reeked like wet coals. Outside, a burning tree lay across the main path. Gouts of smoke poured off of it, but the fire had spread to the brush. The rain flashed to steam as it hit the blaze.

Jinx caught up and gave Rat a shove toward the door. "Come on!" she said under her breath.

They sprinted past the threshold and out onto the muddy pathway.

Rat's shoe slid, and they went down hard. They scrambled to pick themself up, and then a hand reached out to help them.

"That's twice, Evans," Harker said as he pulled them to their feet, his skin still feverish to the touch.

Their pulse skipped, and they wished it hadn't. "Bite me," they said, righting themself.

"Guys!"

Rat whipped around to see Will standing on the grass with Agatha, one hand still raised to cast.

The air went out of their lungs.

Mud streaked his sweatshirt, and his hair was plastered from the rain.

They hadn't actually spoken to him since he'd found them in the woods. They wanted to run to him and apologize, and they wanted to hide.

"He saw us leaving when everyone was moved to Galison Hall," Harker said, following their gaze. "He refused to let us go unless we brought him."

Rat swallowed hard. "But—"

"We need to go!" Will shouted.

Harker hesitated. For a moment, Rat thought he was going to release them, but his hand tightened on their arm, holding them back. "Wait. Rat. The terrors—I didn't—"

"I know," they said. They touched his shoulder. "It's Evening. He told me everything."

For a moment, Harker looked surprised, and then he shoved them toward the path. "Go. I'm right behind you."

They swallowed the urge to pull him after them and ran.

Lightning cracked across the sky, flooding the lawn with light.

Ahead, Jinx had already reached the grass, bounding toward the curve of the pathway in the distance.

Ducking their head against the rain, Rat shot toward her.

She motioned for them to hurry and shouted something, but the words were torn away from her by the wind.

Rat's feet hit the gravel just as the thunder rolled in, distant and low. Rain ran into their eyes. They pushed it away and kept running, and they didn't stop until they had lost sight of the Founder's House.

CHAPTER THIRTY-NINE

Rat slowed in the shadow of one of the classroom buildings, heat pulsing against their skin in spite of the rain. They collapsed against the wall, hand pressed to their ribs, cold water dripping down their face.

They shielded their eyes and looked out. The others weren't far behind them. Farther out, Galison Hall glowed in the distance, the faint sheen of aether marking the perimeter. The rest of the campus was dark.

Rat thought they saw long, low forms moving through the haze of the weather, but it was hard to be sure.

Will skid to a stop beside them. "Rat," he said, breathing hard. "You're okay. I—"

He broke off, like now that he was here, he wasn't sure what to say.

Before Rat could think better of it, they launched themself across the grass, pulling him into a hug. Will stumbled back as they crashed into him before he caught them, still soaked to the skin and smelling of wet ash from the fire outside the Founder's House.

"Fuck, I'm sorry," they said in a rush. "I'm so sorry. I . . . Why are you here? I thought—"

"I looked for you," he said. "After you texted. Rat, if you were really in danger, you could have told me."

Something in them threatened to crumble. "Are we still . . ."

"Political allies?" he gave them a shaky grin.

They buried their face in his shoulder. "Shut up," they mumbled. "I missed you."

Will settled against the wall of the building. "So," he said weakly, pushing his hair out of his eyes. "Is this, like, officially an adventure now?"

As he spoke, Jinx veered from the path and rushed across the lawn.

She caught herself against Rat, and the rain stopped as the spell slipped over them. The cold still clung to them like a second skin, and their clothes had already soaked through, but it didn't feel quite as bad.

"Ice skating," she said, breathing hard. "I've decided. When this is over, all of us are going ice skating."

"I can't skate," Rat said.

"Then you can pay for hot chocolate."

They let out a breathy laugh as Jinx turned to say something to Will, like she'd just realized he was there, and then the enormity of the situation hit them all over again. They weren't going anywhere with her. Come morning, the campus would be destroyed. Evening would stake his claim on the wreckage, and Rat would be shut away in the Council Chambers.

They'd done everything right. They'd gotten the Holbrook Map back and they were halfway to finding the Ingrid Collection. They'd fought terrors. They'd been brave.

None of that mattered, though, because they'd still been wrong.

Rat looked out as Agatha shot across the grass, her braid whipping after her. Harker followed a few feet behind, hands at the ready in case he needed to cast.

Agatha spun and caught herself against the wall. She tipped her head back, letting the rain wash over her. Her knees shook.

"Hey," Rat said weakly. "Back at the Founder's House—I don't know how much you heard. Evening—"

"God, of course it's him." Her voice came out sharp and metallic against the rain.

"I'm sorry. I didn't—" Rat started.

"No wonder he's been circling around you. I should have put it together the moment he set foot on campus. If I just—"

Jinx caught her by the shoulders, grounding her. "Hey," she said softly. "Ags. It's not your fault."

"You don't know how he is," she said, but the edge in her voice had slipped over into panic. "He takes whatever he can get, and he destroys everything else. That's what my family does. He's not just going to go after the Ingrid Collection. He'll make sure the entire school is his, and all of us are either under his thumb or out of the way." Agatha crossed her arms tightly over her chest, and for the first time since September, Rat remembered exactly how small she was. "Fix this."

Rat wanted to sink into the ground.

"What happened when you were in the Founder's House?" Will asked softly, and they realized all over again that he still didn't know the worst of it.

Before they could come up with anything to say, Harker slowed to a stop at the edge of the group.

Everyone got quiet again.

Heat bled off of him from the working he'd done at the Founder's House, and the air hung heavy around him, thick with a smell like doused coals. It was clear that his control was shot. Rat had never seen him try to channel that much power at once, but they'd always assumed that at some point, he'd hit a wall and need to stop to recharge. But instead of running out of power, he'd run out of whatever it was that held it back.

As the rain beat down, he pushed his hair out of his face. His breath fogged in front of him. "So, we're all in agreement, then. This is Rat's fault."

Jinx turned her gaze on him. "You can't stay here, Blakely," she said, but it wasn't unkind.

"I—"

"I know about the deal you made." Something in her face softened, and he sank back. "A common enemy doesn't make us allies. You're going to turn on us the moment you have the chance. How could you not?"

He looked at her like she'd cut him. Like, somehow, sympathy was the worst thing she could have thrown at him. "I . . . you're right." His voice turned cold. "I'll finish this on my own."

"No. You're going to return to Galison Hall," she said. "We might be friends, but if I see you again, I'll make sure you don't follow us."

Rat caught Jinx's arm. "Wait. Both of you."

She turned to look at them. "I'm sorry," she said, dropping her voice. "I wish things were different, too, but we can't trust him right now."

"But . . ."

"Rat. She's right," Will said gently. "I know I don't have the full picture, but I don't think it's safe to keep him here. For anyone."

"I know. I just—" They glanced back at Harker. They didn't particularly care if they could trust him or not. They didn't want him going back out alone. "It was Evening," they told Will. "Behind the attack. He saw all of us, and—I just need a minute. Please."

Harker looked away, his arms crossed tightly over his chest. Fog curled off of him in ragged wisps.

"We can't stay here," Rat said. They looked out at the darkened shape of the clock tower rising out of the haze of rain. "Evening's going to be sending people to look for us, and he knows where the Ingrid Collection is."

"And we do, too," Jinx said.

They shook their head. "He's probably already moving the Lesser Hours to lock down the whole area. As soon as I put my head up, he'll catch me, and he's going to be watching for you, too." As they said it, they felt themself sinking all over again. It didn't matter if they were a key that opened every door. They'd never reach the Ingrid Collection on their own, but even if they waited out the attack, Evening would be there to take them back to the Council Chambers in the morning. "I have to go back. If I don't . . . you all need to get out of here, and I'll—"

"No," Jinx said.

"I have to. This is the only way he'll stop this, and . . . I can cooperate. I don't know. Maybe it won't be that bad."

"You don't know my uncle," Agatha said. "No matter what you do, he'll just keep moving the goal posts. If you go back there, he isn't going to stop until he has exactly what he wants."

Rat shut their eyes.

Jinx lowered her voice. "I told you that we were going to fight, right? So, we can fight this."

"Jinx," Harker said. "Give them a second."

She looked up at him. "You're not on our side anymore."

Rat pulled on her jacket. "It's fine. Leave him alone."

"It's not fine," she said. "I'm not letting you go back there. Do you honestly believe things are going to get better if you give yourself over?"

"I don't care if things never get better," Rat snapped. They hadn't meant it to come out that way, but as soon as they started speaking, they couldn't stop. "If I don't go, Evening's going to have me dragged back to the Council Chambers as soon as he finds me. He'll cut off all my exits, and then he'll come after everyone else unless I do what he wants."

No one spoke. Rat was painfully aware that everyone was staring at them.

"Jinx, he saw you at the Founders House just now. He threatened you. And Will, as soon as he finds out you're involved, he'll be after you, too. And Agatha, you were right. He's planning to establish a presence on campus, so this place will basically belong to him. And—"They looked at Harker, and their voice died in their throat.

They didn't have the heart to repeat Evening's threats out loud. Suddenly, they felt exhausted.

They let out a shuddering breath. "Enough people have gotten hurt protecting me, and I'm so tired of pretending there's nothing I can do about it. Going back with him is the best choice I have."

They'd set out to fight monsters. Maybe they still could, even if it meant turning around and walking back with their head down.

In the corner of their vision, a dark shape swept across the sky. Rat spun as a great black bird cut over the top of the building, wings outstretched, as if it had been watching them all this time, just waiting for its entrance.

The bird fluttered down in front of them and dropped a mum from its beak.

The silence thickened.

Slowly, Rat stepped forward. Jinx's hand slipped away, and the rain crashed over them as they knelt down in the flooded grass. Traces of aether clung to the torn leaves of the flower, and the roots were ragged.

The bird tilted its head toward Rat. Then it was off again, wingbeats heavy on the air.

Rat stared after it. Their thumb traced the line of the mum's crooked stem. An electrical charge prickled up their arm. This was an invitation.

No, they thought. *An offer.*

Isola had been watching. They should have known better than to think she'd ever allow them to fall into anyone else's hands without a fight. She could tip the scales, easily.

They knew the tower. Isola could be bargained with. They would lose, but maybe they could control how badly. Maybe, they could get something back for it.

They already knew what she'd ask for in return. Rat just needed to go to her.

Jinx reached out and laid her hand on their shoulder, her touch light now. Rat could have shrugged it away if they wanted to, but they just rested their hand on top of hers and got to their feet.

If they asked Jinx to fight with them, she would. She'd battle terrors until the sun came up, and when Evening came and dragged Rat back to the Council Chambers, she'd keep fighting. Without question, they already knew that Will would do the same.

But Rat couldn't ask that of either of them. They couldn't ask Agatha, who owed them less than nothing, and they refused to ask Harker, who still had fresh burns on his hands from saving them again, even though he was supposed to be their enemy. They couldn't keep hiding behind other people when they knew how to stop all of this.

Rat thought about the field of fallen stones, and the unfamiliar stars, and the dead rabbit with its eyes like polished glass. They thought about Margaret Ingrid, riding out on a beast made of shadow, with no idea if she'd ever return.

Any doubts that Rat still had broke apart like smoke.

"Rat?" Will said quietly.

"It's alright," they said.

Their hand tightened on the mum as they turned back to the circle. They didn't need to speak. Agatha's mouth was drawn in a grim line, like she already knew. A few feet away from her, Harker watched them, stiff and unreadable, but Rat could tell from the tension in his shoulders that he'd figured it out, too.

Another sheet of rain swept down the path, but Rat didn't feel it now.

"I'll meet up with you guys in the morning," Rat said. "After all of this is over. Okay?"

Harker's eyes flickered to the mum in their hands. "I'm coming with you."

"Fight me, Blakely," they said, because the alternative was admitting how badly they wanted that, and they'd sooner die than tell him that.

Before Harker could dignify that with a response, Jinx adjusted her hold on Rat's shoulder, like she wanted to make sure he'd seen.

"What do you think you're doing?" she asked him.

"You don't need to worry," he said coolly. "If I was interested in handing Rat over to the tower, I would've done it months ago, and it wouldn't have been that hard." His gaze flickered back to them. "I know a way to get to Ashwood. It's neutral ground, right outside the wards. She'll be able to find us there."

Rat could picture the ruined estate, overgrown and crumbling with age.

They hesitated. They wanted to ask him how she'd contacted him before, if there was a way for him to summon her here as a shadow—something safe and easily dispelled that couldn't actually touch them.

But Rat knew Isola wanted them within reach. They'd meet on her terms, or not at all.

When they didn't answer, Harker inclined his head to them. "If you'd rather face her alone, that's your choice."

Rat eyed him warily. Harker wasn't protecting them. He was probably just afraid that Isola would cut a deal with them behind his back and he'd lose the only thing he had left, however broken and vicious it was.

But the thought of going alone clawed the air from their lungs.

Jinx gave them an uncertain look. "Rat," she started.

"It's okay," they said. Far off, thunder rolled across the hills. "There's something else I need you to do. Please."

She exhaled deeply and nodded.

"Evening is going to have most of the Council of Hours looking for me. For all of us, probably. Could you . . ."

"Keep him off your trail?"

They nodded. "Can you?"

Rat waited for her to argue, but she just tipped her head up to the rain. "Yeah. I'm in my element now."

They swallowed hard. Until she said it, they hadn't realized how badly they'd wanted her to say no. They wanted her to insist on coming with them. They wanted her to refuse to let them leave at all, so they could go back to Galison Hall with everyone else, even if Rat knew that wasn't really an option for them anymore.

"I've seen pieces of this," Agatha said, stepping toward Jinx. "I have an idea of where they'll be."

"Thanks," they said, but they knew from the look on her face that she wasn't doing this for them. They turned to Will. "If you want to go back, I know you didn't sign up for this, and—"

"Whatever this is, I'm with you," he said. "Just come back safe, okay?"

"Morning," Jinx said, fixing Rat with a stare.

"Morning," they promised.

Then Agatha looked out at the campus and laid a hand on Jinx's arm. "They'll be fanning out from Galison Hall. We should go now if this is going to work."

"Same," Harker said to Rat.

The minute Jinx let go of them, the rain came crashing back down in icy sheets.

"Let's go," Harker said as Agatha disappeared after Jinx and Will, into the haze of weather.

"Wait. I—" Rat started. They reached for his sleeve, and then remembered that they'd lost the right a long time ago. "Which way?"

He hesitated for just a second, then motioned for them to follow him.

Rat tucked the mum into their pocket and walked after him, out onto the windswept lawn and on toward Ashwood.

CHAPTER FORTY

HARKER BROUGHT THEM TO THE DRAKE.

"You're sure about this?" Rat asked as he resealed the door wards.

Even with the rain hammering down outside, their voice sounded too loud. They'd followed Harker most of the way across the campus in silence, and now that they were alone in the library, they had no idea how to speak to him.

"You should hope so," he said without turning back. Bracing himself against the wall, he leaned in and murmured a password into the door-frame, too low for Rat to hear.

The rain had washed most of the soot from his hands, but by the faint glow of the door ward, Rat could see the fresh burns snaking over his skin. In spite of the heat still pouring off of him, the rain had plastered his hair to his face and soaked through his clothes.

"We should be clear of the terrors here," Harker said when he noticed them watching. "The Drake is under more protection spells than almost anywhere else on campus, but it's best if we keep moving." He took a shaky breath, then threaded his fingers through the air, drawing up a pale will-o'-wisp of spellfire.

Instinctively, Rat stepped toward him. "Are you okay?"

He gave them a look, and Rat remembered they'd broken every bone in his arm less than thirty-six hours ago. They sank back.

"Come on. It's a long way out," he said and started toward the reading room. "I'd say trust me, but I'm not sure you have a choice."

Rat took a last look at the doors and then followed him.

Their footsteps echoed on the polished wooden floors. Rain beat heavily on the skylights, and shafts of dull gray light swam over the empty tables. For a moment, Rat could sense the passages of the Drake opening up around them, sprawling out in all directions.

"It's kind of like we're sneaking into my family's archive again," they said, then immediately felt ridiculous. "Except, you know."

Harker glanced back as he led them across the room. "Fewer stolen books?"

"More death centipedes," Rat said, following after.

"Yeah, well. Sorry if this isn't what you had in mind when you said we should go to school together."

Holding the spellfire high, he cut toward an exit at the back.

Rat started toward it, drawing even with him, but he stopped at a solid row of bookcases instead.

"This way," he said, motioning to them. Before they could ask, he drew a stick of chalk from his pocket and knelt, marking a sigil on the floor in a smooth, practiced motion.

Even now, in the dimly lit stacks of the Drake, the gesture was strangely familiar, maybe because they were so used to Harker casting. Maybe because they knew a moment before he finished what kind of spell he'd drawn.

The way ahead of him opened into a narrow passageway. Bookshelves lined the way, but the books were older, like they'd been tucked away in a hard-to-find pocket of the library and forgotten there.

A cold draft rolled through the aisle, stale and smelling of dust.

He looked back at Rat as he rose to his feet and lifted his chin, and they realized they'd been staring.

"There are a couple of turns ahead, and it's going to get darker as we go," he said. "Just stay in sight of me, and you should be alright."

Rat hurried after him. "This is how you did it," they said, understanding. "When you stole the Holbrook Map."

"The Drake is an old building. I'm not even certain Fairchild knows all the paths through it."

They brushed their hand over the wall of books as they passed. They wanted to ask him how many times he'd gotten lost or trapped back here before he'd found his way through, but a part of them didn't want to know.

They quickened their pace, closing the distance. "How far out is it? To Ashwood?"

"Not as far as you'd expect," he said, and if they hadn't known him, they might have missed the edge in his voice.

They thought of the knight as they'd glimpsed her in his room, incorporeal and wreathed in smoke.

"Have you been back with her?" Rat asked. Without meaning to, their voice softened. "To the tower?"

He hesitated. "No," he admitted after a moment. "Not any closer than you have. I don't have a spell to get there on my own. She usually sends her messengers when she needs something."

"Once she has her heart back, she'll release you though, right?"

"I . . . if I can get it to her then, maybe."

"Harker?"

"There isn't a term for our deal. I'm just bound to her." There was a note of defeat in his voice that they hadn't expected.

"Oh," they said quietly. "I didn't know that."

"Why would you? I've lied about everything the whole time we've been here. I don't know why any of you are still being nice to me."

"Harker . . . last year," Rat started. "I—"

"You needed to protect yourself. It's fine."

"But—"

In the narrow aisle, they felt his skin heat. His face flushed in the glow of the spellfire. "You don't owe me an apology. Anything you've done, I've probably done something worse."

Before Rat could respond, Harker led them down another turn-off, into a room with aisle upon aisle of mahogany bookcases. Even though it reminded them of the reading room, the ceilings were higher, bookshelves tall and narrow, and Rat was certain they'd never been there before.

A cold draft blew past as they made their way in, coming from somewhere deeper within the building. Rat's wet clothing stuck to their skin, chilling them.

They were in deep now.

"Through here." He motioned to them. "It only gets darker ahead. Stay close. It's easy to get lost back here."

Rat flashed a small, nervous smile. "Even for you?"

He exhaled. "I hate that I'm saying this, but what you do is a lot harder than you think it is."

"So, what you're saying is that I'm a better arcanist than you."

He looked down at them like he wasn't going to dignify them and all two and a half spells they knew with a response.

Rat lifted their chin, and Harker bit back the edge of a laugh before he caught himself.

Something that might have been regret flickered across his face, and then his expression smoothed over, and he was all ice again.

Their heart sank. They'd told themself over and over that he belonged to the tower now, but it was still *him*. They'd left him behind more times than they could count, and in the morning, they were going to have to leave him behind again.

"Come on," he said, starting past them. "The faster we get through this place, the better."

Before he could get any farther, Rat caught him by the wrist.

"Rat—"

"You could still come back," they said. Fever pulsed below his skin. Gently, Rat traced their thumb over the inside of his wrist.

He swallowed hard, not meeting their eyes.

"I've seen the door on the clock tower," they pressed. "If I could get us in, if we could find Isola's heart first—"

"We wouldn't make it. You were right. Evening's going to be watching for our next move. The moment we tried, he'd stop us."

"But, if we could—"

"She would know," he said too quickly. His pulse beat rabbit-fast under their fingertips. Even behind the school's wards, he was still bound to her. Isola could still hurt him, long before they ever managed to strike a blow against her.

"She used your bracelets in a binding spell, right? So she can, what? Summon you to the tower? Keep you there?"

"It's already done."

They closed their other hand over his. "What if I could get them back?"

He let out a shuddering breath. "Rat."

"I don't care what the tower wants. I'm not letting her keep you just because she cornered you into making a vow," Rat said. "You promised me first."

Harker looked back at them like they'd finally managed to say something more entitled than *I know the admissions board.* For the first time, they emphatically didn't care.

"I don't think you understand," he said finally. "I'm not doing any of this to help you. I'm not on your side, Rat."

"But—"

He drew himself up, and Rat realized he'd stopped. At some point while they were walking, the stacks had opened into a clearing and the ceiling cut away in a mezzanine overhead. It was even colder here, the darkness somehow thicker than it had been in the hallways.

Slowly, the wrongness of it settled over them.

"Why did we stop?"

"Do you know where we are?" he asked.

"No?"

"Do you remember how to get out of here?"

Rat's throat tightened. They'd lost track somewhere in the maze of hallways and aisles.

Harker had been distracting them.

"Where are you taking me?"

He looked down at them. Heat flashed across their skin.

"Harker." They grabbed on to his sleeve. "Where are you actually taking me?"

He gave them a look that might have been smug, if he wasn't so exhausted. "Nowhere."

"I mean it."

"There's no route through the library. I only know about Ashwood because you told me," he said. "I got lost back here once, and I think it took me three hours to find my way out."

"You can't do this," they said. Panic crept into their voice. "Evening already knows where to go. You're basically giving him the Ingrid Collection, and as soon as he's done here, he's going to bring me back to the Council Chambers—"

"And if Isola doesn't want her heart to fall into his hands, she can use me just as easily as she can use you," he said, but something in his face softened. "I'm already sworn to her. There isn't anything she can take from me that wasn't hers to start with."

"Harker."

He touched their cheek, and if they hadn't been standing so close to him, they might have missed the slight hitch in his breath. "Sorry, Evans. I'm not letting you have this."

The spellfire flickered in his hand as he took a step back from them.

"Hey! You can't—"

They lunged after him, but the spellfire winked out in his hands, and then he was gone, swallowed up by the darkness of the stacks.

"Harker!" they shouted after him, their voice jagged, and they hated him a little more for it.

Their magic pulled at them like a tide, threatening to well over. Something in their chest tightened, but they pushed it back.

Not against him, they told themself. But they thought of the knight again as they'd seen her after the Whisper Ball, smoke curling off of her, and they thought of her hunting dogs, and her crows, and the sharp glint of her teeth. They couldn't let him leave, either.

Their magic pulled at them again, and this time they reached for it.

Their awareness rushed out, every twist and bend of the library's passages taking shape like a tangled length of string, and for a moment, they could feel each impossible turn that would take them back. They knew each corner of the building and every crack that they could slip between.

Movement flickered in the web of passages, somewhere close, and Rat whipped toward it.

Without thinking of where they were going, they threw themself forward. The telltale glow of a dead passage glinted ahead of them, and Rat veered toward it.

Motes of aether spun around them as they rushed headlong into the dead passage. Everything inside of them screamed, but if they stopped moving, they wouldn't be able to start again.

They threw themself around the corner after Harker, but the aisle was already empty.

Rat ran straight ahead. The next passage caught them before they careened into a wall. They braced themself, but then their shoes hit the carpet, and they were in a new row of shelves, still running.

Spellfire flashed past the mouth of the aisle as Harker passed ahead of them, a shadow between the shelves. Rat charged after him, even though he'd always been faster than them and the distance was more than they could close.

As they passed through a third dead passage, Rat didn't even have to think. There was no bracing themself this time. The passage spit them out in the aisle just behind him and they lunged.

Rat caught his shirt.

Harker jerked back. The fire in his hands went out as he spun toward them, twisting out of their grasp, but he was off-balance. They threw themself into him, and he went down, pulling them with him.

Rat slammed into the ground, landing hard, but the library had given way to the rain-slicked boards of the widow's walk.

Rain hammered down on them as they scrambled back to their feet, shoving away from Harker. On instinct, they shot back toward the building as he picked himself up.

Rat threw the door open and burst onto the stairs, a gust of wind howling through after them.

They caught a glimpse of Harker, just behind them. And then, they pulled the door shut.

A split second after it closed, his body thudded against the door, shaking it in its frame.

"Wait!" he shouted.

"No! I'm not sending you back there, you blazing trash fire! Why do you think I'm okay with losing you? I don't care what you've done or how terrible you keep trying to be, I'd still go after you! I would literally always go after you!"

"Rat!" The doorknob rattled, then stuck.

"*Stay*," they said into the door, and they felt their spell take hold, the space around them fixing in place, even as Harker murmured a counter-spell on the other side.

He pulled at the doorknob again. "Just listen to me! You can't go to the tower. She's never going to let you go. You're not like me. You're—"

"I'm what?" Rat yelled, edging away from the door. Now that they'd closed it, the narrow stairwell was pitch-black around them and as cold as the late autumn air outside.

"You were right. Of course you're the one she actually wanted. I thought that if I did what she asked, I could change her mind, but she's never taken her eyes off you. She always wanted you. Okay? Everyone always wants you."

"Good. I'm counting on it." Rat exhaled. "This shouldn't have been your fight anyway. When you get down, get yourself somewhere safe, okay?" they said, even though they knew he wouldn't.

They heard him mutter another spell on the other side of the door, and then the doorknob rattled again. Probably, they'd only bought themself a few minutes before the spell gave out or he figured out another way down. It would have to be enough.

He hit the door one more time as Rat headed down the stairs, and then they made it to the hallway, leaving him behind.

CHAPTER FORTY-ONE

RAT SET OUT ALONE THIS TIME, THE WAY ISOLA HAD taught them once, a long time ago.

The first dead passage took Rat to a narrow staircase, somewhere deep in the earth, the beam of their phone lighting the way. Then, the stairs opened into stone-hewn corridors, and then into aisles of abandoned furniture and the impossible overgrowth of the underground meadow.

A black bird fluttered down, landing on an empty bookcase as Rat waded out into the grass.

"You can tell her I'm on my way to Ashwood," they said. "Let her know I can find it from here."

The messenger blinked at them, and then, cawing, it leapt up, its wings catching the air.

Rat stared after it as it flew back toward the crack in the wards. Then, alone again, their hand went to their compass.

They touched their fingers to the metal case, steadying themself.

You know this place, they reminded themself. *Pretend you're coming home.*

Then, they started out again into the weeds, their hand still wrapped around their compass long after they suspected it had stopped pointing north.

CHAPTER FORTY-TWO

RAT WALKED UNTIL THE GRASS RECEDED AGAIN, AND THE aisles of old furniture turned back to crumbling stone passageways. The ceiling gave way little by little, until there was nothing but night sky and the remains of the rafters curving overhead like broken ribs. Rain fell in heavy sheets.

Rat hadn't gone nearly far enough to have come to the edge of campus, but it didn't matter. The moment they saw the sky, they knew they'd made it to Ashwood.

They slowed as the passage opened into the entrance hall. The last time Rat had been through this room, it had been summer. A curtain of wisteria had clung to the banister of the marble staircase then, and the air had been clear and crisp and faintly sweet. Everything had been drenched in moonlight.

Now, it was flooded with ice water. Bare vines crept up the side of the steps, and a rippling black lake pooled in the crook of the staircase, where they'd once followed Isola as she led them through the ruins, telling them of rooks and old magic and long-absent gods.

Thunder rolled outside, closer than it had been on campus.

"Hello?" they called, giving away the tremor in their voice.

Their voice reverberated through the empty room.

"You wanted to talk! So, I'm here!"

A cold wind whistled over the broken roof. In spite of themselves, Rat shivered. Their sweatshirt was already soaked through again, and the rain traced rivulets in the aether that dusted their skin from the tunnels.

Movement flickered in the corner of their eye. They turned toward the staircase as a bird touched down on the banister.

"It brings back memories," said a voice behind them. "Doesn't it?"

Rat whipped around.

Isola sat perched in one of the broken window frames, like she'd blown in with the weather, a heavy cloak draped over her shoulders and a sword at her hip. A garland of flowers twisted through her dark, tangled hair even though it was too late in the season for anything to grow here, and if she noticed the cold, she didn't show it.

They met her gaze, and she flashed her teeth at them, a little too sharp in her mouth.

For a moment, all Rat could do was stare.

With a slick, animal-like grace, Isola leapt down. The birds that had flocked around her all scattered as her boots hit the ground. "It's been too long."

Involuntarily, Rat took half a step back.

"I was starting to think you'd forgotten everything I taught you. Even after I sent for you, I hadn't dared to hope," she said, her eyes flickering over them. Rat's hair was plastered with rain, and mud and aether streaked their sweatshirt. "But I did wonder."

"You made me an offer," Rat said. "You asked me to go with you, to the tower. I'll—I'll bargain with you."

"I know why you're here," she said, reaching out her hand to them. "But, come with me. You've traveled a long way tonight, and we have a way to go yet."

"Wait," they said, fighting to keep the tremor out of their voice. "I'm—I think you misunderstood me. I'm not looking for a place to hide."

"Oh?" she said. Her eyes lit with a dangerous kind of interest. "But then, you always were braver than you looked."

Rat drew themself up. "I know you have messengers at the school. You saw what happened."

"I might have."

"Edgar Cromwell is after the Ingrid Collection. He wants to use me to find it. He already has my father's map, and if I don't stop him, I'll be taken to the Council Chambers as soon as he catches me. But he's using your creatures. You could tip the scales."

"And why would I do that?" Isola asked, but she said it like she already had an answer in mind.

"Because." Rat swallowed hard. *Favors, but never things.* "If you did, I'd be in your debt. He wants me on his side, but I'd rather be on yours."

She inclined her head, and they knew they'd said the right thing.

"And," Rat said. "Because I know what you're after, and I could get it."

She sharpened, watching them closely, and in that moment, she was every bit a carrion bird. "Can you?"

"You'll leave the school and everyone associated with it alone. You won't set foot on the campus again. All of the binding spells you hold will be released, and you'll return the remains and belongings of any students you've taken." They drew in a deep breath. "And I'll find your heart for you."

"That's a steep price for something you might not be able to deliver on."

"You need my help."

"Almost as much," she said, "as I imagine you need mine."

Rat suppressed a shiver.

"You came to me," Isola said, drawing in. "If memory serves, a friend of yours has already promised to do the same thing. What would I do with another set of hands?"

"Then what else would you want with me?" they asked, but they already knew the answer.

They'd known from the moment they saw her messenger. Maybe even earlier than that.

She gave them a knowing look.

"I'll return to you," they said before they could lose their nerve. "In the morning. Even if we lose. I'll go back to the tower like you wanted. I won't run this time."

Rat lifted their chin, fighting the urge to lower their gaze.

Isola laughed, cold and low. It wasn't a nice sound. "If only I could help."

"You can," they protested.

"You overestimate me."

"But—"

"All of my creatures slipped through the wards. You know as well as anyone that as long as the school is under protection, I don't have much power there." She drew the words out, and there was a leading edge in her voice that set Rat's teeth on edge.

"You wouldn't have sent for me if you didn't have a plan," Rat said. "There has to be something you can do."

"No." Again, her eyes flickered over them. "Not on my own."

Goosebumps pricked up Rat's arms.

Another gust of wind tore through the ruins, tugging at the edges of Isola's cloak. She tipped her face up to the sky, as if she'd only just noticed the weather. "Walk with me."

Rat eyed her warily.

"Just inside, no farther than that. We'll be dry there." She waved for them to follow as she started deeper into the ruins.

They hesitated, but she didn't stop to see if they were behind her. Forcing out a breath, Rat started after, falling into step.

They waited for her to name her terms, but instead her eyes slid over them, curious almost, and she said, "Did anyone ever tell you what my heart was?"

Rat eyed her warily. "It's a secret."

"And do you know the kind of magic it would take to unravel such a thing?"

They shook their head, unsure of where she was going.

"They're shadowy, spiteful creatures, and very difficult to destroy. I suspect it would have been done by now, otherwise," she said.

"Why are you telling me this?"

"Because if someone were foolish enough to attempt it, even if they were to succeed, they'd quickly find that I am not my heart, and that I could live on the vestiges of my power for a long time yet."

Unease pricked through them at the warning. "It hadn't crossed my mind," they said, and her mouth twitched. "There was something you wanted me to do?"

Isola came to a stop under the shelter of the mezzanine. "Take me through."

"Take you through?"

"That's it. Take me through to the campus, just this once, and I'll help you."

"I can't do that," Rat said. "The school's wards—"

"Are a shadow of what they were," Isola told them. "Powerful, maybe, but there are cracks now where there weren't before."

Beyond the overhang, the walls had crumbled away, and Rat could just pick out the shape of the hills through the haze. Far below, a handful of scattered lights showed beyond the faint sheen of the school's main wards.

"Evening's already moved his forces to the center of campus," she said. "He has them watching the clock tower."

Rat hesitated. Telling her any more than she already knew felt dangerous, but she was on their side now, whether they trusted her or not. "That's where the map starts."

"So I've gathered," Isola said, half to herself. She looked thoughtful. "The clock tower is sealed with a loyalty spell. No one who isn't acting in the school's interest can get inside, but it's not as strong as it used to be. If Evening really has a will to break it, I have no doubt he'll batter his way through. But then again . . ."

Her eyes flickered to Rat.

Their stomach sank. "You think I could get in."

"It's old magic. It's a different creature than you're used to dealing with," she said. "Spells like that have a way of taking on a life of their own around the caster's intention."

"Is that good?"

Her eyes glinted. "Intentions can be overpowered or bent. If you can get the protective workings to recognize that you want the same thing they do, you might be able to convince them to hold Evening off. Take the clock tower, and the battle is ours."

Rat hesitated. "You're sure that would work?"

"It's that or overpower them," she said, which wasn't an option. She looked back to the campus below. "Of course, you'll need to break through his defenses just to get there," she said, drawing it out. "I could lend you my power, but I'm not at my full strength. I wouldn't be able to assist you from across the wards, and that still leaves the terrors. I could banish them, but . . ."

"Your reach only goes so far," Rat finished.

"Take me through," she said again. "And you'll have my sword at your side and my power at your call. I'll collect my creatures and clear the way for you."

Rat hated that they were even considering it, but every second they wasted arguing was another second closer to morning. "As soon as you have what you came for, you'll never set foot on the campus or any of the school's grounds again."

"I won't return unless you ask."

"I won't ask."

Her mouth curved in a way they distinctly didn't like. "Then, you have nothing to worry about. Do you?"

"Okay." Rat's voice barely came out. They looked up at her. "I'll take you through, and at the end of the night, I'll return with you."

"That's all I ask." She held her hand out to them, and when the wind caught her cloak, she was every bit the battered knight that Rat remembered from that first night in the field of grass, before they had known to be afraid of her.

There wouldn't be any turning back from this, they understood. But they were a long way past that already.

Rat lay their hand over hers.

With her thumb, she traced an arc across the back of their hand, cutting the sheen of aether and rainwater.

"On the dust of my bones and the stars of my making, I pledge myself to your cause," she said, dipping into a low bow.

A whisper of power shivered through the binding spell, cool and fathomless as open sky.

They hated how much they wanted it.

Her lips brushed their knuckles.

"Rat Holbrook Evans," Isola said. "I'm yours until morning."

Someday, they promised themself, *they were going to knock the tower from its foundations.*

Today, though, they needed her.

Rat drew their hand back as Isola rose to her full height, power still humming in their veins. "Tell me what you want me to do."

CHAPTER FORTY-THREE

ISOLA LED RAT TO THE ROOM THAT HAD ONCE BEEN A study. The broken windows looked out over the darkened sprawl of the campus, and the roof had caved in, leaving the room open to the weather. The remains of the writing desk were still where Rat remembered, collapsed in the middle of the floor, and a few of the empty bookshelves had fallen in now, too.

The room had flooded. Cold water seeped into Rat's shoes as they picked their way through the debris.

Isola walked alongside them, her hand on their shoulder as she steered them through the ruin, like they'd come out to talk with her about the names of stars and long-forgotten places.

"Here," she said stopping among the wreckage, and they immediately knew why she'd chosen it. It was where she'd always taken them to cast.

Rat braced themself as the wind tore past the windows, howling over the empty frames.

"It was her house once," Isola said, and Rat understood who she meant, without her having to say it. "It isn't inside of the school's wards, but it isn't quite outside, either. There have always been too many protections for me to cross onto the grounds alone, but if there was someone to open the way . . ."

She tilted her head to Rat, her eyes bright.

Isola had been waiting for this, they realized. Maybe from the moment she'd first seen them. They had always been adept at finding cracks in the world to slip through, and if they could open a door, then maybe she'd be able to walk through after them.

"I'll try," they said.

They shut their eyes and breathed in deeply. Underneath the musk of rotting wood and the sting of the cold, they caught the familiar scent of aether on the air as their magic flickered in their chest.

Firmly, Isola pressed on their shoulder, adjusting their posture. "Like I taught you," she said behind them, her voice closer than they'd expected.

Rat drew in another breath, the sprawl of the estate taking shape at the edge of their senses the way it had before, more times than they could count.

They thought of the campus. The steep rise of the clock tower, jutting out of the haze of rain, the Drake curled sleeping at its feet. The darkened sweep of the outlying dorms. The office in the Founder's House, with its cluttered rows of bookshelves.

Without meaning to, their mind went to Jinx, and Will, and Harker, and Agatha back at the school, and they shoved the thought away again.

Over their shoulder, they heard a sharp intake of breath, and even before they opened their eyes, they knew what they would see.

A dead passage had opened ahead of them into a second office, like a strange mirror of the one at Ashwood if it had never been abandoned. Papers littered the floor, and a camping lantern still glowed on the desk, like someone had been there moments ago. Behind the desk, a panel in the wall hung open.

Rat hesitated, half expecting someone to peer out from the passage on the other side of the office. Then they realized where they were.

Nervous laughter bubbled in their throat. They were looking at Fairchild's office.

"When you're ready," Isola said.

"Right. I just—I can't promise that this is going to work."

"It will." She leaned in, close enough that her breath curled over Rat's neck. "You were made for this. It was a cruel trick that anyone tried to convince you otherwise."

Rat knotted their fingers into the tattered wool of her cloak. Bracing themself, they stepped forward, into the Founder's House.

For the first time, the thin veil of aether at the mouth of the passage pushed back on them, like the protections that had been laid over the campus understood Rat had brought something that was never meant to come through.

They pressed their hand through the veil again, more slowly now, but it was like trying to push two magnets together, when they wanted to fly apart. The wrongness of it resonated in the hollow of their bones.

"Focus," Isola told them, and they thought of Jinx in the east woods, steadying their arm as she taught them a spell.

They pushed everything else out of their mind. Whatever safety the wards had been meant to secure, they didn't now. Rat intended to go through, and they intended to end this.

"*Open*," they said into the passageway, and their magic rose up to meet it, the jagged edges of the world cracking just a bit farther apart.

Then, Rat didn't think. The aether broke around them like cobwebs, and when they crossed the threshold, it didn't feel like anything at all.

The soft thud of Isola's boots sounded on the carpet behind them. She walked forward, stepping into the room the same way that most people entered cathedrals, craning her neck to take in the high ceiling and paneled walls.

"After all this time . . ." she said to herself. There was a catch in her voice, halfway between hunger and reverence. "Absolutely magnificent." She let out another low laugh. Shaking her head, she traced her fingertips over the polished surface of the desk. "By every star and all of my breath."

Rat cleared their throat. "We had a deal."

"We do," she said, leaning back against the desk. "Lead the way, and I'll clear a path for you."

Rat opened their mouth, but something stopped them. They wondered if part of her could feel it, the pull of her own heart calling to her from across wherever Ingrid had hidden it, but even telling her where the path began felt dangerous.

Except, she was on their side now, and they'd already set their terms.

"If you reach it without me—"

"Our agreement has been met," she said. "I keep my word."

Her mouth pulled taut as something scraped by out in the hall. For a moment, Rat thought it was the terrors. Then Isola spun toward the window.

Rat followed her gaze. A light glinted below. A flashlight on the path, pointed directly at the Founder's House.

"Fuck," Rat said under their breath.

Isola turned back to them, a question on her face.

"I was here earlier, and Evening's still looking for me. He's probably had someone watching the building in case I came back."

Rat half expected Isola to laugh, but she slid away from the desk, her cloak fluttering out behind her. "We have to leave." Her voice had turned serious. "I don't suppose you can get us there the fast way."

"I—" Their magic surged outward, and for a moment they could feel the same path they'd used before, winding down through the building.

Outside, the distinct crunch of tires sounded over gravel, and they realized they'd taken too long.

"Pity," Isola said, taking them by the wrist. She pulled them out toward the hall, her traveling cloak catching the air. "We'll need to move quickly. I'm not at my full power here, and my assistance won't mean anything if we're cornered."

Rat raced after her down the darkened corridor. Aether dusted the way ahead, lighting the wreckage.

At the end of the hall, a terror unwound itself. Its armored plates scraped against the wall with a low hiss as it turned toward them, casting a dim glow over the carpet.

And then, it stopped.

Rat turned back to see Isola, her hand raised like a command. "Take the main doors. I'll be close on your heels."

Rat scrambled back toward the stairs. They caught the rail and threw themself onto the steps. They braced themself for the terror to change its mind and come barreling past, but they didn't look back.

Half a dozen terrors swarmed the lobby, scuttling over the floor and crawling up the walls. The doors had been knocked from their hinges, and half an inch of rain had gathered on the floor. The fire that Harker had set outside had gone out, but the smell of ash still hung heavy in the air.

Rat whipped around, but they knew they wouldn't find another way out.

Something crashed in the hallway behind them, dangerously close.

Rat spun back toward the lobby and bolted.

Ahead of them, one of the terrors turned and canted its head toward them, the others twisting after it.

Everything inside of Rat threatened to revolt.

They flinched back as one of the terrors raced by. Its tail snapped in the air like a whip. Instinctively, Rat ducked, but it scuttled past them toward the back of the building, the others following after it.

Rat caught themself in a crouch, one hand on the rain-drenched floor of the lobby. Their knuckles were bleeding, but they couldn't remember when they'd cut themself.

The beam of a flashlight swept the entrance. "Here!" someone shouted from outside.

Rat scrambled to their feet and launched themself at the door.

Their momentum carried them over the threshold. The rain crashed down on them as their sneakers hit the path. Just ahead, the man with the flashlight moved to block them.

Rat barreled past him, veering onto the grass.

He spun after them. His hand closed on the back of their sweatshirt, and he tugged them back.

"Let go!"

"Rat Evans?" the man said, shining the light in their face. Rain rolled off his gray regulation cloak. "You need to come with me. It isn't safe out here."

"I said let go!" Rat twisted away from him, and a burst of power surged through the binding spell.

Magic poured off of them, undirected and raw. The blast slammed into him, sending him reeling.

Their heart beat in their mouth as they stumbled back. Magic thrummed in their core, but instead of their own familiar power, this was autumn wind and hounds and teeth and the flurry of wings, and they shouldn't have liked it.

Someone shouted after them from across the grass.

Still breathless, they turned hard and scrambled toward the path as the other Hours started after them.

Then, it all stopped.

The flashlights on the lawn swept back toward the building, and a dangerous kind of still settled over everything.

Rat spun back as a great black bird burst through the entrance of the Founder's House. Its wings beat hard against the rain, a sheen of aether flashing on its oil-black feathers.

Isola.

At her heels, a small army of terrors clambered through the doorway, climbing over each other as they poured out onto the path. Their star-flecked bodies glinted in the dark as they snaked away from the building, the low hiss and scrape of their chitinous armor just audible over the rain.

She swept toward the ground, cutting in front of the formation of Hours.

As she touched down, she turned human again, and then she was on her feet, the storm whirling around her like a beast called to heel. She flung her hands out and her power rolled off of her in a wave of wind and shadows, driving the Hours back.

"Go!" she called, her voice rising above the clamor.

Rat turned hard on their heel and shot toward the path, not daring to look back as they ran.

CHAPTER FORTY-FOUR

RAIN STUNG THEIR EYES AS RAT SPRINTED UP THE PATH, darkened buildings rising up around them. The sounds of the knight and the Hours wore on behind them, rising over the wind.

A spell shot past them, throwing up gravel where it struck the ground.

Rat risked a glance over their shoulder.

They'd left the Founder's House behind them, but not far enough. On the low rise of a hillside, Evening had appeared out of the fray, a pair of Lesser Hours close on his heels. The wind tore at his coat as he raised his hand to cast.

They tasted metal. Rat shoved themself forward as Isola swept overhead, maneuvering between the buildings.

In the distance, their eyes found the steep rise of the clock tower, dark against the sky.

Another spell shot over their head.

Rat veered out of the way. Rainwater flooded their shoes as they stumbled off the path into a drowned garden bed, but the attack hadn't been aimed at them.

They looked up as Isola banked after them, the spell slicing the air where they'd been.

They needed to get through to the center of campus, and they needed enough distance from the Hours behind them that they didn't end up surrounded.

You know this place, they told themself.

Ahead, Rat caught sight of a narrow path, half hidden between the buildings.

They started toward it as Isola swept past, overtaking them. She dodged to the side as another spell whistled past her and into the path of another attack.

A sharp tug jolted through the binding as the spell struck, and all of the air went out of their lungs.

Rat stumbled.

Above them, Isola dipped toward the ground, but she was losing altitude too quickly.

"No," they breathed.

They launched themself forward.

She couldn't go down right now. One day, she would die, and they'd make sure it was by their own hands, but right now, they needed her alive.

Isola landed in the shadow of the alleyway with a sick thud.

With a shudder, she tried to lift herself back up, arms shaking. Her wings had turned back to a tattered cloak, her feathers to snarled black hair, now soaked from the rain.

"You're hurt—" Rat reached out, then stopped themself.

"It's just a graze." Her hand went to her side, but even in the dark, they could tell it was deep. She bled starlight and rust. Liquid silver seeped through her fingers and ran down, into the puddle of rainwater at her feet. "Trust me, I've had worse."

"This is serious." Rat said. Across the grass, flashlights roved through the dark, searching for where Isola had come down. Before Rat could think of what they were doing, they started toward her. "We need to go," they said, pulling her arm over their shoulder. "Can you walk?"

Isola allowed Rat to haul her to her feet, resting heavily on their shoulder. She was taller than they were and broader across the shoulders, and they knew they weren't going to be able to carry her far.

"I'll recover," she said, easing off of them a bit. "I'm harder to take down than that."

Before they could move, a wall of water crashed out of the air on the other side of the path.

They stilled as all the flashlights turned toward the sound.

"It looks like we have help," Isola said, and Rat followed her gaze.

Jinx had stopped between the buildings on the other side of the alley, her hands raised to cast. At some point, she'd dropped the working that kept her dry, and her leather jacket was soaked, flapping around her as a gust of wind tore down the pathway. The storm seemed to bend to her as she moved, like it was drawn to her, the rain coming down around her in torrents.

Her jaw set as she locked eyes on Isola, and Rat knew that if Isola hadn't been undying, or close to it, Jinx would have drowned her where she stood.

Rat opened their mouth to explain their bargain, but Jinx just stepped closer, power thrumming on the air around her like lighting about to strike. "Where are you heading?"

"The clock tower," they told her. "If I can get inside first, there's a chance we can hold Evening off."

As they spoke, Will appeared on the path behind her, Agatha close on his heels. "Jinx," he started, his hand raised to cast. "We're—"

He stopped as he caught sight of Rat, Isola still bleeding at their side. He stared at them, like even though they'd told him everything, he still hadn't been prepared.

Before he could move, Agatha leaned in and said something, her voice drowned out by the sound of the rain.

Jinx looked back at Rat. "We'll try to keep everyone off you, but they know you're here," she said, more loudly. She spoke directly to them, like Isola wasn't there.

"She won't set foot on campus again," Rat said quickly, but they didn't know if they were trying to explain themself, or if they just wanted Jinx to know the bargain, in case they couldn't find her again before morning.

"She's going to send the missing students' remains back, and everything she took. All of it."

Jinx's face softened. "Just hurry, okay?"

And then, Agatha took her by the arm, and she was off again, the storm howling after her.

Will gave Rat a small nod. "Go," he said.

Before they could speak, he drew a spell on the air. With the low rumble of scraping stone, a wall of earth rose out of the ground, closing off the mouth of the alley.

Isola looked back at Rat, a too-sharp smile tugging at her mouth. "Where's the other one?"

Silently, Rat promised themself that one day, when she had her heart back, they'd find a way to destroy her.

"We're going," Rat said. Without waiting for an answer, they grabbed on to Isola's cloak and pulled her forward. She staggered, and then she drew ahead of them, lengthening her stride as she moved.

Rat followed close behind her as they made it out on the other side of the alley. Ahead of them, the long, spiny form of the Drake twisted around one edge of the main lawn, and Galison Hall stood at the other, glowing like a beacon against the haze of rain.

Between them, the darkened shape of the clock tower rose up from the center of campus, and a few Lesser Hours spread out on the flooded grass.

It was like they'd guessed. Evening had divided his attention, half of his forces spread out to search for them, the rest standing in wait, the one place he knew Rat would have to go back to.

Isola's magic pulled at them, but they knew they weren't going to be able to blast their way there. The moment they were seen, the rest of the Hours would converge on them, and there was nothing but open space between them and the foot of the clock tower.

As if she'd had the same thought, Isola threaded her fingers through the air, drawing the shadows around them. Her power surged down the binding spell, pulling at Rat like a current.

"You'll need to hold the spell," she said. "It will last as long as you stay focused."

Before Rat could speak, she pushed them toward the path. "I'll draw them off. Go. And don't be seen."

Rat turned back to protest.

"I'll meet you there," she said, with the air of a promise. Then, with a wince, she started forward and turned back into a bird.

Blood and rain and liquid silver rolled off her feathers as her wings caught the air, and then she was off, flying low over the grass.

Shouts rose up as she circled over the Hours, and a spell shot past her.

Rat watched, pressing themself into the building as Isola dipped toward the grass, dodging another blast. She caught herself on one knee, human, the wind howling around her. Magic surged off of her.

They forced themself onto the grass, trying to focus on the concealment spell the way she'd taught them to in another lifetime. The shadows whispered around them like a living thing, the wind whipping past them as they ran for the clock tower.

A stray spell caught the ground ahead of them, cutting a deep gouge in the earth. Rat veered out of the way and felt the working slip.

"Shit," they gasped, but their voice didn't come out. They drew a sharp breath through their teeth as they ran, and they felt the spell fold back around them.

They couldn't afford to lose this.

They fixed their gaze ahead and ran harder, the shadows shifting to cover them. The sounds of the fight washed over them, and they could sense Isola on the other side of the binding, her power a vicious current.

Their lungs ached, their pulse slamming hard and too hot through their entire body.

They shoved themself forward, closing the last of the distance.

Their momentum carried them, and they skid into the side of the clock tower. Their shoulder slammed against the brick.

With a wince, Rat pushed off. They needed to find the door.

They ran their hands over the wall, but there wasn't anything there. "Please," they said under their breath. "Fuck. Please work."

Shouts rose up behind them, cutting above the roar of the wind.

Rat shut their eyes and pressed their fingers to the rain-slicked stonework.

Forcing out a breath, they drew on their magic, and the world opened around them.

Isola's power flooded through the binding, surging after their own.

They pressed their hands against the bricks, grounding themself.

"I don't mean harm," they said into the wall. "I need to make sure that no one else gets hurt. Please."

Somewhere deep in the building, they felt something give, like a lock clicking open.

"Rat."

A gloved hand caught them by the arm, their power snapped back. A moment too late, they realized that they'd let the concealment spell slip.

Evening jerked them back, pulling Rat around to face him. "You seem to be under the impression you still have a choice to make. I assure you, you don't."

"Let go of me." Their eyes darted across the clearing, but they couldn't find Isola in the fight. They drew their other hand back to cast, and he caught their wrist.

"Was this your plan? Strike a deal with the tower, and then what?" He stepped in. "I always forget how little you know about magic. I've been propping up the school's protections for years now. Isola barely has any power here."

They glared up at him.

"I should thank you. I couldn't have set a better trap for her myself."

In the distance, more flashlights appeared between the buildings.

He followed Rat's gaze. "It's over. I won this game hours ago. The least you can do is lose with grace."

In the corner of their eye, the faint, telltale glow of a dead passage glinted against the rain. They glanced toward it, but it was too far for them to reach.

Evening looked down at them, and they knew the expression on his face. It was the same look Isola had given them countless times before.

"*You know why everyone treats you like that?*" Agatha's voice said in the back of their mind. "*Don't you?*"

They shrunk into themself. "No one else will get hurt."

"You have my word." Evening adjusted his grip on their arm. "The minute we're back at the Council Chambers, I'll call everything off. I'll make sure the Council knows your friends had nothing to do with it. By morning, this whole thing will seem more like a bad dream."

"Promise me," they said softly.

"On my honor." He tilted his head toward Galison Hall, and even in the dark, Rat couldn't miss the smug curve of his mouth. "Shall we?"

He rested his hand on their shoulder as he started back toward the path, as if he'd already won.

The moment his grip loosened, Rat jerked away.

Evening lunged after them, but before he could close the distance, a burst of spellfire lit the air. He drew back, and Rat pulled clear of his reach, their shoes skidding on the wet grass.

They whipped back to see Harker close behind them. Ragged, wind-torn wisps of fog rolled off him as he caught them by the arm.

"You—"

"You're not hard to find, Evans. I just follow whatever's trying to eat you," he said, pulling them forward.

When they glanced back, a plain wooden door had appeared on the side of the clock tower, set into the wall exactly where Rat had glimpsed it the first time. But this time, it didn't vanish.

They turned toward it, and a wall of force slammed into them from behind.

They came down hard and skidded across the grass. They pushed themself onto their side to see Harker on the ground next to them. Wincing, he forced himself up, already tracing a counterspell on the air.

"Come on," Rat said, grabbing his jacket before he could finish the working. They shoved themself to their feet, pulling Harker after as Evening advanced on them.

Across the grass, Evening prepared to cast again.

Rat scrambled back as a bird circled low overhead, and then Isola touched down on the grass, bleeding and human again. Her hair hung down her back in rain-slicked tangles, and her cloak was torn and stained with runnels of silver where she'd bled into it.

She raised her hand in a working, the shadows folding around her to shield her from the blast.

She looked back at Harker. "Get Rat inside. I'll hold him off."

Heat pricked the air around him, but he nodded. "Let's go."

"But—" the words died in Rat's throat. A moment too late, they registered the complete lack of surprise on Harker's face. He hadn't found them. Isola had called him here.

She gave them a small, crooked smile. "The clock tower is warded against me. I'm no use to you inside."

Rat stared at her, incredulous. "You knew the whole time," they said, understanding. She'd never actually intended to come with them. It was always going to be Harker. She must have realized they wouldn't have agreed to bring him back to the fight if she'd asked. "You planned this."

"You don't have much of a choice now, do you?" She stepped out ahead of them as the spell wavered.

Harker took their sleeve. "Rat. Come on," he said, pulling them back toward the clock tower.

They felt Isola's defensive spell waver over the binding, and then the low thud of impact behind them as a spell flew wide, driving into the ground.

Rat gave her a last, furious look and broke for the door.

They shoved it open and spilled over the threshold, Harker behind them. Will-o'-wisps of spellfire flared to life around him, washing the entryway in pale, bluish light. A narrow room opened ahead of them, the air stale and tinged with magic.

Beyond, a stone staircase rose up, twisting out of sight.

The door swung shut, but instinctively, they could feel that it hadn't fully closed. The spell that had held it shut had bent to their own magic to let them through, and it had left the way open behind them.

"*Stay*," they said to the door, tracing a spell on the air. They felt it seal, but already, they knew it wouldn't hold.

Rat tightened their hold on Harker's sleeve and started toward the stairs. "Come on. We don't have that much time."

"Do you know what we're looking for?"

They shook their head. "I'm kind of hoping I'll know it when I see it."

"How are you still alive, Evans?"

"Generational wealth?" they asked. Their hand skipped over the banister as they took the first turn of the staircase.

A sharp pull tugged across the binding spell.

"Rat?"

They turned back to see Harker looking up at them and realized they'd faltered.

"It's fine," they said. "We need to keep moving."

"Wait," he said, keeping pace with them. Wisps of spellfire swarmed through the stairwell in his wake, sending shadows shifting over the stone walls. "Isola—did you—"

"I promised her heart back. As soon as she has it, she'll release you from your binding spell, all obligations met," they said. "If you really want to stay with her, you can swear another oath when we're done."

"What did she really ask you for?" he asked, but there was an edge in his voice, like he already knew.

They opened their mouth, but they couldn't make themself say it.

"Rat. What did she ask for?"

"It's already done," they said. "Whether we succeed or not, as soon as the sun comes up. I'm the reason you got pulled into this in the first place, so you can just call everything even. It was always supposed to be me."

"That isn't your job—"

"And it isn't yours, either." Their voice came out hoarse. "You'll have your freedom, and you'll still have Bellamy Arts, like you wanted. I'll be out of your way. You could even blame me for stealing the Holbrook Map. I bet Jinx and Agatha would back you up, and the Council wouldn't be able to touch you."

"Rat."

"Don't worry. I'm sure you'll find a way to make yourself even more of a problem than you already are."

"I'm not letting you do that. I'll—"

They spun on him, bringing him up short. "What? You'll stop me?"

He stared up at them, still breathing hard, his mouth hanging open like he'd run out of things to say to them.

They felt a painful snap as the spell they'd placed on the door gave. "Shit," Rat breathed.

Below, with a sound too sharp to be thunder, the door splintered in. The scent of magic rose on the air, too much and too close.

Their hand tightened on Harker's wrist, his skin still hot to the touch even through his sleeves.

They pulled him forward, pushing themself around the last bend in the stairs. A narrow archway appeared ahead of them at the edge of the light cast by the spellfire, etched in flickering shadows.

Footsteps echoed through the stairwell after them, rising from somewhere farther down.

"Go," Harker said, slipping free of their grasp. "I'll buy you as much time as I can."

Before they could decide what that meant, he'd spun away from them, tracing a warding spell on the air.

They raced forward into a wide, circular room, lit by the glow of the storm. There were windows on all sides, and the air was thick with the scent of dust and rain.

At the center, a spell diagram sprawled across the floor, set into the stonework. The lines twisted around each other like a map of the stars in their orbits.

Rat's footsteps rang out in the heavy, long-unbroken stillness as they walked toward it. They reached for their magic again, still raw from casting, and for a moment, they thought that they wouldn't be able to.

Then it rose up in answer, and the clock tower took shape around them. The curve of the stairs spiraling down beneath them. The high arc of the ceiling, rising into darkness overhead. The wide sweep of the room, and out to the campus beyond.

Rat reached farther, searching for the seams in the world, but this time, the wards pushed against them.

There was nothing else.

No paths left. No extra rooms, or hallways that shouldn't be there.

Behind them, light flared in the stairwell, and Rat realized that whatever time Harker had bought them had already run out.

They spun back as he staggered over the threshold, will-o'-wisps of spellfire bobbing after him. Harker traced his hand through the air, drawing out a spell Rat didn't recognize, but Evening dispelled it like waving away a wisp of smoke.

Harker looked back at Rat, and then Evening's next spell knocked him back.

He landed on the ground in a heap. Before he could pick himself up, Evening grabbed him by the arm. He let out a small cry as he was hauled to his feet.

Spellfire flickered in his hand, then went out as Evening tightened his grip, like it had been choked off.

Harker struggled weakly against him. "Rat—"

Evening wrenched him back, and his other hand came to rest on the hollow of Harker's throat, poised to cast. "This has gone on long enough," he told Rat. "You're going to bring me through."

Harker gave them a pleading look.

Their mouth went dry. "It's not here. There's no way in. We were wrong about the map."

His eyes slid over them. "A step behind again, Rat. You're forgetting, the collection was sealed along with the campus."

They eyed him warily, and then, slowly, they understood. "There isn't an entrance. You're going to break the wards."

"No," he said. "You're going to."

Rat went cold. "I don't know how. I can barely do magic."

"Do you know what kind of spell it is?"

They opened their mouth to argue that they didn't, and then they remembered what Jinx had told them in the tunnels. *That which cannot be taken back.*

"A deathworking," they said, their voice just above a whisper.

"They're costly to break," Evening said. Idly, he drummed his fingers against Harker's arm. Harker pulled back, his jaw clenched, and Evening's grip tightened again. "But then, you have quite the talent for getting places you aren't supposed to. I've always wondered what you might be capable of under the right circumstances."

"Let go of him," Rat said before they could stop themself.

Evening held their gaze, impassive. "You can break the seal, or I can do it the hard way."

Harker bit back a wince as Evening dug his fingers in. He shot Rat a desperate look.

Blood pounded in their ears. "You can't—"

"It won't work," Harker said in a rush. "They don't care what happens to me. They can't even cast—"

He broke off with a cry of pain as Evening traced the line of a spell at his throat.

Evening released him, and he pitched forward, catching himself against the stone floor.

"Harker!" Instinctively, Rat rushed toward him, but Evening stopped them with a warning glance, his hand raised to cast.

Harker heaved a too-deep breath and doubled over, coughing.

Something watery and silver flecked the ground in front of him, glinting in the low light, but it took them a moment to realize it was his. The wrongness of it slithered through them. Without meaning to, Rat thought of Isola, blood and liquid silver running over her gloves. But Isola was whispers and magic and the secrets of long-absent gods. Harker was deeply, breakably human.

He looked up at them, frightened. He moved to pick himself up, and Evening sent another wall of force shuddering toward him, knocking him back down.

"It's a simple spell, but an old one," Evening said to Rat. "It can unravel its target from the inside without leaving a mark." He stepped in, his footsteps echoing in the dim. "It runs deeper than a fleshworking, but I've always found it to be more effective. It's survivable, of course, but only to a point."

Rat's lip trembled, and they hated themself for it. "Stop."

"It's actually rather convenient," Evening said as Harker forced himself up again, his arm shaking. "I doubt anyone will bat an eye if he doesn't make it back out. With his obvious connections to the tower, we might even be able to skip the pretense of an investigation."

"Stop it!" Rat's voice came out in shreds. "I'll try. Okay?"

Evening gave a small, satisfied smile and motioned for them to go on. "After you."

They drew in a shaky breath, steadying themself.

Rat closed their eyes and reached out again with their magic, taking in the room. Now that they knew what they were looking for, they could sense the wards, holding the worlds in place. Like the unsolved piece of the puzzle box that held it all together and bound it from opening.

They felt along it, searching for a crack they could slip through, but there wasn't any.

Their magic snapped back to them.

"No?" Evening asked, disappointed.

Rat shook their head. "I told you, there's no way through."

"Pity." He traced his hand through the air and cast again.

Harker drew in a staggered breath. On the air, a wisp of spellfire flickered and went out as he lost control of the working. Still bracing himself against the floor, he doubled forward and hacked onto the ground. It was a wet sound from somewhere deep in his chest, and something watery and silver spilled onto the stones like he'd choked up a lungful of starlight.

"Stop! Please. I'm trying!" Rat shouted. "I don't know how!"

"Then try again," Evening said.

Rat ground their teeth. Again, they reached for the edges of the wards. For a moment, they could feel all of the fault lines, where the planes jarred against each other.

They shoved whatever force of will they had left against the wards, searching for a way in. Something in the aether shifted, just for a moment, and then stuck fast.

Rat drew back as they brushed up against something cold and metallic. In the hollow of their ribs, a small, mortal part of them recoiled.

The deathworking. Even if the wards might give little by little, this wouldn't.

They hurled their magic against it anyways.

Pain bloomed behind their eyes, like they'd pushed too hard, and the spell collapsed again.

When Rat looked up, Evening was still watching them, like their failure was evident.

"As you'd have it then," he said. He lifted his hand and cast again.

Harker sank back down as he dissolved into another fit of coughs, except this time, there was blood, too.

Before Rat could think about what they were doing, they rushed forward and dropped down next to him. "Harker."

He looked up at them, breathless as another wisp of spellfire winked out. His hair was still plastered with rain, and the look on his face was fury and pleading and spite, the same way he'd looked at Isola that day in the grass. "I'll destroy him," he said weakly.

Another cough wracked through him. He doubled forward and hacked starlight onto the floor.

Rat pulled their arm around him, as if there was anything they could do about it. Power flickered off him like a dying ember, the heat on his skin slowly ebbing away.

They looked up at Evening. "Stop it! You're killing him!"

He regarded them coldly, like they'd entirely missed the point.

Their eyes stung. "I'll figure something out! I'll find another way to do it—I'll go back with you! I'll break my deal with the tower! Just stop!"

"I told you," Evening said. "Open the wards or I will."

Harker sank against them, knotting his fingers into their sweatshirt. "Rat, I still . . ."

"You won't die here," they said, pulling him in. They pushed his hair back. "Okay? I refuse to let you. You can't leave again. You promised me we'd get to the end of this."

He swallowed hard and nodded, heat still ebbing off of him in ragged waves. "Please stay here," he breathed, but his voice came out small and afraid.

Evening traced another spell, and Harker pitched forward.

"Stop!" Rat cried.

Evening gave them another cold look and cast again.

"Leave him alone!"

Their magic flared in answer, battering against the wards, and it was vicious and terrible and *theirs*.

Isola's magic pulled at them on the other side of the binding, and Rat drew on that, too, letting it run through them like falling night and shadows and wind.

The clock tower shuddered around them.

Rat knew they were bleeding power, and they didn't care. It rolled over them in a breaking wave, raw and uncontrolled, and they wanted it to. They wanted to shred through this world and every other one if it stopped this from happening.

Debris rained down from the ceiling. They buried their face in Harker's shoulder, pulling him in.

They wanted him.

They'd always wanted him. Maybe from the moment they'd found him in the stairwell at Highgate, or when he'd drawn the first set of wards for them, or when they'd run back from the tower with him. Maybe even before that, the first time they'd seen him in the school lobby when they'd been electric with jealousy at everything that he was.

They had lost him too many times already. They refused to let anyone take him where they couldn't find him again.

The wards jarred against each other. Rat shoved past the cold wall of the deathworking, and then, like forcing a lock, it gave.

They felt a flicker of power as it came undone, older and subtler than their own.

Then a shock wave rolled through the aether, and the world unhinged around them.

The clock tower lurched, the ground tilting underneath them as something deep in the earth shifted, and Rat's magic snapped back to them. Their balance went out as the floor dropped beneath them, Harker still clutching their sweatshirt as they slid across the ground. Stone and rubble pounded down around them, and dust hung heavy on the air.

They squeezed their eyes shut, burying their face in Harker's neck until silence settled around them.

Slowly, they let themself look. Their arm was still wrapped protectively around Harker, curled against them on the ground. His chest rose and fell in unsteady waves, and the last of the spellfire had gone out.

The floor had splintered around them, the stones jagged where the force had broken them apart. Grass and mugwort grew up between the cracks, like they'd torn a hole to the tower itself, and a flurry of aether curled through the air around them.

In the center of the room, where the seal had been, the ground had opened into a wide stone staircase. Rubble and aether coated the top steps before they curved down into the darkness.

Evening nudged a fallen stone with his shoe, surveying the ruin from where he stood amid the wreckage. A cold gust of wind blew in through the windows behind him, broken now, carrying in the rain and the sharp smell of frost.

"Remarkable," he said.

Rat stumbled to their feet and launched themself at him.

He waved his hand, and a wall of force knocked them back. Rat landed hard, skidding across grass and stone.

Evening gave them an appraising glance, and Rat realized that their lip was bleeding. Their entire body hurt, and dust and grime streaked their sweatshirt, still wet from the rain.

He traced a spell, summoning a flicker of silvery light. "You're coming with me," he said, motioning to them. "Just you. The boy stays."

Behind them, Harker pushed himself up and caught them by the arm, as if he had any strength left to fight. "Wait."

"Harker." Gently, they moved to slide his hand away, but he leaned in.

"You don't aim your spells," he said quickly, too low for Evening to hear. "That's why they're so unpredictable. You need a target."

They opened their mouth and then closed it again as they realized what he was saying.

Rat touched his cheek. "I'm coming back for you, you sodden matchstick."

His expression softened and he looked at them with something dangerously close to hope.

"Rat," Evening commanded.

They dropped their hand. Then, their legs still shaking, they pushed themself to their feet and crossed to him.

Without a word, he motioned to them and started toward the staircase, waving them along.

💀

They followed the staircase down, their footsteps echoing as they went. Aether dusted the way ahead of them, etching everything in a weak, golden light, and Evening's light spell hovered after, casting long shadows over the walls.

The damp autumn air above turned cool around them, heavy with the smell of earth and magic and the dust that had shaken loose when the wards gave.

As they walked, Rat's hand slid back to their compass, but they didn't take it out. They knew already that whatever it showed, even if they hadn't left the confines of the clock tower, they weren't on the campus proper anymore.

"Quickly," Evening said as he reached the end of the stairs. "If you're hoping that Isola will catch up and find you, you're mistaken. The protection spells will be stronger ahead of us, and even she knows a losing fight."

Heat prickled in their lungs as he waved them on. He was right. Ingrid had planned this for a long time. The air on the staircase was thick with magic, and even Isola's presence on the other end of the binding spell felt dull and far away.

Whatever happened, they were alone here.

"There isn't much telling how far we still have to go, and I want to be out of here by morning," he said as they made their way down the last handful of steps.

Below them, the stairs gave way to a wide corridor. The ceiling curved high overhead, bolstered by stone archways, the masonry untouched by time or weather, and a long-settled quiet hung over everything.

The passageway ended in a single pair of doors.

Rat inhaled deeply, drawing on what magic they had left. They felt raw from casting for a moment, but it rose back up, uncoiling in their core.

A whisper of power stirred in the tunnel, waking around them as if in answer.

"It's old magic. It's a different creature than you're used to dealing with."

A shiver pricked up their arm.

Behind them, Evening nudged them forward.

Before he could stop them, Rat spun back, drawing the only spell sign they knew on the air. They aimed their gaze squarely in the center of his chest, and the spell tore away from them like an arrow.

And then, as Evening cast a defense spell with an unhurried wave of his hand, it dissipated.

"You're talented, maybe," he said, "but you're not much of a caster."

They traced their hand through the air to cast again, harder, and sharper.

Before they could finish the spell, a blast of sheer force slammed into them, throwing them back against the stonework.

The pain of impact flashed white behind their eyes.

"Do you honestly think anyone's coming for you?" Evening asked them.

They shoved themself forward, and he cast again.

Their head snapped back against the stones, and the ground went out from under them. Rat grasped for another spell, but they didn't have one, and it wasn't enough.

"No one's here to save you, and whatever the tower promised you, you'll be out of Isola's reach in a matter of hours," he said, stepping forward. "It's finished. You're only making things worse for yourself the harder you fight."

Weakly, Rat fixed their focus on him and lifted their hand to cast, willing their magic to answer. Even if they lost, they wouldn't allow him to have this.

Evening cast again.

Rat flinched back, but the spell dispersed around them.

They opened their eyes.

Again, he drew another spell.

As if in answer, a veil of aether glinted on the air, curving around Rat to take the impact.

Instinctively, Evening reached toward them, and then pulled back as if he'd been burned. Blood and aether streaked his fingertips, slick in the glow of the light spell.

"What do you think you're doing?"

"I . . ." their pulse quickened.

It wasn't their magic. And it wasn't Isola's, either.

A quiet fury flickered across his face as he cut his hand through the air. A shock wave rippled away from him, shivering through the stones of the tunnel, and the same whisper of power they'd felt when they entered the corridor rose up around them.

They had broken the wards, but something in the protective workings had recognized them. Maybe because they'd wanted to keep something from harm. Maybe just because they'd shorn through the school's seal and their intentions had overtaken everything else.

They stepped forward, the spell drawing in around them.

"I—You won't come any closer," they said, and in the quiet of the tunnel, it echoed like a command.

His jaw clenched, but he didn't take another step. The protective workings whispered through the tunnel like a long-sleeping creature just beginning to stir. They were old, and immense, and even he wouldn't be able to match them.

It was the kind of magic that could swallow even him.

For now, at least.

They stepped in, feeling the tunnels bend to them as they moved.

"Maybe Isola isn't coming to find me, but everyone saw the wards go down," they said. "How long do you think we have until Fairchild sends someone over here?"

They held his gaze, fighting the urge to look down as they continued,

"There are two versions of what happened here. In one, you came to my aid after Isola launched an attack on the campus and protected me and Harker, who had no other involvement. You fought her back from campus after she brought the wards down. My family is in your debt, and the school receives you as a hero." Their voice ran flat. "The other version is the truth."

He let out a cold laugh. "Who would believe you? You're a child."

"I'm a Holbrook." Their voice came out sharper than they'd expected in the quiet of the tunnel. "You're welcome to take your chances, but you've been wrong once already."

Evening met their eyes, his gaze steely.

They stared back, unyielding. They had brokered a deal with the tower and slipped past all of his reinforcements. He'd seen them tear through a hundred-year-old deathworking, nearly leveling the clock tower in the process. Maybe a few hours ago, Evening had thought of them as a frightened animal who didn't know their own power, but he'd seen what they were now.

Finally, he stepped back. "I'm going to get through, with or without you. I would advise you to consider whose side you want to be on when that happens."

Then, he turned back toward the stairs, the light retreating after him.

Rat held still, listening as his footsteps receded up the stairs, until that, too, had faded. Finally, some of the tension went out of them, and the protective workings slowly uncoiled, settling back into the stonework.

They knew better than to think he would have left them alone. Already, the Council of Hours must have established a perimeter. Anything Rat left with would probably be taken from them as evidence the moment they set foot outside.

But in spite of themselves, they turned back toward the end of the corridor.

The faint glow of aether lit the way as they closed the rest of the distance.

Rat touched their hands to the door and pushed, but for the first time since their powers had come in, it remained locked. They took the handles and pulled inward, then pushed again, but nothing happened. The strangeness of it washed over them.

They pulled at the last dregs of their power, but they were already overextended, and their focus was gone. For a moment, they could feel the network of passages on the other side, sprawling away from them in every direction. Then the spell slipped away, like trying to grab a handful of water.

All that they knew for certain was that whatever was on the other side of the door, they had barely scraped the surface.

CHAPTER FORTY-FIVE

HARKER WAS ALREADY GONE WHEN RAT GOT BACK. A MUM had been left waiting for them amid the rubble like a promise.

Outside the windows, the rain had finally slowed, and the morning chill carried in through the broken glass. Any sign of the terrors had vanished from campus, like Isola had already taken them with her, and a handful of lanterns had appeared on the lawn below, picking their way toward the clock tower.

Waves of tall grass spilled out from the foot of the clock tower, sprouting up from the wreckage where the seam between the worlds had given way.

Rat looked up to the high rise of the ceiling, half expecting Isola to come sweeping down from the shadows to take them, or that they'd hear the low patter of her footsteps on the stairs, but neither happened.

They were alone. The sky was just beginning to fade outside, and they still had a bit longer to sunrise yet.

Overhead, the bells began to ring in the new hour. Finally, Rat closed their hand around the mum and started back out of the building, into the last hours of the night.

Rat didn't have the energy left to cast, so it didn't take long for someone to find them after they left the clock tower.

They didn't bother trying to explain. They just allowed themself to be led, making their way across campus in silence.

Out of everywhere, Rat ended the night in a reading room on the second floor of Galison Hall, Fairchild's office in the Founder's House being closed.

Spell diagrams and spare lanterns cluttered the tables, where the faculty had set up a makeshift headquarters, but the room was warm and dry, and the moment Rat settled into the window seat, they weren't sure if they'd ever get up again.

Now that they'd stopped moving, exhaustion hit them like a freight train. They could barely keep their eyes open.

By the time they'd arrived, Fairchild had already received an official version of the night's events. She offered Rat a cup of tea from the service that had been set up at the end of the table, and they somehow ended up draped in an extra cloak, which at least was clean and dry. For the most part, Rat allowed Fairchild to talk, nodding through the details about how the Council of Hours had arrived at the campus to handle a breach before the wards had failed.

She paused at one point, almost like she was waiting for Rat to correct her, but they just let her speak.

Before she let them go, Evening appeared in the doorway. He looked like he'd been in the fray, but somehow, the worst of the night had left him untouched, his coat still even, if a bit dirty, and his hair unruffled.

"We're still clearing the debris from the clock tower," he said. "I've already sent over some Lesser Hours to secure the area, but the Council is convening later to discuss extending our investigation. As I'm sure you understand, an attack on this scale falls outside the school's jurisdiction."

"You'll meet with me when I'm done here," Fairchild told him, but they knew from the edge in her voice that it wasn't a battle she planned to win.

His eyes went to Rat, and they half expected him to say something about returning to the Council Chambers, but maybe because of that flicker of fear they'd seen in the clock tower, he just gave them a look that could have cut glass and said, "You were lucky to have gotten away safely tonight."

Then, he'd turned and left.

Rat waited until Evening's footsteps had faded in the hall before they got up. "If that's everything, I should head out," Rat said. "My friends are probably looking for me."

From her place in one of the high-backed reading chairs, Fairchild motioned for them to stay. "Just a moment, before I send you back."

They hesitated.

"Elise is staying in town. The school is still locked down, but she'll be here tomorrow."

"Oh." It shouldn't have made a difference, but the words still hit Rat like a brick. "If you want to send me home, I understand."

"Do you want to go home?"

"I mean, I was supposed to leave yesterday, and I really don't think Elise would—"

"That isn't what I asked," Fairchild said. "Do you know what I saw tonight?" She nodded to the window. Across the grass, in full view of the reading room, the shape of the clock tower rose up against the slowly fading sky. "All of the school's protections are anchored in that building. After the wards were set, the door was sealed so that it can only be seen by people who mean to protect the grounds. In my time here, I could count the number of people who have found their way inside on one hand."

"I was with the Council of Hours. It was probably them."

"By all reports, you reached the clock tower first," Fairchild insisted. "I don't know what really happened out there, but I suspect you're the reason it didn't turn out much worse."

Rat faltered, unsure of what to say. They felt hollow, since they hadn't completely lost, but they hadn't won, either.

"When Elise comes tomorrow, if it were up to you, would you want to go home?"

They thought of Isola, still waiting for them.

For everyone else, the night was over, but Rat still had a long way to travel before the sun came up.

"If I had the choice," they said carefully, "I would have really liked to stay here."

With a small smile, Fairchild folded her hands around her cup of tea. "I'll take it under advisement."

"Thanks. I . . ." Rat forced a smile. "Really. For what it's worth, that means a lot." They turned to go, then stopped themself. "One more thing. My friends. Jinx, Will, and Agatha. Tonight, were any of them . . ."

"All accounted for," Fairchild said. "They were released back to the dorms with the others half an hour ago."

A tension Rat hadn't realized they were still holding evaporated. "Thank god."

"I wouldn't worry. We've already turned up a few groups of students who hadn't been marked in at Galison Hall, and from the reports I've gotten, outside of the clock tower the damage has been . . . light."

"Light," Rat repeated.

"Very light," Fairchild said. She took a sip of her tea. "Almost as if the attack had never happened at all."

When Rat got back to their room, they found Isola leaning against the sill, window open behind her. She was human again, cold-eyed and battle-worn in the early light.

She looked up at them as they shut the door.

"We had a deal," Rat said. "Tell me where to go, and I'll follow you."

Isola stepped toward them, and their breathing stopped. She brushed Rat's bangs out of their eyes. "No, I don't think that you will."

Rat's pulse skipped. "But—"

"You promised me my heart." She dropped her hand, but her eyes were bright, almost like she'd gotten what she wanted anyway. Almost, they realized, like she'd anticipated this from the beginning.

"You knew I might not get there," they said slowly.

"I know the terms of our agreement," she said. "You failed to retrieve what's mine. That is a debt you owe me, and if you want me to uphold my end, you'll see that you find it." She threaded her fingers through the cold, damp air. Harker's bracelets appeared in her hand, scorched black and covered in teeth marks. She held them up for Rat to see. "You'll return with me when I decide, and not a day sooner. Until then, you won't set foot near the tower or any of its outlying lands."

"Wait. Let him go," Rat said. "You won't be able to summon me with those. Give them back, and I'll let you have something of mine instead so you can make a proper binding spell."

Isola looked at them, considering. "Somehow, I get the feeling you'll still come running."

Her mouth curved into something sharp and cruel as she slipped the bracelets over her wrist.

Rat's jaw tightened.

Before they could answer, there was a knock on the door. Their eyes locked on Isola, and instinctively, they shifted to block her path.

Amusement flickered across her face. She gave the door one more look, as if Rat ever could have stopped her, then paced back to the window.

"You should be careful," she said, planting her boot on the ledge. For a moment, she was older than dust and stone, and older than all of the

369

stars that had died for dust and stone to be made. "I doubt you'll be the only one looking now. You live in a wide and terrible world, and you'd do well to remember I'm not the worst thing in it."

With that, she leaned out into the open air, her arms outstretched. The light caught the leather cords still looped around her wrist, and then she leapt.

Before her feet left the sill, she was a bird again.

Then Rat was alone at the open window, with the sky slowly fading to morning and the muddy ghost of Isola's boot print on the ledge.

There was another knock on the door.

"Rat!" a voice called from outside. "Hey! Evans, are you there?"

Jinx.

She slapped her hand against the doorframe when they didn't respond. "Well, I'm on my way back to Galison Hall, so, wherever you are, you'd better meet me!"

Rat grabbed their compass off the desk and shoved it back in their pocket as they whipped toward the door. They'd thought that they were too tired to run anymore, but they were wrong.

They flung the door open as Jinx turned to go. Her leather jacket draped loosely across her shoulders, still muddy from the night before. Will stood beside her in a clean sweatshirt and a pair of pajama pants, like he must have stopped back at Armitage Hall on his way over.

"Wait!"

Jinx spun back to them at the same time Will did, and her eyes lit behind her glasses.

"I just got back," Rat said in a rush. "I was about to come find you guys and—"

Jinx pulled them into a hug. "Holy shit." She laughed. "You're here. I looked for you when they let us go, but you weren't there. I thought . . ."

"What happened?" Will asked. "Was that you at the clock tower?"

"I—" Rat started, then stopped again as Agatha appeared at the end of the hall.

She looked from Will and Jinx, back to Rat. "Oh, good. You found them."

Agatha had scrubbed away the dirt from the night before and changed into one of her long satin dresses that looked suspiciously like a nightgown. If Rat hadn't known better, they would have thought she spent the whole night safely in Galison Hall.

"Evans," she said, then trailed off like she had a question she didn't know how to ask.

"Cromwell."

She hesitated, and an uneasy quiet fell over the hall as it sank in that they were all still short a person.

"He's at the tower," Rat said, even though they suspected she might have already known. An ache settled in their chest. "And, the Ingrid Collection is . . . there was just another door. I couldn't get through it."

"We'll need to find a way in before my uncle does," she said grimly. "And you can rest assured that he will."

Another silence settled between them, sharper than the first.

They would all need to regroup. Later, Rat would need to explain what had happened, about their deal with Isola, and the clock tower, and the Ingrid Collection itself. They'd need to find out what their next move was.

But it wouldn't all happen now.

Finally, Will said, "We were all heading downstairs, if you wanted to come."

"I wanted to see everything while it's still fresh," Agatha told them.

Rat didn't know if they felt ready yet to be back in center campus. "I'll catch up with you."

Jinx gave them a nod, then nudged Will's arm. "Come on, Chen. I can finish telling you about the tunnels."

He gave Rat a last *you know where to find us* look and started up the hall, Agatha close behind. Jinx moved to follow, then stopped. "Rat."

They looked back at her.

"I know what kind of spell the wards are. Blakely was with you when they came down, wasn't he?"

Rat hesitated.

"There aren't a lot of things that can conquer death, Evans."

"He runs on coffee and trans spite," they said. "I'm sure it was that."

"I'm sure." She gave them a knowing look. Then, she turned and started back toward the stairs.

Rat went up to the roof alone.

The widow's walk stretched empty ahead of them, the last traces of fog still curling over the boards. Rat drew their hand along the rail. Overhead, the morning had broken cold and mercilessly blue.

Even from a distance, the clock tower seemed jagged in a way that it hadn't before, like the ground beneath it had unsettled, the facade missing bits where Rat's magic had sheared it away.

Rat leaned out as a gust of wind blew in from the woods, carrying with it the faint scent of mugwort and frost.

They were going to find a way to the Ingrid Collection before Evening did, and they were going to find Isola's heart. Whether they returned it was another question.

Absently, they ran their thumb along the burns on the cuff of their sleeve. They wouldn't be the first person to steal from the tower.

When they were finished, they would make sure they were the last.

They swept their gaze over the campus one more time, their magic pricking in their veins, and started to plan.

EPILOGUE

THE SKY HAD ALREADY BEGUN TO FADE AGAIN BY THE time Isola met him at the retaining wall, the unfamiliar stars vanishing one by one overhead.

Harker looked up at her from where he'd sunk down in the grass, his knees drawn up. He still felt shaky and hollow, and he hadn't slept yet, but already, the campus felt far away, like a story he'd told himself.

"I found this for you," she said, settling on the crumbling stones. She held up his cloak, letting it drape over the side of the wall.

He swallowed the urge to thank her and pushed himself to his feet.

She'd asked him if there was anything else he needed before they'd left, but there hadn't been. He could manage with casting chalk and ink for fleshworkings, and anything else, he didn't want falling into her hands.

It had felt like a weakness, to ask for even this much. He knew she'd only offered for Rat's benefit, but he'd wanted it too badly to say no. His cloak was one of the only things he really had.

"We're going, then," he said, although it wasn't a question.

She'd come back alone, but he'd expected that. If Rat hadn't recovered her heart, she needed them on campus.

It was better that they stayed behind, he reminded himself.

A dull ache settled in his chest, but he tried to ignore it. He shouldn't have wanted Rat to come after him.

He shouldn't have wanted them at all.

Isola drew the cloak around his shoulders, though he knew it wasn't kindness. She held her hand out to him. "Shall we?"

"Just lead the way," he said. "It's not like I could run."

She gave him a small, cruel smile and motioned for him to follow.

Harker glanced once more over his shoulder, as if there was anything waiting there, and then started after her into the tall grass and on toward the tower.

ACKNOWLEDGMENTS

A Hundred Vicious Turns has meant so much to me, and I'm still a bit bewildered to be writing the acknowledgments. There are so many people who I need to thank, but to name a few:

Jordan Hamessley, my agent, who fought for this story from the beginning. It's been such a long road, and I can't begin to articulate how much she's done to make this book possible or how ridiculously grateful I am to have had her in my corner. She's been a sounding board, an editor, an advocate, a level head, and an all-around champion, and I genuinely don't think I can thank her enough.

Emily Daluga, for falling in love with these characters in a way that I could only dream of and for her editorial brilliance in untangling the veritable murder-board of plot threads. I also can't begin to thank her for opening a space for me to bring more of Rat's—and my own—transness to the page, along with all of the other messy queer feelings that I'd been afraid to name. So many of my favorite moments in this book came about in revisions, and it literally wouldn't be the same story without her. (Thank you for asking if there was something between Rat and Harker. Yes. There was.)

The entire team at Amulet—Marie Oishi, Maggie Moore, Deena Micah Fleming, and Andrew Smith—as well as Margo Winton Parodi, Diane Aronson, Penelope Cray, and Charlotte Perez, who have done so much to bring everything together and without whom there literally wouldn't be a book.

Corey Brickley, for bringing Rat and Harker to life in the cover art, which is totally beyond anything I'd dared to hope for.

Stephanie Cohen-Perez and Vida Cruz-Borja, for all of their thought, care, and attention to detail as sensitivity readers, and for helping me to bring the cast of the story more fully and sensitively to the page. Both of their notes have been invaluable, and I can't thank either of them enough.

Hayley Stone, Maiga Doocy, and Karen McCoy, my incredible CPs, for being there whenever there was a plot snag to brainstorm, a book to shout about, or a dragon to be slain. It's meant the entire world, and I genuinely can't imagine doing this without them.

Everyone at the Yolo County Writer's Cramp, for all of their support and encouragement on the messiest of early drafts, even when the plot changed every month.

My parents, for their unwavering enthusiasm, even though I have never in twenty-nine years allowed them to read a single word of my writing. (I love you. Please don't tell me if you read this.)

Emberlyn McKinney for troubleshooting plot points and listening to me talk endlessly about this book, usually in a car, frequently in the middle of the night.

You, and everyone reading this, for following me into this maze of a story. I can't tell you where it ends yet, but I hope you'll come with me. There are still a couple of turns along the way.